Other books in this Series by Julia Caesar
(arima Publishing)

THE TAPESTRY OF TTEN

4. SONG OF SORCERY

BY JULIA CÆSAR

Published 2011 by arima publishing

www.arimapublishing.com

ISBN 978-1-84549-506-0

© Julia Caesar 2011
Book Jacket design (based on original artwork by Hillz Dunsdon),
Chris Howard of Blondesign.
Blondesign@gmail.com

Printed and bound in the United Kingdom

Typeset in Garamond 11pt

Swirl is an imprint of arima publishing.

arima publishing
ASK House, Northgate Avenue
Bury St Edmunds, Suffolk IP32 6BB
t: (+44) 01284 700321

www.arimapublishing.com

Dedication

With apologies to my Publishers who state quite honestly that there is no resemblance to anyone living or dead in this work of fiction. In the main that is totally true, but I kept getting a mental image of the one person who proves the point about that rule. He might have been amused; I hope he wouldn't have objected because whenever I tried to compose a mental image of one character, the well loved and deeply missed face of my father kept intruding into the process. I therefore beg the readers' indulgence in order to dedicate this work to the memory of

DON CAESAR

Member of the Scout Association all his life. As a Scout, Ranger Scout, then Scout Leader, he knew and loved the natural beauty of the world around him. He spent many hours in the New Forest and the Solent training Scouts and Leaders to appreciate how vulnerable our world is. Many years were dedicated to building and often rebuilding the confidence of young men whose lives and families had been torn apart by two World Wars. He gave them the strength to trust their fellows, the skills that might support their outdoor activities, and the faith to follow where truth held sway.

So, with much love, and thankful to have been in his company for so long I pay him tribute in the form of

Draille Skellin
(A First Class Ranger of a different kind)

CONTENTS

Pronunciations

Note: Emphasis or stress should be placed on the underlined syllables. Characters shown **bold** should be hard, e.g. **g** as in **g**o, rather than g as in gesture. Syllables in brackets are soft. e.g. (g) as in gesture

Word	Pronunciation	Description
Adora	A Dorra	Senior Healer at Darnesh
Ahnell	Are nell	Daro's foster brother
Adruna	A droon a	Evil Sorceress (Amethyst)
Anduigor	And wig or	Magical belt clasp
Anempor	Ann em paw	Old Capital of the Azure
Amir	A mear	Zurian Drover
Ashgenar	Ash genn are	Wilderness
Beneva	Ben evver	Guardian of Knowledge
Caranchar	Caran Char	The Town above the Low Pass
Carolus	Carol us	A wandering Apothecary
Cathlea	Cathlyah	Main Northern Trail Stop
Citrine	Sittreen	Lemon like fruit
Decrian	Deckreean	Ritual Tattooist
Dinajh	Dinnar(g)e	water tracts in the Sands
Diras	Deerass	Daro's bodyguard
Djellim	Jellim	Library established in Selesh
Draille	Drayle	Name meaning - Forge
Driands	Dree ands	Date like fruit
Droitch	Droytche	Traditional nomadic yurt
Errish	Ehrrish	The Master Builder of Selesh
Gresshe	Gresh	Clan of the Malachite Sands
Gurayen	Gurry en	Wind of the Azure Sands
Holonogarth	Ho Long aguth	Ranger Rite of Passage
Ikella	Eye kella	Sorceress Ruler of the Opal Sands
Iskilda	Iss Kilda	Omen reader in training s
Inesh	In Nesh	Second Clan of the Opal Sands
Ivinish	Eye vinnish	Beast Master
Kilda	Kill da	Ranger Omen Reader
Myst Cat	Mist Cat	Wild cat with magical abilities
Nightlingby	Night ling bye	Native Owl
Nishanawa	nih SHANN awa	Serve Temple of the Winds
Nishan	Nishun	Dedicated to the Guardians
Othervoice	Other voice	Magically empowered voice
Sandsinger	Sand Singer	Extinct class of mage
Seguidor	Seg wid or	Power focussing artefact
Seobra	See o brah	Wolverine like creature

Skythe	Skyth	Herbal infertility cure
Shalhanhi	Shallarni	Ruling clan of the Opal Sands
Shiarjha	She ara	Guardian of Powers
Soapsand	Soap sand	Naturally occurring cleanser
Sybillsce	Sibillsh	Clan of the Amethyst Sands
Tirjhinar	Tier rinn are	City of the Sandsingers
Tregeth	Tree jeth	Zeglur Breeding station
Vetali	Vett arly	Plant with magical properties
Wutherped	Wuth erped	Armadillo like creature
Zeglurs	Zegglures	Donkey like Pack animal
Zephryn	Zefrin	Single horned Storm horses
Zurias	Zurry ass	Clan of the Azure Sands

Terms of Reference	Definition

Planetary System

Seleus	Solar Body
Pelshar	The world of this series
Jenta	Primary moon
Gatta	Secondary Moon

Special Characteristics of Pelshar

The Source	A universal field of energy which empowers magic users

Sands (In order of precedence)

Opal	Predominately white, iridescent
Azure	Grey blue, shade ranges pale to very dark.
Malachite	Deep green with seams of silver
Cynabarr	Luminescent burnt orange to yellow
Onyx	Dark grey to black
Carnelian	Vibrant red
Tourmaline	Pale translucent green
Amethyst	Translucent shades pale to dark purple

Named Wilderness

The Ashgenar	Rough scrub, mineral deposits & mining spoil

Castes

Greeeyn	City dwelling technologists & artisans
Felmin	Traders, farmers, landsmen
Clansmen	Sand Dwellers, (also known (inaccurately) as Sandsworn)
Rangers	Displaced hunter gatherers living in the Highlands

Time

Sector of the Sand-Glass	15 minutes earth time
Turn of the Sand Glass	Hour
Day	Day
Dawn	Dawn or Breakday
Height of Sun	Noon
Evening	Sunfall
Night	Night
Week	Ninenight (referring to the number of nights)
Journight	Two ninenights
Journey of Jenta	Lunar Month
Rotation	Year

Clans (in order of precedence)   Location

Clans	Location
Shalhanhi	Opal Sands
Zurias	Azure Sands
Greshe	Malachite Sands
Czerezin	Cynabarr Sands
Kora-Mai	Onyx Sands
Jedrun	Carnelian
Quexoni	Tourmaline
Sybillsce	Amethyst

Minor Clans or Sub Sets

Inesh	Opal Sands
Nishanawa	The Ashgenar

Centre of High Magic   Location

Centre of High Magic	Location
Sanctuary	The Heights of Surrandel
Selesh	Mount Torrenesh, Opal Sands

Legendary Locations

Tirjhinar (City of the Sandsingers)	*Whereabouts Unknown*

Animals	(Nearest Earth Comparison)
Irix	Antelope
Coatan	Goat
Dolcan	Spider Monkey
Zeglur	Donkey
Mihort	Black Bear
Biron	Bison
Sandrigal	Snake
Cuirax	Giant Snow Raven
Dorrowen	Cattle
Mystcat	Puma
Cherls	Camel

Mythical Beasts (Depicted in ancient artwork)

Drecon	Dragon
Zephryn	Single horned Storm horse

Classes of Character

Guardians	Tutors of all things Historic, Magical or Mysterious
Sandsingers	Mages, both sexes, uniquely powerful, one to each Sand
Sorceress	Magically empowered Rulers of the Nine Sands
Healers	Women who can use the Source to heal
Apothecary	Pharmacist, herbalist - practitioner of practical medicine
Guaradeign	Town or regional Governor
Servitors	Domestic Servants
Drudges	Menials

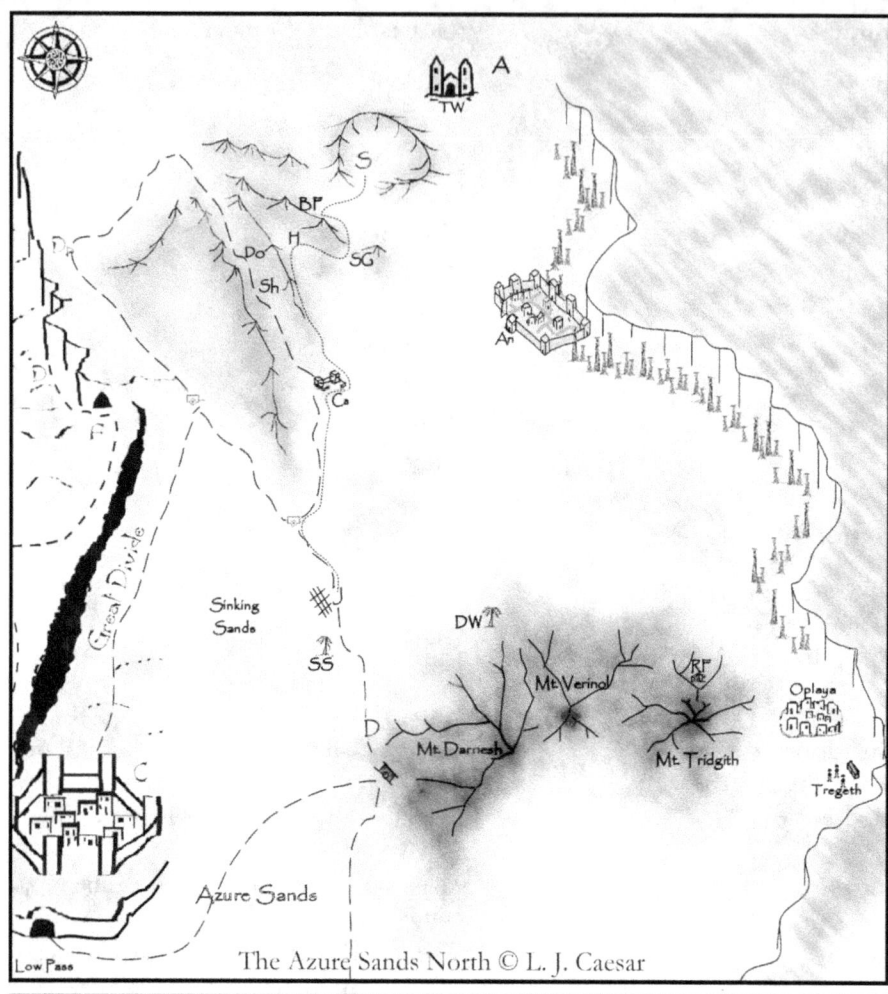

The Azure Sands North © L. J. Caesar

A – Ashgnar
BF – Brus's Fall
D – Darnesh
DW – Drojans Well
J – Jerritol
🌴 - Oasis
S – Scartel
SS – Simlan's Spring
🛒 - Trek Stop

An – Anempor
Ca – Cathlea
🏛 - Droitch
H – Holmgarth
🗿 - Monolith
RF – Ranger Falls
SG – Sholtans Gap
TW – Temple of the Winds
🧍 - Zeglur Breeding Station

The North Eastern Azure Borderlands © L. J. Caesar © L. J. Caesar

A – Ashgnar	An – Anempor
BF – Brus's Fall	Ca – Cathlea
I – Monolith	S – Scartel
SG – Sholtans Gap	TW – Temple of the Winds

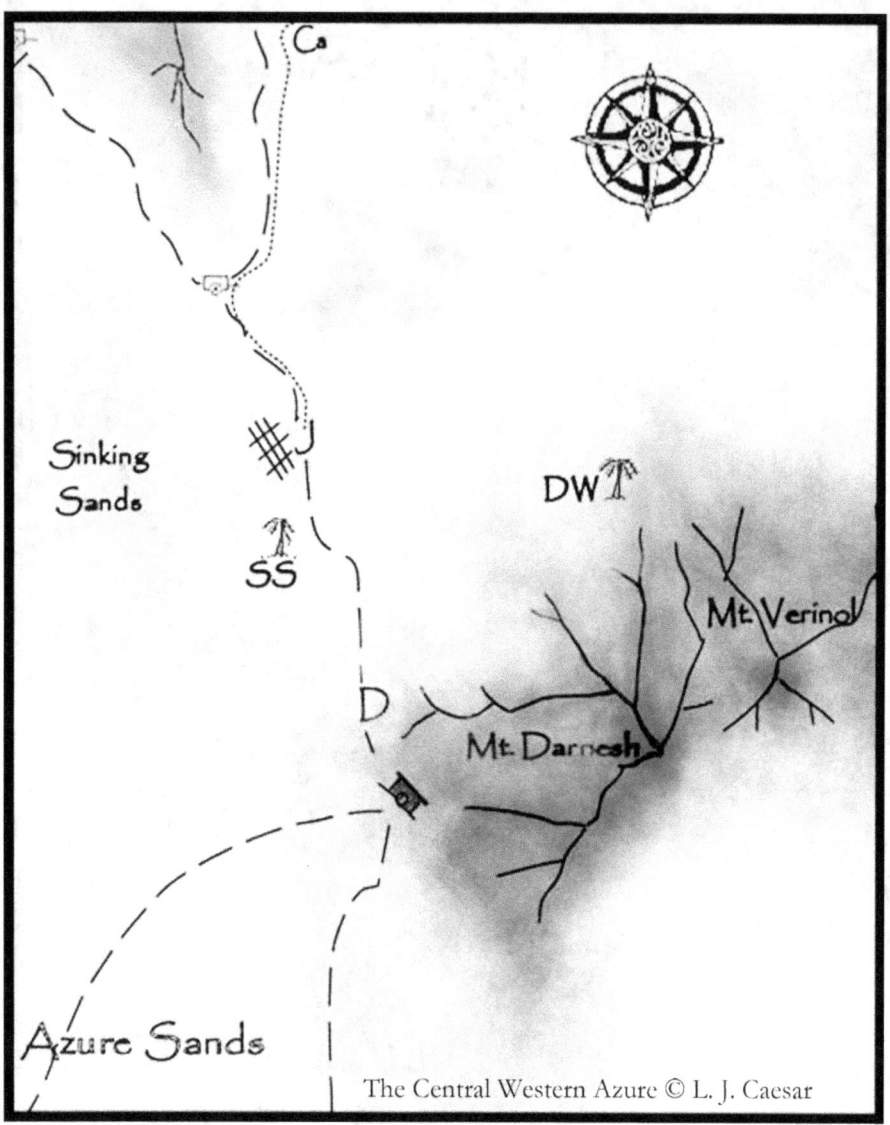

The Central Western Azure © L. J. Caesar

Ca – Cathlea	D – Darnesh
DW – Drojans Well	J – Jerritol
🌴 - Oasis	SS – Simlan's Spring
🏚 - Trek Stop	✳ - Weaver's Holt

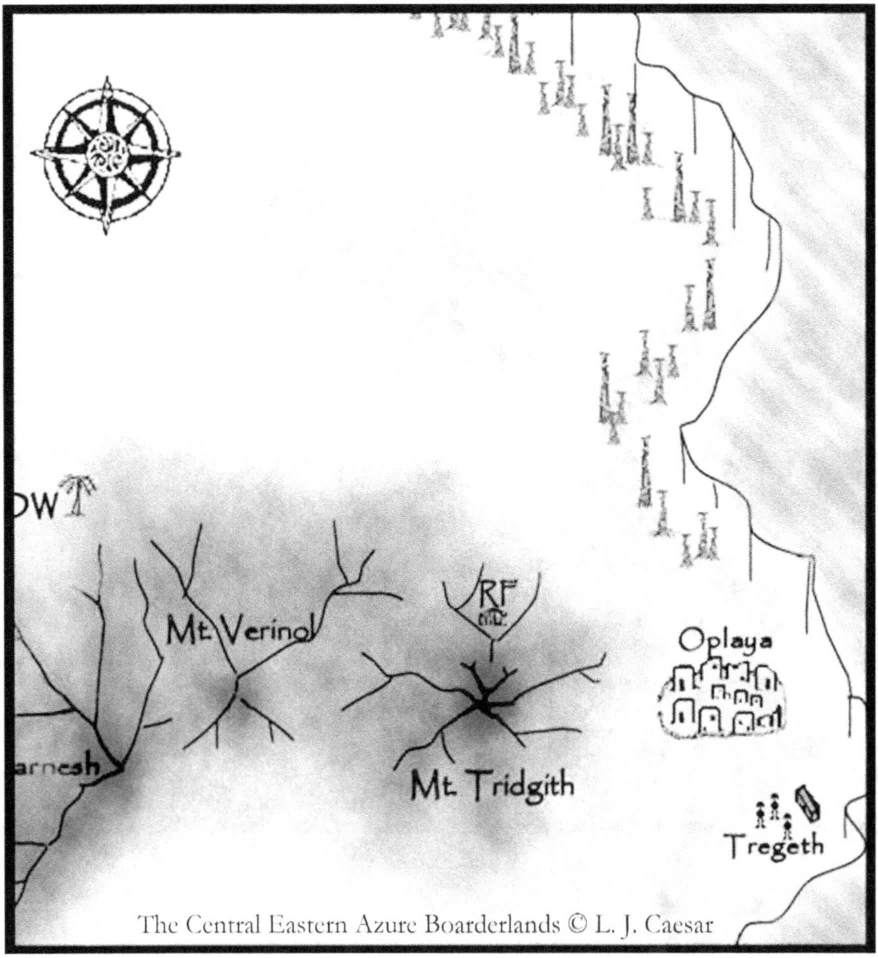

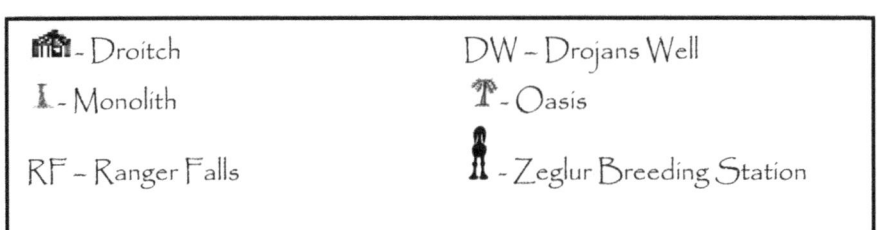

The Central Eastern Azure Boarderlands © L. J. Caesar

Oplaya

Tregeth

Mt. Verinol

Mt. Tridgith

RF

DW

arnesh

- Droitch   DW – Drojans Well

- Monolith   - Oasis

RF – Ranger Falls   - Zeglur Breeding Station

Detailed Map of Holmgarth © L. J. Caesar

▲ - Cave Dwellings	Do – Dovoda
H – Holmgarth	S – Scartel
SG – Sholtans Gap	Sh – Shorronal

PART 1 - THE LONG WAY HOME

Prologue

Written in Ranger script by Anelm Dorenard, Ranger of Scartel.

When my forebears discovered the ridge of the Dorenard Plateau they had to fight against the elements, the terrain and the Clan of these Sands for a lodging. We only brought the Code, handed down from father to son since Cataclysm to guide us. Gradually accepted, we settled this crater amid ancient ruins, before spreading to many other places in the Azure Sands. Here however, with the ghosts of those long dead to advise by their buildings, we have established homes and a way of life. Many of us have married Zurians, despite retaining the wisdom and the Way of the Rangers, but of my generation, I am the last.

When I knew that I was doomed by the marks of plague, I drew up my will, shut myself into my hawking loft, and stayed separate in the hope that my Grandson would survive. I saw him leave unsuspecting, full of excitement as he hauled my barrow filled with grain to the Healer at the caverns. She has taken in many children this ninenight, and I know she will provide for Marran, perhaps harnessing his prodigious foraging talents to good use. I have loosed my hawks, sent them aloft bearing coloured traces that will tell others who can read the code what has happened here, and I have entrusted my message to the stranger Wind that rustles along the roof of my loft, singing me scents of the Opal Sands and safety for the Children of Scartel.

Again I grow feverish, I feel my hands shake and wonder who if any will ever read this, for I know in my heart that they must set a great fire here if they are to save themselves. I will remain here on watch, and trust Solana to light the beacon so that no-one strays into Scartel. This Opal Wind, whispers to me as it cools my fever. I could almost believe what it says, that the children will be safe, that someone will come, that we will not have died in vain, and so as I lie here, I will tell the wind my words, and perhaps my Grandson will hear them one day.

I quote from the Code, the Way I have taught my grandson to behave in the hope of its continuance.

> *"A Ranger is strong, both in body and mind, for he must be able to stand his watch and not fail his Lord.*
>
> *A Ranger provides first, and eats last. His stamina and fortitude must serve those who need protection first. Great power comes from resisting temptation, if a man is greedy, he will gain nothing. The man who waits may feed a village where the hasty loses all.*
>
> *A promise freely given must never be broken. If a Ranger offers to perform a task, then he acquits himself to the best of his ability. There is no place in the Ranger code for laziness, or preferring one task before another.*

*A Ranger above all things is honest, reliable and goes without himself
where another's need is greatest.*

*A Ranger believes in the One. He who watches over the breath of the new-
born Coatan, colours our Sands and shields our skies. We, who follow the
Old Path know of many other things, the magic of the land is ours, the call
of the wild things, the plants and rocks, the winds and trees. This is the
law of the Rangers.*

Thus was the Code handed on, father to son, sat round the fire at night or in
the dim dawn of a misty morning, when the words may be spoken aloud. So I
have taught my Marran, grateful for the son by marriage who not being of our
heritage, has yet insisted that if his son responded to the Calling, he would
provide the means by which the boy could follow in the Old Path. Now all our
dreams have come to dust, and the Lords of Sand have yet to return to their
ancient Halls and homes. I am growing cold, the pain in my joints is very bad
and my scrip holds only a days medication. I carry poisonwood like all Rangers,
but I cannot use it yet. Many is the time I have had to use the kindest medication
for creatures hurt beyond mending, and once I had to loose the bonds of my
dearest one, for she could not birth the child that was to be my daughter Dreean.
The dart so swift, so gentle that she had just time to smile, then my knife
released the new life trapped within, and Marran's mother took her first breath
as Mereth, my dearest love took her last. Not for me yet, though I long to join
her, but I must wait, for the stranger Wind tells of a young Lord coming.

When the one that is foretold comes I do not know, but my friends and
family have watched for him, and so will I, till the last breath fills my lungs. I,
therefore have angled my bed so I may watch Gateway for a sign, and though
the last living have left and I am alone, I will not fear Sundreth, or the coming of
the dark, for a light dawns and with luck my Marran will see it.

This day I think will be my last, for the pain makes me sweat and scream. I
am near the end of my strength, and the crystal chime of dawn was so pure, so
beautiful that I gripped the poisonwood and would have used it then, but for my
friendly Wind, whose name I believe is Mirayen. I found a little water today in
my chilling bowl, with that I will wait until Height of Sun, and when I can signal
with my mirror to tell Solana I must leave. She will already have told my Marran
not to return, and I believe she has warded the village, but if he knew I lived. but
I cannot think of that.

My wits are wandering, I must not stay, but my wind is tugging me, so I turn
to the window once more. Something approaches, a man, a girl, O let the One
not bring them straying into danger.

In the Gateway, an Opal blazes against my Azure Sand. My eyes must be
failing, my wits are scrambled, or am I the Ranger thrice blessed by the sight of
an ancient Anduigor worn on the belt of the Prophecy himself? With him comes

another, shadowed, shaded but glowing still, the right and left hand of power, and unless I dream, the Lords of Sand walk amongst us again.

Now I am content, and my writing is done. Mereth I am ready my love, let death release me on Opal wings which flutter all around as the Wind rustles comfortingly in my loft, my hawking loft, my home...".

Chapter 1 - Song of Sorrow

When Anelm Dorenard's grandson led his charges out of Scartel crater, he had already discussed the planned route with his companions until (as he said), he had succeeded in grinding it into their minds, so that even without him, they could follow the Ranger trail to the travel stop at Cathlea.

"There's little choice.", the nut brown boy argued, drawing diagrams in the sand for his patrol leaders, unaware of the blind Sandsinger's mental touch as the young mage "saw" the path he planned to take.

He continued instructing grimly, "We have to consider the little ones. They have never undertaken Sand walking. Those under seven Rotations have never even left this crater unless they came from Solana's group. We don't use the Sands in the same way as Clansmen, and all of us over twelve Rotations have travelled Ranger routes and know the drill.".

The two adults and nine adolescents had ten times that number to escort, and the young Ranger's brows drew together in fierce concentration as he consulted the Sandsinger.

"Without pack animals, we can't carry enough water to take the Sand route.", he stated flatly. "None of us can navigate an unknown trail or read the sand for dinajh. Unless you can convey us by magic, we have to take the Ranger trails!", and the tilt of his jaw was pugnacious as he made this announcement. Daro considered carefully.

"I agree.", he said slowly, "My real concern is that without sight, I'm a hindrance. I can't clamber about anymore although I'm happy not to have to duck every ten paces!".

His sly reference to the circuitous tunnels riddling Scartel, drew reluctant chuckles, as heads together the seniors planned the first leg of the long route to safety.

"There's a highland crossing with a sheltered depression where we can camp for the first night safely.", said the Ranger boy. "We can refill water flasks from the spring there, staying until early Sunfall when we can climb the next ridge, before going down to Sholtan's Gap. There's an ancient Ranger's halt there, where we'll rest before taking the shortest possible sand crossing into Cathlea.".

They left according to plan, the first short journey taking them higher as they climbed steadily up into the hills, along a gently meandering path into Ranger territory. The falling sun lit the way perfectly, the nine patrols with their leaders made much better time than they anticipated, but, getting excited children to settle in the open, had been a long hard job and tired grizzling youngsters filled Daro and Jalni's minds with apprehension as daylight dawned.

Marran had the way of it though, and soon an ear-splitting whistle drew the patrols up for inspection, and the combined fatigue and misery was overcome as each patrol jockeyed for the Ranger's approbation. Finding roots and a few berries to sweeten their meagre porridge cheered the spirits, and by the time that Marran's foraging party returned the sun was reaching zenith, and the patrols grouped together in shade and slept.

The next stage of the climb was trickier. It would take them along a foot trail above an ancient rock fall, then down a precipitous track to Sholtan's Gap. The party slung re-filled water flasks, backpacks and blankets, and set out, single file in patrol groups. Seniors led, followed by six or seven youngsters, the elders of the next patrol watching those ahead of them, each patrol with a runner keeping in touch with the last. Ahead of the party Marran scouted with Lladro and Torvin, making sure that the track was visible and as safe as possible. In the centre of the party a group carrying babies was brought up by Daro and his Healer, and at the rear came Terris with two other Rangers to make sure that stragglers didn't get left behind, and in that manner they began the climb across the western ridge.

When tragedy overcame them, it didn't come gently. There was no gradual failing wrought upon them by fatigue, or the manifestation of the dreaded plague that haunted their every footstep as they wended their way west towards safety in Selesh. No, tragedy had struck savagely, silencing even the most cheerful chatter, piercing them all with the single terrorised scream as the path collapsed under the feet of Daro's guide. There was a roar of coruscating stones, a chorus of horrified shrieks, a sickening thud, then a pathetic whimper from below.

The Sandsinger cried out, his very protest empowering the protective aura that he cast around the others teetering on the edge of the crumbling track. It formed, a blossom of opalescence, locking them in mid –stride, a span from the edge from which Brus had crashed into the rocks below. Held so, the wail of the distraught and disorientated party mocked the Sandsinger's arrogance, for thinking that he could protect them.

As Daro recovered his balance, he freed the seniors to bring his charges over the gap that had appeared in the path. They formed a weeping huddle, in which Terris, the would be Apothecary moved solicitously, bending over a child here and there, calming, comforting, reassuring, leaving Jalni Daro's healer, and young Marran, to contrive the retrieval of Brus's body, for there was no doubt in any mind that he must have perished. Jalni stood steadily, grim-faced as she payed out the rope that Marran had silently hitched around her body, slowly guiding it for Daro, who took the physical strain of supporting the Ranger who swung perilously off the over-hang below. There was a sheen on Daro's skin, his half open eyes revealed a whorl of fire opal burning in their blind depths, as the muscles stood out on his chest and arms. She trembled, her own hands clawing painfully as she guided the rope, aware that his breath had shortened to tortured gasps. An increasingly panicky mantra had begun to chatter through her mind, "O, how can I help him? What can I do?", when she thankfully felt the light touch of Lladro's hand, as he took up the loose end of the rope, adding himself as anchorman in this silent tug of life and death.

Daro's neck braced backward as a new strain was placed on the ominously creaking rope. His teeth gritted as Marran began an uncertain ascent, then Jalni was transfixed as Daro employed both the ancient powers within his belt clasp and fob, which blazed a line of fire through the hand plaited rope. She heard a hiss of amazement from Lladro as he too felt the whisper of some otherstrength reinforcing their grip, then was caught fast in the gleam of Daro's slowly opening eyes, as the power took him.

Those Opal fired orbs sought her will, subjugating it by the hypnotic flicker of iced fire as his compelling othervoice commanded her obedience.

"Bind your strength to my purpose, subject your will to mine, strength to strength, soul to soul, surrender and know only that you are Opal-sworn bondswoman mine.".

Aware of a gasp of wonder behind her and a whisper of awe from the children, she concentrated, channelling her own not inconsiderable strength into his grip, empowering his tautening sinews, lifting his chest to help him breathe. Thus reinforced, Daro doubled his efforts, drawing Marran over the edge of the pathway and into the willing hands awaiting both him, and the tiny, limp and broken shape he shouldered.

There was no time to waste here, no room to manoeuvre, yet Marran cradled the child's body protectively and in the fading of the day the Rangers face (white beneath the tan) looked shocked as he said gruffly, "He still breathes, but the light is going and we have to make for Sholtan's Gap if we are to stand any chance. This track can no longer be trusted, to try and walk further is impossible, but thankfully I know an alternative route to the camp.".

With the boy's body carefully strapped to his wide shoulders he retrieved his rope and stood, balanced by his staff. Jalni grasped Daro's wrist, finding only a trace of the old nauseated lethargy from spell-casting, and after making them all take a sip of a seemingly inexhaustible flask of snow-berry restorative, she walked on with Daro's arm tucked under her elbow, and for once he didn't protest.

Night was falling, when silenced and shaken, they finally scrambled down a narrow track into the Rangers halt. No more than a group of shallow caves in the angle of an under-cliff, Sholtan's Gap encircled a fire-pit. Quietly leaving Daro and his Healer to relieve Marran of his tragic burden, Terris and the older girls turned towards the caverns, clapping and whooping in the hope that any animals that had settled in this little used camp would leave. Thankfully, the scent of man was still strong, for nothing but a nightlingby flew out of the main cavern, and Terris was able to encourage the children to set up camp within.

She was aware that Daro and his Healer had taken Brus to a secluded cave nearby, that free of his burden, Marran was setting fire to the stock of dried snarflin chips left ready beside the fire -pit, and that Calar (best friend of the injured boy) was being kept busy with the seniors l as the fire took hold. Gentle warmth seeped into the subdued youngsters clinging to each other as they bedded down. All around her packs became pillows, cloaks were used for blankets, soft murmurs escaping the total exhaustion of despair. She settled herself near the entrance, ready to protect them as always, her walking staff close to hand, as Marran banked up the fire to make it last. Slipping the strap of a takran baby sling over his shoulder, to use while foraging, she watched the unusually taciturn Ranger depart into the gathering gloom. Seeing the shadowy figures of the night Watch gathering around Torvin and Rann, she lay facing the fire, struggling to resist the lure of sleep by remembering Scartel and all they had endured during the plague that had made them refugees.[1]

Only children survived. Solana, Scartel's reclusive healer had rescued, fed and comforted them until Daro and Jalni arrived, succumbing to a seizure and dying only days later. Terris and Marran, the eldest of them, had organised the children in the last days of Solana's life, but with the food all but gone, they had been forced to set out across the wilderness. Travelling along the edge of the Azure Sands to the unknown trails beyond, they were seeking relatives, homes and help.

They had known the odds were against them, but Daro, though blind, was Sandsinger of the Opal Sands, so they had been willing to take a chance. Now it had gone horribly wrong and Terris sighed, snuggling into her own coverings. A child hiccupped wearily, another snored and reassured, she drowsed watchfully.

In the cavern they had chosen for its proximity to the fire pit, Daro crouched, waiting for Jalni to examine Brus. Barely qualified, still to take her Song Walk and her Oath, she held the power now. She alone must see what could be done...if anything could be done. His sharp ears caught the familiar sounds as she laid out her equipment. A "clink" as she put out a syndalware bowl, a soft "pop" as she eased the tanbark stopper from one of the flasks, and he caught the sharp scent of porrisroot oil as she prepared to anoint the portals of the child's body. His lips compressed, for it seemed to him that she was preparing the child more for burial than recovery, but he restrained himself from comment, for this was her Sand of birth, and she knew more than he of their rituals. A slither of material told him that she had donned her shantana (covering mouth and nose to prevent infecting the vulnerable child). Soon she would begin her diagnosis, so he sat, shadowed in the cowl of his cloak, cross legged, one hand lightly touching the child's out flung wrist, as he focussed on her. Mind to mind, thought to thought, merged in purpose, one in hope.

Deeply engrossed, Jalni's face betrayed none of her inner trepidation. She bowed her head, forcing her mind to slow, her blood to stop pounding, deliberately matching each breath to the child's, inhalation to inhalation. A frisson of power awakened her to the Sandsinger holding her steadily bathed in that sightless regard, and she relaxed, emptying her mind of conscious thought. Now, she felt for the child's wrist, centring her Voice, seeking the Source with

---

[1] See Another Shade of Mystery © Julia Cæsar 2010

her own skill and launched into an assessment mantra. Her hands evaluated the boy's injuries helplessly, heart weeping for the destruction of one so young. As the hopelessness of the situation was revealed, a kind of calm fell over Daro, who joined the Healer's chant, modulating his empowered *othervoice*, interweaving it with Jalni's until she was able to withdraw, leaving him supporting that precious thread of life faltering beneath his hand.

Time stretched, every turn of the sand-glass seemed like days, and the camp slept, only the dim light of their twin moons touching the cave where the Healer worked and hoped, and a Sandsinger held the threads of a child's life in his hand.

When at last, Daro accepted that the battle was lost, he wept, for Brus had been his self-appointed guide and he had failed him. In the dim light of dawn on that last of days, Brus lay crumpled, breathing in rapid shallow gasps, bones shattered, skin waxen, eyes like black bruises closed and sunken.

Stroking a lock of hair from the child's face, Daro sank into meditation, his own breath slowing to an imperceptible flutter, he searched until at last, he heard the steady voice of the Sentinel, that ancient and shadowy being who had mentored him throughout their time in Scartel.

"I hear your call Ichspeller.", the words echoed in his mind, and Daro concentrated, strengthening that ephemeral link, silently pleading for help.

"I can summon the wind, speak to storms, and restore the light to this world, yet I can't save this child, who has been like a small brother to me. I couldn't prevent him falling, nor mend his wounds, can you?".

In the cavern only the rasping breath of the child could be heard. The greying light might have revealed the figure of the Sandsinger sat as though carved from granite as the occasional sparks flew up from the fire-pit, and still the silence lengthened, the shadows gathered, and there was no answer. Jalni slept exhausted, the camp was strangely still, and then there was light. It streamed as though a myriad stars sparkled to ground themselves inside the cavern, and Daro's senses stirred by the caress of magic, made him relax, surrendering to the presence of his mentor with a sigh of relief.

Slowly materialising beside the Sandsinger, Sentinel raised a hand, bathing the child in an iridescence that flared along every nerve, every sinew, and penetrated that broken shell until the living cells danced in its light. Brus trembled and relaxed, chest lifting, but still the cold sweat of death pooled on his forehead.

Sentinel touched Daro on the arm and whispered, "I can't stay. Walk with me a while.", and turning ducked through the entrance and stood on the far side of the fire-pit. Daro rose stiffly, taking up his Staff and left the shallow cave, to stand in the cool dawn winds, before the heat of day took possession of the Azure Desert again.

"Is it over then?".

All hope had left Daro's voice as he paused to let the breeze freshen his face and dry his tears. There was gentle sorrow in the Sentinel's voice as he spoke softly, inexorably.

"It is not over yet, though his walk on this Plain of Sorrows can't continue. The damage is too great, and without your help his spirit will be lost forever.". He paused, then went on sombrely. "We are not gods Daro though we once thought we were. Our world has paid the penalty for that arrogance, this desolation is the result. You, who have never known the beauty, the fertility, the promise of a world whose name means "Beloved", must trust in what we can show you, and raise the spirits of your people so they may soar beyond their present limitations. Remember my words when you convey that child to the feet of the One.".

For a moment, the blind Sandsinger had the impression that Sentinel was gazing sadly over a wide expanse of blue sand, scattered randomly with outcroppings of savagely wind-carved rocks, then his mentor's voice continued sombrely.

"Though you are Sandsinger, you can't challenge Death, your only power is to challenge life. Death belongs to us all. It is our ultimate right, our ultimate path, it is the Way of all men and even Sandsingers are but men. We can't change death, nor challenge it, nor hold it from its path. Though we live longer through magic, one day all men's paths converge with the way of death, and for that child it will be a merciful release from pain.".

Daro nodded, allowing his acceptance of the inevitable to flood through him. He turned towards the cave again aware that Sentinel was fading like some faint reflection of life, voice fainter, presence thinning as though the winds were disbursing him, but as he faded Daro found himself protesting bitterly, "Am I only granted the power to sing him to death then? Can I do nothing more positive than that?", and as the last trace of his mentor faded, a thready whisper of voice echoed around him in reply.

"Why not try singing him to life Sandsinger? Remember, you can't change his death, but you can change life... Any life.".

Alone again, shrouded in the isolation of mystery, Daro turned and thoughtfully made his way back to the dying child.

As he re-entered the cave, he was aware that the camp had wakened. Marran was stirring their cooking pot over the fire pit, and children were busy scraping roots, crushing nuts and berries ready to add to the Rangers haul. Jalni was awake, and guided him to where Terris was washing Brus gently. He knelt beside her, and heard her murmuring, and then came a whisper, profoundly shocking in its frailty.

"Daro, I feel strange.... Its so dark. Can you make it light?", and the blind man took the child's fragile hand in his as he replied softly, "I can make it light for others Brus, they would see the light, but I wouldn't, and you might not either.".

There was a pause, like the pause between heart beats and the child said slowly, "I must be blind then, or dying?", and the question hung in the air between them, until Daro said heavily, "Brus, I will not lie to you my friend. Some things even Sandsingers can't do. Sandsingers can't use their powers on themselves, so I can't make myself see, and I can't make you...", he paused, fighting for control over his voice, until the child whispered into the darkness.

"Live?", and silently Daro stroked Brus's hand with ineffable tenderness.

The child rested for a while until Jalni and Terris brought his playmates and friends with little treasures to give him. A coloured stone, a feather, muffled farewells, until Daro felt Brus faltering and knew what he must do. A swift sign to Jalni, who brought Calar forward to say goodbye, and then as Terris led him away weeping, his othervoice murmured privately for her hearing only,

"Jalni, I need your assistance. Brus hasn't long now, and I must act if I am to salvage anything from this tragedy. You may not understand what I am about to do, but believe me it is important that I have your support. Will you call Marran to carry the child, and will you lead me where I ask? ".

They went together, Jalni leading Daro, and Marran carrying Brus, out of the encampment, and down a short, rocky scree, to a place where the firm blue sands levelled out in a natural clearing, amongst the towering basalt rocks along the Fringe of these Azure Sands. Without the need for words, Jalni took Daro to the edge of this open area returning to stand with Marran, who dry-eyed but solemn, cradled the child and waited, while Daro took the Heart of Selesh from its mount atop the shaft of his staff. It slumbered quiescent in his hands until he threw the empowered opal down to the ground, crying out as he did so,

"Sorashen! Aris Sorashen!".

As he spoke the ancient words of power, the stone flashed, there was a muted roar and the dark blue sand seemed to shimmer, to shift. The very air swirled thick and viscous for a moment, and about them it seemed that everything had changed. Silently rising from the desert floor, great pillars of opal surrounded them, bathed in a blaze of pure sunlight flowering bushes appeared, humming insects drowsing lazily amongst them. In the centre of the clearing a gleaming dais with an altar materialised, onto which Marran placed Brus. Tenderly the Ranger lifted the boy's limply trailing hands onto his chest, draping the Sandsingers own cloak about him, and murmuring a reassurance before stepping back to stand leaning on his staff, watching intently.

Brus looked infinitely weary now, his eyes still half open had no sight in them, and he rolled his head fretfully as Daro, led by Jalni, came to stand on the plinth beside him. Bending over him Jalni rested her hand on his chest, and closed her eyes before bending to place a gentle kiss on his forehead. As Jalni stepped down to join Marran, Daro spoke, his voice gently enquiring.

"Brus, you once heard me sing in magic. Do you remember?".

The child murmured wearily, "I remember. We were frightened, but you showed us that Sandsingers used good magic, and don't hurt children.".

There was something in Daro's voice that caught the attention of Marran, Jalni, and now Terris and the other children, as they approached the quiet clearing.

Silently and smoothly, the plinth on which Daro was standing with Brus, rose out of the sand, was continuing to rise, until it dwarfed the ancient monoliths of the Azure sands. Strangely the Sandsingers voice was in no way diminished by the distance, and could be heard clearly as he spoke.

"Brus, if you trust me not to hurt you, I will Sing to you of another life.".

Then came the boys voice, a little sleepier, a little slurred as he whispered, "I know you won't hurt me… You're my friend, but I wish I could stay with you.", and to this Daro's magically enhanced othervoice said softly, "I can't help you live as Brus my friend. I can't challenge death, but I can change life and so…", an Opal aura like a beacon shone out over the Azure Sands, and the gathering below saw the distant figure of the Sandsinger open his arms to the wide heavens above.

They felt the tingling of growing energy spreading through the rocks, through the sand, through themselves and the very air they breathed, leaving them resonating in thrall, as they heard in its full power, the magical othervoice high above them. There was a calling in the air, a summoning of some kind, and there, floating lazily in the thermals above Daro was a Cuirax. Far from her own lands, the snow raven sought others of her kind, on pure white wings, with eyes full of fire. To those below, it seemed as if Daro was but waiting for some sign, and as soon as the Cuirax gave out her fluting call, echoing it in great peals through the magical canyon below, he turned and lifted Brus high above his head, and began to sing.

The words of power made the very air shimmer around them, the melody was old, older than the rocks, haunting, lonely and yet full of hope, full of life… As Terris, Marran and Jalni looked up to the spire of rock where sparkling patterns of energy now created a vortex above Daro's head, the outlines of Brus's body seemed to glow, to coalesce, and then suddenly the Sandsinger's cloak fell, freely fluttering its way to the ground and high above them, two great snow ravens spiralled lazily around the outstretched hands of the Sandsinger. The song that had set the rocks around them ringing was fading…fading…and the altar monolith was descending silently, as swiftly as it had risen, bearing only Daro back to them. Of the child there was no sign… just the calling of the Cuirax twirling in the thermals above…

"Kiragh, Kiragh.", one called, and the other called back, "Brus, Brus.".

Chapter 2 - Continuance

As the Sandsinger stepped down off the altar stone, he extended a hand to his staff, which rose from the sand beside Jalni and flew (as if magnetised) by silent command, slapping into his palm with an authority of its own. No sooner was it in his hand when there was a shimmer, a blurring of the eyes, and the opal based canyon ceased to exist as if withdrawn into the Opal power-stone.

Even as Marran wordlessly stepped forward to guide the mage, Jalni saw children rubbing their eyes, and her gaze met that of Terris, who, with a flick of her head, indicated that she intended to return to camp. Nodding agreement, the young Healer stared skyward, but both Cuirax had departed, and she shook herself out of this state of semi-trance irritably and ran after Marran and Daro, catching them as they returned to the smaller cave.

Sagging against the wall (face guarded, eyes closed), Daro seemed devoid of energy; all magic depleted and Jalni hastened to prepare a restorative. Joining Terris at the camp kitchen created by Marran's crew, she found water already boiling, so it only took minutes to prepare the herbs she carried in her scrip. Adding a generous dose of "Sandsinger's Friend" which, she devoutly prayed, would alleviate Daro's obvious distress, and allow him to sleep.

Going back to the cave, she added solinspice to sweeten the drink, then set it aside to cool before she found that Marran had prepared a bed, then helped the exhausted man to strip and wash. Daro was half naked and she drew in a breath of shocked pity, for the Sandsinger bore the marks where the rope had burned into the skin of shoulder, neck, and forearm during the rescue. His knees were bruised and like all of them his legs had been scratched and cut from the scramble down the gulleys, but what really riveted her gaze was the evidence of deep and dreadful injury to his flat stomach and chest. Eyes blurred as she realised those injuries mirrored those borne by Brus, before the mornings events. The young Ranger, always particularly gentle on Daro, stilled with shock, and for two seconds she stood aghast, but as she drew breath to make comment, Daro touched his Seguidor. His Anduigor added its own signature, glowing under his fingers, as the torn skin closed and the bloody tracks scored across his chest faded. In deep awed silence Marran drew a clean dry robe round the Sandsinger, but Jalni, tears welling, had to turn away to control her breathing, her thudding heart, as her realisation of what his magic cost him dawned on her.

Daro took the bowl shivering, barely noticing the additional ingredients as he drank. He had withdrawn from them, and it was not long before Marran deftly caught the mage, supporting him as he slid into sleep. Between them, Daro was manhandled into the bed of dried grasses, covered in his cloak, his boots placed close to hand and left drowsing. Rejoining the others, still quiet with the wonder of the morning, they became aware of their own lassitude and settled down to rest until the desert cooled, and decisions could be taken.

The children reappeared after Height of Sun, sitting or squatting in the shade talking softly with their friends. Marran and his patrol quietly left the encampment, bent on foraging along the edge of the desert, and Jalni shuddered as she contemplated what they would add to the cooking pot. She was developing a positive distaste for meat, and idly wondered if Daro's own allergic reactions were influencing her choices, remembering how Brus had abandoned his favourite food in order to emulate his hero. Ambushed by a clear memory of the boy's shaggy hair, tilt tipped nose, and deep green eyes, she looked away from the fire, straight into the eyes of Terris, and remembered something she ought to do.

Shading her eyes she considered the would be Apothecary steadily. Terris, from being sunk in some reverie of her own, looked up expectantly, as she realised that Jalni wanted her attention.

"Is there something you need for Daro, Jalni?, she asked brightly, adding, "I noticed he seemed to be in pain when he retired. Is there anything we can do to help him?".

Jalni (abandoning professional reserve) admitted, "I don't know, but as you already know about Daro's diet, I can tell you that he takes a very vital restorative after prolonged spell-casting. I have some of his Apothecary's making, so I will give you some, and instruct you how to use it, in case something prevents my doing so.".

She knew that she could have done nothing less with the events of the morning painfully fresh in their minds, and the two girls shared a meaningful glance as the Healer continued, flipping open her scrip and withdrawing an apothecaries slip. Their heads close together, Jalni revealed the contents, taught Terris to "test by sight, test by smell, and test by taste", before she refolded the slip and gave it to her.

"Should Daro need this, he will be showing signs of fatigue or distress. If he is shivering, clammy and cold mix a little to a firm paste with water, then add boiling water and the rest of the slip. If he recovers quickly you need not give more, but I'll give you three slips just in case. He can take up to two full doses in quick succession, particularly if he is physically injured or sick.".

She shuddered at the memory of the injuries she had seen transferred to her lord that morning, but said nothing, continuing to mentor Terris.

"You can add the resulting liquid to any available liquid, warm or cold as a mild tonic. He can drink milk which is a blessing, for without that nourishment he might not have survived infancy.".

She caught the astonished look of the would be Apothecary and grinned.

"I imagine he was a very trying child, and he's not much better in the adult condition.", she pulled a face, allowing a little sisterly familiarity to colour her voice.

"I nursed him through a serious illness recently, so he is still weak and needs your care Terris. I am grateful for any help I can get.", and took great pleasure from watching the girl silently form the word, "Weak?", in awed contemplation of what their Sandsinger might achieve in the peak of health. They continued to discuss Daro's diet until Marran and his contingent arrived bearing aromatic fungi, wild nuts and biroots which the children clamoured over enthusiastically. In astonishment, Jalni and Terris realised that day was ending, the shadows were already creeping into the encampment, and Daro still slept.

Mildly alarmed, Jalni crept into the cavern and stood for a moment observing him. He slept sprawled on his back, arms above his head, the covers disclosing his chest and upper abdomen which was smooth, the skin unmarked, no sign of the grievous injuries she had witnessed, not even a bruise. Jalni shivered, aware that forces greatly beyond her understanding surrounded her patient and turned away to joined the others, feeling oddly excluded from the tantalising mystery that was Daro.

Little groups of children were assembling, travel packs in hand, having brought wood, more of the seemingly inexhaustible supply of the desiccated fungi that they called snarflin to burn, along with dried grasses for the kindling store. In accordance with desert law the camp was constantly restored in readiness for their imminent departure, or for other arrivals. Marran moved from patrol to patrol, making sure that every group had a length of rope, (fashioned by the seniors) from the tough fibrous reeds that grew through the Sands along these Fringes. They had been hard at work, one group succeeding another under the watchful eye of the Ranger, or one of his Nightlingbys. They had amassed a huge coil, from which Marran was cutting and dispensing lengths, making sure that they were better prepared for when they ascended to the Highlands again.

Seeing Calar busily running errands for the Ranger, Jalni bit her lip against the memory of a pair of merry eyes, and continued to rub corrisroot salve into the legs of the smaller children, whose unseasoned limbs had suffered most. Terris rolled clothing into packs, as a patrol carried on stirring pots and fetching water for Brisha, their leader, who seemed intent on following in Terris's footstep. Jalni grinned at her friend conspiratorially and nodded towards Brisha saying in a low voice.

"I see you have an apprentice Terris.", and was taken aback when the girl said (without raising her head or altering the rhythm of the braiding that she was contriving around an oddly shaped pack).

"I have an apprentice? Good healer, examine your memory and see who it is she worships for truth! It is not I who she talks incessantly about, it Is not I that is possessed of more grace, more beauty, more skill, more dedication than any seen in this Plain of Sorrow! It is not my name that crosses her tongue, trips lightly off her lips every time she opens her mouth...oh no my Healer friend, I don't think she looks to me!".

Jalni was puzzled, looking up to see Brisha and Lallee, heads together whispering and giggling even as they stirred dishes for the evening meal. Her eyes dropped to see the Sandsingers specially marked bowl being cleansed with soapsand, with an intensity of purpose and devotion to thoroughness that she found touching in a child of no more than twelve namedays, and said incredulously, "Daro? She's crazed Terris. A child could never aspire to that sort of power. It would surely kill her! Besides, we don't know if there can be more than one at a time, or even if women are admitted to those ranks.".

She wondered suddenly if she should tell Daro, then ducked as a soft burrin moss was tossed at her. She caught it deftly, staring at Terris who was chuckling.

"Oh Jalni!", she gurgled, "You are clearly unaware of the effect you have on several of my young women. I have them queuing up to tell me how wonderful that one of our Sands serves the Sandsinger. How gifted you must be, because he trusts you and only you. Night after night they see you tend him, and day after day you are at his beck and call. You are so meek, so properly behaved towards him, and so beautiful that they think you the epitome of all that they want to be. No, I have no potential apprentice, but I could name you three!".

She cheekily poked out her tongue at the bemused Healer, who watched as Brisha, Lallee and a shy girl that she thought was called Erinim giggled and blushed and darted stolen glances at her, inwardly groaning at the thought of Ikella's reaction, should she discover that Jalni was the object of hero worship, for meek behaviour and instant obedience! Not quite sure if she was numb with disbelief, or stupid with fatigue, she had just decided to allow her reputed skill to stand, when she became aware that Marran had called the Nightlingbys to attention, and that they were stripped to the waist, for the ritual of evening exercise.

Packs readied, Terris had summoned the older girls to eat the foragers stew, water was drawn and still Daro slept. Jalni stood undecided, the fire lit up the darkening arena of the camp, they were shielded from casual view by the immense outcrops of rock surrounding them and she felt safe here. She moved restlessly, wondering if they were indeed going to travel that night, seeing that stars were beginning to appear, when she felt a tingle along her ears and realised that an amused voice was complaining in her mind.

"Jalni?", he said sleepily, "Why am I still in bed? Where's Marran? Where are you all?", and a little relieved, she hurried to see that Daro was nearly dressed, his bed tidied and that he seemed well recovered.

Keeping her expression blank, she bobbed a curtsy, saying submissively, "You called me Lord?", and lowered her eyes to her twisting hands, refusing to meet his compelling othergaze, although her treacherous body tingled with the memory of it. Her breath shortened, her cheeks flamed, and she didn't feel his presence until a warm palm was laid against her forehead, and in a voice which crackled with apprehension he demanded anxiously, "When did you start feeling ill Jalni, what have you been eating??", his concern was so genuine that she immediately regretted playing games with him, but found herself confessing truthfully.

"I am not unwell my lord.", she said as humbly as she could.

"However, I heard that a number of young women hold my abilities in high esteem. They also seem to believe that I am to be admired for my behaviour towards you, and that my general grace, beauty and intelligence are things to emulate!".

She snorted derisively, then (for reasons unknown) a tear trickled down her cheek to meet the Sandsingers fingers where he still held her face tilted towards his. He was still, his eyes closed, and then they opened and lost in a torrent of emotion Jalni was drawn into his arms, and his mouth descended ruthlessly on hers. His lips tormented her senses, tantalising, invasive, but oh so tender and with a reluctant groan, she gave herself up to them.

He kissed her until she thought she could die happily, then, as the wave of desire flooded through her, tiny tender kisses traced her throat and she felt her heart hammering, breasts crushed against his chest, hands entwined in his hair as he straightened. He touched her lightly on the nose, and his inner voice murmured intimately.

"Well little one, perhaps they will think you are ministering to me now, but we had better not tell them how!".

That mocking voice in her head was like iced water in her veins, followed by a rush of red hot anger. Mutely, she tore herself from his arms, turned her back and stood trembling, still throbbing to the song of desire, troubled by her inability to make friends, and confused by the misperceptions laid at her door by the impressionable teens outside.

"Is this some sort of joke?", she asked herself bitterly, "Does he toy with me for his own pleasure? Is he testing me to see if all I am capable of is to be a bedmate, a plaything supplied for his own gratification? Are we all simply toys to him?".

She had whirled away from him, and stood resentfully staring into the shadows at the back of the shallow cavern, one hand to her mouth as though she could deny the burn of his kiss – the other clutching her cloak across her bosom as if she could defend herself against the arousal that he had instigated. She almost felt his presence behind her, then shockingly did as he pulled her roughly back against him, bending his head to tease the crook of her neck with his tongue.

"No. No!", her voice was husky but certain, and he reluctantly withdrew his hold on her.

"Jalni, I care for you, perhaps more than I knew.", his voice was hoarse, and she turned to see that he was struggling to keep control over the situation, hands fiercely clenched to his sides, face darkened.

"I know that you don't care for being bound, and that you would willingly walk away given the choice, but I have no choice and neither do they.".

He gestured in the direction of the darkening camp, just ten paces and yet a whole world away as he fought the urge that had nearly undone them, finding his balance as desire ebbed. He sat on a flat rock and said quietly.

"I know that this is difficult for you to believe, but the girls are right. You are greatly gifted, graceful, and beautiful, which is why Ikella wished you on me in the first place, more as a test of my strength of purpose than yours. She didn't know whether Healing was your true vocation, so I must test your calling while we travel. I can already tell her that you are quick to anger or to love, that you are fearless, funny and so female it frightens me. That you are my own true bondswoman, that I trust you with my life, and quite possibly my heart, for even Sandsingers need to be comforted, loved, desired.", his voice had dropped sadly, and Jalni suddenly saw that a very human need for comfort in his loss had provoked this situation, and smiled tentatively as he sighed and said regretfully, "I'm sorry, I didn't think this would happen. I just wanted someone to hold, someone to love, but this is not the place, or time, and I have behaved badly.".

His voice sounded uncertain, and Jalni found herself reaching for his hand and saying softly, "I know. All these things in good time and now is not the time?", she repeated Ikella's favourite mantra, and was rewarded as he grinned in perfect harmony once more.

She guided him out of the cave, into the arena lit by the fire pit, and the Children of Scartel rose as one, bowing to the Sandsinger respectfully. Stunned, Jalni faltered to a stop, aware that Daro couldn't see this deeply moving tribute, even as her tremulous inner voice projected her thoughts to the young mage.

"Ichspeller! They bow to you. ", and the wonder trembled through her words.

"In the memory of Brus, they bow low.".

Daro paused, his head inclined as though he listened to her speaking voice, then he stepped forward into the light. He raised his right hand, with fist clenched to his heart, then (fingers lightly curled) to forehead, finally extending it, palm up to the children, in a graceful sweeping gesture that returned the salute in the manner of the Opal sworn. He pivoted on his heel to take in the entire group, ending with his back to the track, facing the open desert.

At that moment there was a sighing sound and the evening breeze sent up a little ripple in the dust at the Sandsingers feet, and Daro knelt in a single fluid movement, touching his forehead to the sand and the others followed his example. It was simple, silent, but his prayer to Gurayen, the wind of the Azure Desert was heartfelt for all of that, although Jalni, found herself wishing that he had spoken aloud so that the children could share the moment.

As soon as the breeze died away, Daro stood, and she moved allowing him to take her arm, following as she picked her way through the gaggle of hungry children, into a circle of travel packs set up for them to sit on. As she settled him down he murmured quietly, "They all heard me Jalni. I spoke so that they would all understand that I would give my life to return Brus to his, that I have dedicated the rest of this journey to his memory, for I consider his sacrifice more, much more than any of the Winds deserve.".

Chapter 3 - The Old Path

Jalni shot Daro a curious glance. "Does he imagine he can issue such a challenge with impunity?", she wondered, grateful for the emergence of a stammering Calar, whose tentative approach to Daro acted as a distraction. She watched curiously, seeing a very chastened soul, as he knelt on one knee before the Sandsinger trying to thank him for helping Brus. The sight of the pugnacious orphan, who had constantly sparred with Brus, and defied anyone to make him obey "some old Sandsinger", almost reduced her to tears, as he apologised, but Daro knew what to do.

He reached out, touching Calar's forehead at third eye, placing the unmistakeable signature of the Opal-sworn there. Calar's eyes blazed with pride as the Sandsinger bent to place the kiss familiar on a cheek too immature to shave, then she saw him gulp, and laughter rang out from his entourage, as Daro said plaintively,

"Must I bond everyone in order to get a plate of stew?".

They were close to the fire and children were hastily queuing for food, patting travel bags into place for their friends, or eating. Jalni who carried their small carry-sack extracted Daro's spoon, a horn travel mug, and went to stand in line for food, but was waylaid by Brisha who shining eyed was bringing a flatwood with the Sandsingers dishes laid out for her to inspect. Jalni smiled and looked approvingly at the bowls as Lallee tottered under the weight of the ancient tray.

She spoke thoughtfully, "Brisha, the flatwood is a brilliant idea, but it is heavy, far too heavy for one so young, and I don't think even Lallee could handle it when the dishes are full.".

She paused and contemplated the problem.

"I know", she spoke brightly, "Why don't I carry the flatwood, then if you follow my directions to the letter, you could serve Daro's meal yourself.".

She thought she would laugh at the child's reaction, but unaccountably found herself fighting back tears as Brisha stammered, "I can assist you Healer Jalni? Won't the Sandsinger be angry?", she sounded nervous, but was extending the flatwood to Jalni as she spoke, and it was plain that the girl thought her day was made.

She quietly followed Lallee to where Terris was ladling food into the children's bowls, already starting on the second of the large vessels that they had filled with the fruits of their foraging, and when Jalni rested the flatwood on the edge of the stone fire pit she smiled approvingly.

"Hello girls.", Terris said lightly, "Are you helping Jalni?", and amidst a flurry of shy nods, and self-conscious tucking back of hair, continued smoothly, "The small cookpot to the left is for Daro, Brisha. Jalni will taste it, and add what she must to make sure that he keeps healthy.".

Carefully shielding a smile of amusement, Jalni took her cook spoon from her belt, held it closely over fast boiling water, shook the condensed steam from it and stirred Daro's pot, before taking a spoonful of the aromatic stewed fungi and putting it into her own tasting bowl. She followed the code of the Healer meticulously.

"Examine by sight.", she murmured, moving several chunks of biroots to one side and looking at the resulting red liquid. "Examine by smell.", she cut a piece of mushroom, lifting it on a skewer to inhale the delicious aroma. "Examine by taste", and happily taking up her spoon, carefully composed a collection of every ingredient, and chewed then thoroughly, swallowing gratefully.

Terris swiftly re-arranged bowls, saying happily, "When Jalni is satisfied with flavour, texture and seasoning, the Sandsinger will eat. She will fill his bowl ready to serve him, and will again taste his food in front of him, with a single spoonful in that small bowl. No-one touches Ichspeller Selunsanni's food but Healer Jalni. ", she smiled at the low chorus of gasps, and showed Jalni a third cookpot in which clean hot water bubbled, and Jalni took over, instructing briskly.

"Add red hot stones to that Lallee.", then at the child's obvious bewilderment said, so that Brisha and Erinim too could hear her.

"Daro's bowl rests on the top of that, hot steam from the water rises and …", the girls chorused in happy enlightenment, "Keeps his food warm?", and Terris turned away to hide a grin.

Brisha bowed her head in obedience to Jalni as she measured and stirred, giggled when stemmis leaves turned the boiling water brown, and gazed with horrified concern as Jalni placed a small tasting bowl on the freshly laden flatwood.

"What if we got it wrong?", she agonised, and flinched as Jalni chuckled darkly.

"Then you will only poison the Sandsinger's Healer, not the Sandsinger.", she pointed out caustically, adding, "I am of little account, but without Daro this world could die. This may seem like senseless ritual, but it is the Way.".

Brisha was shocked, but dutifully obeyed every instruction that Jalni uttered, and soon they were making their way back to where Daro was chuckling with the older boys, who queued for food last, according to their custom.

He took the bowl with consummate care and Jalni was pleased to see that Erinim (the youngest of the three), had dropped back to busy herself finding clean folded cloths. She took them as they were proffered and protected both Daro's hands and clothes as he took the hot bowl and sighed with pure contentment.

Brisha watched Jalni taste his food, gaped when he tapped Jalni gently on the hand, playfully insisting that she had stolen the best piece of his fungi, until Jalni drew all of them to one side, and completely over-awed the girls by sharing her bowl with them.

"A master should always feed his apprentices first", she murmured, "for without apprentices to help, what good is the master if there is too much work?"

Lallee asked the one question she dreaded.

"Are you Daro's apprentice then?", and she drew her brows together thoughtfully.

"I don't think so Lallee.", she confessed, "I don't think that you can learn to be a Sandsinger, or we would have more of them. We know so little about the far past, but Daro believes that there were more Sandsingers then. He is the first for a long time, and we don't yet know how he is called to this state of being…".

She spoke slowly, unwilling to discuss matters of which she knew little. Lallee stretched her arms luxuriously, and completely shattered Jalni's inner composure by announcing seriously, "Healer Jalni, I think you are very brave. Sampling food for someone as important as Daro is a very dangerous thing to do, unless of course you prepared all the food yourself. I don't think I want to do that, and I don't want to cook the dinners either…No!", she paused and then said in a very practical voice, careless of who heard her.

"I think I'd better be a Sandsinger myself !".

Behind her Daro, taking a mouthful of his stemmis, caught his breath and choking and spluttering had to hide his amusement from the oblivious child.

The evening passed, the obligatory cleaning of cooking pots was completed by Marran and his group, the Ranger using this time to teach the younger men about camp cleanliness.

"Many may pass through Sholtan's Gap until the high trails open again, so we must clean the cooking pots, for they will be needed. Start with the biggest pot, scrape any remaining food on to the fire, or get it inside your stomach. We can't afford waste, and you will soon walk off the extra! Leave no scraps to attract vermin or scavengers, use or burn, that is the way. Take the soapsand that lies under the greenrock at the base of the cliff, and tear up some long groundroot, rub the soapsand into the pot walls with that until it is greasy and soft, then use water, sparingly mind, and remove the soaped rubbish, tip it into a smaller pot, or one that is overburned, and while you tackle the next one, that will sit and soak and be easier to clean. Make sure that you can see, feel and smell nothing in those pots, then, dry them thoroughly, turn them on their sides and let Gurayen help you. When the pots are dry, go to the soft sand and fill them to the brim before storing them in the main cave where we found them.".

Brisha watched them, turning to Lallee,

"Why fill the clean pots with soft sand Lallee?", she asked plaintively and Lallee hastened to explain.

"Soft sand is very strange. It is like dust really, and occurs near greenstone deposits. It will prevent poisonous creepies (like scalebacks) making their homes inside the pots. Soft sand won't cling to the pots, empties cleanly, and will suck down and kill larger vermin, so that others are warned off.", she explained succinctly.

"Oh.", said Brisha, mentally filing information away with a decisive nod, "That's all right then.", and turned to Jalni, dropping a bob of a curtsy.

"Please Healer Jalni, may we be freed to find our packs and prepare for travel? I am mindful that my group friend Sherimin has looked after our set, while we assisted you, and if you are not in need of us now, we would like to go and help her.".

Jalni looked back at her steadily.

"I believe I can spare you Brisha, but I must ask permission to dismiss you.".

She stood, and made a graceful curtsy to Daro, who was facing the desert, a frown on his face as if waiting for something to happen.

"My lord?", she asked softly, wondering what he was listening for, "May I dismiss my assistants to their own duties now, or do you still require their presence?".

For a moment Daro seemed bemused, and then he cleared his throat and asked.

"Are you satisfied with their performance my Healer? Did they work well for you, did they leave everything tidy and clean? Were they obedient to your decree?".

He was wonderful, Jalni decided, looking at his innocent face. She could detect no mockery there, and the children were quivering in an agony of anticipation as she took her time before speaking.

"My lord, they were everything that Terris told me they would be. Of course you know Lallee well, and even she was no trouble at all, though I think you may need to guide her ambition a little.".

Behind her she could sense the irrepressible Lallee shaking her head vehemently and smiled. It was just her imagination, but she could hear the girl saying firmly,

"No, I think I'll be the Sandsinger.", and prayed that thought would not meet Daro's ears.

Brisha nearly fell over when Daro said severely,

"Lallee needs to be careful what she thinks. I can hear you clearly young woman!", and Jalni turned in time to see Lallee trying in vain to conceal her blushes.

"Most odd...", the Healer thought, and then realised that she could possibly hear some of what Daro heard, through their bond... and thinking about the interlude in the cave, she too shivered and blushed, but not with guilt.

"Brisha!", Daro had turned his attention to the younger girl, "My poor Healer is over-worked and needs an apprentice of her own. Would you like to take a trial with her?".

The child was as white faced as Lallee was pink, she dropped to her knees covered in confusion, and kissed the sand at Daro's feet, gabbling happily.

"I, my lord?", incredulity filling her voice, "I can be Healer Jalni's assistant?", and Daro, mindful of his duty, straightened from his comfortable slouch on the travel packs and said formally.

"You will have to obey her every word, instantly. You will attend her regularly every day, after you have performed your own daily duties. Your fellows will not regard your new status highly, if you leave them with more work than is fair. You will be bound by oath and bond to Jalni, as she is bond to me. You will see and learn much, and speak of nothing!".

There was an odd note in his voice and Jalni glanced up to see the brief glitter of Opal in his eyes, and stretched out her hand, obedient to the voice in her head that said softly, "Stretch out your right hand Jalni, touch your forefinger to her forehead at Third Eye, and say the words.".

Numbly, feeling as if she too was in a trance, Jalni obeyed, feeling an odd tingle in her finger as she touched the child lightly.

"Bend your will to my will, your hand to my command, your thoughts to my thoughts and know yourself bond to me, bondswoman mine.", and the child knelt, waiting for Jalni to say more. The tingle along Jalni's ears increased and she repeated his words, slowly and clearly.

"Now you are my assistant Brisha, you will need to listen for my voice. If I call you, I will expect you to come instantly, and not bring all your friends as well. Healers above all things have to conduct themselves carefully so that the sick can have confidence in them, the injured know that they are safe. You must conduct yourself in manners at all times so that others can learn from a good example. You may hear our lord call for us both sometimes, and you must attend, whatever else is happening. Do you understand me?".

The child whispered attentively, "Yes Healer Jalni, I hear and obey!", and Jalni said briskly, "That is good. Now go and celebrate!", wincing as Brisha raced towards her friends whooping and shrieking with pent up excitement,

"I'm bond! Bond to Healer Jalni. Terris, Lallee, Erinim I'm going to be a healer, a healer just like her."

Amazed at the lack of resentment at the imposition of Daro's will, Jalni turned to see that the mage had cloaked himself in his Opal aura and was looking somewhat sad and pensive. She reached out to touch him, but hesitated as his thoughts whispered in her head, curiously strongly despite the shield of his aura,

"Now that is how a bond should be.", and her throat tightened as a sense of his loneliness touched her.

Once evening chores were done the boys in Marran's group returned to their elaborate exercises; clad only in long travel pants caught loosely at the ankle, they stretched and flexed arm, stomach and chest muscles to limber up, and then began on the specialised link movements of Zurian Warriors. They were not many, these striplings; perhaps nine at the most, they faced Marran, proudly; crossed their arms across their chests and stood straddle-legged, ready for the word of command. Marran was somewhat taller, if only five name days older than his faithful band, but he was every inch the commander. He stood facing them, and Jalni noticed how carefully he observed them, checking posture, composure, attitude. Then, when he was sure they were ready, he brought his own right hand across his chest in salute and commencement of exercise. The whole arena glowed with the leaping flames from the fire pit, the others just dark silhouettes against the hot red heart of it, the leaping gold of it, the flicker and sparkle of it, then Marran raised his hand in a complex gesture, and there was a low staccato drumming, as the girls created a rhythm for their men folk, and the air around them began to hum.

One of the older girls stood, folded her hands and raised her voice in ululation in which both celebration and mourning for their friend mingled. A soft thrumming from the posturing bodies, their stamping feet and snapping fingers built up, Torvin, Rann, Lladro and Marran leapt and whirled in some dervish descant, the sands gleamed bluer, the shadows lengthened and in the dark a voice spoke.

"We that belong to the Old Path greet you, Children of our children's children. Let the Ranger Code and Ranger Ways see you safe back home.", and into the fire-light clad in the leather jerkin of a bowman, walked a Ranger.

Chapter 4 - Holmgarth

The visitor stood just over a hands breadth above five and a half spans, lean yet sturdy, dressed in patch dyed blues which had permitted his unseen arrival. Short dark hair receded from a noble brow, under which highly intelligent eyes sparkled from the weathered complexion of one who lived in the open. His air of unhurried calm was impressive as Marran and Torvin ran forward to intercept him. Laying a short bow on the ground in front of them, he waited quietly, empty hands displayed, while Rann circled to join the others.

He seemed relaxed, though his hazel eyes were watchful and Jalni, aware of the subtle shifting that had hidden Daro from the stranger's view, felt the hugely increased tension as she sidled forward, determined to see this Ranger clearly. The visitor, (boxed in between a well heaped fire and three younger, taller and presumably faster males than he), seemed supremely confident, and Jalni was possessed of the strange conviction that the Ranger could defeat any or all of them with one arm tied behind his back. She held her breath as laughing eyes, oddly familiar eyes, smiled directly into hers, as his finely moulded mouth quirked in amused tolerance. A slight shrug said, that he accepted the boys were trying to be men, but if ever she wanted a real man, he stood in front of her.

"Hmmph!", came the caustic comment in her mind, and alarmingly, the stranger's eyes strayed momentarily to the quivering group that shielded the Sandsinger. Submerging Daro beneath then, Lallee and Brisha sat on his lap, Erinim leant against him with Calar and friends, until Daro had all but disappeared beneath them.

The Ranger said calmly, "I give you greeting kin to kin, is there a Dorenard amongst your number, or a Skellin? My name is Draille Skellin. I have come in answer to a summons from an old friend.".

The small group at the fire rearranged themselves as he extended a gloved arm, and looking earnestly into Marran's eyes, threw back his head to emit a strangely haunting whistle. Nearby a nighthawk shrilled, then jesses flowing drifted into land on his outstretched arm with a gentle tinkle of her tracking bell. The man stroked her head gently with the crook of a finger, and then Jalni caught sight of Marran's face. He stared at the hawk, longing, grief stricken, yet hopeful. The Ranger smiled, face lighting up, laughter lines around his mouth creasing, eyes crinkled, as Marran admitted gruffly, "I'm Dorenard.".

Gently transferring the hawk to Marran's gloved hand, he said softly,

"Anelm loosed his hawks and they found us. We have journeyed far and wide to intercept you, but you took the high route. We had no idea that so many of you survived.".

His glance swept round the camp, noting kindling and burnables replenished, taking in the camp kitchen, the readied packs, and said slowly.

"Who is trail Leader? Camp Captain, Quartermaster? How many scouts have you, and who is Ranger?".

Marran shuffled, explaining diffidently, "We're a bit of a hotch potch really. I am Camp Captain, and Trail Leader. Terris is Quartermaster, Torvin mirrors me on Night Patrol, Lladro and Rann are scouts and Calar is my runner, but we have no Ranger. I was promised to Findar Helebran before plague took my family, but I had no sponsor. I am Marran and Kreel here was my Grandfather's hawk.".

It was a long speech for the normally taciturn boy, and Draille's hand which had risen to support his chin, now thoughtfully rubbed his upper lip as he considered that information. Marran stood gentling the hawk, and then he said quietly.

"If you can help us Ranger Skellin, we will share what we have to hand, find you a bed and food for Kreel.", and Jalni suddenly saw how responsibility weighed on Marran's shoulders, and understood his longing for advice. Slowly she felt the camp relaxing around her, and then Marran's head lifted, and he whistled shrilly.

The children rose, silently slipping into patrols as the Ranger turned towards Daro, who sat forward, into that trail honed perception. Draille Skellin stared up the slight rise to where the Sandsinger waited.

"He might as well have been sat on a throne.", Jalni marvelled. It seemed as though the entire pile of travel packs glowed. Daro's Anduigor gleamed softly, echoing the Seguidor which flashed at the base of his throat.

The Ranger bowed respectfully.

"Lord of the Opal Sand.", he turned bright knowing eyes on Jalni, "Lady.", he inclined his head in acknowledgement, "We have waited many Rotations for your return. I praise the day that the Lord's of Sand walk with our kin again.", and then, as if Draille had not interrupted their celebration of Brus's transformation, the camp enfolded them, and a blanket was produced, drinks and bread arrived and once more the events of the day were retold, in mime, in dance and then Daro stood, taking Jalni's arm and came forward to the fire, and the familiar ritual of the bedtime story was repeated.

Jalni led Daro to one side of the natural arena in front of the fire-pit, conscious of the gentle shift of the hawk, as it rocked on the temporary perching post Marran had provided for it. She was uncertain of hunting birds, and chose to stay out of its way, crossing to sit with Terris, aware that Marran and his Nightlingby patrol stood, elegantly poised on a terrace above the fire. Their heads bowed as from the dark shadows, Daro's voice whispered a prayer, gently hovering at the edge of hearing.

There was no obvious sign of magic, yet every word thrummed in their minds as he conjured the memory of Brus, and how he had left them. Jalni saw him clearly, running, leaping, shouting with laughter, leading Daro so proudly. Then the fragile broken shell, the dying whispers, the final farewell, and an extraordinary stir began as the children remembered the Cuirax and its fluting call.

They could hear it in Daro's remarkable *othervoice*, even as the Nightlingbys stretched their arms, and fluttered their hands simulating wings in a slow whirling exercise seemingly supervised by the Ranger. They were all aware of the intensity of emotion as the last part of the story was told, and it seemed to Jalni that as Draille and Marran positioned themselves for a jongleurs throw, in which one would impel the other high into a somersault, that something else was planned.

As Daro's voice rose to a soaring crescendo, the wind stirred the embers into leaping flames, Marran was poised, and Draille suddenly ran towards the boy, somersaulting high into the air above Marran's head, then pivoting. One foot was cupped in the boy's hands, and Marran smiled as Draille appeared to take flight, soaring high over the fire, arms positioned precisely like some raptor's wings, as he vanished into the dark. Daro was still "in magic", and his voice held them in thrall, but Jalni, suddenly "aware", in a way that she had never been before, caught sight of a deserted perching post, and wondered if they would ever see Draille again.

Somehow the entire camp seemed to know that there would be no travel this night. In silence the Children of Scartel collected packs and blankets, retiring to the larger cavern, Terris bringing up the rear, and Jalni's last sight of the arena, was the Night Watch, banking the fire against the night, shooing stragglers to their beds, and Marran, staring out across the sands as though straining to see one who had departed. She took Daro herself to the temporary washdown and latrine, sensing that he didn't want to talk, and in companiable silence they readied themselves for bed, returning to the cavern in a sort of sleepy domesticity, that Jalni found strangely comforting. She waited for Daro to settle down and was touched when he submitted docilely to the suggestion that sleep came before study, slipping the small book he treasured into his pack without demur. Jalni slid her tired body into her own blankets, and indifferent to the hard ground slept, rousing to a light touch as Marran woke her around first light.

The boy's face looked different, and coming fully awake, Jalni saw with a strange thrill that he wore the blue dyed designs of a ritual warrior. He raised a finger silencing her, and beckoned her to follow him, sliding out of the cavern to find that the Night Watch had been replaced already, that Rann wore Marran's half dyed jacket, and that their trail leader was stripped to the waist, his whole body adorned with the dappled blue shadows of a Ranger camouflage. She stared at him in bewilderment and then the man hunkered over the wakening fire stood, and she glanced up into Draille Skellin's calm face.

"He has withdrawn from conversation Healer.".

The man's voice was low, emphatic as he poured a little water into a shallow bowl and took up a razor. He indicated the silent boy who sat stoically permitting Torvin to rub some compound into his feet.

Draille's voice said steadily, "I am to instruct you, stay with you in his stead, and lead you in his wake as he takes *holonogarth*, the Ranger's ritual challenge.". Jalni was horrified, she knew that all Ranger's submitted to a test of trail worthiness, but she also knew that few took the test before their thirtieth Rotation, if they survived that long, and something of her reaction must have shown in her face, for Draille said with conviction.

"He is ready Healer. I know the preparations that my good friend Anelm put him through. He has no fear of Sundreth, or of death, and begs you to understand that this Walk is for his Grandfather, that his spirit might soar with that of Brus Skellin, my grand nephew, whom your Lord freed yesterday. Where one goes, so goes another, and Dorenards and Skellins have always wandered the trails of the One together.", he moved swiftly to stand by Marran, and Jalni saw with relief how gentle was the hand that cut the boy's hair, shaving it bristle short, but for one long strand at the nape of his neck, which he deftly plaited, embellishing the plait with two feathers, one large, snowy white, the other small, mottled blue and bronze, and without a word Jalni knew one to be Cuirax, the other Nightlingby.

She watched numbly, as Draille readied the boy. He could take nothing but a belt and knife. She watched as Draille took from his own pouch, a thin pliable cord, wrapping it round the belt and securing it firmly. He watched as Lladro and Torvin booted him, drawing out a strangely fletched dart, capped with tanbark, and secured it to Marran's belt, all the time murmuring in the boy's ear as he worked. Then he was ready, gloved, booted and supplied with what was allowed, his braid gently adjusted to swing over his shoulder, and he stood before Jalni, and casting an agonised glance at the cavern full of sleepers, raised a hand to Draille who spoke softly.

"I have taken my vow, and may not speak amongst men until I complete *holonogarth*.", said the Ranger's voice, and Jalni instantly understood that he spoke for Marran.

"This is my living will, bequeathing all I die possessed of to Terris Amstellern, who is the mate of my heart. She knows nothing of this choice, and will require a friend to help her understand that I couldn't leave our Sand without preparing to bring my people back. As you are bondmate to the Lord I would serve, I beg you to tell him that I do not desert him, but must finish my training before another life is lost on this trail!", and in a mist of tears, Jalni saw that Marran felt responsible for Brus's accident.

She cleared her throat and said slowly and deliberately, "You are not guilty of any fault Marran Dorenard. You do not have to do this, but if it be your will, then I will bless your trial by Gurayen, the Wind of our Sands, by the Azure itself, and by Mirayen the Wind of the Opal, whose Lord I serve. I will relay your words to those who should hear them, and will follow Ranger Skellin's advice, taking your brothers and sisters in Sand to safety.".

She watched silently as Marran knelt before Draille, saw the Ranger's face still in prayer, and then watched the brief arm clasps of his Nightlingbys, and then, in the blink of a tear-filled eye, Marran was gone, into the grey dawn light, out of her view, at his waist a poison-wood dart.

Feeling as drawn and haggard as an Elder, Jalni crept back to bed, and was only wakened by the touch of an amused mouth, as Daro kissed her nose. He crouched beside her, and in the distance Jalni could hear excited children readying themselves for travel. She shot up to sit shivering in a keen dawn wind, and ignoring Daro's look of enquiry broke the news of her morning triste with the Rangers. He sighed deeply, but heard her out, saying only, "We'll clean Sundreth's kitchen over this once Terris finds out!", and to be true, he was right. She ranted for a good sector of the sand -glass, fixed Daro with a look filled with withering contempt, and said,

"I knew you were tricky my Lord, but at least I know he loves me!", as with mingled anger and fear she cleaned every vessel in the camp twice over, earning Draille's approbation until she snapped at him.

"Mages, Rangers and Healers alike. Put them in a bag, shake them up, and whichever comes out first, you've still got trouble!", so they left her strictly alone, until Height of Sun had passed.

A whistle summoned them all back to the cooling fire-pit. The morning labours of the foraging party had replenished kindling, snarflin chips and strikestones. Draille had taken the awed youngsters away to teach them how to find even the faintest trace of water, and they had returned to show Jalni that they now carried several pieces of odd reedy grass, with which they assured her solemnly, they could tap the light surface dinajh or underground aquifers that snaked invisibly beneath this arid landscape. They had however not been all that hungry, and Draille suggested slyly that finding a nest of sharrabugs, which they roasted on hot stones was to blame, and while Draille's new conquest's slept contentedly, she had rescued Daro and insisted that they sleep in the shade of their own cave, but now it was time to move on, as the desert cooled and they prepared for the short sand crossing to join Marran, at the beginning of the unnamed canyon, that sliced through the rising land and took them within an hour of Cathlea and safety.

Daro and Jalni stood waiting for Draille to summon them, as the Ranger gravely inspected patrols, and made sure that Sholtan's Gap camp was left as they found it. Glancing across the empty fire pit, the Healer saw Terris anxiously minding the Flyby patrol, girls of only five or six Rotations in age, who hung at her skirts wide-eyed and wondering. Draille headed towards her, followed by the Patrol leaders, and announced.

"We are Sand walking today. Its not far, and the Sands are cooling. However, none of your patrols have a Flyby for luck.".

He winked at Terris, who said solemnly, "How sad, after all the work we put into giving them wings.".

Jalni explained to the puzzled Sandsinger that each child had a "trail flag" attached to their backpacks. As Torvin and Terris unfolded the bright pennants, Daro's lips pursed and a small breeze fluttered them bravely. Then, as excited children shrilled, the Flyby's (one to each patrol) were lifted on to teenage backs, and at the Ranger's whistle, once more the Children of Scartel moved out on the next leg of their journey.

The sand crossing was utterly uneventful, the children walking in pairs were nevertheless surprised by how often Draille made them stop, rest and drink. The Ranger however walked amongst them, teaching as he went, so that they soon learned that without plentiful supplies of water they would dehydrate just sitting in the Sands. This area was reasonably level, and Daro walked easily, but amused the children by occasionally imitating the cry of a Cuirax, then adjusting his direction minutely, until Draille trotted back to the end of the line where Rann and Daro walked to investigate. When Daro explained the trick of bouncing sound back against the sheer cliffs of the Drekkens, the Ranger was quick to grasp the principle, and Jalni sighed as they trudged along with a cacophony of bird calls rising in their wake, rolling her eyes at Terris, as a shout of laughter accompanied the mournful cry of a Zeglur! She murmured confidentially, "May the One take pity on the Wanderer band that kidnaps those two!", at which Terris quite forgot her anxiety over Marran, and responded innocently.

"Oh, they leave the insane to wander. They'd be far too difficult to control.", and giggled as Draille jogged past them.

Shortly thereafter, a shadow on the horizon became visible, growing out of the sand as they approached. A dark Highland stretched like a finger into the sands, and they stopped staring at the obstacle. Daro and Rann caught them up, and as Jalni took Daro's arm again, he murmured, "We walked the long way round apparently. Draille says that if we head for a place where the face of the rock shows white, we will see a dead tree. This marks a crease in the land and a deep canyon where the Rangers have their training ground. It is where we will meet Marran after he completes his *"holonogarth"*. We are invited to rest, take what Draille calls the "high route", and then make for Cathlea by a well walked trail.".

He surprised her by gripping her arm tightly and saying with deep satisfaction, "From Cathlea I can summon local assistance, get a message to my Songfather, and summon the bloody Guard if I want to! I can do without all the stress and worry for at least two nights, I'm shockingly tired!", and threw Jalni's composure to the winds by hugging her. However, no-one noticed, for their eyes were on another Ranger striding purposefully towards them.

The single toned whistle that Marran had taught them rang out, and the children stopped dead in their tracks as Draille ran forward holding up his hand to indicate "Halt!". He waited without turning his head to check on obedience, he didn't have to, and Daro lifted his head, unerringly following the Ranger's progress as Draille went forward alone to meet the stranger. Jalni caught a look of intense concentration on Daro's face, but he turned to her seconds later, and said shortly,

"They talk in riddles, using symbols in the sand, and that is their right. I was only able to find out that Marran started trial this morning, has not yet completed it, and survives with no injury. What their plans for us are I don't know but I don't think Draille has told them who or what I am.", and Jalni shot him a glance.

"Draille is returning already.", she muttered, "I think that he would find enhanced hearing a discouragement to trust.", but Daro said without a trace of shame.

"I know I can hear him, and I, Healer Jalni would equally find Draille's knife in my ribs a discouragement to breathing.", and Jalni felt his fear for the children touch her also.

Draille approached Daro, slowing to a walk ten paces away, saying quickly,

"All is well.", he seemed to hesitate for a moment and then said cautiously, "I did not reveal your name or status Lord, not knowing your wishes in that respect. You have not shared your familiar name with me, so I have no right to use it. Garald, my second tells me that young Dorenard is resting. If you follow me in single file, we can meet the boy at the end of the canyon. May I tell his sweeting what occurs before her eyes burn my brain to sand?".

Daro laughed, clasping the Ranger's arm warmly, "Call me Daro my friend. You have shown yourself to be wise indeed. I can disguise myself and you are right. I can think of good reasons for doing so from time to time, although many already know me as Guardian Ikella's son, they don't know I am Sandsinger yet, and very few know I am blind!".

Draille touched his hand to his heart and said quietly, "It is my privilege to be admitted to your confidence Daro.", then blinked at the magical shifting of Daro's clothing, the dimming of Anduigor, and muttering, "Deo me!" ,turned back towards a pale faced Terris to give her the glad news, and lead them into the Ranger training grounds.

The last two hundred spans seemed like a ten day march to Jalni, whose concern for her friends over-rode her natural curiosity. She guided Daro, feeling his hand on her shoulder as they followed Draille's instructions to walk single file. With babies slung in takran slings they filed through a narrow sliding gateway, passing (apparently) through a solid rock wall, overgrown with stinging ivyvine, and fronted by distinctly unfriendly thorn bearing bushes. Avoiding dense grass like plants of particularly noxious colour, and noting bright red spines along patently poisonous leaves, she communicated her concerns to Daro silently, with the realisation that "speech without speech", had its uses after all. She was rewarded by the tensing of his fingers on her shoulder, then a subtle flickering radiance "fizzed" along her skin, the children ahead of her grinned as the magic surrounded them also, and she was not surprised to see Draille stop, waiting for them to catch him up. His face questioned Daro silently, and the mage said softly, "Few, if any of them have ever left Scartel. They have little awareness of danger, and there are too many to take risks with. I can't protect them all the time, but we can spare no distractions today.", to which Draille responded with a curiously sweet smile.

"You're right Daro, our legends, handed down from father to son, tell us that we once came here after a natural disaster destroyed our home. Many of our forebears lie in perpetual peace close to their descendants, and it was from here that our settlers found Scartel. All our younglings finish training here, and in that respect, your boy is very strong in the craft, and so I welcome you to Holmgarth to witness Marran's final trial.".

As he finished speaking he held up his arms, and to Jalni's surprise seemed to be communicating in some way with others. "Above us?", she questioned inwardly, and smiled with relief as she saw Torvin grinning at Lladro, Terris nodding and Rann positively bouncing on his toes.

"I hope the children understand this arm waving.", she grumbled silently at Daro, whose voice, overlaid with amusement, said privately,

"Draille has signalled ahead that we are to be given every assistance. Latrines, beds, drinks and food are waiting somewhere ahead. Calar can teach you this signalling system.". Then a vine was swept aside, and Jalni suddenly realised that the real rock face was riddled with caverns, that Rangers were on every level above them, as they passed from the broad false passage inside the concealed gates, through an arch and into the strangest place any of them had ever seen.

They were poised high above a natural ravine on a broad walkway that had been formed partly from a natural stone ledge, and partly man made. She had never seen such a green place before, and her wonder must have communicated itself to Draille Skellin, whose Second, Garald now stood my his side. Jalni blinked, she hadn't seen him arrive, and knew by the quirk of Daro's lips that he had heard her thought. She turned back to the view over the valley.

The children were hanging over an immense wooden railing, and Jalni stepped forward to join them. Calar came to Daro's side, and said thoughtfully, "Brus would have loved this.", and proceeded to describe what he saw to the blind Sandsinger.

"It's a very deep valley Daro. Like a dark crease in some places, but in others it is very green. On one side there are very high cliffs, the rock is sandstone, and seems to be riddled with caves, but they are very high, and I don't see how anyone could live in them practically.", he paused, head tilted, an enormous frown on his face, and Garald seeing his puzzlement stepped forward.

"Is there anything I can tell you about Holmgarth my friends?", he asked in a cheerful voice, and Calar's face brightened. "I was just describing what I can see to my friend Daro, can you tell me what I am looking at. It is very different here, lots of strange things I have never seen before.", he admitted gruffly, and Garald's eyes flickered over Daro incuriously, then he asked gently.

"Have you ever had sight young man?", and Daro grinned saying perfectly easily.

"Oh yes. Up until Jentaroth last I was fully sighted, but you know how things go?", and Garald said in a very practical tone of voice.

"All too easily I'm afraid.", and proceeded to enlighten them as they walked along what he told them was the High Route West. His voice carried clearly and soon the entire group heard about Holmgarth, as they progressed along the right hand side of the valley. Garald's voice floated to them clearly as he led them in a hushed attentive pack.

"Ranger legend has it that we came here after some terrible disaster, bringing with us only seeds, the contents of our packs, and eleven families. Our leaders were Anelm Dorenard, his eldest son Marran Dorenard, Draille Skellin and his youngest son Brus Skellin. Those names are still Ranger names today, and I believe you know Marran Dorenard who undergoes *holonogarth* or trial by nature today. On the left side of the valley is the Citadel of the Dead, below which is our training and testing ground. You will see many plants here that grow nowhere else, for here is what we believe to be the last remnant of the river Opaz. This once carried water from the High Range above Sanctuary all the way to Selesh. This valley is home to the last Ranger settlement, but from here, we hope to find other places where our plants, our animals can survive, so that our planet can repair itself."

There were wondering faces and subdued comments from the gaggle that trailed behind Garald, then he was turning away from the dizzying drop to the valley floor, and ushering them through another archway cut into the sandstone, and they were in an immense cavern, into which light streamed through narrow wall apertures. Their guide waved a hand.

"Make yourselves comfortable.", he invited, "Ranger families who settled out of the Garth stay here when their men take the trial. You will find facilities beyond that curtain, blankets and beds for babies, drinking water for hot drinks will be here in minutes, and light food. Ranger Skellin must supervise the last stage of trial for your friend, but he will join us later.".

The air was clean above Holmgarth, and as patrol leaders sorted patrols into order, Calar took Daro away from the bustle to lean on the rails. The boy stared across the valley where he told the mage he could see it curving away in the distance below. He said thoughtfully,

"I didn't know Brus came from such an important family. Garald tells me that Draille Skellin is leader to all Rangers, and is the only Ranger living to have taken every section of *holonogarth*.". He didn't seem to notice the expression of deep concern that crossed Daro's face, but continued.

"Garald says that only a first-class Ranger can be elected as Ranger Leader, and that there are only three Second Class Rangers at the moment, Marran's Grandfather was the exception, but when his wife died in childbirth, he devoted himself to the child, and ranged no further than the first post outside Scartel. Marran being five Rotations older, I didn't know him socially, but I knew Ranger Dorenard. He taught me and Brus to fly hawks.", his face blazed with a sudden quiet joy.

"That's what was so utterly brilliant about what happened to Brus.", he confided, "He used to say that if he had to live in another form he would choose to be a hawk.!", and then stilled, seeing Daro touch fingers to heart, head, lips, and asked respectfully, "Did the One guide your hand in that Lord?", and Daro nodded solemnly.

"May the One always guide my hand so.", he murmured, and turned to meet the bright knowing eyes of Garald who was hurrying towards them.

"The last stage is about to begin.", he announced and let out a shrill two toned whistle, then as the children swarmed out to peer down into the testing ground a strange hollow note sounded across the valley, and Marran's last trial began.

Chapter 5 - Sword of Honour

Garald said quietly, "You may observe from the family viewing point, but you mustn't interfere. No sound, no communication of any kind is permitted. It is very hard on young children, so while most of those are asleep our women will watch over them. Your teens can come with me for an introduction to this process.", and smiling continued..

"Ranger Skellin invites you elders, the company of Nightlingbys and young Dorenard's woman, to join him where he supervises this challenge".

Turning to an agitated Terris, who twisted her shawl uncertainly, he said kindly,

"Don't worry about your Rangerling's. Treyan our Bard is going to make a saga, and they will help her. We will take them down to the Holm, feed them, let them groom the animals with our own youngsters, and they won't miss you at all.". His voice was hypnotic, deliberately pitched and seeing its calming effect on her friend, Jalni glanced at him suspiciously, then Daro spoke firmly.

"Thank you Ranger Garald.", he murmured, employing magical "persuasion of voice" quite casually. "Calar can guide me, and Terris can join young Dorenard's patrol or sit with my Healer, who will be glad of female company.".

The voice was mild, conversational even, but such was the compulsion to obey that Garald threw the blind man a sharply perceptive glance, as he slid open a door concealing the continuing walkway. Calar moved forward smoothly, positioning himself so that as they turned on to the descending steps where Draille Skellin waited, one of Daro's hands rested on the boy's shoulder and the other grasped the handrail. They moved forward confidently, heads close together as Daro received instructions, then as the Sandsinger gauged the drop onto a short platform where the steps changed direction, his cloak fell apart and the gleaming Anduigor came into view. Jalni, stood next to Garald caught his gasp, and at the same time Daro raised a smiling face towards them, magic alight in unseeing eyes.

Turning to the bemused man, Jalni said quietly, "You appear to be signally favoured Garald. My lord does not reveal himself to everyone. Respect that confidence by treating him normally until he decides that Pelshar is ready to believe in Sandsingers again.".

She was rewarded by a low whisper.

"Healer, I will know nothing until your Lord tells me differently, but this day will live in memory always.". He turned, gathering teens around him, ushering them to vantage points higher up the unusual ledge, as Jalni clattered down the stairs, running to catch up with the others.

This section of the platform resembled a large roofless box. Looking curiously at one long wall which didn't match the others in height, Jalni tried to see how this "observation post" worked. The odd "room" admitted the bright afternoon light despite its curtained entrance, but with no window, Jalni couldn't begin to understand how they could see Marran's progress, and with difficulty restrained her impulse to demand answers to a hundred questions.

"It certainly isn't going to be through that gap.", she admitted privately, eyeing the shortened wall and realising that even stood on the long bench that Draille was offering as a seat, no-one was tall enough to see out. Sounds from the steep valley below filtered in, a sough of wind, odd chirps and flutters, the light rattle of stirring vegetation, but as the silent Nightlingby patrol settled down, Jalni still stood, staring around curiously.

The entire structure was made from closely woven branches plastered with mud, much like summer foragers use. These walls, dappled with the shadows of overhanging vines seemed to take up the aspect of the natural stone of the cliff it clung to, and as her awareness grew, she finally understood that she was inside what must appear to be a natural bulge on the face of the cliff below the extensive walkway.

She caught Draille Skellin's calm smile, and was totally disconcerted as he bowed to her, encouraging the Nightlingbys to follow his example with a gesture of his hand. Blushing furiously, she dropped into the space at Daro's right hand and hissed at the unabashed mage through gritted teeth.

"You do me too much honour Lord.".

Uncomfortably aware of Draille's amusement, she leant forward to examine one of the long upright boxes mounted at eye level in front of her, as the Ranger's low voice instructed.

"We keep a vigil of sorts for your brother Ranger.", he told the awed Nightlingbys. "He must resolve a puzzle, and your behaviour is part of his test, for a leader must instil in his followers the qualities he most prizes. At this time, all that he has learned will be tested, and all that he has taught will be proved.".

He paused, moving to the end of the bench and sitting on a high stool pulled up close to one of the strange boxes. Adjusting his position with a little wriggle, he brought his eyes level with the lower end of the box, apparently peering into it before he looked around the group and explained.

"Through the viewing box, you may keep the watch with Marran Dorenard as he strives to answer this last challenge. Every Ranger test is in itself complete, and each test is as different as the Rangers tested. Most of us take our *holonogarth* in stages, progressing towards this point gradually as experience grows, however, there are exceptions. The last Ranger that completed every stage together was Marran's Grandfather, who would have been our leader, but his woman died birthing their child. I took the long route to become leader, nearly thirty Rotations to fledge!".

He grinned, holding out a hand on which was tattooed a feather descending from an intricate braid. Jalni's eyes widened as she finally understood the symbolism connecting this tattoo with the plait that Draille had woven into Marran's hair only that dawn.

As Draille peered at the long box before him, they mimicked the action. Immediately, there was a hastily suppressed chorus of gasps, for reflected in a small panel of polished metal they could all see Marran. Draille continued his instructions solemnly.

"This is not magic, just a trick of mirrors and angles. You can quietly look through a viewing box, but remember this is a vigil. Any distraction affects its outcome. Please remember that not all of us here can see, and Marran's lady is present!".

His cool scholarly manner diffused natural excitement, as the Nightlingbys shuffled forward, securing viewing boxes, seats, and making room for Terris. Daro leaned back and said softly,

"Why don't you come round and join Jalni? There are enough viewing boxes as I don't need one.", and Jalni shot the Sandsinger an approving glance as Terris slid in beside her, and peered at the reflective metal panel, blinking in surprise as she saw Marran's image displayed.

Surrounded by low scrub and sparse grass like plants, he sat cross-legged, surveying a clear area of astonishingly unmarked sand, and anxious to see more Jalni bent over the nearest available viewing box herself. Almost as though she peered over Marran's shoulder, she could see that he sat facing the far end of a cleft, sheer sandstone walls towering above him to left and right, ahead of him the sandy clearing, and then a dense tangled mass of swinging vines, no doubt attached in some way to the slender arch formed by the close proximity of the walls that overhung his position. She moved irritably, and Daro's voice filtered through all the other distractions in her mind.

Their Dream Walker has placed Marran in a light trance, so that he cannot be distracted from this task. Nothing he has previously used as a tool on his journey so far may be used during the last stage of his *holonogarth*. He must review the tasks he has completed, drawing on that experience. All his previous tasks have combined elements of mental process and physical solutions, but this one is different. When he is ready to proceed, he may do one of two things. He may pull on that rope to signal Draille that he has a solution, or he may take the poisonwood dart that he hasn't used and throw it at that board. If he does that he is admitting defeat, and cannot ever progress beyond this point.".

She grumbled silently aiming her thoughts like barbs.

"He is too tired to make sensible decisions. I wish I could get closer to him. He appears to be sweating, yet he is only sitting. I know nothing of this Dream Walker's talents, but he seems too stressed for my liking."

She turned away from the viewing box abruptly demanding, "Is this more of your magic my Lord?", but Daro shook his head.

"Not guilty.", his voice quivered on the edge of humour. "This is Ranger knowledge, thousands of Rotations old, which they have adapted specifically to this site, to this purpose. Can you see Marran clearly?", he asked anxiously and Jalni felt his tension in the warm thigh that trembled against hers.

"Well enough.", she turned back, and found that the box was mounted quite loosely as it swivelled in her hands, and she gazed anxiously into the viewing plate, and immediately froze as a wutherped scrambled past the tense figure below, and bolted out into the clearing. As soon as the pathetic bumbling creature's armoured feet took it away from the edge, the sand rippled. The wutherped, (a favourite pet amongst children), wrinkled its long nose, and as its tail started to sink, turned pathetically frantic eyes skyward. In mounting horror, Jalni stared transfixed as the scaly backed creature reared up in terror, but it was already too late, and despite its desperate struggles, is sank inexorably below the surface. There was a tautening of young backs, a constraint that touched the previously carefree atmosphere of the observation post, and Daro's head raised, his eyelids fluttered and Jalni caught his hand urgently.

"What happened?", his whisper was shrill with concern, as Jalni hastened to explain, feeling the sweep of his power touch her as he commanded, "Just visualise it, I'll follow.".

She ran the mental images through her mind, and heard a pitying hiss, then abruptly he was gone from her, a hand gentle on his guides arm, and she saw that young Calar was convulsed with silent sobs. She rummaged swiftly in her scrip, finding a twist of chorovin root, and reached Calar, breaking off enough for one dose and pressed it into his hand, before turning to a white faced Terris.

"Here.", she pressed a strip of the odd pink root into the girl's hand, "Chew this, it will ease the stress, moisten your mouth, and doesn't taste too bad either, but Terris didn't seem to hear her. She muttered so low that Jalni could hardly distinguish the words.

"O may the One protect all his creatures.", she recited the child's prayer, "May he guide us away from Drum Sand, Sinking Sand, Fire Sand, and the dark places where Sundreth holds sway. May Seleus guide our days, and Jenta guard our nights, until our paths bring us home to those we love.", and Jalni bowed her head as Daro reached across her, clasping the girl's arm in mute sympathy.

The company watched as Marran rose, placing two large twigs to mark the point where he had sat, and moved around the arena, testing, touching, bending plants to outline the area of the sinking sand. Finally, having discovered that they extended from left to right, and up to what seemed to be an impenetrable tangle of vines, he returned to sit once more in contemplation of the puzzle. They watched fascinated by the thoughts playing across Marran's familiar friendly features, now masked by the blue pigment markings of this trial. They saw bright ideas flicker in his eyes, cautious hands touching belt, patting pockets, and watched the painful maturity of solemn thought paint a second mask of determination on his face. Still they kept the Watch, silently supporting their Captain, easing cramped muscles with tiny movements, hardly breathing in the intensity of oneness, radiating their belief in Marran till it filled the observation post with a light of its own.

Marran brooded, then rose again, and picked up three small fist sized rocks, hurling one directly at the foliage shrouded area ahead of him. It rebounded with a resounding "thwack", then sank with a disgusting "glug", and if it seemed to Jalni that the sinking sand chuckled as the stone sank, she saw the same conclusion in the sober eyes surrounding her. Then, quite suddenly, Marran threw the other stones in quick succession. The first penetrating the vines to slither down and into the sinking Sand, then the last, which returning as if catapulted to clatter against the wall to Marran's right. He shrugged, then squared his shoulders having obviously come to a conclusion. Jalni saw Draille Skellin brace himself, and then a horn sounded, and a trapdoor which none of them had noticed dropped open. The Ranger rose, held up a hand and said softly into a silence sticky with anticipation.

"Stand. Hold still and keep quiet. Until the horn sounds twice and I return the test is ongoing. When I have heard the solution he has come to, I will summon our Keld and you will ascend to the level above. I think you might call a Keld, a Council of Elders, and as this is Ranger business, you will forgive me my Lord if I announce my findings first to our own.".

Daro smiled and said quietly, "We will withdraw while your deliberations are made, but know that I am responsible for all the Children of Scartel, and consider that as a brother Nightlingby, I should be admitted to your confidence as soon as possible.".

Draille Skellin blinked, caught the pugnacious expression on Torvin's face then said uncertainly, "You fly with this patrol my Lord?", and Daro held out an arm where Jalni saw two paling wounds, and understood that Daro was bound by blood oath to the patrol in a way from which she was excluded. Physically resisting a surge of jealousy as she examined Daro's arm, she ordered brusquely, "Next time you want to die of blood poisoning, let me at least dress the wound so your mother will know I did my best.".

Draille chuckled softly as he descended a ladder below the trapdoor, and left them to return alone.

They ascended to the upper level in silence, each wondering what was happening in the testing ground, and Daro found no difficulty at all in encouraging the teens and the Nightlingbys to enter the guest chamber they had left only that same afternoon. No-one spoke, they just huddled together in patrols, and Jalni persuaded Terris to wrap herself in her cloak and doze while they waited.

The horn blew twice. Urgent, demanding, then the curtained entrance was thrust aside as two beaming Rangers called them out into the weakening light of early evening. They bowed, and said simply,

"You are bidden before the Keld to see your brother Ranger elected to the Tawn, the brotherhood of Rangers.", and as Calar threw a cloak round Daro's shoulders, and led him out, Jalni and Lladro assisted a shaking Terris to her feet and followed in her wake. The whole of the walkway was thronged with Rangers, and Jalni, wondering, saw that amongst the men in the patch dyed blues, there were women as well. Grouped in entrances she hadn't even noticed, women were holding babies, youngsters crowding round their ankles, but what drew her attention were the tall lithe group who shouldered bows, quivers hanging from their belts. Daro had stopped, quietly encouraging a nervous Calar, and she tucked his hand into the crook of her elbow, as he chuckled at his guide.

"Calar got cold feet over some "fierce ladies", he explained in a quivering voice as a fuzzy image of Ikella's Second watch drifted into Jalni's mind, accompanied by the warning his Songfather had impressed on him at much the same age.

"Better to die in combat than drown in honey!", said the mage in a fine rendition of the Apothecary's voice, and ignoring Calar's aggrieved expression, Jalni led her Lord forward, chuckling. Smiling Rangers ushered them to a pile of animal hides and they found themselves at the widest part of the walkway, sitting alongside a circle of Elders who had to be the Keld. The atmosphere was expectant, the Nightlingbys gathered behind Jalni and Daro shifted, and Terris passed through, as a horn blew three times and silence fell.

Towards the back of the Keld gathering, a curtain was pulled aside. In the doorway stood a young Ranger, wearing the familiar patch dyed blues. At her friends awed whisper of "Marran. Deo me, is that my Marran?", Jalni looked up, to see the metamorphosis from boy to man. He gleamed, from nut brown hair to warm brown eyes, bronzed skin glowing, flushed with pride, lambent with joy, and then by his side stood Draille Skellin. He raised Marran's hand in his own and cried out.

"Brothers all, welcome to the Tawn one who was trained by Anelm Dorenard to be a brother to all present. He has brought to us the Children of Scartel, descendants of the first wave, most assuredly our own, although their journey has not been without loss. He wishes to dedicate his transition from Rangerling to Ranger, in the memory of Brus Skellin, who was lost above Sholtan's Gap. May the memory of my kin live forever.".

Draille touched Marran's arm, and together they strode into the circle of the Keld, and a man rose silently to greet them, passing something draped in a bright blue cloth into Draille's arms and with a shock Jalni saw that the man was none other than Garald, who now wore over his blues, a fantastic cloak of animal fur. She gaped as she realised that Garald was in fact the Dream Walker of the Rangers and reached out to touch Daro's hand.

"Let me show you, and you can share your ears.", she suggested and concentrated, streaming her perceptions as she heard the low voices conferring with the Keld.

Marran was reciting something, and as it unfolded she realised that he was proving his patrimony working through generations of his Ranger forebears, and as each generation was told, the Keld leaders nodded and chorused back, "To the glory of the One, to the sorrow of Pelshar.".

She was startled to hear in Daro's soft inner voice, "That is a tradition worthy of inclusion to all cultures.", and then more wistfully, "How I wish I knew my forebears in that manner, but I don't know who my father was, or is, so I can never participate in such an act of remembrance.", as Draille stepped forward to speak. This time the voice rang out, echoing across the cleft that was Holmgarth.

"There are three generations living who can give thanks for the life of Anelm Dorenard, who withstood the temptation to leave Scartel when the plague came, and who unselfishly sent from Scartel all the food he could muster, to the Healer of the Sands who resided in the caverns above with her orphans. This Healer, gave her life so that our children survived. Ranger Dorenard told us that much with messages sent by hawk. In the persons of Anelm Dorenard and the Healer we mourn not just the passing memory of our settlement of Scartel, but also the passing of a breed of people whose courage and fortitude create legends.".

Draille raised a hand, and a haunting call sounded down the valley, followed by a nighthawks quaver, and then as Jalni felt the hair rise on the back of her neck, there was a whirr of wings, and Marran thrust out an arm as Kreel dropped onto his gauntleted wrist.

"Aah.", the sigh went round those gathered as proudly Marran displayed the hawk (who had it seemed) chosen her new master. Then Garald relieved the puzzled boy of Kreel, as Draille Skellin turned and murmured something to a woman wearing an ornate pouch. She stood to join him, grasping Marran's wrists, turning them this way and that, before nodding and returning to her seat. Daro, who had fallen silent hunched forward, and for the first time Jalni became aware of his voice in her mind.

"That will be their Decrian.", he murmured, and Jalni stared at the Elder, noting the slender fingers, and the steady gaze of the ritual tattooist, as still engaged in conversation with Marran she took something from Draille's hand, and appeared to be measuring Marran's wrist. Beside her, Terris whispered,

"Jalni, what's happening?", she begged, "I can't hear because the boys are so excited. Torvin says that Marran will make Second Class Ranger, but I said he couldn't because he is so young, besides he hasn't got a sponsor.".

She was so anxious that she ignored Daro, who, head tilted "listened" to the Keld as they deliberated, heads bowed together with Draille. The Sandsinger said very gently,

"Terris, slide forward and sit with me and Jalni. I believe that we might see more from here. There is about to be some ceremony, and you shouldn't miss that.".

Terris, totally focussed on the building light as great torches were lit, hardly noticed the little shimmer in the atmosphere around her, as she murmured.

"Thank you. I can definitely hear and see better from here. I just wish the boys would settle down, they are terribly over-excited.".

Jalni caught the gleam of teeth as Daro grinned, felt the Nightlingbys subside into a magically enforced silence and then a low drumming began, torch bearers encircled the Keld and Marran Stood Alone in the circle. From out of the dark a voice began to chant, slow movement was perceptible beyond the lights, and then Garald appeared at one side of the circle, and Draille took up position on the other, as a full patrol of Rangers, stripped to the waist encircled Marran, and in the flickering light of the torches began a slow exercise routine, every step of which seemed to be an instruction to Marran who stood until the formation lined up on either side of him, providing a perfect passage between Draille and Marran. There was a single whistle, at which the guard of honour froze, and Daro "felt" the Nightlingbys quietly stand and slide out of their position behind him. Jalni, alerted by Daro's alarm, turned and found that one of the women Rangers was beckoning them, and rose silently, dragging Terris with her.

"Calar.", she hissed, "I'll take Daro, you bring Terris.", and so it was that they were brought in to the ceremonial circle of the Keld. They fell in behind Marran, and for a long moment the boy looked stricken as his erstwhile companions surrounded him, but Daro gripped his arm, and Jalni heard him clearly as Marran turned toward the blaze of torches, clearly torn between the two halves of his life.

"Go brother, go into the light.", said the mage, "Fly free little Nightlingby, you are fully fledged now.", and it seemed to Jalni as if Marran heard someone else in Daro's voice, perhaps felt the embrace of the Grandfather he had loved, for he drew himself up, squared his shoulders and leapt from the Nightlingbys to join the Tawn, completing in six strides the symbolic journey between childhood and maturity. As Draille clasped arms with Marran, there was a resounding cheer, then Garald came forward holding the strangely wrapped bundle in both hands. He placed this at Draille's feet, and then took from his pouch something that flashed in the light and Terris gasped as Marran knelt and bowed his head.

"O Deo me!", she said, one hand trembling against her mouth as Torvin, Lladro, Rann and Calar turned faces bright with incredulity towards her.

"Ranger First Class!", Lladro hissed, "Marran did it.", and stared transfixed as Marran's trail plait was shorn, and held aloft with its brave feathers twirling. Terris said very softly,

"O that's wonderful.", but she sounded wistful as she watched Draille fasten Marran's trail plait to his right wrist, "but he won't want me now. He can have his pick of all the girls, and besides we will be separated by Ranger duties and training walks.", she sniffed fiercely suppressing tears, but Daro turned to her and said briskly.

"I don't think you'll get rid of him that easily Terris.", he turned back asking querulously, "For the love of the One, won't someone tell me what is going on?", and then Garald was there and saying anxiously,

"Will the one called Daro lead Ranger Dorenard's patrol in to meet the Keld?", and Torvin stepped forward to guide Daro and organise the Nightlingbys. Terris blinking rapidly was persuaded to sit by the woman Ranger who had remained as Garald led the boys away.

"Rest and get your breath back my dear.", she said kindly, and pressed a drink into Terris's trembling hands. "I'm Sushanna, Apothecary to Holmgarth, and you look like you could do with a restorative.".

Jalni's hand hovering over her scrip dropped away, and the woman smiled at her, murmuring a conventional "By your leave Healer?", and Jalni suddenly yearned for a restorative herself.

"Look.", said Sushanna, and both girls turned to see Draille Skellin holding aloft a sheathed sword. There was an odd tingle of anticipation as Draille lowered the scabbard until the harness fitted neatly onto Marran's shoulders. He adjusted the sword until it lay along the boy's spine, hilt accessible to hand, as a disembodied voice declared,

"Now is the time to send forth Trail Blazer, the sword of Marran Dorenard the first. In the hands of another bearing his name, our Sword of Honour goes forth upon the trail once more. The young Nightlingby is truly named, for Marran means Sword Bearer, and there is not one here who doubts his worthiness to carry the honour of all Rangers to those who know us not. Who will sponsor his trail walk? If he be present, let him make himself known to us.", and Jalni felt a frisson of energy brush her hair into life, as the Lord of the Opal spoke quietly.

"My name is Daro bin Selesh.", there was a brief stir in the gathering gloom as Rangers leant forward to observe this phenomenon, for everyone had heard of the child adopted by Ikella. Daro cleared his throat and began again.

"I return from collecting the Children of Scartel. I hoped to protect their interests while my mother sought relatives to guide and guard them. I hold surety for Selesh, an offer to stand sponsor for Ranger Dorenard and all those children who have returned from Scartel into the bosom of their Ranger kin. The hand of the One hovers over them truly, for the Guardians undertake to assist those who would foster or adopt these children according to the Way.".

In the silence that followed this announcement Calar whispered despairingly, "What about the Clansmen in our midst? What will become of the girls who want to train as Healers, Apothecaries? I am Sandsworn and must stay with my Lord, but Lallee is Greshe and wants to go home. Brisha follows you Healer, and Erinim…", he stuttered to a stop, then choked out piteously, "I'll lose her. She'll stay here with the Rangers and I just found out she loves me!".

Jalni's eyes met those of the Apothecary as Sushanna's deft hands prepared a drinking horn with another restorative for the shaking boy. She thought bitterly, "How easily adults make decisions that will affect a child's whole perception of life. How little we know of their wishes, loves, or fears.".

She watched the Keld draw in, the rearrangement of seating as a great throne like chair was placed in the centre of the circle, flaming torches ensconced around it, while Marran, Draille and the Tawn gathered on piles of skins conversing with Daro, who seemed grave but attentive. The young Healer, aware of Calar's distress, was remembering abruptly how events had swung her between delight and despair in her own youth, and found herself wondering what her life would have been like had she understood the adults who made the decisions, giving her the life she was now pursuing, and something whispered in her mind.

"You must face it, face your past as these children have to face their future. If you don't, aren't you conniving with those that decided who you were, and what you would become? Have you lost your courage utterly Jalani del Orto? If a blind man can face the past of an entire world in order to correct the decisions that threaten to destroy us now, why can't you face your own past and find out who you really are, and what you will become?", she absently drank the restorative that a perceptive Sushanna pressed on her, then shaking her head at such introspective rambling turned back to watch the next stage of the evening's ceremonies.

Chapter 6 - The Turning Point

Jalni drew her cloak on as the air cooled. All She could feel the sense of preparation as Rangers conversed with their women, and gathered their families closely around them. A large brazier brought into the circle of the Keld and close to the central chair, had been lit, in preparation for the forthcoming rituals. Two solemn faced attendants produced a free standing frame, drawing it up to one side of the chair, and as she watched, a slender girl with serious eyes arrived, discarded an impressive scarlet cloak, and with assistance slipped on a garment which covered her from neck to ankle in soft supple leather. One attendant caught her hair in a snood, another assisted as she plunged her hands into a bowl of reddish brown liquid, and as Jalni watched, she held up her hands for the Keld to inspect. Into Jalni's mind, the Sandsinger insinuated his familiar voice.

"She is Iskilda, Decrian in training and her task this evening is to prepare all the tools and equipment for their Decrian. Her hands have been cleansed with something they call "Drying liquor". If I am right that would protect anything she touched from any infection she carries. All the instruments that the Decrian uses are kept in this liquor throughout this process. I don't know enough about it but it is essential that infection is kept at bay.".

Staring past the Ranger's Apothecary, Jalni saw Daro sitting cross-legged amongst his fellow Nightlingbys. Rann sat in Torvin's stead, beside the Sandsinger, freeing Torvin who standing with Draille, had drawn Lladro into consultation. Simbel and the other seniors assembled anxiously, but as she wondered what was happening, Sushanna turned a smiling face to hers.

"They must choose Ranger Dorenard's successor from amongst his old patrol. It is an essential part of this process. The fledgling must ensure the safety of his fellows before he leaves the nest, and this will be the last they see or talk to him for a while, for once he passes into the hands of the Tawn, receives his emblem and is shod for the trail, he becomes the property of the Dream Walker. He will take the Old Path north, and will not return to Holmgarth until a Rotation has passed, taking him beyond the fellowship of children and into the company of men. Before he leaves he will be given one night with his woman, but his patrol must say their farewells now. It is the way of the Rangers, all our young expect to enter a patrol and train until this point, but only ten in a thousand Rotations have ever flown so high, and I saw it happen!".

Jalni's eyes took in the joy and pride on the woman's face, glanced around to see it mirrored on others, and gulped remembering no such fellowship in her own family or Clan. She dismissed that thought, preferring to remember Marran's awe when he first understood that Daro was Sandsinger, and heard the mage's voice saying soberly,

"Even more remarkable, Marran did it without magic!".

As Jalni felt the wave of pride and affection warm his blood, she privately considered that the combination of Ranger "oneness" with nature, coupled with Marran's own clarity of thought and strength of purpose had given him access to some kind of *"other magic"*, and heard Daro chuckle grimly.

"Try that idea on an empowered Sorceress!", he remarked and Jalni withdrew the thought with a little shudder as she recalled a pair of enraged green eyes!

She grasped Calar's hand as the crowd shifted and swirled about them, then she realised that they were being guided to sit beside Daro and the boys. She caught a word here and there as families settled on gathering rugs to witness the ritual tattooing of Marran's rank. Marran had called Daro forward to join in the private consultation amongst the Nightlingbys when Jalni found Draille Skellin bowing courteously to her. She smiled shyly, as he asked permission to sit with her but his first words riveted her attention utterly.

"I wished to ask your advice before I bring a matter close to my heart before the Keld, or raise the hopes of Ranger Dorenard unrealistically.", he announced, leaving Jalni to stare in bewilderment, while he mustered his thoughts, his face sombre.

"Those who died at Scartel were not honoured in death, which weighs heavily on my mind. We are not of the Sands, nor of the earth above the Sands, we are one with the Winds and the highlands of our world, and our ancestors lie here amongst us.".

His hand indicated the opposite side of the cleft, picking out the shadowy evidence of very high caves on the face of the cliff, and Jalni suddenly saw that these were rock tombs. Draille nodded at her intake of breath, and then said slowly, "Young Dorenard told me that your Lord and he set the prescribed fire, that with Daro's help, even the stone burned, and for that I praise the One. However, we want to rebuild at Scartel, and when I asked Daro when we could retrieve the ashes and bring our kin home to the burial grounds of our forefathers, he told me to ask your advice.".

Jalni stared at him, convinced she had forgotten something that she had learnt in Scartel, but as she strove to recall it, all she could remember was the lectures that Andria had delivered on the handling of disease, the disposal of infected material, and the preparation of the dead. She cleared her throat carefully, and suddenly didn't want to meet Draille's liquid brown eyes, for his kin lay in the remains of Scartel village.

"I would advise caution where plague is concerned.", she began and Draille nodded. "Remember that this particular contagion took the adults, not the children, and your families here would be at risk if contamination was transported home.".

The Rangers knuckles whitened as he clenched his fists, but there was no flicker of reaction on his face, so she continued, feeling more confident as she spoke.

"How long would it take to prepare sealed tombs?", she asked softly, and Draille's face went blank, then he protested, his voice quiet but emphatic.

"Sealed tombs would deny our kin contact with the soil, the air, the sounds of life. They would be better left in the ruins of Scharatel, thus rendering that place doomed to die uninhabited than to seal them away.". He sounded so outraged at the concept that Jalni glanced at him, saw the pain in his face and relented.

"Ranger, I mean your dead no discourtesy and because of what you say, this is my advice. Leave the ashes for five Rotations. Scartel is protected by my Lord's hand, and well guarded. Every Rotation go to the Heights of Scartel, avoid the crater and the village but go and restock the Healer's beacon. From the watching post look down towards Gateway, and while you see any green glow from the ground do not return to the place where the village stood. When that vanishes you may take up the ashes and the burnt remains. Send word to Selesh and my Lord will assist you. the ashes should remain sealed but could be placed in stone caskets, that is natural, sealed with tanbark stoppers and junifray wax they would be safe enough.".

He seemed to be thinking over this advice carefully, and Jalni added hesitantly, "Your Decrian understands the use of "drying liquor". All those engaged on that task should wear permeated masks, gloves soaked in the liquor, and be instructed to bathe in the lower caverns before returning here.", and finally satisfied Draille thanked her gravely, and had just turned to Calar, when a horn blew, a tinkle of bells sounded and the Keld returned, the Decrian amongst them.

She was magnificent. Tall, with a mane of black hair, she shunned the shadow of her cowl, showing herself to be a woman of middle years only in the dusting of silver at her temples. She too wore the leather robe under a cloak of brilliant scarlet as she stalked forward to the very edge of the brightly lit circle, poised overlooking the strange green cleft that was Holmgarth, now fast disappearing into the night. Then, the strangest thing happened. There was a sudden hush, then a low pitched "Whoo hoo", and into the light floated a Nightlingby. The soft creamy plumage of its belly and under wings gleamed, the blue flash across wings and tail feathers contrasted with the tawny flight feathering as it flew the length of the valley, and hovered briefly back winged in front of the tattooist. Marran, caught in the arms of his patrol seemed to grow taller, more resolute, then as from further away the fluting whistle of a Cuirax sounded, the new young Ranger drew back from his patrol and walked calmly to where Terris knelt by Sushanna.

Jalni's heart lurched as she saw Sushanna hand Marran a twisted drinking horn, passing through the liquid a braid constructed of tiny flowers. This was solemnly bound around Marran's forehead and another braid was given into his hand. This one he passed through the liquid himself and bound around Terris's brow. She came to her feet, face radiant as Marran took her right hand in his and offered the drinking horn for her to sip from. Her free hand rose, slid over the one in which he held the horn, and to resounding cheers the young couple drank together. Jalni, close enough to touch Terris saw proud happy tears on the girls face, and was suddenly very aware of Daro, whose mind had turned back to a small room in Scartel. She felt the wash of desire touch her also, then it fled into the night on the words.

"Yes my love, we too have unfinished business!".

Marran took Terris proudly on one arm, and made a slow circuit of the Keld, accepting their congratulations as he presented his bride. When they returned to the Nightlingbys on Jalni's right, Torvin stood, and with a wrench Jalni saw that Torvin wore Marran's prized emblem on a thong round his neck. As Torvin brought the patrol to the salute, Marran reached out, touched his once cherished emblem, a Nightlingby carved in wood by the hand of his own Grandfather, then he spoke, his young voice serious.

"Little owls, fly safely with your new Captain. Listen carefully to your older brothers and stay safe while I trail the Old Path north. Care for the young ones in the other patrols, keeping the memory of our patronage and the secrets of Scharatel to ourselves. The Tawn will guide you, but it is agreed that when I return and when you are old enough to accompany me, I will return to Scartel and we will rebuild. I will be away a long time, during which we will all learn of other things, but we will meet again. I will bid farewell to the younger patrols later, but know this, in leaving my wife with you, I am trusting you with my most cherished possession. You will obey her in my absence, follow your new Captain and train hard!".

As one, the entire patrol, including Daro struck open palms to hearts, and chorused obediently, "Yes Ranger Dorenard.", then Jalni saw the momentary confusion, and the bleak realisation strike home, clouding the young Ranger's face. He now filled his Grandfather's shoes, and the thought was almost too much to bear. Then Lladro said comfortingly, "You know that because of your success, his name will never die Marran. He laid your trail back to our brothers, perhaps he knew that we walked with a greater protection than he could give us.".

Draille Skellin murmured softly to Jalni. "That boy is a natural Dream Walker!", and she was amused as he hastened to attract Garald's attention, but took that opportunity to retrieve Daro and Calar. Cushions and trail blankets had appeared, Terris was enthroned amongst the Nightlingbys, and then the youngsters appeared led by a group of Ranger teens wearing half dyed blue to signify the beginning of training. Brisha came directly to Jalni, Lallee settled near to Daro, Erinim sank to her knees by Calar, and they all stared at Marran who stood looking quite frankly appalled as he realised that he had to go through the ritual application of his tattoo quite alone. Cut off from his childhood companions, not yet part of the Tawn, he stood forlorn for a few moments, and then Garald detached himself from Draille, swung his furs about his shoulders and the drums began.

It was the strangest ritual that Jalni had ever observed. A seat had been drawn up near to the Decrian. While they had been otherwise engaged the woman's long hair had been plaited and bound in a snood. The Scarlet cloak had been removed and hung from her chair back, and her arms had been plunged into a vat of "drying liquor". There was a clean clinical aroma tickling Jalni's memory and for a moment she fancied that she was in one of Ikella's famous clean rooms dealing with an infected wound. Daro's hand found her own, and quite naturally she began streaming what she could see along that strangely intimate link they had created. They watched Iskilda sliding the unusual frame into place so that the Decrian's instruments could be laid out in what Jalni perceived to be shallow trays into which Iskilda had poured liquor. She commented on the roll of material that the girl was cutting into strips.

"I think that is for wiping away excess pigment from the skin. My grandfather had a Drekken tattooed on one arm. Serba angered him once by saying that he fainted when they wiped the red pigment from its wings. My mother told me how he punched her for saying he thought he was bleeding!".

Daro's voice was curious in her mind. "How odd it seems to me to embellish what the One made beautiful in the first place. I would be fearful that the Decrian might slip, ruin the design, and yet I can see the beauty in the craft, and I suppose the decision to create a skin record marks a turning point in ones life.".

Draille had approached them silently, and as if aware of their internal conversation, stood waiting intent on speaking to Daro. The young mage smiled up at the Ranger's inscrutable features, then the man spoke softly.

"Lord of the Opal, I ask very humbly your indulgence for our Decrian. She knows you only by your admitted rank, but senses that you hold the secret of young Dorenard's new emblem. It is my belief that she would take your counsel on the matter of the ceremonial point.", he sounded awkward, and Jalni sat forward, and said swiftly, "My people choose a tool made from natural substance that forever links those tattooed with the tool and the symbol of their choice. If a man has a running hound as his emblem then the tooth of a hound would provide the point. It seems that either Marran has no idea of his emblem, has not recently dreamed in a manner that Kilda can discern his emblem, or is uncertain of a choice offered. As his sponsor she may believe that you know something that could help her decide the matter. Shall I take you Daro?", and so they followed Draille into the brilliant light surrounding the great chair.

Garald stood behind Marran whose forearm was supported on a frame. His upper wrist and hand were stained with the liquor, but he sat calmly rested against Garald's supporting torso, and Jalni could see no sign of outward agitation. He too wore a leather apron, across which several lengths of white material had been laid, and then Kilda spoke, and her deep voice startled Jalni, snatching her attention away from the boy.

"It is rare for the new entrant to the Tawn to know his emblem my Lord.", the woman said in a practical manner. "They have been through their *holonogarth* and are both confused by their change in status and by fatigue. It is nearly always a friend or relative that reveals the emblem, and whereas I would have called the one named Torvin, Ranger Dorenard asked for your help in this matter. He was Nightlingby, and therefore as the trail blazer of a new wave of Rangers he cannot choose his old emblem. He tells of a strange dream in which a dying friend changed into a snow Raven, but they are white and I cannot use that colour. We can influence many pigments but white is not one of them. His recent dreams have always been of storms, travelling, and you but there is no obvious link in his mind. Can you suggest anything?".

Daro was silent for a moment then his inner voice said ruefully in Jalni's mind, "I have the answer, but how many more will have to know who and what I am?", but Jalni never got the chance to answer for as Daro's eyes opened revealing a blaze of Opal, there was a long mournful howl and she saw Garald pale, gripping the boys shoulders. Hidden in the closeness of their intimate circle, Kilda's jaw dropped, and Jalni linked to those who now held the mage's hands also saw an ancient rock painting come to life. First what appeared to be dogs bounded forward and were no dogs but wolves! Ancient wolves, huge wolves ridden by Rangers, then from the heart of a billowing storm came the Zephryn, the single horned storm horses ridden by a man with Opal in his eyes, and behind him another wolf, ridden by a boy, wearing a sword strapped to his back. The dream faded, Daro's eyes closed slowly and Kilda looked at Draille, unspoken questions in her eyes. Garald straightened, stepped forward and clasped Daro's forearm in the traditional manner, barely breathing, "Thank you, thank the One!", as Draille said cryptically, "They have been no further into Holmgarth than the visitors area and the observation platform.".

Kilda nodded, then spoke briskly.

"Then we must act on what has been revealed here. I have known those symbols all my life, and could tattoo them in my sleep.".

She sat up, and said briskly, "Well my Lord, Draille will undoubtedly tell you the legend, but I must go to work. You two Nightlingbys have given me much more to consider than I had ever dreamed of. Now you must answer me one question apiece. I will ask your emblem once and only once. You will give me your answer in a single word and then we are done for now.".

In Daro's mind her voice was as serious, as intense as he had ever heard his own mother's, and in that moment he felt so connected with Ikella that his heart jumped. Kilda spoke solemnly.

"My Lord sponsor, what emblem shall Marran Dorenard take to his grave?", and Jalni felt the delicate shudder as Daro said in a considering way.

"Wolf, SheerWolf to be exact.", and in response to the same question Marran blinked and said breathlessly,

"SheerWolf, if it please the Keld!", and Iskilda reached out and selected a pouch emptying various points into a bowl filled with the sterilising liquor. Kilda herself reached into her ornately decorated scrip and produced a point holder, which she wiped with an impregnated cloth, and then a stone palette supported by the frame was swung into place and the sterile points moved so that the Decrian could reach them easily. Draille, Daro and Jalni settled onto cushions nearby and Garald was bracing Marran again, as the night, breathless with anticipation closed in about them.

Iskilda stretched the skin on Marran's upper wrist saying softly, "Rank first.". The Decrian lifted slender tongs from a basin, fitted a point soaked in the full blue pigment of a fledged Ranger and bent over Marran's wrist. For a fleeting second the boy trembled, then Garald's hypnotic voice floated down the cleft, taking Ranger and Clansmen all, on the Old Path of Rangers long past.

"Now has the fledgling flown. Now he must face the turning point between the life of a child and the birth of a man. A Ranger first Class, known by his brand, by his deeds…".

The voice drifted on. The boy relaxed and the Decrian, hands steady began to outline a triple braid. The voice recited old deeds, ancient legends as the boy's hand was turned and flexed. The skin was stretched as the point kissed the skin, christening the clean flesh with a tracery of feathers. The boy breathed deep ragged breaths, a cleansing cloth dabbed, the brazier flared, and the point turned and flicked, then turned again. The feathers grew along his hand. The voice now recited the patrimony of the man whose head slick with sweat was braced, while bright eyes focussed on the point, the turning point as it coloured his rank in deepest blue.

In the night families came and families went. Children wrapped in trail blankets slept and the Decrian worked the braid around Marran's wrist. In the morning he slept, pillowed in his wife's lap his wrist bound with damped bandages, His back protected where his new emblem lay. His faithful patrol stood guard around him, and in the dawn a Sandsinger recalled a voice saying,

"Lord of the Opal, when the time comes I know your emblem and will stand ready for your call!".

Chapter 7 - Farewells and Promises

The cat stretched, luxuriating in the comfort of a warm bed. He didn't want to wake, but he had dreamt, a dream of warm hands, Opal eyes and a soft voice in his head. it wheedled, coaxing then *compelling* his attention. His eyes, blurry with sleep opened, nictating membranes sluggishly retracting as he stared around his lair seeking "He who called", to no avail. His tail lashed crossly, it had been a very good dream, his head lowered as though he sought sleep again, but half open eyes still watched hopefully.

His human companion had stirred on the platform above his lair. The rumbling rasp of Chrism's snore had abated, and the cat purred contentedly as a large gentle face appeared over the edge of the bed, hanging upside-down, full of anxiety.

"Tummy-ache fellah?", a deeply unmusical voice growled enquiringly, "I told you that gulley-hoppers had to be eaten fur off! Shall I come and rub it better?", and the cat, whose stomach was perfectly comfortable (though full), uttered an inviting "Puhrr aow", and the lesser demigod of his existence rolled backwards off the platform, still wrapped in his sleeping rug, and snuggled down beside the mystcat. In no time the gentle belly rub had turned into a game of "Touch paws, pat nose, grab and growl", and the large herders hut shuddered from the onslaught of thumps, giggles and satisfied bellows as a barely matured mystcat pounced on his devoted keeper. Eventually even Chrism had to admit defeat as they sprawled out of the decently curtained sleeping area onto the floor of the main hut. He lay full length where Echo had knocked him flying, and wondered why he felt as though he was being watched. A shaft of early sunlight reflected off a polished metal plate, and Chrism stared at it, before picking it up to rub at the image that appeared there. As he did so the mystcat slunk out of his lair, to stand on his hind-legs, forepaws draped affectionately over Chrism's shoulders, nuzzling his head while they both stared at the image of a single gleaming eye.

"Finally I get some attention!", the half aggrieved, half amused voice exclaimed, and the mystcat yowled, deafening Chrism, who blinked once, then with the direct simplicity of a late maturing child exclaimed, "Daro!", joyously turning to search round the living area, leaving the cat to stare mesmerised into his Lord's remotely viewing eye. Eventually, convinced that their sworn Lord was not physically present, Chrism returned to where the mystcat reviewed the simple instructions he had received. Daro had simply visualised a party travelling together, using the well remembered images of sunrise, sunset, with twin moons rising to indicate a journey of a few days distance. He used images of Ikella, Shiarjha, finishing with Jashell, Indeera and the guard, until the cat's ears twitched excitedly as he understood the final image, then Echo yowled softly as the eye faded.

At this, Chrism bent over the plate and said cautiously, "Daro. Where are you?", and heard the weary reply.

"Not far from home now Chrism. Tell Jashell and Indeera to bring the Watch to Cathlea, two sleeps from now. Lown must get word to Seris Ikella to prepare. Go, hurry and tell them we are safe.".

Then he was gone, and the gentle faced man wept disconsolately and a confused mystcat chased his tail, the dust motes in the sunlight, and anything else that moved while he waited for the guards of the Second Watch to patrol the waking slopes above Selesh.

Far below the path leading to the herders hut a woman frowned, wearily rubbing her face. She brushed her fingers through her thick silver mane of hair, surveying her image in the polished metal mirror propped against the wall in the treatment room. She had slept badly, and resolving to retire once Seleus baked the Sands she ruled into its noontime incandescence, grimaced, mentally berating herself for complaining of the heat, when until recently, her entire world had brushed the depths of celestial Winter, hidden from their sun by a shroud of debris. She ruefully rubbed her aching back and stood, thinking that it was ever thus with Pelshar. Too much cold, too much heat, too much Sand, too many to feed or heal. They also had too little fertile land, too little information, too little contact with other Sands and far too much worry. Disgusted with her morbid turn of thought she turned towards the door, but before she could reach it, the latch clicked and another entered.

Beneva said impulsively, "Oh, the Source was so disturbed that I cancelled class. I should have known it was you!", and Ikella, face inscrutable beneath a mask of weariness said testily, "Just what do you mean by that!", her head tilted imperiously as Beneva responded gently.

"You are agitated 'Kella. I suppose its over that dratted boy of yours again?".
The Sorceress enquired harshly.

"Who else rouses lightening in his wake? A runner from Tirjella says that Solana died not long after Daro remembered to tell me they had made Scartel safely.". She tried to keep her voice level as she continued,

"I know only that they have left Scartel. When the beacon burned blue, they sent help, only to find the village razed and warded, the caverns deserted and no clue to follow. They didn't take the Western route, unless they are invisible. If they went north they could be anywhere in the Drekkens, I just don't know where.".

Beneva said comfortingly, "Daro has more than the usual bag of tricks to fall back on my dear. Jalni is a strong and determined woman, and they will manage, let us go and make sweetdrinks, take a nap, and if there is still no word when we wake, we will scry for him.".

The latch clicked, then in the dusky light of the afternoon an Opal eye peered from the metal mirror, gazed around the deserted treatment room, blinked then closed. A minute later it had disappeared entirely, as Selesh slept through Height of Sun.

To the north-east and far beyond the Great Divide, secreted in the hidden valley of Holmgarth a man flexed cramping hands and exclaimed softly and profanely.

"Hadda's balls!".

Daro, who had sat cross-legged on his pallet bed for hours following Height of Sun, groaned involuntarily as his finger joints cracked and popped. He stretched his neck, rotated his shoulders and returned his attention to his hands, rubbing his thumb joints, freeing the muscles that had frozen into the odd position he had assumed. Ruefully accepting that there was much more to learn about remote viewing than Sentinel had told him back in Scartel. He tilted his head, listening to the sound of steady breathing as he stood still flexing the hand that had cramped so painfully. The low call of a Nightlingby sounded and in the shaded cavern, Daro's teeth gleamed as he grinned, wishing that it had been that easy to rouse his mystcat!

He sidestepped, reaching towards the wall where his staff was propped. Crooking a finger which glowed as the plain looking staff leapt to his hand, guiding the blind mage effortlessly to a curtained entrance. Carefully lifting a fold of hide, he left the cavern he shared with the exhausted Children of Scartel, pausing on the sun beaten walkway outside to await developments.

A blue clad shadow detached itself from the wall where it leaned and in two strides became the man who had summoned him. A hand took his arm and Garald stepped in, raising Daro's hand onto his shoulder as he led the mage along the walkway. There was a low murmur of, "Mind your head Daro.", as Garald swept aside another hide hanging, then they were standing on a hide rug in front of a gathering of some kind. Daro waited calmly, head tilted as he concentrated, hearing the minute shifting that told him that he and Garald were not alone. The silence persisted as he pivoted slowly, catching a scent here, a sound there, and then he bowed to the assembly saying quietly to Garald.

"Do I understand that we are with the Council of Rangers?".

He stood relaxed yet aware of the scrutiny of others, then Marran's familiar voice replied.

"Yes Daro, the Keld are gathered to ask your will with regard to the children. They understood your wish to return them to their kin, but not your wish to sponsor them. They have always kept themselves free of any preferment to the Sands and it troubles them that the Guardians want to change that balance. They will not discuss the matter directly with you because although you have shown your authority to act for Seris Ikella, they cannot believe that she understands what she has undertaken.".

The serious voice said softly, "They have never been exposed to magic, and although rumours of her powers reached here after Partition, they cannot give credence to something they have no understanding of. Entrusting the lives of Rangers to the hands of one whom they have never met would not be possible. However, I have persuaded them that you are a different matter.", adding hastily as Daro's brows drew together ominously, "Not that I have in any way revealed how different you are, although I think you might have to!".

Daro frowned, then asked abruptly, "How come you here anyway? Aren't you supposed to be having one night with your wife before you leave?", and Marran smiled.

"We can wait. We must settle this matter now, and it is better done with only the Keld present. You are in the presence of Ranger Leader Draille Skellin, Dream Walker Garald Lightfoot, Decrian Kilda Pagthorn, Trail Finder Cobbold...", and the list of names rolled as easily off Marran's tongue as if he told the ancient history of his ancestors. When the eleventh name had been given, the new young Ranger paused awkwardly, and Daro greeted the Keld.

"I am at your disposal good Councillors.", as he might have greeted the High Council of Selesh, then wondered how to proceed, until Draille came to his rescue.

"You are welcomed amongst us Son of the Opal. I will speak for the Keld, and Ranger Dorenard who knows your ways will explain anything you do not understand, but first our Dream Walker will tell you the history of our kind and how we came here.".

Daro felt Garald touch his arm gently and allowed himself to be guided into a surprisingly comfortable seat. Marran came and sat at his feet, and then to his immense surprise he realised that Garald had come behind him, much in the way that he had braced Marran through his tattoo ritual. He forced down a flicker of panic, then Garald whispered gently,

"By your leave Lord?", and at Daro's silent nod, skilled fingers found pressure points on Daro's forehead, and into his mind drifted the most extraordinary images.

He was looking at what appeared to be a world on fire. Towards him raced beasts he couldn't even begin to identify, as flaming rocks hurtled from the sky and the plentiful grazing all about them singed and burned. He felt compelled to run himself but was anchored in the vision, hearing Garald's persuasive voice completing the patrimony of the frightened Rangers as they swarmed past him, and then as the earth beneath his feet shuddered and rent asunder, he felt himself falling, down, further and further, into the depths and knew that he was falling into the Great Divide. Garald's fingers at his brow sustained him, and soon he found himself wrapped in a great cloak of some soft hide, sharing a piquantly flavoured dish of some stewed vegetable. It was the oddest sensation that the Sandsinger had ever experienced. The waking mind told him that he was safe in Holmgarth amongst friends, but his dreaming mind walked a world he had never seen, ate food he could only taste, and discovered sensations he had no knowledge of. Days and crazy nights filled with brilliantly flaming objects streamed past the Sandsinger's consciousness. Once it seemed to him that he woke, then he found himself dodging between rocks, hiding from some airborne threat, and all the time he was plucking at plants, harvesting seedpods nuts and berries, dropping them into a pouch as he ran. Somewhere in that journey of the mind he felt the Anduigor at his belt tingle and his hand raised to his throat touching the Opal sector of his Seguidor as he verified the truth of this inner vision, and then he was stumbling into Holmgarth, exhausted, soaked in sweat, and hearing a voice declaim.

"To my sorrow I have brought you only death my friends. I thought to serve my fellow Ranger as well as my Lord of the Sands, and I was mistaken in my faith. They have passed from amongst us now, those troublesome ones who have failed our world so badly, they and their magic have gone forever, and we are left alone to rebuild our beloved Pelshar. I, Anelm Dorenard take my oath upon this sword, that never again will I so recklessly depend on things not of this world, that all my faith will be in Pelshar and the realities of life. To that end I pledge my line. Here in the Vale of Holmgarth I will dedicate myself to salvaging what we can, growing and sharing what little we have, until the One guides us back or sends us a sign.".

Daro gasped as once more the strange rock painting he had dreamed under Kilda's influence ran through his mind. The wolves, the Zephryn and two men riding flickered through his entranced mind, and then the Seguidor "twitched" out of his grasp, and he was waking to the dying cadences of Garald's hypnotic chant, and froze in shock at the Dream Walkers last words.

"One comes out of the night, unpractised in the craft, a child amongst dangerous men yet in his hands he holds the future of Pelshar. This sign will walk the night, lighting our darkness with his courage, inspiring the people to use the power we carry within to save our world. This sign shall make himself known to us, and respect for our world will make him one of us again.".

Daro's eyes flickered and opened, ablaze with shimmering Opal as the Keld rose and bowed to him. He leant back against the comforting body that supported his head, somewhat bemused by the low apologetic voice saying softly.

"This is foretold my Lord, and if this revelation had not been intended, my dream trail would have had no effect on you. I am privileged by your trust and pray that you do not think I have in any way betrayed you.".

Daro suddenly felt very bereft as Garald's light touch was withdrawn. For some strange reason he craved physical contact, and then it suddenly occurred to him that with the Rangers, he had never avoided it. He remembered how comfortable he had felt around the children. Examining his recollections he realised quite suddenly that he had not had to shield himself against touching or being touched by any of them. He remembered the warmth of Draille's forearm against his own as they exchanged greetings, the sensation of tousling a child's hair, the ministrations of Marran in the most intimate services during his illness, and suddenly understood that the Rangers were so "grounded", so at one with Pelshar that here at least, he could be a man amongst men without fear of influencing them, or being overwhelmed by their untrained emotionality. He sighed, feeling himself quiver with reaction, then Marran's sword, lying cradled in that young man's lap, sang a thready whisper of sound, and a tense silence was shattered by a quavering howl from the ravine below.

The Keld were on their feet, Draille Skellin grabbed Marran raising him from his position at Daro's feet, as the curtain was swept aside and a bewildering number of laughing excitable Rangers peered in. Daro was shielded from their gaze by Garald's protective body however, and he heard Marran say reassuringly, "Draille will deal with that lot, we will be going down to the Holm, Garald has much to tell you, show you even. I will go and get Terris, she will wake Jalni and stay with the little ones until the Trail Finder settles things.", and so it was. A confusing number of Rangers departed, half the Keld with them. Outside on the walkway the Tawn gathered their newest brother, and as the day sank to a close in Holmgarth, Torvin and Terris took charge of the children, conducting them through a myriad of hidden passages down to the base of the cleft and out where an apparently green and fertile area was being cultivated. Garald walked back to where Jalni (still confused with sleep) led Daro, and said quietly,

"Healer, if you will walk with my wife, I will guide Daro, and describe for him.". Somehow Jalni was not surprised when Sushanna appeared, and readily accepting this solution they followed in Draille's footsteps. They were headed towards rising ground until a path opened up leading into a narrow defile covered with scruffy brushwood. Daro walked trustingly behind the Dream Walker, one hand on his shoulder as the path narrowed, and then they were in a clearing, vegetation under their feet and a sheer rock face rising ahead of them, inset with low cave entrances. Rangers milled about these, and Jalni saw that a low bench was stacked with joints of meat, and understood that some sort of animal was kept here as Garald came to a halt saying sharply over his shoulder.

"Stand quite still, no matter what happens. ", and then Trail Finder Grobold was being towed towards them by an immense wolf. She was panting, determined to elude the huge hands that clung so purposefully to her coat. She stood at least fourteen handspans high at the shoulder. Tawny eyes surveyed the approaching party along a silvery muzzle, and as Jalni's breath caught in her throat, the Sheerwolf lowered her head and rumbled contemplatively. the Trail Finder staggered to a halt, reaching up to lock his fingers into the thick pelt, leaning against the great she-wolf as she eyed the muscular strength of Garald, then deliberately turned an enquiring snout in Daro's direction. She snuffled delicately, licked her lips and whined softly. Grobold shifted his hold as she gave out a throaty growl of enquiry, and Daro lifted his head. The she-wolf tensed, then leaned forward and rested her great head against Daro's face. The almond shaped eyes opened, and the wolf crooned softly, then just as Daro was getting used to the experience of feeling fur pressed into his cheeks, she lowered her head still further and nuzzled at the Seguidor at the base of his throat. Daro felt movement at his side and then the wolf transferred her interest to Marran, nuzzling his hands and groaning happily, before she trotted off, dragging Grobold with her. She moved so silently that Daro missed the direction that she took and turned a bewildered face to Garald.

He whispered uneasily, "Something I did?", but the Dream Walker laid a silencing finger across Daro's lips, and then Grobold and the wolf returned as silently as they had departed. She carried a cub by its scruff as she trotted straight past Garald and Daro, to lay the whimpering cub at Marran's feet. The boy crouched swiftly, touching the cub gently on the nose, letting him take the human scent in before the cub lifted its head and laid his snout against Marran's nose, sharing its own scent with the young Ranger, while gazing into Marran's eyes in some curious intimacy that brought a lump to the throat of all that saw that exchange. Daro who could not, felt the tremor in Garald's hand and understood that something rare and precious had occurred, and felt his own eyes sting with the frustration of exclusion. Then there was an audible gasp around him, and the she-wolf was returning, pressing into the blind mage until he knelt at her feet. Garald's voice echoed oddly in his mind as the Dream Walker said urgently.

"Stay very still Daro, Endrusus is entrusting you with her only she-cub. This is an honour beyond any we could give you. This cub is the last she will bear for she is aged and must soon return to the Eternal Snows of her kind. Remember how Endrusus greeted you? Let the cub get your scent by holding your hand to her nose. She will press her face against yours snout to nose, and though you cannot see her eyes will stare deep into your soul, as she gives you her scent and her secret name. You are the only one to know that name, it is what you call when she is old enough to carry you through the Sheer.".

The surrounding Rangers saw the young mage reach out confidently and find the cubs nose. They smiled at the surprise and joy on the blind man's face as the cub laid her muzzle against Daro's face, and if only a few had bonded a Sheerwolf they all understood the wonder of hearing that voice in one's mind declaring, "I'm Gray I think! I promise to be a good girl like Mother told me!".

Then the dream visions returned. With the soft fur of Gray pressed against his face Daro felt an immense surge of power. He was running, along the edge of sleep, with a wild dream of riding endlessly along some boundary that his very speed prevented him from crossing. He felt a deep thrumming as his paws touched the ground, there was light ahead of them, the wind streamed through his fur, her fur tickled his nose, and he sneezed breaking the dream, as his head lifted from the communion with the cub. Garald's voice was low but sustaining.

"Now you understand the bond of the wolf and have experienced the Sheer you will understand how it is that Rangers cling to the old ways. If summoned a Rangers Sheerwolf will take him through the Sheer to where he is needed. This has led to the rumours that a Ranger can be in two places at the same time, and as I know that Clansmen protect their own mysteries, we don't tell anyone how we achieved that reputation.".

They all saw the young man chuckle, fondling the startling silver pelt that had marked this cub as something special. They all saw Ranger Dorenard hand his new friend over to his keeper with a reluctant sigh, then they were leaving the wolf pen, walking back into a crowd of children all anxious to find out what was happening to them. The Keld were waiting grouped in the shade of an entrance on which the Dream scene of Sheerwolves and Zephryn galloped endlessly into the future, and Daro sensing Jalni's sudden interest reached up and lightly touched the carved and painted frieze. His fingers brushed the outline of the delicate legs, traced the shoulder to the head and as he touched the single horn, smiling to himself there was a distinct growl of thunder overhead.

Afterwards, Jalni realised that she had seen several members of the Keld smiling and nodding, but she was torn in so many directions as the children flocked around them. All but the very few clans folk were staying in Holmgarth with their kin. Marran was half distraught at their imminent departure, half joyful that he was to be their leader in the future, and she kindly left him alone with Terris to make their plans. Sushanna confided that she thought Terris would make a very good Healer, vowing that she would train her as an Apothecary herself before sending her on to Selesh. Brisha held Calar's hand and trembled as Daro looked for his guide, but then Draille was by Daro, and speaking solemnly.

"Calar is a Clansman, but he has lived in a Ranger community all his life. He was stepson to a Skellin and we would like to train him another Rotation or two. He is all that is left of my own kin at Scartel, and I would welcome him here. I will stand surety for him my Lord, and return him to you able to hold his own in any community.", and Jalni with relief saw Daro nod in agreement. He raised a finger to Calar and when his reluctant guide approached he said gently, "I need someone Sandsworn in Holmgarth Calar.".

He appeared to be giving the matter great thought, brow furrowed as he said.

"Did you realise that through marriage your mother was Ranger Skellin's cousin? No? Well it's a fact, and to make matters worse he tells me that Brisha won't stay without you, and she as you know must be looked after until she is ready to return to Scartel. The only way to deal with all these problems is to leave you here young man, but can you bring yourself to stay?".

Jalni sent him images of herself doing cartwheels all around the Gathering Square of Selesh and saw him bite back a chuckle as he succeeded in gaining agreements from the boy.

"Yes!", he would stay and report back to Daro when needed. "Yes.", he understood that he would have to obey Draille as the father he had never known, and might even have to agree to formal adoption as a Ranger, and "Yes.", he knew it was a bore, having to look after a girl but Brisha was special and Jalni would be sad if he let her down. Exacting promises of good behaviour from all the Children of Scartel, and clasping arms with Garald, Draille and Marran, Daro and Jalni took their farewells before a sadly depleted company swung out through a cunningly disguised gap, to find themselves on the track to Cathlea, only two hours before sundown, with an hours walk ahead of them.

Chapter 8 - Confrontation at Cathlea

As the sands thinned to a border track skirting a finger of rising land, the travelling group had shrunk to less than three patrols, made up of Solana's orphans (who had elected to stay with Daro), a few Zurian children who had relatives beyond the Azure and a cluster of what Daro called his special cases. Jalni, surprised at Calar's meek acceptance of a role caring for young Brisha, had discovered that Daro was more perceptive than she suspected.

"I couldn't embarrass the boy by throwing him into Erinim's arms could I?", he told her as they ambled towards the grey shadows of the next headland.

"He'll mature in his own time. They are very young and calf love may not last. However, this way, I get regular reports on all of them, and Calar takes responsibility seriously, which won't hurt him!", and with that, Jalni had to be content.

She was restless, somehow feeling as if all the purpose had gone out of her life, and she cast a glance over the straggle of children, and felt very inclined to turn back. Something in her manner alerted Daro to this uncertain frame of mind, but he chose to ignore it for the time being as he concentrated on trudging alongside Rann. The quietest Nightlingby had shyly revealed a longing to travel and study, so, with the eager pursuit of knowledge at Selesh in mind, Daro had welcomed his company. Thus they entered the last short stage of this "Azure journey", back to Cathlea first, then with the help of Ikella's Guard, back to Selesh in the Opal Sands

The Sandsinger, Jalni, Lallee, Rann and Motri steered, coaxed, and sometimes carried the remaining refugees as the trail stop came into sharp focus on the horizon, although Jalni became increasingly reluctant to leave her native sands with every step. The weariness born of great excitement and too little sleep affected all of them and Jalni carried the youngest on her shoulder, where she had lurched, training huge brown eyes on Daro's face.

Despite encouragement and exhortation, their progress was slowing. The group struggling down off the sands towards a Fringe track was turning anxious eyes to sullen skies. Jalni's legs were leaden, almost as if the sands were clinging to her, as she realised that every step took her towards the Opal and her return to Ikella's authority. She stiffened her resolve, and pausing to shift the weight of the sleeping child on her shoulder felt something stir beneath her feet. The ground was reverberating, faintly it was true, but something was behind them.

The boy leading the patrol ahead of her, turned fearfully as she crouched placing her palm on the sand. Two strides behind her Daro came up, and in her mind his urgent voice asked, "Wanderers?", and Jalni, alert once more to that indefinable sense of being watched, followed and hunted as a fugitive herself, trembled as she remembered to stream these impressions to the blind mage. As Motri panted back to take the baby, Jalni stood, glancing swiftly around them.

Behind and to their left the open sands rolled into the distance. To the right a hostile cliff face soared, a solid barrier which held itself aloof and impenetrable, no path, passage or handhold visible. Rann, facing back down the track, heard the approaching "thrum", as if many feet ran in their direction and paled as teens corralled smaller children protectively. There was a sudden whisper of wind, the air hot and ominous stirred as a growl of thunder sounded overhead.

Jalni tried to keep her inner voice from squeaking with fear as she said swiftly, "No place to hide. We either stay or run.", as Rann silently indicated a small cloud of dust rising along the track behind them, the sudden terrorised babble of the children finally decided the question and they ran towards Cathlea and what they perceived as the only safety in sight.

For Daro this race was terrifying yet exhilarating. He hadn't moved so fast since the night he came into power, and as his mind touched on that subject, his power rose within him, steadying and guiding him. Rann held on to one sleeve and he strove to keep his balance with his Staff. His stride lengthened as the steady thrumming of hooves began to overhaul them, he "stretched" his perception, trying to get some sense of what pursued them but felt only the joy of speed, the feel of warm blue sands beneath his feet, the bond of trusted companions. As the first building loomed out of the shadows, the breath was sobbing in his throat. He could run no more, they were caught. Then he heard shouts of laughter and relief as cavorting, snorting and stamping they were surrounded by whickering mane tossing Zephryn.

Rann doubled over gasping, as Daro, laughing with joy and relief ran past him, round the corner of the great courtyard and stopped dead in his tracks, as the leader of the Wanderers awaiting them rose, and a familiar velvety voice greeted him.

Almost as the mage realised they were not alone, Jalni arrived, children clustered around her, and the delighted babble that had arisen after the appearance of the Zephryn died into frightened silence. Daro heard Jalni curse, and then Bernot spoke.

"Welcome friend.", he said comfortably. "We have been watching, waiting and praying for you. Come to the fire, let your babies rest, your teens bathe and eat while we give thanks to the One that any of you survived the plague.".

Stunned into silence they complied. Children were lifted into gentle hands. Packs were passed to Jalni who offered their meagre rations to a smiling woman who seemed to be in charge of feeding everyone, and soon she discovered that Trellin was Bernot's wife, and the mother of the child who had confidently crawled into Daro's lap. She watched in a daze as some of the men present went out amongst the Zephryn, checking their legs, looking at teeth and quieting the restless creatures until Daro stood and fussed them. As though caught in some dream, she watched the herd trot away into the dark. The weariness of body and mind washed over her, although she managed to hold herself together until the children had been fed, washed and put to bed in one long hut. Then, reeling with bewilderment, she sat on a blanket close to the fire-pit and listened to

Bernot reciting the prophecy he had told Daro, heard the grave calm questions from the families grouped around him, and finally, too exhausted to care what happened next, slept.

In her dreams she travelled. Sometimes she walked, sometimes she ran, but wherever she went, she was always moving. Onward and outward her dream spirit drove her, great cliffs soared over sands she had never seen, mountain peaks glistened, great ravines fell into darkness, yet all the time she was searching. She had no idea what she was looking for, but it was precious and she was so lonely. Everywhere she roamed she felt "outside", excluded, yet even as one voice told her to stop, another drove her onward. Sobbing she woke, huddled in her blanket and sat where she had fallen asleep trying to make sense of her dream. She absently set about collecting dew, wringing it out of the condensing strips that had been hung from a frame, collecting the precious moisture in a pannikin, reluctant to draw water from the precious reserves for her own use. Absently she checked her backpack relieved to find that she had enough dry rations for three days, and turned her face toward the deep blue desert. On the outer edge of the trail stop she paused to consider what she was about to do, and as she did so a small dawn breeze stroked her face dry of the stupid tears that threatened to undermine a decision that had been slowly forming over the last few days. She remembered the heart-breaking courage of Brus as he whispered, "I wish I could stay with you!", and caught her breath on a sob.

"It won't do to wake Daro.", she schooled her emotions grimly and took a few tentative steps out of the trail stop, glancing up at the clearing sky. She saw with relief that she could indeed steer her way by the stars she always thought of as Rowin's Eyes and set her feet on the route back to Jerritol. Back to her roots, to the beginnings of what made her what she was. Jalni had finally realised that she had to go back home, to face the past and bury it. or undo the damage that had sent her endlessly searching for peace. She paused in the shadows of the last rocky outcrop, quieting her quaking emotions then strode forward into the early light of dawn, unwinding the Rotations with every step as she walked into her past in search of her future.

As soon as he woke, Daro knew she had gone. Since they left Scartel he had felt some inner turmoil that she shielded from him. He "reached" for her, seeking perhaps the whisper of her perfume, the tingle in his blood when their minds locked, but there was nothing, only the emptiness and desolation that her presence had replaced. Closing his mind resolutely to the urgent desire to weep, to howl, to throw himself out into the cool blue dawn and call the Zephryn to search for her, he was trembling with the effort to control himself when Rann tapped on his door and entered saying urgently,

"Daro, we have visitors. They are very insistent on seeing you.", then his voice died on an affronted squeak as Jashell thrust the door open behind him, and knelt, head bowed.

"Ichspeller!", she said with relief, "I am in advance of my Watch who travel with Healers, supplies for a ninenight, your Sandsworn man, and that damned cat!".

She gulped, apparently on the brink of unburdening herself of other news, then Jashell the imperturbable, the calm face of stoicism burst into tears, as Daro sat, swathed in blankets demanding imperiously,

"By the fist of the One! Tell me Jashell. What ill news do you bring now?".

As the signet ring on his left hand flared into life, Daro's head tilted questioningly, and his eyelids flickered and opened as a whorl of opal appeared. As a child pretending to look through some aperture, he joined forefinger to thumb and pressed the encirclement to one glowing eye, touching his Seguidor lightly with the other hand, and queried tentatively.

"Mother?", but the voice that replied was not Ikella's. Into that dusty dawn Beneva said quietly,

"Daro, whatever is happening at Cathlea, the guard and Indeera can manage. They will bring the children back to Selesh, but you must come now with Jashell. Your mother is gravely ill, may have been poisoned. Word reached us that the Gattarene plots the downfall of Sorcery, but Ikella was off-sands. Dear old Eshima comes to the end of her life and your mother went to visit her, returning quite out of sorts. She had a fever rising after Height of Sun yesterday, and this morning we could not rouse her. Daro, we need you here quickly.", hearing the last ominous words, the Sandsinger's face grew cold and hard, the glow of his *othergaze* positively glacial as he lowered his eyelids, and stretched a cramping hand.

Between Daro's finger and thumb a sparkling web spun, then it was gone as Beneva's voice faded. Rann held out a hand and said softly, "I will assist my lord Daro to dress and prepare for the road, someone tell Jalni to get the children together.".

They were all shocked when the Sandsinger's voice came. It was unnaturally harsh as he said bitterly.

"You can't tell Jalni anything! She's left me. Mother could be dying and Jalni's left, so has anyone anything else to add to this bright and shining day?".

PART 2 - FOOTSTEPS IN THE DARK

Chapter 9 - The Retreat

Afterwards, Daro was always to think of this end of the journey as a retreat. He physically felt each step of the process as though it was a desertion. As his new friends from the Felmin farming communities, and the small band of Wanderers disbursed, he heard the muffled confused chatter of those who would remain until Indeera's party arrived. His face was glum as he heard a wail of indignation, but he had no time to make the round of farewells. He hardly had time to check his flask or sling a backpack before Jashell was impatiently jogging on the spot, anxious to return. He would have prepared her for his slow progress, but she forestalled him.

"Ichspeller, legends abound with my people, one of which concerns a secret way between Selesh and the Ashgenar. I plan to prove the rumours to be nothing but dust swirls in the Sand, or reveal a truth that has been buried in the mists of time.".

She was mysterious, but resolute in her silence, and Daro felt a pang as he wished Rann farewell, and took Jashell's shoulder in his grip. They left the waking compound walking fast, but it was not long before the pace slackened to a crawl, as Daro was reminded how unfit he had become since losing his sight. Jashell seethed silently as he stumbled along, and then she said slowly as if the idea had just occurred to her, "What if I teach you how we hunt with the Sorrel hounds? If I am "the hound", and you run in the harness, I will be able to warn you when we need to be careful, and you will be safer within the lines.".

They paused, where he had met Bernot and Trellin. Reminded of his scramble to the Sands from the crumbling Dorenard Trail, Daro was wondering how Jashell planned to progress on the precipitous track above, when the Guard Commander spoke.

"We won't be going that way so you won't need your Staff either", she said gruffly. Producing a leather trace from her carrisack. As Daro dematerialised his Staff, she was telling him that she had "borrowed" it from Rowbet, and he deduced that she was laying it out, and smiled as she referred to it as a "hound line". He heard clasps worked together, the "clink" as they engaged, then she tapped him on the shoulder twice to let him know that he should stay still as she passed a loop around his chest saying briskly,

"Work that under your arms, over your shoulders, letting the line lie against your back. I want you to feel the tension as I take up the slack first".

He obeyed silently, feeling straps slide around his chest, under his armpits as Jashell stepped into the opposing harness and raised it to breast height. She fiddled with a broad leather belt, sliding it up to connect to the "line". There was the soft "whirr", and snick of fastening buckles at which Daro touched his

Seguidor, hastily drawing strength as Jashell walked forward until he felt the tension on his improvised harness. She called over her shoulder.

"Stand now, get your footing and make sure your flask and pack are secure and won't interfere with the line or your movements. When you are ready tug the line.". He carefully swung the small pack, adjusted his flask, and wriggled his toes down into his boots, tugged the line and concentrated as her voice instructed him solemnly.

"As I move forward, you hold each side of the line with your hands, and match my paces. It will feel odd, but we are running on the level and I will call any change of direction or pace. Just keep your feet lifted, hold the line and try not to fall!".

Horrified at the idea Daro retorted, "I'll try, what about you?", to which Jashell responded with grim amusement.

"I will make a special effort Ichspeller, for the bottom of the Great Divide is a long way down.", and then they were moving, pace for counted pace as Daro leaned back against the unconventional harness and muttered softly, praying that his powers would engage should either of them stumble.

He was literally being towed along when Jashell called a halt and allowed him to sink gasping into the shade of a rock. She opened her carrisack withdrawing a tiny flask which she unstoppered with her teeth, pouring a little fluid into her palms, briskly applying this to the burning calf muscles of Daro's legs. He yelped as the cold bit, then grinned with relief as Jashell said sternly.

"You need exercise. Toning those leg muscles can't hurt your dignity, and might yet save your life.".

Ever the Guard Commander, she growled softly as she hunkered down beside him, and without a "By your leave", reached out and calmly took the measure of racing pulses. Silently rising, she came to stand behind him, checking the trace, adjusting a twist that threatened to rub a sore under his arm, speaking brusquely.

"Deshun Ikella still trains regularly with the Watch. I am convinced this may have saved her life (and yours) during the Great Storm. Now you hold the power and the trust of my people as well as your own, the loss of your sight must not mean the shortening of your days. It is no use being able to restore the light of Seleus to a world, if you can't move your own body fast enough to catch the words of a dying woman. Seeing is only one part of your life, don't neglect the rest of your body because your eyes don't work! Now, stay still and I will massage your chest and back, get those lungs working and then I will stretch your legs.".

So saying she followed up her words with swift actions. Strong hands pummelled his back, kneaded and squeezed his muscles until the blood sang in his veins, then she had him stand, raising and lowering his arms, filling his lungs and stretching his sinews till they cracked.

"After which,", he later reported to a bemused Guardian, "Being towed on a Sorrel hounds line at a smart gallop was as nothing to a full session in Sundreth's torture rooms."

He raised an admonitory finger at that point and commanded, "Don't ask me where I ran Aunt Beneva, for I really don't know. I was too exhausted to try and follow the twists and turns of that strange route, and besides I promised Jashell never to reveal what is known only to the High Priestess of her Clan. I don't think that path had been trod in Rotations and we were running, so any impressions I gained were fleeting and had no relevance, other than I sit here and Ikella still lives.".

He leant wearily against the wall and thought again of the thing they had withdrawn from the heel of Ikella's foot. Holding the bowl that Mina gave him, he had caught a distinct acrid scent. He heard the Healer's description numbly, recognising this weapon as the tip of a Ranger made poisonwood dart, concealing his dismay as best he could.

Many long hours and a tumultuous High Council session later, Diras led the Sandsinger into Ikella's bedchamber, where he could rest, close to her sickroom, within call if needed. He understood the fear that prompted Beneva to triple the Guard. He was personally thankful that the Gate in the Rock was restored to full working order as he lay fully clothed on his mother's bed, not expecting to sleep. In the guardroom Jashell was relieved by Sorrill who called the reserve to patrol the village. As Diras draped a cover over Daro however, he was too tired to review this strange disjointed day, and was only mildly surprised to realise that he hadn't thought about Jalni once. As the door closed, he smiled, picturing his faithful Diras sleeping across the threshold and slept.

At the end of the corridor, Driss stared savagely at the duty roster and wished for twenty more Guards. In the labyrinth below, Healers came and went under the watchful gaze of the guard, while Selesh slept uneasily. Across the Gathering Square through the double doors of the underground pastures, there was unexpected activity as a dark clad man led a Zeglur out, making the briefest exchange with the Watch Commander as he turned towards the village.

Not long afterwards Daro woke, wondering what had roused him. He ignored the musical tinkle for as long as he dared, before sliding out of the covers. Wriggling his clothes into some semblance of order, he summoned his Staff, and as the Heart of Selesh blossomed into life, the door opened. She stood in the ante-room and with one ear tuned to her direction, he filtered other sounds besides the tiny tinkle as she shifted position. He gave no quarter, surging into power without warning, as he detected a decided absence of bodyguards.

She gurgled appreciatively.

"My oath! What a big bad Sandsinger you've grown into!", but he restrained a grin by scowling, and she continued more soberly.

"You need me in this Selunsanni, even if you don't like it much. I see my successor has deserted you?", and as if a long awaited answer had arrived, Daro nodded and seemed relieved.

"You lied to my mother.", he remarked conversationally as she took his arm, and then as she moved he stopped her. "Feydora, what are you? Ghost? Shade? or ...", and despite his power he felt a chill touch his soul.

"I am a lesson Selunsanni.", she retorted, "and if I lied, you stole my trophy!", and he was aware that she meant the powerstone of his Staff as she continued smoothly.

"I am no threat to you or your people, nor am I a danger to she who will succeed to my Sands.".

He held up a silencing hand, slowed his heartbeat and forefinger to thumb, raised his hand to one glowing eye, true-sight engaged. She was revealed in all her finery. Veiled, wearing the oath cloth and Ikella's sigil to boot! He considered his impressions and couldn't restrain his amusement.

"Very tasty!", he mocked.

"Blonde hair and bells on a warrior?".

"Which only you are aware of Selunsanni.", she hissed, as the glow of his Staff faded, and Diras returned to the ante-room. Totally ignoring Daro, his bodyguard nodded to Feydora.

"Annis.", she questioned with pleasure. "I didn't see your name on the duty board, but thank you for relieving me.".

Realising that she couldn't see him, Daro urgently checked himself as Diras asked.

"Does my lord still sleep?".

As a cold shiver chilled that worthy, he gathered himself as Feydora replied.

"Yes Commander. Guardian Shiarjha tended to his feet and he didn't stir. He is well tucked in and we are advised to leave him resting. I have to return to patrol the village, do you stay on Watch, or shall I arrange relief for you?".

Daro held his breath as Diras walked right past him, and stuck her head round the door. Feydora sketched a symbol, somehow enjoining Daro's compliance, as she placed a picture in his mind of his own sleeping form, together with a glowing shape. He touched his Seguidor where the hub "fizzed" against his skin memorising the symbol she had conjured, receiving a warm glow of congratulation from her, as Diras said softly,

"Poor lad looks dead to the Sands. If the One wills a good night for our Deshun, I certainly won't wake him early.".

Involuntarily Daro touched a hand to heart, lips, and forehead invoking the deity, as he tried not to wonder if he still lived. By all the test's he knew, he was awake, not walking the Plain of Shadows, and his truesight had revealed no threat in Feydora's presence. He listened as the women saluted each other, and nearly jumped out of his skin as he was gently drawn through the doorway, Feydora grasping his quiescent Staff to guide him. Outside Ikella's household slept and yet with guards everywhere, Daro was unable to stop Feydora or challenge the veracity of her alta ego "Annis". Supposing that she was kidnapping him from under his guards nose for a good reason, he tried to relax, passing through the outer doors to the Djellim before he realised that they were going nowhere near the village. He could sense the Council Chamber as they passed through the glowing shield, but had no time to analyse this when his Staff trembled as the powerstone woke.

Beneva stood as "Annis" led him to his chair, the door sealing itself behind them. Daro reached out, sliding a hand along the chair until he located the Staff holder, clipping it into place before facing both Guardians, aware that neither of them had noticed the "Inesh" warrior as she withdrew to a corner. Daro waited until Shiarjha whispered an apology.

"I'm sorry for all the mystery.", then Beneva added glumly, "We have opted to consult you in this manner before your mother wakes up, and forbids us to speak.".

Lapsing into uncomfortable silence Daro waited, sensing a rift between the Guardians and braced himself, as Beneva prompted.

"Hasn't it occurred to you that your Songfather is nowhere to be found in the midst of a medical emergency?".

His blood ran cold as he spoke heavily.

"Oh Deo me. Have I then returned too late to see him again? Was that why High Council was so dismal? No wonder no-one wanted to speak, and we achieved so little.".

He cleared a suddenly constricted throat continuing thoughtfully.

"Why wasn't I told earlier? When they told me of Ikella's collapse.", he was bewildered and it showed, lines of

distress replacing those of fatigue as Beneva sighed and explained awkwardly.

"Carolus lives Daro, but not here. Your mother has removed his privileges, banned him from Selesh, and will no longer use his knowledge or remedies, even to save her own life!", and as Daro half rose, his face displaying incredulity, the Guardian of Knowledge said sharply, "Sit and listen. She is too ill to answer you now. Let her rest, she has paid dearly for her anger.", and as he realised the folly of storming off to demand explanations, Shiarjha took up the story.

"She has been brooding about your situation. Trying to work out what sparked your fascination with the past, and blaming herself for exposing you to magic. She blames your Songfather for your determination to travel, citing his stories of ancient places as the core of your obsession with Sandsingers. She kept very quiet about this until you and Jalni had left, but when Carolus and Olneth returned at Beneva's request, then she refused the old man admittance. He wasn't permitted to collect his own belongings, and Olneth was told firmly that his presence would be limited to the pastures and his tent if he kept such bad company. Her words were set to a scroll, forbidding everyone to offer him accommodation, but of course he owns the "Cross-Eyed Zeglur", so Nadra and Beven have their landlord in what was Ahnell's room.".

She bit her lip, but the blind mage just smiled gently as his friend's name was mentioned, then he sighed reluctantly.

"Aah.", he made the word sound very profound, then added, "I suppose your purpose is to get me to talk to her?", but Beneva shook her head.

"No, that would do no good. She has her mind made up, and you know better than I to flout her will. It would create a crisis of trust. We don't even know if age or illness is to blame. No, carolus has done nothing to deserve this, and she must resolve it herself, but sooner rather than when it is Too late.".

Shiarjha spoke into a cold and shimmering silence, "How are your feet by the way?". Daro was aware that his feet tingled, but all the pain of his days travel had gone, although his legs felt "odd". Shiarjha chuckled as a succession of expressions crossed his face, as he considered that some unknown power must be in play.

"Yes indeed!", she said enigmatically, then Beneva suggested quietly. "Annis, we are quite safe here without your having to stand guard. Why don't you take your report to Driss, then when you return to the village it won't delay you further."

"Annis", strode out of the Council Chamber, with a swift nod and then Shiarjha turned to Daro, and to his surprise took hold of both of his hands. He felt the feather touch of her mind, and then her voice said clearly,

"Don't fight me Daro. This is something that I have learned to do in Sanctuary, and you of all people should understand that as Guardian of all Powers, I might actually know something that can help you.".

He stretched his neck, relaxed his shoulders and said under his breath, "Mechta solus.", in the way he had been taught by Sentinel, and their minds were one. Beneva watched as the young man's hands grasped Shiarjha's, saw his knuckles whiten, then felt a frisson of fear as her Sister Guardian gasped at the revelation of his power. Closer and closer their heads bowed, there was great concentration on Daro's grave features, only serenity on Shiarjha's and then, the Staff that had glowed softly since he had arrived, woke. It was flickering brilliantly as Daro raised his head looking dazed, and then Shiarjha smiled, sliding back into her seat and rubbing ruefully at her wrists.

The Sandsinger sat, communing with his Staff momentarily, then he extended a hand and gentled her wrists until the impressions he had left vanished.

"Sorry.", he commented shortly, "but you took me by surprise. I had no idea that you carried such information. I will make use of it, and thank you.". His eyes were closed now, the Staff gleaming fitfully, as Beneva remarked.

"Entrusting such information to every generation of Guardians has ever been our Way. However, in our particular case we might have recognised, (with every Guardian being Opal born, one of us Sorceress of this Sand), that something momentous was afoot, but…", her voice failed to silence until Daro prompted.

"Beneva?". She blushed, laughing as she recited some dogma from memory, jolting Daro with the uncanny rendition of his mother's voice.

"There is no such thing as a Sandsinger, and as for such a thing being male, I should order you to wash your mouth out Beneva!".

Daro grinned wryly. "Let us hope that prejudice can be overcome.", he murmured quietly, and the thoughts of all present turned to the sickroom where Ikella huddled, weeping and confused by the terrifying prospect of an assassin in their midst, surrounded by guards, yet feeling very alone and vulnerable.

A footfall sounded in the outer Djellim, and the Sandsinger turned towards the door and stood, grasping his Staff before he said to Shiarjha.

"I must put this matter to rights. I will go to Selesh Minoria, taking my Songfather's possessions with me. He is owed an apology for this injustice, and I'll need Annis to guide me. Understand that I don't need your permission either of you, so I didn't ask!".

His voice was gentle, but his manner was implacable, and the two women nodded as Annis and the Sandsinger turned towards the corridor where next to the guardroom, Carolus maintained his quarters.

Lown, first of Daro's Sandsworn, was waiting outside the Apothecary's door. As the door opened to Daro's touch, he lifted a lighted taper to the glow basket, as Daro's powerstone slept once more. There was a backpack beside the door, a peg where clothes were hung and a board game on a table. Lown slid game board, boxed counters, bagged tiles and dice, into a cloth pouch, pulling the drawstring tight, before tucking it all into the backpack, padding that with clothing. Daro waited as Annis packed another bag, then they left, nodding to a guard who barely noticed them. Lown strode ahead, leaving Daro with his guide.

Taking a chance Daro said conversationally, "Do I talk to Annis or to another?", and the woman who guided him smiled in the shadows of her veil, and said softly,

"You speak to Annis, servant at the Temple of the Waters, member of the Inner Court. I and my sisters carry the spirit of the sand when it chooses to reveal itself, and in certain locations it walks free, impressed on the memory of this world.".

She turned him towards the entrance out into the Gathering Square, and Daro felt her change under his hand. The light clear voice said, "Remember what Shiarjha taught you. Imagine the sand is frozen, feel the Stillglass on your legs. When you feel the sand freeze beneath your feet, place your hand on that wall and push.".

Daro felt his feet turn numb, remembered the chill as Jashell ministered to his legs and recited the words Shiarjha had placed in his mind, and pushed against the wall. He felt solidity waver, and choked back a cry. He was travelling freely, gliding through walls, doors, solid rock. Out of the Gate in the Rock he flowed, dimly aware that his powerstone still slept, and then Feydora chuckled saying in his ear impudently.

"Oh yes my lad. There are many things that you can still enjoy. Riding the sands using true sight means that you can get about quickly. When you engage with your Sand using Stillglass you become invisible unless you light your powerstone. That was Shiarjha's secret. However, Stillglass has many other applications for you to explore. As the members of the Inner Court discovered, enhanced meditation techniques revealed many facets of this mystery we call Pelshar.".

Her voice died away, as Daro, shivering with cold, found himself in the marketplace at Selesh Minoria. Ahead of him Annis raised a hand in swift salute as she turned towards the barracks, then Lown, holding the Apothecary's pack, was knocking on the door of the Cross-Eyed Zeglur, and Daro waited in the shadows, as footsteps sounded on the inn's flagstone floor.

Chapter 10 - Into the Past

Daro stood just out of sight as the bolts were withdrawn on the other side of the door. His heart beat uncomfortably and he wondered for a wild moment if he should have come. He hadn't seen his Songfather for Rotations, since they had parted company in the Malachite Sands during that strange interlude in the first Rotation of his exile. He wondered guiltily if the old man had changed and couldn't restrain his imagination from sketching a frail disappointed ancient, hair and beard unkempt, limbs shrunk mind doddering. Then the door swung silently and a man stepped out.

Daro was filled with apprehension as he recognised Olneth's low voice exchanging greetings with Lown. If his Songfather had taken deep offense, Olneth might very well forbid this visit, but it was not so, for as Lown pushed his hood back to display Daro's sigil, Beneva's spy smiled and took a step forward. As Daro stepped into the light however, the inn door was snatched open and a small feminine form ran past Olneth and threw her arms round Daro, weeping and murmuring little endearments. For a moment Daro was shaken by the intensity of her emotion, then his arms slipped around her shoulders and his voice was choked with tears as he hugged her close.

"Dear Nadra, Little mother. I am so very sorry that I couldn't bring him home to you.", he whispered, kissing the hands that cupped his face anxiously. "I should have come earlier, but I am back now, and I will visit as often as I can."

For a little longer they clung to each other, then Olneth and Lown gently intervened.

"Lord, these streets aren't safe.", Lown urged. Olneth stepped round Nadra, and said softly, "Let's go in, out of the chill and into safety. Nadra please, I beg of you. Beven will have my head if you take ill.", and so encouraged, Daro threw his cloak over his old nurses shoulders and she guided him into the silent inn. He allowed Lown to divest him of his cloak, while Nadra fussed over him, then Olneth tapped him on the arm, and he was drawn through a doorway, down a step, and into the kitchen. It was warm, smelt of baking bread and drying herbs. It was large, accommodating a number of people, and Daro paused, listening, trying to identify those present, as Lown turned him towards a hearth. Somewhere he caught the distinctive smell of hot metal and racking his memory for names said gravely, "Good morning Farandel, how goes the forge?".

Into the surprised silence, the Master Smith said happily, "Good day my lord. The forge is fine, and will be finer now you are home and well again.". Suddenly tongues were loosened around the big table as Lown guided Daro to a seat. Nadra bustled off, leaving Daro as Beven arrived. Ahnell's stepfather was to Daro's mind somewhat quieter, cautious of his son's friend perhaps, but still friendly. Then Daro felt a rough sleeve brush him, and said swiftly, "Ivinish my friend.", hearing the low chorus beyond, as he turned a laughing face to Rowbet.

"You need to count your traces after Jashell visits you Master Driver.", he said solemnly and was in the midst of a hilarious account of his journey back with Jashell, when there was the sound of feet descending the wooden steps at the rear of the room and silence fell. Daro rose, stepping aside from the table and hesitantly turned facing the Apothecary. He breathed in a scent like wild berries mixed with crushed herbs, and knew his Songfather was unchanged. The wiry old arms opened and wondering Daro caught Carolus to him, disguising his surge of emotion by muttering the comment,

"Now I'm taller than you old man!", and pictured Carolus twinkling as he replied cheerfully,

"and I seem to remember telling you that no man is too tall to be put on his back if he steps out of line young man!", and the moment passed, as the gathering chuckled. Hand drawn into the crook of his Songfather's arm, Daro was returned to his chair and drinks were produced. Daro sensed movement at his elbow, heard a rustle of paper as the faintest scent touched his nostrils, and as Carolus stirred the cooling stemmis into which a full slip of Sandsinger's Friend had been emptied Daro recalled the oddest phrase from his childhood and tilted the sweetest smile at his Songfather, raising his cup and saying happily.

"Ah yes, I remember. Boy's milk. Now I know I'm home.", and so saying took the next step into his future.

A Sand away, as dawn struck rising dunes of Azure blue, a lonely figure was preparing to walk into her past. She shivered in the cool air, resolutely hefted her small backpack and munching on a handful of dried berries clambered stiffly to the highest point and stopped to survey her surroundings. She lent on a slim walking cane, face inscrutable as she reckoned her distance from Cathlea, from the children and the man who haunted her dreams. She had wakened in the night, wondering what he would say or do if she turned back, but even as she wriggled her hip seeking a more comfortable position, she had known that he was no longer there. She fell asleep almost immediately, huddled into her blankets, lulled by the song of the wind bewailing the loneliness of the trail stop. Bereft of children, bereft of travellers, bereft of Sandsingers, she sighed and slept. She woke with the dawn, faint chiming of sand buried crystals stroked her memories of home, and she shivered with astonishment as she realised that she had substituted Scartel for the childhood home that she remembered.

"Jerritol.", she murmured, trying the word she had eradicated from her vocabulary for size, and was amazed to discover that it no longer stuck in her throat. The wind tousled her hair encouragingly and she found herself smiling as she headed down-dune into deep desert territory, totally unaware of being followed.

The mystcat was confused. Over the past two days he had walked into the place of man at his keepers heels, submitted to being collared, amusing himself by draping his lengthening body across the dais in Ikella's audience room while perfectly sensible (though half-clad) women, talked to each other but ignored his flickering ears. He sulked while Chrism went to find his family, but when Lown arrived he drew himself up, curled his tail around his legs and pressed his head against Lown's chest and growled. Lown glanced down, saw anxiety radiating in the cat's eyes and questioned his brother urgently.

"Chrism, did Daro call you?", he asked quietly, trying hard not to sound concerned, and Chrism's simple homely face broke into a joyous grin.

"When I woke up he was in the plate.", he agreed. "He said to tell Jashell something, but I forget what. It was about children I think, but Daro hasn't got any children.".

Lown fought down a feeling of foreboding as he struggled not to alarm this gentle giant of a brother, remembering the debt they owed the Sandsinger who had released Chrism from the bonds of incoherence, giving him a purpose in life. Slowly he elicited the story, and looked up to see that his blind father had somehow persuaded Indeera to come to the audience room. She was squatting on her heels staring at the mystcat as Chrism wailed crossly.

"I don't know! I don't remember! Don't pick on me.", and slouched off leaving his brother frustrated and angry. Indeera said very softly,

"Lown, don't fret him. He can't help it, and it will upset the cat. I will stay here, but I need you to fetch Shiarjha and Beneva. Ask them to bring a scrying bowl and Stillglass with them, then alert the watch Commander and tell her I may have orders for her in two sectors.".

Lown stared at her, but seeing her fondle the pendant that proclaimed her High Priestess of an Inesh Temple, and eyeing the ritual spear she carried nervously, he decided to do as she requested, departing the hall to spot his brother happily turning a skipping rope for a gaggle of girls.

He was subconsciously chanting the old skipping rhyme to himself when he summoned Shiarjha, who drawn and haggard kept a vigil of sorts in the Infirmary. Like so many of those who bustled about their lives, he had been totally unaware of Ikella's perilous situation, all else paled into insignificance as he realised that they might send him packing, in the light of this revelation, but Shiarjha leapt at the chance of relieving Ikella's concerns over Daro's whereabouts. Less than half a sector later they followed him, precious objects collected from Ikella's study under the brooding eyes of Driss, making a swift exit to find Echo and Indeera. She had been busy, soft cushions had been moved to make several seats facing the dais. Ikella's state chair had been moved and Echo sat proudly where the great chair had commanded all eyes, and the Guardians looked around them, faintly puzzled as Indeera explained the outlandish incense, the unusual chants arising from a small congregation of Inesh. every one of them wore blue amulets, and Lown flushed with excitement as he accompanied the Guardians to their cushions, assisting Beneva to place the sand-paste bowl she carried on the dais in front of the cat.

Shiarjha raised smiling eyes to Lown. "You are First among Sandsworn Lown. You may stay amongst us, but I need not remind you that your silence is enjoined.".

Lown took up a place at the petitioners rail, and watched as Indeera poured a little clear liquid from Shiarjha's flask into the bowl, and the cat bent its head and stared into the Stillglass. Tension built, glows flickered and then a clear voice said,

"We are not far from home. Tell Jashell and Indeera to bring the Watch to Cathlea in two sleeps, the few children we have to find homes for are very little and need carrying. Bring Healers, supplies, yourselves and that lump Chrism. Tell my mother we are safe, that I love her and will be back to torment her before this ninenight is out. Tell her I have found my Azure Singer!", and then the cat's eyes blazed just once and both Guardians stared in horror at wristlets that flared a network of lace on their hands.

"She sinking.", Beneva spoke sadly, as members of Indeera's Temple rose to their feet. "Get Jashell.", she commanded, "Summon Andria, Felaya, and Tisanna then go. You all heard the message, though we must train the messengers, at least Indeera knew what to do!".

Lown lurched to his feet. "I will help get Chrism and the cat ready.", he said, and that was all that Echo remembered. They had left heading for the Dorenard Plateau by way of Fronish, where a tail lashing, nose quivering night had ensured that Echo had the scent of his Lord firmly in his mind again, but he had found himself following a tingling nerve jolting perfume that rose in waves from the wrapper on the kitchen chair at Fronish, and had spiked in Cathlea, where his lord was not! He yowled in disappointment when they entered the trail stop. Chrism argued that they should remain and wait for Daro, but Indeera was no fun at all. The children all stared at him, so he'd slunk off, following the trail of that scent until he heard Chrism bellow. He remembered how to shift shades then, following the one they called Rann silently, blurring his coat to match the Sand, stalking them until Chrism said heavily.

"S'not fair. We should stay. Indeera should leave us alone. Echo and I are used to it, we don't need anyone else.".

Rann had disconcertingly winked in Echo's direction (as if he could see him!) then said kindly, "But Chrism, I need your help. You are big enough to carry two tinies at once, and even I can't do that. Besides, us men have to stand together!".

Echo had thought of shifting shade again, but seeing Motri link arms with Chrism, and Rann laughing affectionately, he turned away to set off on an adventure of his own.

Jalni moved on, much as she had on that first uneasy morning. Cathlea still called her back with its mixture of trials and blessings, which threatened to undermine this strange new confidence, as she pictured those she had left behind, eyes filled with silent reproach. She staggered to a stop at the crest of the next dune, staring around curiously for this part of the Azure was totally different to the Fringe where most travellers clung to the rise of their highlands. The explorer in her noted tracks, footprints left by some desert dwelling animals crossed her path, as she cast about for any sign that she was approaching human habitations.

To be true she enjoyed the silence of the sands. There was no call on her to help with scratches, bumps or bruises. She hadn't used her scrip for at least two days, so the medications stored there would last until she could replenish them, although she didn't relish attempting to make the Sandsinger's Friend tonic. At this point she stopped dead, mind overwhelmed by the image of Daro's face. She knelt clutching her body, heart thudding to the memory of his kisses, as a half forgotten incident seized her mind.

"Become my willing bondmate.", his voice shaking with emotion was as intimate as if he still held her. She "saw" the brilliance of his Opal eyes, the tender curve of his mouth as he bent to caress her, then his voice was saying softly,

"You will find your true path soon, and I will exert no compulsion.", he had sighed wistfully, and Jalni wondered dismally if that was what she was doing here, amidst the half-remembered torment of that event.

"Am I finding my true path?", she asked herself, struggling to recall if she had become not only the Sandsinger's bond-mate but his bedfellow? She couldn't recall exactly what had transpired, so deeply confused and wearier than she had realised, the young Healer had decided to rest when a movement below attracted her attention. She slid back, flattening her body to the grey blue Sands that matched her clothing, and trained her eyes on the lone stranger.

She saw the traditional short tunic and bound leggings of a Guildsman and glimpsed dark hair worn long, as she narrowed her eyes straining to see more clues to his identity, then with a start she recognised the paler blue jacket of an apprenticed Weaver.

"Sandrigals!", she swore, "I must be closer to Jerritol than I thought. This one could even be coming from the Weaver's Halt there.", a low internal chuckle filled her body, and fighting for self-control over self-congratulation, she never saw the direction from which her attacker sprang. Completely taken by surprise, she was flattened, gasping for breath below something that held her down snarling. She struggled ineffectively, then a low muttering began, and her blood ran cold, as she remembered tales of insane Wanderers, struggled. The weight on her back lifted, seemed to bound away, but as Jalni freed her mouth from the

Sand she'd nearly suffocated in, it pounced again. This time, she "heard" the joyful "mantra of the mind" from whoever was killing her.

"Gotcha. Can't wriggle now Lady Blue…Puhrr aow", purred the voice in her ear, as tumbling the hapless Healer down the dune, Echo leapt after her. As the mists cleared, Jalni half rose and scrambled backwards from the rippling shimmer of the air, crying out in relief.

"Echo! Stop it you behemoth.", then before she could stop herself, she said sharply,

"By Gurayen's own breath! Stop. Right Now!", and the sand shivered as Echo shifted shade and stood revealed in the rippling male majesty of young mystcat. However, before either of them could draw breath, the stranger sprang out of nowhere, a hoarse grunting cry on his lips, and to her horror, Jalni saw the blade in his hand. Her mind whirled, the sand shifted to match the shimmering spiral of her thoughts, as around the newcomer sprang an Azure shield. It spun him back on his heels, thwarting each lunge of the knife, then as the bewildered girl staggered upright, the cat lay down, neatly tucking its paws under its chin, surveying the stranger placidly. Jalni fixed Echo with a stare, gritted her teeth and spoke uncompromisingly.

"You brought that on yourself, you lunatic animal. Now, thank your lord for me and tell him that we are not far from Jerritol. When I have settled matter's there, I'll be able to re-enter his service.".

As she became aware of the man disarmed by the sand squall she reached his knife at a run, putting her boot firmly on it as he reached out.

"There's no need friend!", she exclaimed, and broke off, looking into his face helplessly, for he wore her own father's well beloved features! Her shock must have conveyed itself to him, for as she stared transfixed, he touched his own face as if he would explore whatever she was looking at, then taking his hand away again, he emitted a strange note of enquiry. Jalni's mind reeled, common sense arguing with the hopes and fears of a bereaved child.

"Perhaps Rowin's injuries left him as simple minded as brain fever had left Chrism? Was it possible that Sowdin and Serba had used that excuse to defraud their son of his inheritance.", but as he moved, she realised that although very like him, he was not as tall. She stared into his eyes, as the mystcat sidled behind her, hiding itself from the man, whose hands made pleading gestures. However, as she stared distrustfully into his oh, so familiar face, he carefully positioned himself, took a deep breath and announced (in the flat nasal tones of the profoundly deaf), "Orto.", and pointed to himself, repeating the word emphatically. "Orto".

Jalni, avidly drinking in his features, thought numbly.

"I'm Jalani del Orto, my father and mother were Rowin and Viness del Orto, and here is a man with my father's face, saying our family name, apparently unable to communicate further.".

She watched his fingers flickering absently and was startled when the cat suddenly reared up, leaning his not inconsiderable weight on her shoulders and peered at the stranger with interest. Jalni smiled encouragingly, pointing to the sand where a distorted shadow made up of her own and Echo's bodies stretched as Seleus rose. Immediately, her companion pointed excitedly to Echo's rapidly twitching ears, grunting as if in agreement. Jalni shook Echo off her shoulders, as she saw a familiar gesture and sitting abruptly, tried to recall the intricate fingering of handcode. It was getting hot, so she absently shrugged back her cloak and rolled up her sleeves, picturing the movements involved and was taken aback as a strong but shapely hand grasped her arm. He bent his head over the symbols that ran from wrist to mid knuckle, making strange crooning noises under his breath, then the cat joined in this odd game until thoroughly bewildered she withdrew her hands, and refused to let them continue. The cat removed itself, padding over to sit on an unmarked piece of sand, where it pressed its forepaw into the smooth blue surface. He threw back his head, yowling softly as their new friend inscribed several symbols (which Jalni knew were on her arm) into the sand, then nodded to the cat and chuckled.

Jalni, hot, thirsty and bewildered, was slipping into one of those strange half thought, half dream sequences that allowed her mind to catch up with current events. She must have come to herself just a second later, and the strangest thought had struck her. The cat's ears were twitching purposefully, sometimes its tail lashed, up and down in a highly unnatural movement. Reminded of the Inesh hand code for "rations", she absently framed the movement with her own hands. The Guildsman cried out, a short muffled bark that seemed to indicate pleasure, for he clapped his hands, and painfully slow in his movements began to laboriously ask questions.

"Who you?", he asked. Jalni struggled to think how to explain. She'd give him her official name, she decided, for if he worked at the Weaver's Halt, he might know of her. She tapped the back of her hand, to signal the beginning of a new word, then touched her sternum in the universal signal for "me". Tucking her right thumb inside the curl of her left hand, like a baby in a shawl, she indicated that part of her name meant "little". Her companion nodded, then she mimed a weaver, touching his jacket, pointing at him, then pretended to throw the shuttle with her right hand, while lifting a heddle with her left, to open the warp. After several attempts she received a puzzled look and a brief nod. She then continued to mime, until the man's face cleared.

He grunted, then said in that hoarse toneless drone, "Orto.", proudly touching his chest to emphasise that "He was Orto!", and Jalni caught the hand and held it, as she repeated her mime of "Jalani", adding the slide of finger to palm that indicated "family", saying clearly "Orto", and pointed to herself. He looked so shocked that Jalni could have laughed but she persisted, using hand code that didn't lend itself to this purpose and pantomime to convince her new friend that she was already named del Orto, and that she was not actually proposing marriage, but when he finally understood, he became oddly withdrawn and sat brooding for a while.

The sun climbed, Jalni's back grew hot and uncomfortable, then the stranger shrugged, rose and sketching a graceful bow, invited her to follow him. With huge misgivings, some four sectors later, he led Jalni, (with Echo in tow), down a deserted dusty street, and right up to the doors of her childhood home.

She felt frozen, could hardly believe what was happening, and wile every instinct encouraged her to turn and run, the curiosity of this encounter screamed synchronicity at her, and remembering Ikella's lectures on the subject of magic and synchronicity she decided that if magic was afoot, then it had drawn her, the mystcat and the man she now called Orto together for a reason. She thought fiercely, directing her thoughts to Echo.

"Shift shades my friend. Whoever opens that door won't expect your kind to be asking for shelter.", and grinned as Echo flexed something and melted, becoming one with the shadows cast by Seleus in his noontime glory. Footsteps clattered inside, and before Jalni could prepare herself, a well maintained door swung open, and a voice said brightly, "Orto? What brings you home so soon? Did you change your mind, because if you did, I have never been so relieved.".

Jalni standing silhouetted against the glare in the doorway, caught hand movements that accompanied this conversation, and frankly stared. This was neither Temple talk, as imported by the trusted suppliers to the Temple of the Winds, nor was it a warriors hand code, so limited in what it could convey. This was obviously a full language and the interest on her face must have shown, for the man who spoke seemed quite self conscious.

"I apologise Healer.", he said gruffly, "I didn't see you there the glare outside is so bright. did you come to trade with us?", then his eyes widened as he took in Jalni's hands and the swatch of material she had withdrawn from her carrisack. He stuttered to an uncertain stop, and then, as Jalni stepped forward into the light cast from the garden window, he gasped and bowed.

"Mistress del Orto?", he asked, voice rising to a squeak. "Mistress Jalani? Is it really you?", and Jalni remembered the defiant Weaver who had left the garden gate open a crack, urging her to take the bundle he carried and run before her Grandfather returned from market. She gazed at him, trembling for as he moved she saw one shoulder rose unnaturally high, and that the hand on that arm was twisted and clawed. Tears rose in her eyes as she beheld the violence that had been done to this skilled craftsman, and she blinked them back as he remarked,

"Now don't take on. It saved me from duty shifts, and hasn't stopped me teaching! Wasn't your fault I let him catch me out. He's working Sundreth's mines now for his pains, and that's all I ask!", and the matter was closed. She ran all the names of the Weavers that she remembered through her mind and placed him, as she said faintly,

"Edrith, thank you. Thank the One that you are still here, for I don't recall many of the others.", her voice failed, and then Edrith said cheerfully, "Then you've a might of catching up to do Mistress.", he indicated Jalni's silent companion airily, as he delivered the most shocking news without a blink.

"It's a good thing your Uncle found you before Height of Sun. Now, come you in, and take some refreshment and rest. Your factor will be here before Sunfall, and will tell you all the news, and I will find Orana and tonight we will feast.".

Jalni could hardly take it in. No wonder the stranger looked like her dear father, and momentarily her eyes sought the family funerary plot, beneath the citrine tree just outside that garden window, but the tears blinded her temporarily, as she turned to "Orto". He smiled tentatively, then opened his arms and Jalni ran to him, clinging to the only relative she had, home at last.

When Madiv returned with the dyes he had gone to collect, the Weaver (now well established as the Guilds caretaker in Jerritol), seemed pleased to meet her. He was a neat, brisk individual, smartly dressed in cloth of his own weaving, everything about him precise and self-contained. He surveyed her with curiosity, for he had been well tutored by Rowin's faithful servants and knew much more of her grandparents through the depredations visible in the accounts he had inherited. However, he made no attempt to take Jalni through such a distressing catalogue of waste immediately, preferring to leave her with Edrith, Orana and her uncle, as she re-explored rooms that had been part of her darkest memories. She stood on the threshold of her old bedroom, touched to find the wall drawings that her mother had painted to amuse her baby, still fresh and bright.

Orana, who had cooked and cleaned for the del Orto household said defensively, "We left them so that your room would seem familiar when you returned, but of course, being beyond the Sands in our own grief, none of us thought about you having grown to womanhood before that happened. would you like us to clear it all away?", but Jalni was sitting on the small bed, clutching a faded ragdoll to her and crooning softly.

"Nina, Lina, Ruamina be my friend today...", the door shut quietly as the house staff withdrew, and Orana whispered over her shoulder to Edrith as they descended the steps to the kitchen once more.

"Poor child. Well I remember hearing that song from the old storeroom when that brute shut them in, after the Master died.", and Edrith swiftly translating for Orto, was touched by the sympathy on his face. Orto's hands flickered, and Edrith nodded.

"O yes. Orto knows the Way of Sorrow. He says that many of the orphans that lived with his Healer friend came like that. Too fearful to make friends in case they died as well, turning to toys or pets for love.", Orana had reached the bottom of the stair and turned, drawing Orto into her realm with a smile. She spoke simply but directly, and Edrith signed for her, smiling.

"We mean no disrespect to your family Villeth.", she said (using the name by which Orto had once been known), "but we suffered dreadfully under Sowdin and Serba. Your late brother, his wife and child more than most. We loved that child, having none of our own, and now we have her back for a while, thanks to you.".

They followed her into the kitchen, and were sat drinking stemmis, when Jalni joined them. She wandered in, and it was clear that she had been crying, but it would seem that those tears had been a release. She had washed her face, taken advantage of a breath of fresh air during which time she had paid her respects at Rowin's grave, and sent the cat to catch his supper, before slipping inside the garden room, face resolutely turned away from the sight of the storeroom where she had been imprisoned with her dying mother. Now she was ready to eat, to talk, and was handing over her ration pack to Orana when Madiv wandered in and slowly Jalni began to piece together what had happened after she ran away.

Edrith spoke drily and fast, not wanting to upset Jalni again.

"Well Mistress.", he said deferentially, "The old witch laid about her with a whip!", and Jalni, seeing his face darken, reached out across the scrubbed slab they leant against and said simply, "Edrith, there is no need to revisit those times. They can't hurt me anymore and I refuse to allow them to reach beyond and hurt you again. They went to the Sands long since, I have healed, and so must you.".

He sighed, then added, "Mistress, I totalled our losses as three house staff, two Weavers and more thread than I could tally. I took my witnesses to the Guild courts and they issued an edict banning Sowdin and Serba from the Azure. The Guild raised a levy on all his property, and when I thought I could recover I asked for a journeyman to help me rebuild.", he saw the bewilderment on her face and explained.

"She drove the servants into the street with a whip. He screamed and ranted at them, saying that you had been hidden, somewhere on the premises and that someone would pay for that. He drove us out of the weaving sheds and dyeing rooms, laying about him as he went.", his voice had dropped with the pain of the memory, and Jalni recalling her Grandfather's inclinations shuddered when Edrith said quietly.

"Then he seemed to go very quiet. Spoke softly and reasonably, apologising for losing his temper. We all went back to work, I came into the house to try and find you, while he grabbed bags, clothing, and your Grandmother. They left, saying that they would go looking for you, with some of their crew. They rode away a-Zeglur back, after sending round as an apology, a hot spiced drink. We know now, that it was drugged, leaving us unaware that they had set fire to the weaving rooms.".

Jalni, cold with horror, heard Edrith state in a matter of fact manner,

"My shoulder and arm broke when we jumped from the roof. If the house hadn't been so solidly constructed of stone, we wouldn't have survived to get there. Those who perished were locked in the weaving shed, they stood no chance, and meanwhile your Grandparents escaped. We heard that they had been seen at odd times, and then that they had perished in a landslip. Begging your pardon Mistress, we celebrated then, and laid flowers on your father's grave, for Sundreth's revenge may be slow, but it is inevitable.", he paused and then said in an oddly muffled voice.

"Then of course your Uncle turned up!", and Jalni, for once relaxed and enjoying herself, leant back against the settle carved by her own father's hand, listening to Orto's story.

Madiv told it gravely, sketching symbols on his hands so that Orto could follow the tale as it slowly unfolded. He drew a picture of a small family, headed by an autocratic old Weaver, who in his latter years had been so crippled by the painful "bone-rust" disorder, that he could neither set a warp, nor grasp the heddle. He had tried to teach the craft to his only son, but Sowdin had no head for patterning, no patience with thread and was a bully to boot. The six daughters with whom he had been blessed wove for him then married, and as the grand-daughters arrived so depression sank the old weaver's spirits. Had his brutish son bred daughters, the Weaver's Halt would have been willed back to the Clan, or left to the Guild, but despite their differences, Sowdin and Serba had boys. Two of them, Villeth and Rowin, three Rotations apart, bonny and bright, and secure in that knowledge, Sowdin's father left his own house in the village to Sowdin and Serba, and the Weaver's Halt to whichever of the boys completed their apprenticeship with the Guild of Weavers first, with the provision that the legacy had to pass to the other brother should anything happen to the first.

"It was that provision that Sowdin took such exception to, because when the time came and the old man died, the Weaver's Halt, passed in trust to whichever of the boys had the talent to follow their Grandfather. At the time it didn't seem to matter much, in fact Sowdin was a minor warlord with a band of disreputable followers with which he handed out summary punishments for his overlord far to the southern Sands.

"However, he disgraced his overlord, and was dismissed, packed back to Jerritol where he wasn't even elected on to the village Council. With no means to support his family, Sowdin was forced to live as a lodger, minding the Weaver's Halt until one of his son's could take the apprenticeships their Grandfather had paid for.".

The dry voice paused and Jalni saw the beginnings of the terrible breakdown in her family and turned stricken eyes to Orto, whose mouth turned down at the corners as he saw her distress.

Madiv sipped at wine that Orana had produced and said thoughtfully, "You know that Sowdin went to study at the Guild himself don't you?", then shocked them all with a strange laugh.

"He said that he wanted to create a family archive and knowing that he had no talent at the loom, wondered if he might study a year with their archivist so that he would know the best methods for preserving patterns, dye recipes, and weaving methods. Strangely enough he was good at it too. He helped salvage many records, painstaking in his scrutiny, showing particular interest in old weaving methods.", the neat little man leaned forward, translation for Orto forgotten as he clasped his hands together enthusiastically. Jalni reached out, clasping Orto's hand as Edrith took over signing and Madiv said with fierce indignation.

"Of course we should have known that scoundrel was up to something, but he had left the Guild, at least ten Rotations before anyone noticed that all the records about a remarkable weaving had vanished, along with his father's deed of trust!".

A kind of shiver passed over Jalni's neck, a breeze tinkled the wind chime that still hung in the citrine tree above her father's grave, and she felt the magic caress her skin as Madiv said sorrowfully,

"Now we shall never be able to re-create the Tapestry of Tten".

Chapter 12 - The Tapestry of Tten

Jalni felt the hair on the back of her neck rise. She had no idea what made her tingle with excitement, but it was all she could do to keep her voice steady as she asked curiously, "The Tapestry of Tten? What in the Sand's name is that?".

She was profoundly disappointed in the answer, because it seemed that Madiv didn't really know either, but as a second drink was proffered, he did his level best to explain.

"Well…", he eyed her judiciously.

"Its Weaver business really, but you being the legal Holder for the moment, I guess I can trust you in confidence.", and continued to do so as she glanced up at her Uncle strangely embarrassed.

"I don't know what those Seleshanni have taught you Mistress, but in our Sands, long ago, we had the growing of plants that were used in weaving great tapestries. These were used to line bare walls in the great Halls of the period, and have served to teach us much about our world, and the way weavers used to work. Fortunately, one of these was bequeathed to the Guild, and shortly thereafter another was discovered at Anempor together with ancient writings.".

Jalni could predict what was about to be revealed as Madiv concentrated, frowning as Edrith signed for Orto. He cleared his throat awkwardly, then went back to the story.

"You understand that this situation has its roots way before you youngsters were born.", he said. " We were still building the new Guild Hall at Darnesh at the time, and had no place to hang such enormous weavings. For Rotations the Clan had been excavating there, because as you know, Mount Darnesh was severely damaged during Cataclysm, and most of the ancient development had never been explored or charted back then. Anyway, Deshun Tirjella allowed the Guild to look for a dry storage place in the Lower Halls which Master Janureth had only just declared safe, so we went exploring.".

Again his slender hands gripped each other in suppressed excitement, and Jalni's skin prickled with the presentiment as he continued.

"We found a very suitable place!", he announced, and for the first time Jalni recognised the impishness in the flicker of deep-set brown eyes, as he described the moment.

"I was there Mistress, I saw Master Weaver Toldran open a small door inset into a far greater one at the end of a passage. Every new Weaver, all the apprentices and most Masters were there, spread through the levels, looking for a room that was cold, dry, and tall enough for hanging brackets to be installed for the two ancient tapestries. We also wanted temporary storage for the archives, and enough room for our archivist and his assistants to work. Master Churien was our Archivist then, and his assistants rotated duties with classes, for in those days only apprentice Weavers studied our records.".

His bird bright eyes smiled as he described the events, and Jalni began to reckon Rotations. She knew that the Guild of Weavers, housed in a magnificent Hall faced the Market Square in Darnesh. She also knew that it had been used as a temporary nursing and feeding station during the Great Storm, because she had seen the plaque erected to commemorate that event, and she had only been about ten Rotations old then, travelling with Serba to buy dyes. She struggled to remember more, but her eyes glazed with the effort, and she could only comment.

"That must have been ten Rotations before I was born.", to be greeted with the news that it was nearer twenty! She subsided into silence and listened.

Madiv continued.

"I only had three Rotations of dealing with historic techniques, but what greeted us that day completely re-wrote everything I'd learned. for when the door was opened Master Told run had found an ancient store, possibly even part of an earlier Guild Hall.". He drank deeply, wiped his mouth, and continued quickly, anxious not to lose his audience.

"Well, it was far easier to utilise this store for records than it was to preserve them in a building site, so we moved there.". He paused, seemed to look internally, and then said slowly as an aside.

"It occurs to me that you young things wouldn't know that Darnesh at that time was only just being adopted as our official capital. There was a wealth of building, excavations to put up with, but Deshun Tirjella was adamant that her seat of power should be where most people could gain access, so we moved from Anempor to Darnesh, and there we stayed. She was right you know…", he said thoughtfully then carried on briskly.

"Master Toldran persuaded our Deshun to open up level Four for use, we found plenty of rooms and supports for large Tapestries. Each one of which can be moved for study under the expert eyes of its own Keeper.".

He broke off apologetically, rubbing the bridge of his nose with finger and thumb as he considered his next words, trying to keep the information both scholarly and easily absorbed by avid listeners. He nodded to himself, stretching his fingers to frame more complex shapes for Orto.

"You will discover that ancient weavings have to be protected from dust, mites, damp, light, humidity and human interference, so that the minimum of disturbance is inflicted on fragile threads. The other tapestries that we found there that day required many Rotations of study before we knew what a treasure house we had stumbled on you see.".

He looked up, ensuring that he still had their undivided attention then carried on.

"All records now occupy another Hall in the same gallery, with plenty of room for students and master's to come and go or stay and study. However, now we also have guards! No-one other than an articled Master is allowed access to ancient records and even they are searched every day entering or leaving. It is very disturbing, very disturbing indeed.".

Orto shifted uncomfortably, and his face was shadowed as this last sentence was signed, but Madiv said abruptly. "No blame attaches itself to you or your surviving family Villeth. We know that you are victims as well, but it is necessary however for you both to understand the sequence of events. Perhaps you have questions you want to ask?", and Jalni said rather hurriedly.

"You mentioned other tapestries besides the two you had to store. How many were there?", and Madiv's mouth twitched with laughter.

"Far too many for Master Toldran's peace of mind.", he grinned, "There were seven, just glimmering in the dark, waiting to be studied, but there were three supports left untenanted. We hung our two as soon as Master Churien said we could, that was when we recognised that in that Hall we had a record of the colours and weaving techniques of every Sand, and yet there was one missing!".

He turned a puzzled face to Jalni and said uncertainly, "I believe this is where a rumour sprang from, which has enough elements of truth in it to set solid sensible citizens searching for the tenth tapestry. One of your Guardians mentioned a "Tapestry of Tten" to Master Churien long ago, and we suppose they are the one and same thing. The Guild Masters believe that a tenth tapestry might hold the answer to the riddle of the Cataclysm.", he leaned back on the settle unaware that he had drawn gasps from his audience as he remarked.

"Speculation was rife at the time that it not only tells the story of the event, but would provide valuable information that could prove what changes took place in the environment. We have friends in the cities who know about fibres, and who could find out more if the rumours are true. Putting it frankly Mistress, it is worth a fortune to any man who could find it and restore it to the Guild. We believe that Sowdin found some records in his father's possessions, and that when he studied with Master Churien he uncovered not only those from Anempor, but something we knew nothing of. The man was mad, totally obsessed of course, but he destroyed not only the hopes of an old wise archivist, but a whole world's chance to discover its history, along with his entire family as well.".

The clear voice was full of condemnation and Jalni found herself reaching for Orto's hand as the last words were signed, and he clasped her hand briefly, then turned an inquisitive face to Madiv and began to sign questions faster than Jalni could follow.

She saw, "What happened to me?", and watched Edrith closely. He said gently, "We all thought that you'd died Villeth. You had a terrible fever, a streaming nose, then a dreadful red rash. Serba nursed you night and day, she even paid a woman to care for Rowin they were so afraid he would catch it too. when several children of the village died, they finally took you to a Healer, somewhere north of here. Your Grandfather (who loved you dearly), was dreadfully upset. You would have been three Rotations old, it was nearly

Jentaroth, and all the wooden Zeglurs on Pelshar couldn't rouse you, though old Zonelas carved a new one each day to tempt you.".

Orana interrupted. "He never recovered you know. When Sowdin and Serba came home and told us that you had died before they could get to the Healer, he said "Not my boy!", and sat carving Zeglurs till the day he died. I never heard him utter a word afterwards.".

Jalni saw Orto's distress, and "reached" for his signature in the Source, connecting so powerfully that tears sprang to her own eyes. He swung away, covering his face until Orana took something from a shelf, and pressed the most exquisite wooden Zeglur into his hand. As he took it in trembling fingers, Edrith began to sign again and Jalni, still connected to the Source "saw", before she heard.

"That was the last one he made. He loved you always, never believed that you had gone to the Sands.", and the group expressed silent sympathy, gripping his free hand or a shoulder as Orto wiped his face and signed his thanks.

It was getting late now, and Jalni could tell that Orto was very tired, the emotional revelations about his family seemed to have completely exhausted whatever reserves he was drawing on, and besides she had to see to Echo. She touched Madiv lightly on the arm and said softly.

"We have a lot to digest Weaver Madiv. We had never met before, and I think that my Uncle needs to rest now. Is there somewhere that we can sleep and recover? We would be a better audience for you tomorrow.", and it was so. Edrith lit Orto's way to the guest room upstairs, while Orana and Madiv bolted the doors and the gates. Jalni went out with them, drawn to the citrine tree, where her mother's wind chimes still tinkled, and as the factor opened the garden room door, she called to him.

"If you are retiring, leave the garden door open. I just want to be alone for a while.", and his light voice fluted back to her.

"Take as long as you need Mistress. Orana and Edrith have quarters behind the Weavers shed. I alone sleep in the house, in what I believe was your father's workroom. It has made an excellent study for me, and I keep a bed there. If you need a maid we can hire one in the morning. Good Night!", and he was gone.

The cat purred in the dark and relieved, Jalni squatted on her haunches and ran her hands down his silky back, seeking the spot that he couldn't reach on his own, and the purr grew throaty with contentment. Presently she found that she was in a kind of reverie, lulled by the wind, the chimes and the soporific purring of the cat, so she tucked her feet underneath her and meditated. It seemed so natural to be here, at one with her Sands, surrounded by loyal friends and then she shivered and half asleep rose, walking towards the storeroom in which her mother had died. The door opened silently and framed in the light of Jenta was a mattress. She slipped across the room, and lay down, pulling the pillow under her head and slept, the warmth of the cat curled against her back and the scent of citrines in the air.

Dawn found her still sleeping, one arm curled under her face. Only a soft tap on her door alerted her to another's presence, and for a moment her eyes were dazed as she lifted her head realising where she was. The tap came again, and she rolled over and sat up, trying to think how to explain the presence of a mystcat, who seemed barely awake himself. The door opened quietly, and framed in the entrance was her Uncle, carrying a cup of hot stemmis. He grinned at the sight of the sleepy cat, placed her drink on the floor and retreated, closing the door as he returned to the house. Jalni prodded Echo awake.

"Come on lazybones. Shift shades and I'll open the gate so you can go and catch breakday for yourself.", she said conversationally.

The cat yawned and stretched, standing, to arch his back, spreading huge forepaws to display massive claws. He sat, tail curled around him, blinking as his gaze turned on Jalni. She froze as he "rippled", an extraordinary glow appearing in his eyes. Almost as if she was experiencing it for herself, she became aware of a very full stomach. She concentrated and found a deep desire to sleep off the very satisfactory dinner he had caught that night, and "knew" that he needed no assistance to get over puny garden walls, that gully hoppers were his favourite food, and that he planned to sleep under the bushes in the garden. Then he was gone!

She had told him to shift shades herself, but she never saw him do it. She stared into the shadows, wondering where he was, as a thready yowl came from outside the store.

"Sandrigal's!", she swore softly to herself in the privacy of the necessary. "What wouldn't I give to have that ability. I wonder if Daro knows how to do that?", and giggled, imagining the furore if he started "shifting shades", round Selesh. Then, humming happily, she walked towards the house determined to help Madiv piece together the rest of Orto's story.

In Selesh, there was already a furore. Not because Daro had "shifted shades", but because he had completely vanished!

Diras was the one to make the discovery, staring in disbelief at Ikella's unoccupied bed. None of the normal investigations could produce the Sandsinger, for there was only one way in or out of the Guardian's bedchamber. Rotations ago Ikella's dressing room had been redesigned so that her study could be enlarged. Now the secret passage between Ikella's suite and the Library was well known to her guards, and the regular patrol of the ancient warren of passages had neither seen nor heard anything unusual.

Diras licked dry lips, as she defended her decision to allow the exhausted man to sleep on in his mother's room, beginning with the fact that she had not left the ante-room of Ikella's suite after seeing Daro spread-eagled across the bed with her own eyes.

"However.", she'd reported gloomily to a furious Jashell, "Even a Sandsinger needs the necessary. I couldn't stretch credulity past Height of Sun, and went to investigate, in case he was unwell. Our Deshun is thankfully still too tired to be troubled, and I dare not rouse the Guardians, who've been standing watch over her all night.".

She stood, (every sinew taut with suppressed anger at Daro's duplicity), listening as her Commander vilified all magic-users, whilst studying the previous night's duty roster, stabbing a finger on the wax tablet in front of her.

"He left Ikella's sickroom with you?", she demanded and Diras murmured, "Yes Commander.", in reply.

Jashell snorted derisively.

"A quiet voice won't turn away *my* wrath Sub-Commander Diras.", she snapped.

Diras leapt to attention, bellowing her response at parade ground volume. "I hear and obey Commander!", and Jashell raised a frail hand to her aching forehead and resting it against the cool rock wall, shuddered, saying suggestively,

"Shall I dash out my brains now, or let Deshun Ikella put a period to my existence (and yours), when she finds out we've lost a perfectly good Sandsinger?", but before Diras could reply, she advised sharply, "If I were you, I'd write my will and start thinking up excuses!". Her dark eyes swept over her discomforted junior, then, her voice changed hopefully as her finger traced another name on the duty list.

"Did I hear you say that Annis saw him sleeping too?", and Diras said slowly,

"Yes Commander, so did Guardian Shiarjha. She treated his legs with that new compound of hers. Annis reported as much to me when she returned to patrol the village. She left precisely as the Gate reported, entering the Barracks to change a broken bootlace before Height of Jenta, returning to patrol Selesh Minoria until dawn.".

"Could Daro have slipped past the Watch without help? Did anyone search the pastures before Olneth took herbs to the old man last night? He needed a Zeglur to transport them, but did anyone search the panniers?".

Then as Diras blinked in surprise, Jashell clapped her hand over her mouth in dismay.

"O Deo me! It is such a short time ago that he and Ahnell would have done such a thing! I can hardly believe that Daro is blind, and Ahnell is dead. I must be sliding into elder confusion!".

They stared at each other sombrely as Jashell pointed out.

"We might never find out how he went, but there is no sign of him in Selesh. If someone told him of the rift between his Songfather and Ikella, he may have gone to find him. However, I think it unlikely that he could get to the Cross Eyed Zeglur alone, or if Nadra and Beven would welcome the cause of Ahnell's death under their roof again. My problem is this, do I raise a panic and upset Ikella, or do nothing, and put my lord in danger?". Full of foreboding they stared at each other, and in the guardroom the silence was profound.

Jalni tapped on the kitchen door, sticking her head around it as the most delicious aroma tickled her nostrils. Orana smiled cheerfully, and set hot bread on the table, scooped a spoonful of citrine curd on to it, and set a platter in front of the hungry girl. Edrith, who was busily wiping down a bench turned as she sat in the corner of the settle and said gently,

"Did you sleep well Mistress?", and Jalni saw that they knew where she had slept and blushed.

"Thank you both.", she replied, knowing who had provided the mattress and pillow, suddenly shy in the face of such understanding, and Orana said softly, "It was nothing my dear. I just thought that you'd like to be close to your parents, though the One only knows what that wicked man did with your mother's body. ", and in the silence that fell, Jalni heard her own voice.

"Dear Orana.", she murmured. "That is precisely what I came home to find out, and believe me, I shall not rest until they are reunited.". She felt the colour rise in her cheeks, but couldn't have known how her eyes blazed fervently blue in the wake of this pronouncement, but she had found her purpose and with it a thread of power tinged her voice with conviction.

Later, as she helped the others piece together the last part of Orto's history, she began to feel the tingling sensation again. A feather touch at her neck aroused her to new awareness as Orto signed and Madiv talked, filling in what he could, in a clear unemotional voice.

"He remembers the wooden Zeglurs and being swung high in the air, by a man who made him laugh.", and added thoughtfully, "That might have been Keddic, our thread merchant who adored children. He often swung young Villeth till he laughed. Serba often blamed him for making the boy too excitable!".

However, as there had been no reaction to the name of the merchant Orana said comfortably, "Perhaps Villeth was too young to remember, also recall that the severity of the illness might have affected his memories as well as his hearing!", and looked to the Healer for confirmation. Jalni wrinkled her brow considering.

"Yes indeed. There are many childhood illnesses that can have terrible side effects, most of which are associated with high fevers. You must all realise that a high fever of any kind can even cause death in an adult if left unchecked. If only we understood why so many diseases seem to have occurred in the Rotations since the Storm, but we don't yet, though it is my intention to finish my training and work on the solution to that problem.", her eyes blazed blue and as her words were signed for Orto, he reached forward and gripped her wrists, smiling at her as he made a simple sign, which Orana translated swiftly.

"I am proud of you child!", she said, and ever afterwards Jalni wasn't sure if she spoke for herself or her uncle.

Edrith coughed and said apologetically, "We of course knew only that Sowdin and Serba returned saying that Villeth had died before they found the Healer, and from then on no-one could do anything right. She was alternatively tearful or angry, which we put down to grief. He was either withdrawn, or scolding old Zonelas, who had entered his elder childhood. I remember the Guild lawmaker coming to talk to him about the Halt. However, when he couldn't persuade Zonelas to countersign his will, procedures were stopped. As I understood things then, Sowdin had asked the Guild to put his name in Villeth's stead, making himself first legatee. They could have appointed him as Rowin's Trustee, but when Zonelas refused to accept that Villeth had died, the lawmaker went away, telling Sowdin that it was too late for the terms to be altered. I think it was about then that I started to wonder about Sowdin's mental health.".

Madiv asked gravely, "Was that about the time of our first stewardship?", as Orana interrupted briefly, clearing platters and setting down drinks. Outside the little town was springing to life. A market was being set up along the street, and already vendors were exhorting customers to buy milta flour, murl juice, or cheese. It was only in the kitchen that time stood still as Madiv explained how a man had waged war on his own children.

"We had to take charge immediately, for Sowdin had only ever worked as an enforcer, far to the south in the region of Asrujen.", he announced to a sea of blank faces, (signing this with difficulty). "As I told you, he was a natural bully, and he hired out with his crew to anyone who needed strong-arm tactics. He'd take money to move Felmin peasants off prime hunting land, collect rents, debts, taxes and so on, but he'd overstepped the mark the year after Rowin was born, and returned here to live off his father. That would have been about sixteen Rotations before Partition, if I reckon rightly.", he announced, unaware of Jalni's amazed face as he went on.

"Zonelas only put up with his nonsense for the sake of the children, you see Sowdin was the only male amongst six daughters. He'd exhausted one fortune trying to persuade one of them to marry a Weaver, and the other he invested in guild management for his Halt. Our first Steward, a man by the name of Chorill was happy to work here indefinitely. He was Sybillsce, and a skilled exponent of double weaving. He looked after both weaving shed and dye rooms, and some of his more learned writings are still used at the Guild Hall today. He was a wonderful businessman, and the Guild were entirely happy to leave him in charge, and he in turn seemed settled, but his wife and child were not. They eventually returned home, where sadly Chorill followed them about seven Rotations later.", his head bowed as he admitted, "We have no way of knowing whether he still lives of course!", and a chill touched the atmosphere as minds turned to the Amethyst Sands, now excluded from the Union, through the heresy of its wayward Sorceress.

"As you know gentles.", said Madiv the Weaver abruptly, "Villeth here turned up at Darnesh telling us of dire problems in Scartel, and before we knew it, our new Healer Hall was inundated with some feverish plague. I haven't been back to Darnesh until yesterday, when I heard that the Healer of that place had died, along with every man, woman, beast and child of the village!".

Jalni felt rather than saw the reaction to Edrith's flying fingers, for with a crash Orto shot to his feet, throwing his chair backwards with his momentum. His face was contorted with grief and rage as he brought his fist onto the table with a mighty crash, then crying out incoherently, he ran, blundering to the front door and lurching away, towards the unfeeling Sands, where the silence was broken only by the deaf man's sorrow.

Chapter 13 - A Weft of Weavers

Jalni's face was sober as she rose to her feet and slowly followed Orto as far as the door. Peering up the bustling street outside, she failed to spot his pale blue tunic and turned back, knowing that she could put him right about the children later. He would mourn Solana's death in his own time, in his own way, and her eyes were wet as she considered that the aged Healer had been the only mother that many children had known. She closed the door reluctantly, and found Edrith and Madiv waiting to pursue Orto on her orders. She caught Edrith's sleeve and said urgently.

"Let him go. He has to absorb the news alone. I believe I can find him when I need him.".

She left them in the passageway, and went into the long garden room, leaning against the window frame (eyes closed). She sought the cat in the swirling patterns of energies, sensing the signatures of pinkly peppery firebush, the cool clean stroke of the citrine tree, then a warm curl of somnolence, lying against the baked stone wall. Using only the fingers of her mind, she ruthlessly "poked" Echo in mid-snore until he opened an eye lazily. She "poked" him repeatedly, until he sneezed and sat up, awake enough to hear her thoughts.

"Our big friend is very sad. His other friends have died and he goes to the Sands to mourn.".

She found that she was thinking in short clear sentences and deciding that this was like talking to a child, asked simply, "Will you track him? Keep him safe until I fetch him?", at which there was a faint reluctant growl. Receiving (almost immediately) the mental image of Orto's reactions during their earlier encounter, she hid her relief at finding she could communicate and decided to get stern.

"for the sake of the One!", she exclaimed, "Are all males as pathetic? He has left his belt and knife here, besides he knows you won't hurt him now. However there could be sandrigals, scalebacks, seobra's or robbers out there, and although you are only a kitten, I thought you braver than that!".

The cat wavered, climbed to its feet and stood, hind-legs braced as he sharpened his claws on the wall. Jalni glanced behind her, up the passage where Edrith and Madiv consulted, heads together, eyes watching her, and took a risk. She raised the shutter slightly, as if taking a breath of fresh air, and furious with the cat's delaying tactics, threatened meaningfully.

"If you don't want to find your claws blunted, your fangs withdrawn and the pride of any male anatomy shortened, you'll take yourself Sand-wards my lad and seek the man. Keep him in sight and safe for me, and call when you find him!".

He hissed reluctantly, then Jalni felt for the Sands and it was as though the garden rippled in her mind. Echo leapt for the top of the wall, shifting shades as he landed gracefully. Where he passed the air shimmered, but all Jalni heard was a muted yowl, and a random thought.

"That's all we need! Two of them.", as the concerns of the day rushed in, sweeping this odd comment right out of her mind.

She honestly didn't think she could concentrate on the rest of her day, but when Madiv gently suggested that until Orto returned they should continue the working round, she found herself seizing on the suggestion. Orana picked up a basket and bustled off to market, and Edrith made his way to the Weaving shed, as Jalni helped Madiv enter the record of the dyes he had brought in from Darnesh the previous day. She marked the numbers off steadily as he bent over boxes containing plants, powders and pigments, and in some ways she was able to see some likenesses between the tasks of the steward, and those she had undertaken at Selesh, putting together ingredients for dyes was much the same as for medications, only the end result was different. The morning passed as Seleus rose, and gradually it was borne in on Jalni that the marketeers were departing, Orana's kitchen was creating mouth watering aromas and Orto still hadn't returned. She excused herself to Madiv and slipped out in to the garden, finding her way to the storeroom, and peering in through the window saw a pale blue back, lying on the mattress, and heard the hiccupping sobs with relief. She was about to reach for the cat, when it remarked from a corner of the storeroom.

"Easy to track. By the first rock he found. Very sad, many small people kitts dead.", said the voice in her mind, and Jalni knelt digging her hands into the blue -grey soil and radiated warmth, peace and "felt" the tension in Orto's body ease, as he slid into sleep. She rose silently, dusting off her hands and returned via the washroom to the kitchen, then after a simple bowl of soup, she slept until Orana's gong woke them to return to work in the mid afternoon.

Madiv was talking to a fair haired woman, dressed in the loose blue tunic favoured by female Weavers. She was expostulating vigorously, arms thrown up in disgust as Madiv clicked an enscrasure against his teeth, one arm folded against his chest supporting the other elbow. As Jalni glided quietly down the passageway, neither of them seemed to have noticed her, and as a particular snatch of conversation caught her ears, she slid into a patch of blued shadow and stood still, listening.

"Well Master Steward.", the thin bitter lips twisted. "You may support the claim of the Holder, but I do not! Neither does my weft of Weavers. Villeth del Orto is at least apprenticed to the Guild, and as his Grandfather willed it, so the Sorceress should rule. Tirjella, on the other hand is a Healer, and my guess is that our revered leader will protect her own. After all, she'll obey Selesh, no matter what the right's or wrongs of it are. With my face bared to Gurayen and my hand on my heart, I can't see Tirjella allowing Villeth's claim to disenfranchise the Guild of Healers, one of which is getting fat on our labour, and that, my friend, will split the Weaver Hall from nape to navel, you mark my words!".

Jalni's heartbeat slowed, as the woman's words sank in, and she shifted deeper into shadow, listening intently as Madiv's clear voice rang out contemptuously.

"If you stirred your dyes as well as you stir trouble Renna, we would be able to produce a better standard of goods. A holder of a Halt doesn't have to be a Weaver. They could be retired, a babe in arms or yet unborn, as was our current Holder when Zonelas died. Provided that the Guild have the right to supervise the Halt through a steward, as in this case, that is all the Guild require. My function is to manage this Halt under the guidance of a far larger Weft than you will ever control. Better you women go home and make babies, than stay here and make trouble for everyone. I believe that Lady Tirjella will take good advice over this, including talking to the Holder and her Uncle. She is older and infinitely wiser than either of us, so stop tangling your warp unnecessarily and don't forget that it is entirely possible they might sort it out themselves..".

The woman moved into a patch of light and Jalni stared at her, noting pinched nostrils, the hectic flush on pale cheeks, the angry glitter in brilliant eyes. Then she was speaking again, a low stream of invective that made Jalni blush.

"Well.", she snarled, "I have as much claim as they! My mother swore on her deathbed that Sowdin fathered me. He made provision for me in his own will, and paid for my indentures, acknowledging the relationship in kind, if not in kindness. However, because he jumped the trave with Serba, her children inherit while I get no part of this Halt? I think not my Masters all, even if I have to invoke share holder rights to break this Halt apart. I am a daughter of Clan Zurias. Pure of blood under Gurayen, yet this Halt passed from my older brothers to a half-blood bastard who can't even weave. Now if I let that lie, while they eat well and live in luxury, then I am not my father's child.".

She seemed to be staring right through Jalni as she rasped, "That Healer bitch had better believe, if she thinks she suffered at Sowdin's hand, that was only the beginning of her nightmare!".

She shook off Madiv's restraining hand and flounced past Jalni as if she wasn't there, disappearing into the depths of the garden, leaving only the crash of the garden door in her wake. Jalni, feeling as if she floated in ice, held her breath as Madiv passed her on the run, muttering furious imprecations under his breath. She leaned against the wall, wishing herself anywhere but here, and as she did so, became aware of the cat. He was close to her, the gentle thrum of his purr comforted her as she stared listlessly into a copper mirror, seeing nothing, not even her own reflection.

"Very interesting…".

Jalni jumped almost out of her skin as real words sublimated the throaty purr of the Mystcat. "Very interesting.", he repeated, somewhere close at hand. "I never thought of shadow shifting in daylight. How do you do that?". Jalni stared at a mirror plate showing nothing more substantial than the reflection of the room around her, and shuddering with cold, fainted clean away.

She came round seconds later, feeling sick and stupid. Orana was bending over her, clucking solicitously, fanning her with the towel she normally wore over one shoulder as she tended the kitchen. As she struggled to force down her nausea, taking control of the spinning sensation in her head, Jalni's mind raced through the disconcerting "conversation" that she'd just held with a mystcat, who now of course, was conspicuous only by his absence. Reluctantly, she allowed Orana to help her up to the nursery room, lying obediently on the small bed as the windows were shaded, and tried to get her buzzing brain around the fact that somehow she had tapped into yet another strange ability without any idea of doing so. The room was dark and cool, Orana had tiptoed away muttering when Jalni gave up the struggle, and allowed herself to slip into a light doze on the thought that she could have done with Daro's help to solve this puzzle. She curled up, feeling the soft texture of a pieced quilt enfolding her and smoothing the familiar material under her hand, floated away on the thought that something very strange was happening to her.

On the other side of the Great Divide there was a bustle and stir in the main street of Selesh Minoria. The Second Watch shepherding a gaggle of children, (some mere babies in takran slings), had just passed through on their way into the fortress. That they were expected was not in doubt, for as they turned towards the Gate in the Rock, Jashell had mustered the guard outside and they stood to attention, as a pretty girl in a silvery robe came smiling to welcome Daro's orphans home. Tired and thirsty the last three patrols were ushered into the cool inner sanctuary of the junior school of Healers, where they were bathed, fed and left together to sleep as Seleus slid towards Sunfall.

In a backroom of the "Cross Eyed Zeglur", Daro was waking, aware that he was not alone as he struggled upright. His Songfather leant over him and the younger man flushed with embarrassment as he realised that he must have fallen asleep in mid-sentence.

Carolus laughed softly. "Well my boy, just be thankful that these old bones still have enough flesh on to pillow your head.", he groaned ruefully as Daro pulled him to his feet solicitously,

"Are you alright? I can't think what came over me. I should be used to long nights and physical activity by now!".

Carolus snorted. "Well, that's as maybe young man, but this last five nights, you have lost your Healer, and therefore access to restoratives, run half a Sand to your mother's side, and endured enough emotional jolts

to make a weaker man buckle. Now, I can help fix that temporarily, but you still have a road to travel until your recovery is complete.".

He leant forward, studying the dim glow at Daro's throat and said abruptly, "While I go and get the makings together, why don't you slip out through that door into Beven's yard? Lown will guide you, and I can bring you a sweetdrink out there. You need some fresh air, sunshine, good food and contact with the sand to refresh you. By the way, where on Pelshar did you find that bauble you have taken to wearing round your neck?".

Daro chuckled. "If I told you I found it twisted around the horn of a Zephryn, you wouldn't understand what I was talking about Songfather.", he teased, but had he been able to see, he might have questioned the sudden stilling of the old man's face as he responded.

"I expect I won't understand much of what you have experienced.", the Apothecary retorted, "but don't you for get that I once had the run of Sanctuary and the confidence of the Guardians. I think I can still be of much use to you my boy, but somehow I have to get past your mother's current mood.".

He opened the door passing Lown who entered to guide his Lord into the yard. Daro cocked his head as the Apothecary's parting shot floated back to him. The dour prognostication caused a muscle at the side of the Sandsinger's mouth to twitch, as the usually musical voice rasped gruffly.

"and even if I were Sandsinger myself, I'd take a deep breath, and half eternity to bend that woman to my way of thinking!", followed by some muttered comment about the immovability of Mount Torrenesh, and the implacability of the Winds, then the kitchen door shut, and silence reigned.

They had finished their drinks and Daro was turning his mind to getting back to Selesh (and the regrettable explanations that would be demanded of him), when Nadra came into the yard. She spoke urgently to Lown, who had risen at her appearance, returning directly to Daro frowning.

"Trouble!", he interrupted Olneth's convoluted tales of adventuring.

"Already?.", Daro responded, sensing heightening tension. The shoemaker's son grimaced, altering the shape of his mouth so that Daro "heard" the scowl that crossed his face.

"The bloody Watch has tracked you down Lord!", he grumbled. "Sorrill and Diras are drinking in the bar, my watcher tells me that Jashell is in the Marketplace with a patrol and I saw Jerint walk the passageway behind the yard, not a sector ago! It isn't that they shouldn't find you here, but it will look as though you've taken sides if they do, which could spoil any chance of Master Carolus returning in my lifetime!".

Olneth grinned at the assembled company suggesting, "Shall we show Daro how ordinary men disappear before their very eyes?", as Carolus stood.

"Come my boy.", he murmured and Lown took Daro's arm, following hard on the old man's heels as he continued instructing Daro.

"The passage is very narrow.", he murmured. "We only found it after the innkeeper at the "Wandering Apothecary" started to extend his cellar. Poor Geffrodus was mortified to find himself in a passage leading to ours. We think it was used long ago to smuggle destreigned goods into Selesh, but had collapsed through disuse.".

Daro heard a "click", a growl as a panel slid aside reluctantly, and then the warmth of the sun was cut off as they stepped cautiously in the Apothecary's wake. The passage sloped down steadily, and Daro heard odd rustlings as something scuttled ahead. He detected the faint waxen scent of the Apothecary's torch, grinning in relief as he realised that the passage was reasonably tall, having developed a positive antipathy to banging his head on low tunnel roofs in Scartel.

With quiet efficiency, the panel had been reinstated as the Sandsinger, (his guides shoulder under his hand) proceeded into the depths single file. His Songfather's voice quietly advised.

"Careful now. Keep your voices down as we pass the hold below the Watch room.", and amazed Daro realised that a gentle curve had brought them below the Gate in the Rock, and into Selesh itself. They passed through a massive portal, then the passageway was behind him, and he became aware of a faint chiming sound as Olneth behind him whispered.

"Steps ahead Daro.", and a toe-stubbing three flights later, another door slid open, into the late Master Builder's experimental forge. He knew the scent of it immediately, fine metallic aroma's mixed with firestone, ash, and wood shavings. He caught the pleasant smell of drying hancharr (a plant much favoured by brewers), and lifted his head, knowing that Beven who had been a smith, and who now used Errish's workroom and forge for his own pursuits must be present.

Beven said mildly, "Good. You got my message then?", and Olneth, bringing up the rear said briskly, "We did indeed.", adding shortly, "I must go back now. It would be stupid to raise suspicions by not returning as I left, with a Zeglur and panniers filled with preparations. I'll see you in the marketplace old man!", then turning he clattered back down the stairs, as Carolus closed the panel behind him. Lown grasped Daro's sleeve.

"There is a way from the pasture to the spring.", he hissed, "Errish uncovered it when he made the hotfloor for the Hall of the Healers. We can go that way, through one marginally risky area near the pools, then into another passage that leads into the Eyrie. Yon daft Apothecary found it when Master Errish was building here!".

They were moving steadily now, Daro's hand on Lown's arm and Daro was suddenly aware that he hadn't taken leave of Carolus. He resisted Lown's guiding arm fractionally, and his First said gruffly.

"Don't concern yourself with Master Carolus. He said to tell you that he'll see you later. He was here in his youth, and knows more about this place than any other, and has his own ways of getting about. He will speak to Shiarjha then he will come to you. My job is to get you into your own suite, and then we can relax.", and chuckling grimly at the expression of joyful complicity on his Lords face, Lown led Daro through the secret passages riddling his home.

Chapter 14 - Adruna's Warp

Jalni woke in the stillness of her old nursery, uncertain of where she was. The day was far into the evening and from where she lay, she could see the brilliant streaks of approaching Sunfall in the skies above Jerritol. She drowsed briefly, then the sound that had roused her came again. Swiftly, she knelt, peering through the window, down into the short alley that bordered the house, and found herself overlooking the entrance to the weaver's courtyard. Despite the advancement of night, she could see most of the area formed by three large weaving rooms, Edrith's shop, various living quarters and the shed that housed threads and spare looms. She concentrated, certain that what she had heard jangled still in her head and sure enough, it came again, the sound of tortured metal and wood. Moving carefully, she became aware of footsteps stealthily approaching. Silently raising the half drawn shutter, she made out the shape of Edrith's head as he paused in the shadows below.

"Psst! Edrith, look up.", she hissed, freeing her hands as the long pale oval turned towards her. Hastily signing the additional word, "Danger!", so emphatically it could have been a scream. She scanned the surroundings seeking the cat, as Orto came to kneel on the bed beside her, hands flashing as he conversed urgently with the aging Weaver. Jalni, aware of substantial damage being done in the loom loft, heard a throaty rumble borne by the Source, with immense relief.

"Bad people break things.", emerged from their link and Jalni realising that the pale blur on the loom loft roof was Echo, suggested slyly, "Echo play snarl and pounce?". There was a seconds pause then she heard the query.

"For real? Claw and kill, or pounce and play?".

It was not language in words, but the thought was clear. Jalni sighed as she saw a second shadow creep up to join Edrith. Orana held a large kitchen weight in one hand as she courageously went to help her husband. In that moment, Jalni hardened her heart.

"For real Echo. Bad people hurt friends and cats, so be careful.".

She streamed an image of broken looms to the mystcat, hoping that he would pounce on the unsuspecting vandals as they left the loft, for fear of him impaling himself on the working gear below, but hard on the heels of her thoughts came piercing screams. Orto raised the shutter as she jumped off the bed, and swinging himself over the sill, dropped into the alleyway below, calling up to her with a soft coughing grunt of reassurance.

Rolling her eyes at such foolhardy behaviour, she whispered.

"To the glory of the One.", and slid out of the aperture and into her Uncle's strong arms, gulping in relief as he set her down easily, allowing her to run behind him to a scene of utter devastation. The wrecking crew had spared nothing. Stretching frames, thread spinners, and hanking frames were smashed to smithereens. Anything metal was buckled or wrenched from wooden mounts, looms ready for another weaver destroyed where they rested, and standing transfixed in a corner, three women dressed as youths cowered away from the snarling ferocity of a mystcat. At Orto's rapid entrance Echo bellowed a yowl of frustration, leaping for the ladder that led to the roof. Orto ignored him, advancing on the three cornered vandals, holding them with the fire in his eyes and the gleam of the knife in his hand, as Jalni bent over their felled companions. However, even the immediate presence of a Healer could do nothing to restore life to two of Renna's Weft of Weavers.

Madiv, in company with Tetro and Danic, (the other time-served weavers) came running from the inn along the street where they were taking supper, apparently fetched by one of the dyers. The Steward's face was pale and clammy with shock as Jalni stepped back from Echo's victims, who sprawled in the wreckage that they had created, impaled by the weight of the leaping cat on the very weapons they had been using to wreck the looms. The Healer stared at the blackened metal bars they had used, seeing one edge tempered and forked like a prising bar, the other flattened to create a hammer and wondered if these were mining tools. She had seen similar items in the Ashgenar as a very small child. Madiv's voice, thinned with strain, was nevertheless calm and controlled. He rounded on the other three members of Renna's weft, completely ignoring their state of imminent collapse and spoke brusquely.

"Pull yourselves together.", he advised, followed by a soft aside to Edrith. "Get them inside quickly. I don't want them slinking off to find the hell-cat that set this in motion.", and Jalni stared at her Steward with a new respect. Orana was bent over one of the still figures on the ground, as another of the weaver's closed dead eyelids over staring orbs. He spoke curtly.

"Hell-born perhaps, but don't stain our cat's with the blackness of that ones soul!", at which Madiv's mouth thinned as he ordered.

"Danic, take them into the garden room. Lock the doors and get the shutters down. Guard them, I don't want Renna getting access to them before I can get word back to Darnesh. Master Cruin at the Stewards Hall must be advised and it is very possible that Master Nimm will send word to the Clan. We could do with some more security here as well.".

He turned measuring eyes on Orto, then shook his head and said quietly to Jalni.

"I must have private words with you Mistress.", adding almost as an afterthought, "I am ever watchful of the Gattarene's hand in this Halt.", he spoke conversationally, but his words fell like icy tentacles around Jalni's spirit, as they moved away from the scene of sudden outrageous death in the yard, toward the house where plainly Madiv sought answers to questions. He continued thoughtfully.

"When Villeth del Orto turned up at Darnesh with word of plague in Scartel, Deshun Tirjella had him segregated in case he brought the sickness with him. He was ill, but mainly through dehydration and exhaustion. He had not ventured into other communities for fear of carrying contagion, so had not been able to get more water or food. One of our journeymen found him in extremis and managing to get water into him, ran back to the Guild and raised assistance. The Healers took him, but not before he told my journeyman a very odd kind of story. He reported it to Master Nimm, who is the Head of Guild, and he took it to Tirjella.".

Jalni shivered, just the mention of the black-hearted Sorceress of the Amethyst had reminded her of Tjerri, who had the most gruesome fund of horror stories with which to regale the dormitories at the School of Healers, where she and Jalni had trained and where Tjerri had died. She listened intently as Madiv, unaware of this reaction told his tale.

"It seems that on his journey Villeth saw a woman dancing with shadows in a place we call Dark Springs.". He had paused by the door into the house and Jalni stopped to listen to his low emphatic voice.

"It has become an evil place Mistress. The very sand is sick, all around what my Guild Masters tell me used to be a good watering place.".

That strange frisson that Jalni had begun to associate with some element of mystery, shivered along her scalp as she listened to the story of the exhausted man as he struggled towards Darnesh with his plea for help. She could almost hear the wind playing across the darkening Sands, the brief glimpse of water nestling in some shadowed hollow. Her head turned, tracking Orto as framed in the doorway of the loom loft, he adjusted a ladder so that he could climb up to block the hole through which Echo had entered the loom store. She could imagine his thirst, the joy of finding the strange oasis, only to discover discoloured sands and dying vegetation, overlaid with a stench that defied description.

She dragged her attention back to Madiv's voice.

"Fauggh! Don't ask me what has caused it Mistress, but the water is contaminated. Whatever evil permeates the place hangs over the pool like a miasma. Where animals have drunk, their carcases have further soiled the spring. Great yellowing grasses with slimy brown roots encroach at one end, but nothing there lives. Villeth was so dehydrated that the temptation to drink was almost irresistible, or so he signed. He thought he must have fainted, but when he came round, what he saw was unbearable.".

They had squatted, talking in low voices by the back step, and the dying light caught the gleam of fear in Madiv's eyes as he brought the scene to life, hands flickering as of habit he signed the words he spoke.

"Villeth had resigned himself to dying of thirst when a woman arrived on a Zeglur.".

Madiv's voice, now tight and hard shook with fury.

"Luckily he was too weak to appeal for help or we might never have heard this tale.", he remarked. When understanding came, she shivered, wondering how Renna would have reacted to her eavesdropping on her earlier outburst. Madiv's words reclaimed her attention.

"As soon as he described her, I knew it was Renna. She rode my own Zeglur between Jerritol and Darnesh at the Rise of Moons some six ninenights back.".

The Steward's face darkened as he explained angrily.

"I am tasked with finding out more about her, which is why I haven't broached the matter directly, in case I forewarned her that she is under investigation, but although part of another story, she had been sent to deliver an order, but went missing. Two days later, she dragged herself to Darnesh, saying that she'd been attacked, losing both order and beast as a result.", his jaw clenched as he said coldly. "However, I now believe that the truth of the matter is entwined with tonight's wickedness.". He stared at his hands blankly, then cleared his throat, saying uncomfortably, "Deshun Tirjella sent her Truth Finder to listen to Villeth's story, she was so concerned. Master Cruin made sure that Magdurah confided security concerns to her Captain of Guard, and he came visiting.". He grinned, admitting shyly, "He's my son you see!". and Jalni let him continue.

"Villeth thought what he saw was a vision or a dream, and did nothing as she dismounted and stripped. The moons had risen by this time, and he saw the woman lead my poor beast into the pool herself. She was stark naked and chanting, so thinking he witnessed holy ritual, he was about to turn away, when she whipped out a knife and cut the poor beast's throat, drinking its lifeblood before bathing herself in that noxious filth. She sang, dancing under the dark glow of Gatta and although I am persuaded that some of this might be hallucination, he told Magdurah that dark shadows "in the shape of men", arose from the lake and danced with her.".

He shuddered, whispering self-consciously, "When my Master's told me what occurred next I could hardly tolerate Renna's presence. I would not speak of it to an unmarried innocent, but as a Healer, you know well what men and women do together".

His face flamed in the light from the window above, then sickened he turned away, muttering.

"Forgive me Mistress, but now I'd better go and see what the human cost of this woman's perversions are before we are all caught in the twisted threads of Adruna's warp!".

His hand touched heart, lips and head, expiating his sin in naming the Gattarene. Then he rose unsteadily and went to question the three remaining craftswomen. They huddled together, sitting on the floor of the unfurnished room and wept. Madiv eyed them with disgust.

"Did you think that dressing as young men would cover your tracks?", his voice flayed their overstretched nerves, but he was merciless. "How did you think to evade Guild justice?", he snapped, adding more mildly, "Or didn't you know the penalty for destroying a man's working tools is death?".

They moaned, clinging to each other and rocking in terror as Jalni interrupted, voice hard and edgy.

"One of those stored looms was my father's. It would have passed to my Uncle when he qualifies.", at which a snigger rose from one of the group.

"Renna says dummies can't learn crafts!". She continued to mutter resentfully.

"He's too stupid to talk that one! Can't believe anything he signs either. Not fit to be apprenticed, let alone Holder! Besides, he's officially dead! His own father swore to it. Renna's next in line, ahead of that Nishanawa bitches base-born get.".

She was obviously so used to referring to Jalni in this fashion that her voice sounded bored rather than vicious, but the hand that flashed out of the dark and slapped her face certainly woke her to the peril she stood in and a wail of fright left her, as Jalni reaching for the source to help calm her own temper, became incandescent in the light of one dim candle. She felt the air tease her neck, her hair positively crackled around her head in a nimbus of fire and her eyes blazed arctic blue in a chalk white face as she purred invitingly.

"Ah, so nice to find out in what esteem the legal Holder of this Halt is held.", she remarked into the nerve-shredding silence that followed the slap.

"May I suggest that you restrict your foul mouth to making comments that you can validate. Such as the last time you drew breath without screaming? I hate to remind you, but apparently life gets very hard once your gizzard's torn out and your lungs decorate the Gates at Mount Darnesh!".

The throaty purr continued as she scythed through the girls resistance effortlessly, tasting their terror as her eyes blazed, lambent with power.

"Now talk to me of Renna. What are her plans and where is she likely to be found. Speak now and honestly before I summon the Guardians to rule on your fate.".

The girls buried their faces sobbing desperately, then a strange thing happened. Bethig, the youngest of the three said faintly,

"I'm so hot!", and grasped at the neck of the jerkin she was wearing. The other two stared wildly, as smoke poured from their companion, who screamed, stark terror gripping her as flames burst from her body. Only seconds separated their death's. In front of a house full of horror stricken witnesses, the remainder of Renna's Weft of Weaver's burned and died, before their secrets could be told. Encapsulated in icy blue fury Jalni stared into the shadows and wondered who to blame.

Madiv's voice came shakily through the roaring in her ears, and she stared at him, trying to make sense of what he was saying.

"Mistress, Mistress Jalni. I must report this to Deshun Tirjella, the Guild, and these poor benighted children's families. What in the Nine Sands am I to say?", the light clear voice trembled and Jalni, ever the Healer reached for her scrip and withdrew a handful of slips containing a variety of restoratives. she handed them to Orana and said clearly.

"No-one leaves the Halt tonight. It is far too dangerous and we have all had a dreadful shock. I will speak to the Guild and Deshun Tirjella. Orto must check the Roll of the Dead, and present himself to the Guild, and Master Madiv, you will have to organise security not just for our Halt, but for the village, so I need you here to talk to the Elders. for now, Orana make hot sweetdrinks adding these restoratives. Edrith and Orto can walk the perimeter of the Halt and lock up, Tetro and Danic can get all the evidence together in the main house. I need to see clothes, weapons and tools from that weft of weavers. What has been done with the bodies of the two who disturbed that mystcat?".

Gradually some sense was made out of the disorder. Madiv rolled his eyes at the darkened patch on the flagged floor of the garden room where three girls had spontaneously burst into flame, but thankfully said nothing as Jalni steeled herself to sweep together the ashes, placing them in a funerary urn that Orana produced with a small grimace. It was she who told them that none of the five had families that she knew of. It had been one of Renna's boasts that she had deliberately chosen orphaned girls for her weft, saying that the traditional group of weaver apprentices would become the family that none of them had known. That she looked after her weft well, and that they adored her was not in question, but what strange hold had she over them, that they believed they could break every Guild law, impervious to retribution.

As Jenta rose above the Weaver's Halt, followed by its surly twin, the compound was secured. The Weavers took their restoratives and drank in the moonlit garden. One by one they departed to the courtyard where they worked and lived, conscious of strange sounds beyond the wall..

"Don't worry, that's our friendly mystcat.", Jalni soothed them. "I have a feeling he'll keep Renna at bay.". Her confident voice reassured them, as she slowly signed her words to her Uncle, who happily restrained his mirth as she deliberately showed him a pair of crossed fingers before she started to sign.

"Oh yes.", she said airily. "The Ranger's told us that Mystcats (once used by hunters) could easily be tamed, if young enough. I never saw one in Scartel, but I have no doubt that they spoke from experience. Perhaps the one that helped us tonight is but a kitt seeking friends. If it is comfortable round men, it poses no danger, and I for one would prefer it patrolled the compound than wake with Renna's knife at my throat.".

There was a scurrying sound on the far side of the wall as she spoke, a soft short yowl, a snap followed by a scrunching sound, then loud contented purring. Edrith, who had blenched, said softly. "One less gulley hopper to eat my solben crops?", and Jalni nodded poker faced.

"Indeed.", she agreed solemnly, knowing how precious the plants were in the production of blue dyes.

"Aah.", sighed Orana.

"Then the kitt is welcome here. I shall let the village elders know it belongs to Mistress Jalni and must not be pursued.".

They drifted off to bed as peace settled over the Halt, but the night was young and other players waited to exercise their influence over Jerritol.

Jalni knelt in the darkened nursery, waiting as the tensions of that dreadful evening relaxed. Orana had impetuously hugged the young Holder as she went to her home in the compound, whispering thickly, "May the One forgive them for straying from the Way.", her voice choked with tears, as Jalni placed the urn in her father's garden.

"They will be forgiven, for what happened here was none of their doing.", the young Healer replied gently. "They were drawn into some terrible tangle by one who knew better and strayed from the Way deliberately. I have no doubt, they did not know what was happening to them. It was not self-immolation to escape questioning. This was some evil perpetrated upon them, and for that I look to Renna for explanations!".

Orana had stood quivering as she spoke and Jalni was aware from the stiffening of the housekeeper's body that Renna could expect no support in that quarter.

"To be lonely, unloved and unrecognised by your own family is no sin my dear.", Orana said simply, making Jalni wonder whether she referred to the Weaver or herself, then the woman said in a voice devoid of all emotion.

"However, to fall into the kind of wickedness that Villeth witnessed and then drag other innocents into that coil behind you, is unforgivable. I'm not a vindictive woman, but Sundreth's mines are too good for the like of that one!", and Jalni had pressed her hand in mute sympathy as Edrith took his wife away.

Now she perched on her bedroom sill, gazing out over the deeply shadowed garden, waiting for something to happen beyond the sleeping compound. A light step told her that her Uncle was restive also, but her head never turned as he quietly entered the room, coming up behind her and pressing her shoulder. He was fully dressed and Jalni saw the glint of moonlight on the blade of his knife and smiled wryly. They stood, scanning the night until something in the darkness moved beyond the storeroom where two bodies lay dressed ready for burial.

She felt Orto shift and raised her hand to grasp his, using Inesh hand code to tap the sequence very rapidly. "Stand still!", she ordered and thankfully he froze. As two sets of eyes accustomed themselves to the angles and shadows near the storeroom, the movement came again. A stealthy figure rose from ground level to peer in through the window, then a frenzied howl of anguish raised the hair at the nape of Jalni's neck. There was no sanity in that ululation. Nothing other than thwarted ambition, rage and grief was expressed in the depths of the garden below. She gripped Orto's arm unnecessarily hard, but he still stood immobile as, from the direction of the Weaver's compound, feet came running.

Renna was too quick for them, by the time Tetro and Danic arrived, she'd leapt over the wall, fleeing into the night. Still Jalni kept her grasp on Orto's arm, until she "felt" the cat loping silently along a ridge, crossing the place where Jerritol ended and the blue sands began. They slid together out into the village in pursuit. Orto, intent on protecting his new home, Jalni determined to identify and destroy the taint of evil that had shattered her family, before it threatened her Sands.

Chapter 15 - The Heart of Darkness

They slid quietly along the track out into the Sands, leaving Jerritol, with all its memories and sad concerns behind. Jalni felt incredibly alive, the night enfolding her in its blued embrace as though she were the desert itself. Shrugging off that depressing day like an irksome garment, she went lightly on the balls of her toes, slipping effortlessly through the shadows, headed for the ridge where she knew Echo waited. Orto (following within arms length) never attempted to influence her, which, Jalni considered a touching testament to his faith in her judgement, as they were brought to a stop by a ferocious snarl nearby.

Putting out a hand to stay Orto, she felt his hand-code enquiry. "Cat feeding?", he had tapped, but there were sounds and noxious smells that told her otherwise. Wondering wildly if Echo was capable of killing (or eating) Renna, she was tempted to creep forward and find out, but Orto's arm was like a metal bar as he swept her off her feet, and leapt aside, as a brutal blood-flecked muzzle thrust through scrubby undergrowth. They were only seconds from death as a half-grown seobra sprang, foul saliva dripping from its blackened fangs.

Still connected to the Source (which allowed her to track Echo), it was Jalni who grasped the air with clawed fingers, twisting her hand in a complex movement. It was Jalni who ducked, as a snarling creature was catapulted past them propelled by the fist of mighty Gurayen's fury, and it was definitely Jalni, who sat on the ground and vomited as the wolverine-like creature spasmed in its death-throes not three spans from Orto. Solemnly, he placed both hands together and bowed his thanks, before kneeling in mute prayer as the sickened girl clambered unsteadily to her feet.

She swore softly as she took in the muscular strength of the beast that had attacked them. She saw the foam flecked jowl, smelt the foul stench of its breath still hanging in the air and nearly jumped out of her scattered wits as a smooth voice trickled into her mind.

"Nice kill.", Echo remarked approvingly, stepping daintily out of the dark and brushing himself along her legs as he came to survey the corpse. The throaty purr sounded horridly like a chuckle, but Jalni, disgusted with the thought that *she* was responsible for the animal's death, was not listening to the cat.

"Come away.", she ordered brusquely. "You can come back to gloat later.", and turning abruptly she began to move into the Sands proper, leaving the track and her strangely assorted companions behind. When they caught up with her, she had tied her old dark jerkin around her waist by its sleeves, loosened her hair and removed her boots. Bare feet planted in the sand, she seemed abstracted, standing in Jenta's silver glow surrounded by a pale Azure toned luminescence. She seemed to grow taller and stronger as they watched, and Orto came to a stop, staring at her, his friendly face bemused. Echo thought testily.

"That's all I need! Hunting the night with a sand thralled girl in tow!", but he was purring with admiration as he crept into the faintest of aura's and laid his head at his Lady's feet.

She bent and touched him lightly. "Echo, listen!", she whispered as the cat picked up the low thudding. "She's riding somewhere isn't she?", her hands caught hold of Orto's as she walked her fingers over his palm, trying to communicate her fears to him, but astonishingly, he grinned and shook his head. He tapped laboriously.

"Not…", followed by her own interpretation of the word "riding".

They had to wait until the moon was bright enough to see his gestures, as he mimed "driving", embellishing wildly with a flourish of invisible brimmed hats, the flick of a whip, and finally Jalni understood. Somewhere in the desert a night drove was taking place. He was hysterically funny, pulling long Dorrowen faces, bracketing fingers to brow in imitation of horns, but she had to restrain him, when a sour sound caught her attention, and the cat stiffened.

"What is it?", the Healer hissed, pressing Orto's shoulder, a silencing finger to her lips as he raised a questioning eyebrow. The cat flattened himself to the ground, the other's following barely a second later as a cacophony of mournful shrieks was followed by a wail. It seemed to Jalni that the sound was rhythmic, building in volume and intensity across the dunes. Semi stunned she "poked" the cat until he twitched, then she saw that the sound was a weapon. Echo's ears were flattened, a little trickle of blood stained his nose, and his eyes were dazed. Quickly, tearing her jerkin free she hastily wrapped the heavy cloth round Echo's head, in a desperate attempt to block out that screaming pulse, avoiding wildly flailing paws as he attempted to dig himself into the sands in a vain attempt to escape. There was pain in Jalni's ears, it hurt to breathe, hurt to think and she knew it must be so much worse for the cat. Her hands came down, clawing into the dune as it rose above them, a note like a clarion call burst from her lips, then the Sands shivered under her feet.

She was drifting, recalling the peace and tranquillity of Holmgarth, as silence fell like a blanket, stopping out the dreadful sounds and relieving the pain that threatened their very existence. She felt strangely surreal, as if time and place had no hold on her, the Sands were her only reality, then a strange phrase sprang to her lips.

"Braquerum victis!", she cried aloud as the Sands settled and hearing returned. There was a shriek of defiance in the distance, but Jalni didn't care, all she could think of was Echo and she recovered her stance to an upright kneeling position and ran enquiring hands over the limp body at her feet. It was anxious moments until she detected the faint purr, then he twitched under her exploring fingers and with relief she heard his "Purr aow?" of enquiry.

She had hardly registered the fact that Orto was no longer with them, she just bent over the Mystcat, sobbing with reaction, as she tried to tune her voice to the requirements of a non-human. She miraculously found the note, cradling the great head in her hands as she launched her *othervoice* into the space where the kitt curled, shuddering with shock, unaware of the Opal sheen spreading across Echo's half-open eyes. She was singing cool pain-relieving threads, struggling not to overwhelm her patient when Daro's anxious voice made itself heard.

"Jalni, whose hurt?", he demanded.

She reacted automatically, streaming her impressions without considering that Daro was half a sand away. He said urgently, "Are you still under attack love?", and the tenderness in his voice nearly undid her Healer -trained calm. She forced her inner voice to behave as she reported the events, but she was aware of rising hysteria as somewhat non-committal responses jangled her lacerated nerves.

Eventually she demanded, "Daro, where are you?", and laughter bubbled in his voice as he admitted, "I'm in the Djellim with Beneva!".

"For pity's sake!", she blurted, so used to the casual relationship that she and Daro shared, as he chuckled, saying gently, "Don't worry. I've taken a look at him. My dear girl, your diagnostic skill is amazingly accurate, and your reactions are faster than his. Echo will live and hear again perfectly, but you are at risk if Beneva is right. What you heard sounds uncannily like the description of an ancient artefact called the Heart of Darkness. We don't know how it works, save to say that once that noise begins the first effect is that every animal or bird in its vicinity dies. The second effect is that whole areas of land are depopulated, presumably because where no animal life exists, men don't remain. The third and final stage is the death of anyone foolish enough to defy the fate of the others. That is what I fear will happen in the Azure if we can't find out what this damnable thing is or who is using it.".

Jalni said hesitantly, "I hunt a renegade Weaver. She would be a good candidate, tonight having abandoned her crew to their deaths by ordering mere apprentices to wreck the Halt at Jerritol.".

She frowned, trying through a veil of exhaustion tinged with nausea, to concentrate on being accurate. She heard his voice dimly through the roaring in her ears.

"Jalni, dearling, touch the Sand. Sit down, or lie down, bury your hands and take deep breaths. I will help you.", and she sat abruptly, trying to let go of the Source, as she rolled away from Echo. The mind numbing experience faded as suddenly as it had come, then Daro's inner voice said sternly.

"too little to eat, too little to drink, what in Nine Sands do you think you are doing to yourself. For the sake of the One, take a restorative! In fact young woman, take one of mine! It will keep you going longer than anything else at hand for the moment.", and sitting dizzily, she obeyed the tense voice in her head, grateful that he didn't sound angry with her. She rested her head against Echo's flank, as the Sands shivered.

She must have dozed after choking down the powder from her scrip, but he was still in her head when she roused, feeling as though a door had closed on something evil. She sat up, glad to find Echo snoring lightly, and saw her Uncle approaching. He was in a state of high excitement and it was all she could do to contain this as she relayed some of her experiences to Daro, concentrating on the fact that she was related to Solana's missing helper. Daro didn't comment other than to tell her that he knew and trusted the deaf man, then he suggested waking Echo.

She bent a fierce diagnostic stare on the sleeping cat, and one ear pricked, slowly followed by the other. He scrunched up his face, slowly blinked awake, nictating membranes clearing as he sat up, surveying them through lazily blinking eyes. He was mildly confused, his head swung from side to side as he took in a long breath, then suddenly Jalni "heard" the connection form.

Daro's calm voice said, "Good fellah! Are you feeling better now? ", followed by a rumbling moan at the back of the cat's throat. Daro responded quickly.

"I know. Ears hurt, head hurts too, but there are plenty of gulley hoppers out there!", and Jalni smiled at the cat's twitching ears. He turned a mildly reproachful look at the young Healer and complained throatily. "Ouh, purr aow!", and Jalni swung round, just in time to see Orto's moonlit hands sign.

"Sorry fellah! They're all dead!", and Jalni saw that he had dropped at his feet an assortment of small mammals, and groaned in disbelief. She needed to talk to Daro, but how could she with Orto around? He wouldn't understand magic, she couldn't explain Sandsingers in signs, so she knelt in the Azure desert and wondered exactly what to do next.

Orto decided the matter. She became aware of a muted conversation going on, ears twitched, then skilled hands flickered. More ear twitching provoked Orto into face pulling, his mobile mouth turned down at the corners and then he caught sight of Jalni's bewildered face. He pulled a long mournful grimace, placed locked fingers to his temples to signify "horns", then he rolled up his eyes till the whites showed, choked and toppled face down into the Sands. Jalni, nerves already at full stretch shrieked.

"Orto!", flinging herself on him, feverishly checking pulses, then becoming suitably indignant when he sat up, odd little choking sounds bubbling up irrepressibly, until she realised he was laughing. She angrily swatted him, determined that he should learn not to tease a Healer that way and was stilled by the expression on his face. He mimed the drove again, complete with Dorrowen, Biron, carts and men, before "dying" with suitably horrific noises that sickened Jalni as she whispered.

"All of them? O Deo me! Orto, you can't be serious?", but he was, and the mood changed as Gurayen whined across the sands of death.

The drove had passed Jerritol and Jalni let Echo cast about for the scent, before warning Orto.

"When we get there, don't let the cat eat anything until I inspect it!". It took several attempts to get this across in sign, but she persisted. They walked on as Jenta rose towards its zenith, when glancing up at the ominous aspect of Gatta, Jalni was forced to question her imagination, for it was haloed in Amethyst tones.

She signed the words "Dark Springs?", as she saw the black bulk of Mount Darnesh glint in the distance under Jenta's light. Orto replied reluctantly, tapping her hand signing "Yes.", followed by something she didn't understand, as all three of them prowled stealthily down the long ancient ridge that led in that direction, and found the drove.

It wasn't large, just pathetic. Several herders with their prized animals, heading for the morning market in Darnesh. Two sand carts, dragged by Biron, five men and a teenaged boy, all dead, with horror imprinted on staring eyes. The cattle had died where they fell, udders full of milk, and with increasing anger Jalni realised that they had been heavy with young. That there would be sorrowing families comparatively nearby, she did not doubt, sending a prayer winging skyward as she helped Orto turn carts into pyres. She worked in icy fury, stripping the bodies, salvaging food, clothes, goods for the families, soon to bear the sorrow as the Clan made the necessary identifications. They watched them burn, as Orto butchered the animals, giving Echo his supper without glancing at Jalni's offended face. They had located a seam of stone not far from the site, so Orto sent the cat scurrying along it and was delighted when Echo returned with damp fur.

Jalni bundled then buried the evidence, then followed the Mystcat, finding a small pool, not more than two handspans wide in the shelter of a rocky ledge. She watched numbly, as Orto collected water in a shallow pan, stripping to wash away the blood. He was well muscled and moved easily, betraying none of his forty Rotations as he slipped into the jerkin he had removed before his night's ghastly task began. He refilled the pan, solemnly offering it for Jalni to wash her own hands, carefully pouring the tainted water into the sand well away from the pool. He had pulled on leggings and boots, signing the need for four or five more helpers with carts to retrieve the carcasses, when Jalni heard a wild lamentation, followed by feverish chanting.

Instantly she clapped her hands over her ears, as the sobbing ululation arose. She was almost grateful for Orto's affliction meant that he could not hear the prayers to Gatta, could not be corrupted by the overt sexual innuendo promising sacrifice for gratification. The voice rose on the edge of frenzy, until Jalni fairly thrummed with fury. She was praying for it to stop so hard that she almost missed the quavering moan as the wind rose and her sands surrounded her in a shuddering pillar of power. Had she known that she blazed Azure from the corona of her hair to pale bare feet, perhaps she wouldn't have felt so terrified. However, inexorable fate was driving her onward and all she could do was to gasp "Daro!", invoking the name of the Sandsinger in anguished appeal as Gurayen (the wind of her Sands) and those sands themselves pitted her against her most implacable foe.

Renna waited at the edge of the contaminated oasis, as the dark moon Gatta inched towards its zenith. Jalni half lifted, half driven inside a whirling pillar of sand could see streamers like flames surrounding that orb and found herself fancying that the night sky was lighter than the threatening aspect of their second moon. Outlined with rippling tongues of deepest purple it pulsed ominously rising in blackened majesty, dominating the night sky with an awesome display, reflected in the sickened pool below. Jalni found herself listening to the rising chant that poured from the exultant woman who swayed at the waters edge, stark naked, arms lifted to Gatta, she was reciting some litany of evil, as she danced.

Mind struggling to repulse a strange lethargy Jalni cried out in relief as Daro's voice urged.

"Don't look, don't listen, close your mind dearling! Think only of your Sands, hear only the song of sunrise in the crystal, the voice of Gurayen in the dawn.".

She flushed cold, feeling in the contact with the Sand beneath her feet a torrent of pure energy rising. The lazy flicker of the pillar of power changed, roaring around her with renewed vigour as hand in hand with her Lord, Jalni went into battle. She knew that Daro was there, if only in spirit, for she felt his hand close around her arm in its old familiar way. She caught his sunny cinnamon scent and her head lifted proudly.

"Well done dearling.", he murmured, "Now, cut her off from the light of Gatta, permanently!".

She remembered launching herself forward, anchored in faith to her Sands she whirled the wind, chanting his name. The sand pillar rose and spread, no longer a light shield but a battering ram, spreading in height and width before engulfing Renna in its path. Jalni saw the woman draw something out and hurl it towards the pool, but the wind caught it, and tumbled it towards the screaming woman, and then the pillar changed. No longer protecting Jalni, it encapsulated Renna, forcing unwilling feet into the noxious pool, driving her inexorably towards the middle, cutting a swathe in the waters themselves. She stretched her own hands to Jenta, words bubbling to her lips as a silvery gleam answered her plea.

"Extoroth, lumis dey Gurayen!", she pleaded and the brilliance increased until she could see clearly, then the voice of her Lord commanded sternly.

"Atash vauntesh demotrix!", as the water boiled and seethed in the pool. His whispered aside to Jalni made no sense, but she obeyed blindly as he said urgently.

"Seize the Sands dearling. Seize the Sands and don't let go!".

She fell to her knees, thrusting empowered hands into the Sands as they shivered and leapt in her grasp. There was a roaring sound, a hissing like steam, and she opened horrified eyes on a scene out of nightmare. The poisoned pool caught in the spiral of wind was spinning, the sand caught in the squall was cascading, mixing with debris, chuckling glutinously as it fell landwards. Too late Renna del Orto saw the truth as her feet were dragged down. In vain she swore, pleaded and cursed as the quicksand formed beneath her, taking her down, cut off forever from the object of her arcane worship.

"She died as she had lived, bitter, twisted and hating!", Daro murmured in Jalni's ear. "That was bad enough, but she turned her venom on the Sands of your birth and that I could not permit dearling. Beneva has sent Shiarjha to Darnesh. She will be there by evening tomorrow. She will explain my intervention without revealing its source, for I don't think Tirjella could deal with the rise of a practitioner in the dark arts, and with Sandsingers at the same time.".

The wind (or Daro) stroked her hair and kissed her cheek, then he was gone, leaving Jalni to pick up the threads, where only the contaminated oasis remained.

Chapter 16 - A Teaching of Principles

In the crowded bar of the Cross Eyed Zeglur, an irate voice rang into one of those gaps in conversation that draws every attention to the speaker. Jashell, slim as a lance and as beautiful in anger as Patris had ever seen her, stared incredulously at the company of carousing men.

"You celebrate someone deliberately giving his guards the slip in the middle of an emergency?", she demanded, colour mounting to her high cheekbones. "Ichspeller Selunsanni left us needlessly searching Selesh until I followed a hunch. I came to escort him home, only to be told that my lord has taken himself (and the Apothecary our Deshun banished) back to his Eyrie!". Her eyes sparkled dangerously as she spat fury.

"For the love of the One! I have a potential assassin on the loose, and only half the Guard I need. Am I to suppose he turned them both invisible and walked passed a doubled guard without us noticing?".

She stood imperious as ever, feet braced apart, the scarlet cloak of a Commander thrown back to emphasise her remarkable physique. It was all the traders surrounding her could do, to keep their eyes off her magnificent bosom as it rose, almost as dramatically as her temper.

Ignoring the placating offer of, "Ale to slake your thirst Commander?", from the flustered barkeep, she demanded to see the Inn keeper or his wife without delay. Nadra came through a bead curtain, her face pale but determined as she faced the scowling warrior.

"How can I help you Commander Jashell.", Daro's old nurse asked gently, as silence fell over the gathering. Feeling oddly "wrong-footed", Jashell decided to be challenging, and spoke somewhat harshly.

"I suppose you're familiar with Lord Daro's latest escapade?", she demanded, but Nadra refused to be intimidated.

"If that includes a duty visit to this house of mourning Commander, the answer to that is yes.".

There was pride and sorrow in Nadra's voice as she continued defending her nursling stoutly.

"I saw neither how he came, or how he went. Beyond the bar, in which we have been comforted by the constant presence of friends, we have behaved in accordance with the Way, not leaving our home until we felt the time was right to celebrate Ahnell's life. Hearing how bravely my poor boy died has allowed us to face our grief, and if Ahnell's blood brother came to us privately, that was no more than his duty, and no business of our Deshun's Guard.". Her eyes didn't waver before Jashell's as she added.

"In the words of an ancient game, "As Sandsinger's come, so do they go", and it is not for the likes of you and I to question my lord's whereabouts!".

She smiled serenely at the defeated warrior, begging softly.

"Don't scold him Jashell. He told us that his mother and her Sisters in Sorcery are endangered. Your place is to keep our Deshun safe and let Daro look after the rest. He needs only loyalty and love to do his work, not the hindrance of rules and guardrooms.".

As she saw the confidence of love in Nadra's face, Jashell came to a decision. Expending no more energy on the subject, she spoke to Sorrill briskly commanding.

"Exercise abandoned Sub - Commander. Dismiss the Watch extending my compliments. The usual reward will be behind the bar tonight!".

She reached for a small tablet tucked into her belt, sighed, then marked it with her seal ring, tossing it behind the bar to Nadra, who simply inclined her head gracefully, departing to order another of the Commander's kegs to be broached. As the street door announced Jashell's departure, normal conversation filtered through to a discreet corner, where a small shelf hid Nadra's treasures. Smiling tenderly, she kissed the tips of her fingers, touching them to a tiny box that Ahnell had made in celebration of his adoption. Content in the knowledge that she continued her dead son's devotion to his Sandsinger, she went to the kitchen and wept.

In Daro's Eyrie, a muffled snore betrayed the Apothecary's presence. The old man had fallen into a light doze (as the elderly are inclined to do), curled into a chair in Daro's great room. He had tucked his robes around him neatly, accepted a sweetdrink, as the vessel materialised in Daro's hand, and now his gentle relaxation formed a comforting descant to the Sandsinger's troublesome thoughts.

He considered the sparse information bleakly. Ikella had access to magical artefacts and powers which he had no experience or knowledge of. He'd assumed without any great leap of imagination, that one of these was in play at the time of the attack, although due to the dart not penetrating properly, she had barely flinched, unaware of the poisonwood's insidious effects until a day and night later. Another thought crossed his mind.

"What if there was no attack at all? She might just have trodden on a discarded dart!", but in his heart he remained unconvinced and this lack of conviction spilled over into his determined efforts to find a motive for such a betrayal.

"Why would a Ranger try to kill Ikella?", he questioned. "It's pointless, unlikely to succeed and yet it nearly did!".

He frowned, turning ideas around in his head seeking a motive that was compatible with Ranger beliefs, and failed to find one. He shifted restlessly, so many viewpoints to consider, so many lives hanging on his grasp of their principles, belief practices and cultures. He sighed, thinking things through again.

"To attack a Guardian knowingly is suicidal.", he compiled his list of reasons thoroughly. "To attack a Sorceress would bring down retribution on either Clan or Sand and is incompatible with sanity. To attack an elderly woman was incompatible with the Honour of Life, the principle belief structure of the Rangers, so unless I am to believe that such a homicidally inclined Ranger plots not only his own death but the downfall of his race, the whole story becomes so improbable, I can't believe it.".

He started violently as his Songfather applauded, almost as though they had been engaged in conversation.

"I agree my boy! It seems highly unlikely that a Ranger is involved, but someone definitely wants us to think that way.". The old man sat up yawning, pointedly ignoring the suspicion on Daro's face.

He seemed to unfold, tottering to his feet, where he stood stretching luxuriously. He flexed long slender fingers till they snapped and cracked. wriggled his neck, shoulders and back until there was a muffled popping sound and he groaned with relief.

"Sands and shades of stone! I grow old and bone stiff from all this sitting around waiting for you to grow up and realise who holds the balance of power here.", he complained without rancour, "Now you have taught Jashell's crew not to waste their time chasing around after you, what other lessons have you in mind?", and Daro's head tilted in appreciation.

"Perhaps a short teaching in how to avoid upsetting She who settles accounts in Selesh!", he suggested, scoring a palpable hit as his Songfather snorted.

"No doubt using your own success as an example?", and Daro winced, but countered the argument with a sharp protest.

"It's a matter of principle Carolus. I know the truths that you taught me, but she doesn't. To her, I got hurt trying to fulfil what she suspects to be your own crazy dreams! Only I know the truth and I'll defend you where I can, but I can't rescue you if Mother throws you to her Sisters in Sorcery!".

A gladiatorial glean came into his Songfather's face, and he chose his words very deliberately, hoping to provoke a traditional response from his poker-faced Songchild.

"Wouldn't want to be rescued from some of them.", he challenged and Daro chuckled.

"No. I guess you'd endure Deschina and her Maidens and possibly enjoy Idirina's intellectual qualities, but dear man, consider who'll replace Mother if you drive her beyond endurance.".

He shuddered affectedly remembering his last encounter with a particularly precocious young Sorceress-elect, adding thoughtfully,

"Of course, that might be amusing for a while.", with such a malicious grin that Carolus sobered abruptly. He suggested warily, "You'd be surprised at the change in Suraya my boy.", as Daro let out a short crack of laughter.

"I'll lay you a Zeglur to a pound of bread that she'll get more of a shock than I will when we meet again!", the Sandsinger retorted rudely, and triumphantly stuck out his tongue, bringing the friendly contest of wills to an end, as the steady tramp of regimented feet swung into his ante-room, breaking the mood.

Daro stood, one hand delving deep into a tunic pocket, seeking items to remove. It was withdrawn with a little grunt of satisfaction, as a Staff materialised in his other hand. Under the quizzical gaze of his Songfather, Daro allowed the Staff to lead him to what he called his "Trophy Table", reaching out to deposit a handful of unusual coloured stones, a single white feather, and an elaborately pierced ovoid created from a deep glossy blue-black substance. Carolus tutted mildly as Daro tipped the collection into a sand-paste bowl, but Daro ignored him, gently winding a cord threaded through the ovoid into the base, fingertips gleaming suspiciously opalescent as he set the collection in place.

"Quiari.", commanded the mage sternly as some of the stones rolled and settled to anchor the cor, and Carolus grinned, casting a discreet glance at Daro's new collection of souvenirs. At the brisk tap on the door, Daro rolled his eyes, and sighing raised a reluctant hand to admit Jashell.

"Good Sunfall Master's.", she greeted them cheerfully, then turning to Daro she bowed.

"My lord, forgive me but Mina says, you recognised the weapon that was turned on our Deshun. I believe that more information is required before any direct pursuit can be made, but in order to defend Selesh adequately, I need to redistribute the Guard.". The tacit appeal for him to understand the exigencies of her situation was not lost on the Sandsinger, as keeping voice level she continued.

"If my lord will permit the loan of his own Chapter of Guard, I will set about the strengthening of border controls, so would-be assassins won't be encouraged to sneak around Selesh. However, if my lord wishes to assist us in any way?".

Daro was amazed but sensibly kept a straight face. "Selesh Minoria can take care of itself.", he suggested. "Let the Guard look after the barracks, and let the old men be the eyes of the village. They'll love it, particularly if you allow them to parade with the Guard.", he waited while Jashell thought this through and added gently. "They know all the highways and by-ways, all the good hiding places and they could relieve each Watch of finding out who strangers meet or drink with. Their observations won't be so obvious either!".

Jashell grinned in wry recognition of this point, saying thoughtfully, "If they can be persuaded that they are not to challenge or fight, merely to observe and report, we could even use younger men. The "Old Guard will after all need a runner or two!", and so it seemed one of Daro's lessons had been understood, as the air of aggrieved hostility slipped from Jashell's shoulders.

The approving murmurs of both men encouraged her to place a tablet on the table. Daro heard it click on the surface and fought down his frustration.

"Who normally signs orders in my mother's absence?", he asked, as he considered his place in the new hierarchy with unexpected repugnance. Jashell replied.

"Somishen Shiarjha takes care of those responsibilities, but she begged me to consult you, reminding you that she is summoned to Deshun Tirjella's Hall in Darnesh. She told me that you would understand that she travels the Old Path!".

Daro had instantly withdrawn from the reality of that room. Utterly still Opal clad hands held her orders, brilliant Opal glazed eyes stared into infinity, and for a mind-numbing second Jashell felt the edge of a storm sweep over her. Then it was gone as Daro smiled saying apologetically,

"Sorry Jashell, I just needed to check how these get done!", pressing his insignia into the tablet.

"Apparently they think I'm grown up enough to do this, so provided you explain what I'm signing, you can come to me directly. Beneva says that might be easier until Deshun Ikella is recovered. By the way, my revered mother is sitting up, demanding my presence so I shall take these to her, and see what else I retrieve from her memories of returning from the Carnelian Sands. Will you come with me Songfather? Perhaps she will have forgotten her decision by the time we leave her.".

Jashell's face was thoughtful as they rose, but she said nothing until Daro took the Apothecary's arm for guidance. She then said uncertainly, "Don't let her think that I wilfully disobeyed her orders lord. She is usually just, but on one subject, and that is your safety. She blames herself for letting you fall into the hands of Master Carolus. She thinks he gave you ideas, inspired your search for power, creating the situation that cost you both your sight and Ahnell. She cannot see as we Inesh do, this was your destiny.", she knelt suddenly, and Daro found her clinging to his hands.

"Lord, she freed us on your first name day. Don't let her repeal that decision because you brought Carolus into Selesh without her permission!".

He was shocked, saying abruptly, "Never! She would never do that Jashell!", hoping he was right as she departed, taking the duty Chapter with her. He sighed as they turned into the corridor linking the Eyrie to the rest of the community, and said heavily.

"It never occurred to me that Mother might blame you when I returned somewhat impaired. I apologise sincerely for that oversight, but I was a trifle preoccupied at the time.", his rueful chuckle took all solemnity from the words, although Carolus realised that the sentiments expressed were indeed profound. The young voice continued wearily, "I never considered that she might react equally badly if she believes that Jashell deliberately disobeyed her! I shall take steps to inform her otherwise, if she is able to take notice, if not I'll let Beneva know. How is it that helping one person can upset another so badly? It's a nightmare!".

They walked silently towards the sickroom, each sunk in his own thoughts trying to prepare for the next step on this very uncertain Way.

Perhaps they shouldn't have been so concerned, for when Daro entered the room, Ikella only had eyes for him. The Apothecary slipped silently into the preparation room, and taking the nod from Mina, gathered a pestle and mortar to grind the potion she was working on. Ikella, embracing Daro said caustically, "I see you old man, sneaking in when you don't think I'll notice you.", but the words held no sting, so emboldened, Daro gathered her frail hands together and said.

"Don't be such a scold Mother. I heard that you were ill unto death and when I found out that Carolus was not treating you, I ordered him here to see what he could do. He has greatly enhanced experience of places and plants outside our knowledge, so here he is and you must endure his presence for your own good.".

She leant back against her pillows exclaiming "Pshaw and if wishes had wings, Zeglurs would fly!", but submitted suspiciously easily when Carolus left the preparation area and taking her wrists deftly read her pulses. He signalled to Daro (with a subtle tilt of the head), that they should withdraw, but Ikella put a stop to that, remarking severely, "Dear friend, I am too tired to fight all of you, but please confirm if only for this brat's benefit that I have Rotations left yet and Suraya's return is not imminent!", at which Carolus chuckled lightly.

"You are undoubtedly right my Deshun.", he returned, but added firmly, "That is provided you rest, take your medication and nourishment. I have added a little extra to Mina's prescription, which should perk up your appetite. If you are able to sit out of your bed tomorrow and take a turn round the room the day after, you should be able to go back to your own quarters soo.".

She eyed him dourly, saying that she thought a glass of red berry wine would do her more good than any medication, subsiding into her pillows when the Apothecary agreed. He, greatly pleased with this, went to arrange it, while Daro took Ikella's hands and kissed them, saying indulgently, "Dearest, could you manage just a little business if I tell you all that has passed, and you just listen?".

She nodded, so he told her that the Children of Scartel were nearly all accounted for, having relatives to care for them. She listened mutely as he outlined his decision to repatriate Ranger children with the Rangers of Holmgarth, only bringing the last twenty or so with him. She didn't enquire about their disposition so he left that for another day, but showed an interest when he told her that Jalni had acquitted herself admirably. He told her that the Healer had gone to Jerritol to find out about her surviving family, and that Shiarjha was travelling to Darnesh at Tirjella's request. To all of this she nodded comprehension, but showed no particular interest in any of it, lying quietly, holding his hand until Carolus returned with a glass of wine.

She responded to this quite well, her colour rising from faded parchment to faded rose, and it was with a thankful heart that Daro listened to Mina telling his mother how much better she would feel with some food and sleep. The two men crept away as Andria brought in a bowl of soup, but Daro was sufficiently shaken by his mother's frailty, to feel the need for a breath of fresh air. They wandered out into the Gathering Square, just as the summoning bell called End of Day, and drudges, servitors, forge workers, and all poured out behind them. A few noticed Daro and smiled as he wandered arm in arm with the aged

Apothecary into the covered pasture, where they slipped unnoticed into the shadowed arena beyond the traders quarters, and under the strange fluorescence of ancient crystals, made their way silently through ankle high grazing to the far pastures, where a Master Spy waited.

In his permanent tented home, a tall serious faced man noted numbers, using a fine enscrasure on a narrow wax tablet. He held up a silencing hand as Carolus arrived alone, having left Daro stroking a new-born Zeglur in the paddock. Olneth was frowning over his entries, muttering somewhat obliquely, "That's ten in the last ninenight!".

Carolus was at his side almost immediately, taking the tablet and demanding sharply, "Who?", then a moment later he strode to a scroll map weighted down on a table. They stared down gloomily, until Carolus announced.

"Daro must be told. I can't see how, but I'm sure it connects with this attempt on Ikella's life.".

His finger traced a line which intersected with the unmistakeable outline of Mount Darnesh. He looked searchingly at Soloria's one-time Captain of Guard and asked.

"Ten exiles with blameless reputations have gone to Darnesh, for no apparent reason in the last few ninenights. Do you think someone stirs sleepers?". He frowned irritably then as a thought crossed his mind, he bent over the map again chewing a lip as his fingers flew over the parchment, until a mildly amused voice enquired.

"Did you call me old man?", and Daro appeared Staff in hand, as Olneth stared guiltily at the map.

"Trouble?", he enquired, to which Olneth said defensively, "Yes lord, and to my shame, my Clansmen may be involved.".

Daro leant over the map table where Carolus brooded. The story was simple enough, Olneth's "spotters" had traced unaccountable movements of Sybillsce refugees. Like Olneth himself, they had been exiled from the Amethyst Sands at Partition. Men and women who had no sympathy with the unhappy Sorceress who had brandished her heresy in Ikella's face on acceding to the Staff, now they had to know if Adruna had planted them in the Opal, and for what purpose they travelled.

Daro's Staff remained quiescent until he placed a hand on the map, then the Heart of Selesh woke, flickering through subtle shades until it settled on a delicate blue. Nodding to himself, the young mage held his free hand over the map, and beneath his hand, it sprang to life. From lines on parchment miniature mountains grew, great fissures opened and movement became apparent.

Olneth shrank away from the table, his face alight with wonder as he saw something bright moving along the Azure Sands bordering the Great Divide. At his suppressed gasp, Daro said calmly, "That's Shiarjha, travelling the Sheer!".

Carolus (who had simply bent closer to the living map), grunted.

"With one Guardian the victim of a poisonwood dart, is it right to entrust another to the Rangers so soon?", but Daro forebore comment, for the light of the Staff had revealed a number of glittering strands, all leading to Darnesh, all Amethyst in colour.

Carolus hissed, and leant forward peering down thoughtfully. He tracked a ridge that crossed the desert, towards Mount Darnesh, then swooped away towards a darkened hollow that glittered abnormally. Olneth (forgetting his awe of magic) stepped in whispering, "Simlan's Spring?", to an emphatic nod from the Apothecary.

"Yes...", that worthy agreed, watching his Songchild warily, for there was the most unholy expression of glee on the mage's face. "Its an odd, out of the way oasis. Very rarely used, but useful if you come off the old track to Darnesh. It had unusual mineral properties if I remember correctly, but unless you were a dyer, or wanted to grow Ritash, the water was only good for animals, or patients with bowel blockage! It fell into disuse after the Storm (which had in any case half buried it), but now it shows Amethyst black.".

He stared at the place contemplatively, then Daro sighed and straightened, the light in his eyes fading as his power-stone slept atop his Staff, and the map shifted back to parchment once more.

"Yes.", he agreed, "All that is perfectly true my friends, but there is more, and none of it good!".

Touching the dimly gleaming Seguidor hanging round his neck, Daro breathed deeply then, seemingly refreshed, settled back on the divan which had witnessed many strange events in his life. Carolus (perched on a nearby stool), said encouragingly,

"Seems to me that you've some idea of what's going on in the Azure?".

Daro didn't reply for a moment, concentrating on dematerialising his Staff, swapping it for a mug filled with stemmis, but as similar drinking vessels appeared in his companions hands, Olneth recoiled, to a chorus of, "Don't drop it!", as the spy blinked uneasily at the steaming contents, before joining his friends, to hear Daro's theories.

Daro gained his companion's rapt attention by explaining Jalni's experience as simply as he could. The youthful voice grew animated over Echo's part in the tale, but when Daro laid bare the effects of the Heart of Darkness, his Songfather grew stern.

"If dark power was concentrated, fed by ritual sacrifice, then subjected to particular influence, it might create a vortex. Height of Jenta last night leads to a very propitious aspect with Gatta, and given the use of an artefact of such power ...", the old man's voice tailed away and he shuddered. There was horror in eyes that Olneth had never seen burn with such lambency, as Daro sighed and rose to his feet.

"Don't worry about that. I am certain that they have lost the artefact. Thanks to the impatience of an unstable woman, they failed to pull together all the elements to establish a well of evil. The artefact is in safe hands and the one who tried to use it, fell into quicksand and died.".

Daro's face had assumed his "set in Opalstone" look, that had so enchanted his mother once, and Olneth shuddered as the mage spoke in a voice devoid of all emotion.

"In the vast deserts of our world there are remnants of the world from which we are descended. With such remains there are secrets, valuable beyond compare. Imagine knowing not a day would pass in which you would be hungry, cold, every day filled with choices. Wine, water, women, food on the table, and plenty for all. Imagine finding power beyond your wildest dreams. In the heat finding cold, in the cold finding warmth, and knowledge beyond anything available today. Such power in the hands of one committed to good is frightening enough, but in the hands of one committed to self-gratification?".

Olneth stared at the boy he had known from childhood and trembled, moistening dry lips as he asked in a whisper.

"Do you talk of Sorcery my lord? Or...", his voice tailed away uncertainly as Daro chuckled derisively.

"Olneth my devoted one! I speak of the power called the Source, of Sandsingers and Sorcery, of pure minds and corruption, and the principles of balance. I speak of a time when all men and women could feel the power, when it was woven into the very fabric of society. Of a time when the Sands were clean, and knowledge freely shared by all castes. I am the first step back to such a world, but first, I must deal with those who would destroy our world from within.", he held up a silencing hand.

"Through a quirk of synchronicity one threat has been removed, although the cost in lives has been far too high. Shiarjha will comfort a group of very disappointed Sybillsce who I believe were lured towards Simlan's Spring with the promise of messages from loved ones.".

He read the astonishment from his companions easily. "I don't imagine everyone of Olneth's Clan to be a follower of the dark path.", he said softly, as Carolus propounded a terrifying explanation.

"Is it possible that she planned to massacre the exiles? If she could somehow implicate the Rangers as the attempt on Ikella seems to have done, such an act would not only teach those who rebel a terrible lesson, but would establish the fact that although shunned she can reach far beyond locked borders..".

Daro, voice oddly taut said thoughtfully, "to add to our problems, some act of arcane serendipity contrives to place Draille Skellin, Ranger leader as Shiarjha's chosen guide. Thus placing him in Darnesh at precisely the time that suits Gattarene causes best! ", and the complexity of events was revealed.

There was a hiss as Olneth tallied effects. "Shnah mahj.", he swore fluently, sounding doubly foreign to sensitive ears.

"A Guardian murdered in the Carnelian Sands. Poisonwood used on the victims of this Heart of Darkness, including Zurians and Sybillsce. Another Guardian at risk. The Clans would turn on the Rangers and each other!!".

Daro's face was bleak as he said slowly.

"Unthinkable isn't it? However, one thing becomes obvious. The Gattarene has followers abroad in other Sands. All we have to do is to identify and deal with them. I can assure you that the Heart of Darkness has been rendered unusable, and placed somewhere very safe! Olneth, you may travel to Darnesh, consult your fellow Clansmen, it will suit my purpose if they know how close they came to becoming victims of the Gattarene plot. Tell them they are welcome to return and see what you can make of them.".

Then, ignoring the catch of breath in his Songfather's throat, Daro returned to his own cogitations. Making a circle of thumb and forefinger, he searched the Azure Sands with the eye of his mind, and found his love, his Azure rising snoring gently on the shoulder of his friend Orto, who strode towards the main street of Jerritol, carrying the exhausted girl in his arms, careless of who saw the Mystcat prowling at his heels.

Chapter 17 - A Lesson in Forgetfulness

When the visitor arrived at the Weaver's Halt in Jerritol, she had been preceded by a score of gossips from the marketplace. With dignified discretion, Orana endured their curious solicitude for the Steward, the Weavers, "old Aunt Taccobi and all, then shut the door on spurious melodramas connecting unnerving shrieks and dead seobras to their house. Retreating to her kitchen (with mounting dismay), she was immediately pursued by yet another knock at the front door.

Snatching it open, she revealed a man whose patch dyed blues blurred the distinction between his shoulders and the desert horizon beyond. Fascinated, she'd "frozen" in mid greeting allowing him to slip in. With only a murmured, "By your leave Mistress?", he'd checked the immediate area then returned to usher in a woman who swept past into the garden with neither greeting nor explanation.

"Just a slip of a girl too! As if they owned the place themselves.", Orana protested indignantly to Madiv seconds later. but the Steward remained calm. He tidied his work into a drawer, laid down his quill and stoppered the ink he'd only just made with a sigh, and rose to join her.

"They might bear messages for Mistress Jalni.", he observed, but stopped by the garden door, with an odd expression on his normally well schooled face.

"Well?". Orana seeing herself as Jalni's only female protector, was agitating at his elbow. "Is Jalni there, or shall I find her?".

Madiv stepped to one side so that she could see that the blue clad stranger blocked not only their path into the garden, but their view of it as well. Flushing angrily, she would have bypassed him via the garden room, but Madiv indicating a silver seal fixed to the frame, gently propelled her back down the passage to her kitchen where she demanded.

"Who are they Madiv? Why are you submitting to this invasion? Have they any right to treat Weaver business as their own?".

"Sssh Orana.", Madiv said testily. "Let me think. Its not often we are host to one who commands a Ranger! I think perhaps our Holder has friends in high places. Now, have you made bread?".

Refusing to speculate, he insisted Orana prepare to entertain, while he, (ignoring her resentment), hovered in the doorway positively quivering with curiosity.

They heard Jalni's voice, followed by a deep chime as the visitors re-entered the garden-room. Shortly thereafter, soft chanting filled the hallway, then two voices entwined in shivering harmony, (the soft rolling weave of *othervoice* to *othervoice*). Doors opened and shut as the sound cascaded out into the garden, over to the old storeroom, then on, out into the Weaver's quarters until, with the bustle of the street, it quietly disappeared. The other sounds of the day filtered into the house as Orana stopped holding her breath, and sagged against the settle with a hiss.

"What on this plain of Sorrow was that?", she demanded but Madiv had no answer, for none had ever heard a Guardian perform a ritual exorcism. When it was over the soft burr of voices returned to the garden room, and Orana turned as Edrith stuck his head through the half-opened doorway.

"Mistress Jalni asked if you could rustle up some ginger and citrine tea before her guests push on to Darnesh? She wants to demonstrate your skill with the blending Orana, and asks Madiv and Villeth to join you, so take the flour off your nose woman!".

He grinned at the expression on his wife's face, then retreated, as wondering who in Azure graced their home, Orana bore a tray of refreshments into a room flooded with light. Shutters, (closed since Rowin's death) had been opened to let the sights and sounds of the garden dominate. A gentle breeze rattled leaves against the unglazed frame, and the Ranger leant against the wall, drinking in the sunlight. Sat on a low bench under the window was a young woman in a silver robe, Jalni at her feet.

Bobbing conventional greetings, Orana laid her tray on a side table, before a strange idea possessed her. She'd compiled a list including Healers, Tutors, even the Council of Nine, but had never considered a Sorceress as a likely visitor before, and couldn't resist a furtive glance. She saw hair double braided in Sanctuary's tradition, an Opal *redic* suspended on a smooth brow, and warming drinking bowls automatically, continued to wonder whose purpose they served.

Jalni came to her apologetically.

"Dear Orana, I'm afraid we've put your routine through the wringer. With a disturbed night, half Jerritol gossiping, topped by visiting Guardians, I must be quite beyond redemption.".

She grinned over her shoulder saying provocatively, "Seris Shiarjha, you will have to report me sadly awry when you next see your Sister Guardian. It may cheer her to know that although I do my best to obey her commands, I will ever be a scapegrace!".

Staring in disbelief, Orana heard a sympathetic resonance in Shiarjha's voice as it bubbled with hidden laughter.

"I will certainly tell her that you tumble headlong into mischief the moment her eye is off you my dear. You see if I don't! Now, let me try this miraculous remedy for myself. Will you make it to Orana's instruction while I watch?".

Orana supervised as Jalni selected a very fine Azure tinted bowl and cut three slivers of fresh citrine. Crushing the juice into the steaming infusion, she added porrisroot sap to sweeten the drink, then taking a deep spoon from her pouch, she sampled the result. Accepting the bowl, Shiarjha remarked softly,

"Daro may set his own traditions, but employing a food taster isn't one of mine.".

145

Abruptly changing the subject, Jalni introduced her Uncle, her Steward and Orana with possessive pride. As Shiarjha sipped her drink, the men made their bows, Orto's hands flickering in swift signs. Then Orana made her curtsy and was rewarded by Shiarjha's particularly sweet smile.

"Orana, I am sorry that you have been so upset by recent events. Shall we forget all that and talk only of your skill with this infusion? I wonder if you would permit me to use the recipe to tempt patients lost appetites.".

Shiarjha's steady grey eyes dominated Orana's bemused mind, her soft implacable voice guiding troubled thoughts with consummate ease as she invited, Tell me, can it be made with dried ingredients?".

Caught in the grip of Shiarjha's power, Orana forgot fear, trepidation and death as she explained the infusing process. They debated the merits of steeping Seerus pods in the boiling water to "smooth" the tang of ginger, as the ambiance of that unhappy room changed and Orana, focussed on shimmering wristlets ceased to worry about Renna or her apprentices.

"After all, they are at liberty to take their skills where they want to aren't they?", she argued with Edrith later, "I think it very mean spirited of the girl to go without so much as a by your leave, but I'm more worried about Jalni. She's really unsettled, even though she has leave of absence, she doesn't seem to know where she belongs, although it was kind of her friends to call on us.".

Edrith nodded from the comfort of the settle in the main kitchen. All was quiet, Height of Sun had cleared the streets, even the visitors had gone. Madiv had seen them off in company with Villeth del Orto and young Jalni. The weavers had cleared the spare billet and now slept in the forenoon. In the desert Gurayen blew Sand over the tracks. In his workroom Madiv prepared a report for the Guild and in the kitchen Edrith settled himself to snooze. He would take over Madiv's duty, once the sun was off the Sands. Now he drifted into a speculative doze, dreaming of working examples for a new Weft of apprentices. Hoping their Weaver would be less abrasive than the woman whose name he had already forgotten, he closed his eyes and slept.

Chapter 18 - The Return to Other Ways?

Having successfully stolen the household's memories of Renna's fate, Shiarjha slipped away towards the next task, thanking the One for Jalni's impassioned cry for help. Now all she had to do was to soothe Tirjella's jangled nerves, find out what subsequent issues troubled Beneva, and obey Daro's exhortation to protect and guide Jalni! Smiling wryly, she wondered how many more impossible tasks she could undertake before supper and clung grimly to the sway backed, shuffle footed Zeglur, as Draille coaxed it into a run.

When they swung abruptly off the track beneath Mount Darnesh, directly into a Gathering Square, she gulped in surprise. Unguarded, open to the skies, it stood, surrounded by huge stone buildings, free of the massif, yet connected, as if sculpted from its rocky heart.

Discreetly applying just a film of power to assist her understanding, her eyes sought familiar features, and it was with a chill recognition, she realised she saw Selesh without an approach, the Gate in the Rock, or entrance tunnel.

"Without the great outer cavern at all.", she murmured, and Draille Skellin, plainly in tune with her train of thought murmured in reply.

"Indeed Seris Shiarjha, we have always known something very terrible must have driven us to hide below stone, but I keep praying that we can all regain the open lands and skies without fear, though perhaps not in this much company.".

Darnesh bustled around them, everything exposed. An open forge, a community kitchen, men herding animals, and suddenly revolted by noise and confusion, Shiarjha longed for the peace of her enclosed community.

The Ranger interpreting her sudden pallor correctly, spoke to a passing drudge.

"Can you deliver a message to the Healers?", he asked, producing a ripe greenfruit from a saddlebag to tempt the grubby child. She peered at him distrustfully, then gave a quick nervous nod.

"Which Healer?", she asked, looking relieved when Draille replied, "The first one you meet?".

"What message?", she muttered, as Draille (eyeing her judiciously) decided to keep it simple.

"Just find a Healer and tell her to come to the Square on Guild business.", he suggested. She repeated, "Guild business?", then Draille put the greenfruit into her hand. She retreated, holding it out of his reach, and demanded, "All of it?", not giving him chance to change his mind.

When he agreed, she swooped away triumphantly exclaiming "Mine!", as she went in search of a Healer.

Less than half a sector later, a young Healer approached, becoming huge-eyed and less than graceful, as Shiarjha revealed her wristlets. Thankfully recovering her equilibrium swiftly, she escorted them up a shallow flight of steps into another level, where the hurly-burly atmosphere of the Gathering Square faded into insignificance. The young escort hesitated as they entered a waiting area, but Draille needed no prompting. He fell back, leaving Shiarjha in familiar surroundings and went to stand peering back down the short ascent as if he hankered for the open air. Shiarjha (knowing that he watched for Jalni and Orto who had fallen behind), allowed the novice to precede her, through carefully fitted doors into the familiar antiseptic scents of an Infirmary. Her young escort paused for a fraction mustering memory then turned with the briefest of smiles to announce formally:

"Guardian, Deshun Tirjella is on her way here already. She comes to see a patient whose case is so desperate, she will welcome your advice.".

The pale face flushed with the impropriety of her next sentence, but she pursued the matter, doggedly determined to do the best for both her patient, and Sorceress.

"It would be the greatest kindness to the patient's mother, who has already lost more than anyone should be expected to…", and broke off, blushing under Shiarjha's raised eyebrows. A child of no more than fifteen Rotations, she raised beseeching eyes to Shiarjha, adding ingenuously, "I'm Adeya should you need my name.", then lifting her chin and summoning serenity of expression, she slipped into a room two doors to the left.

Shiarjha solemnly studied her surroundings, forcibly reminded of Selesh and another student Healer not so far away, resolving as she did so to ask Tirjella to keep a watch on Jalni. This introspective mood was soon broken by the rapid slap of approaching sandals as Tirjella arrived, followed by a senior Healer. Letting her companion precede them through the door, Tirjella confided rapidly.

"I have never been so relieved to see you Shiarjha. My Sands are much disturbed with murder, mayhem and missing messages, alongside a triple tragedy which I doubt my ability to prevent.".

She opened the door into an anteroom, briskly stripping off her robes and stepping into tan workwear, reaching for a pot of sithabalm as she explained soberly.

"Three major events brought about my request for assistance.".

She briskly enumerated, whilst cleaning her arms.

"One. We experienced a local fluctuation in the Source, so brief it might not have happened, but for the toll of Tekrun's Bell.".

She studied Shiarjha's reaction judiciously, for the Sister's of Sorcery seldom remarked on the ancient artefact which accorded magical significance to otherwise common events. After a brief pause she continued.

"Two. (Which brings Selesh into the circle of events). Mina's ward returning to Jerritol with her Uncle, discovered the massacre of a drove. Every human, every animal dead, with no obvious cause!".

The Sorceress turned bright knowing eyes on Shiarjha, and slathered her arms with antiseptic gel, as she mused aloud.

"Is it coincidence I wonder that in the night there are infernal sounds that cause sheer terror in the most placid beasts, or that at least twenty high ranking Sybillsce of the old order have taken up residence in the area? The dark gathers Shiarjha and if it gathers in my Sands, I will need Sanctuary's help. I hope your news is better?"

Shiarjha crossed her fingers, wishing Jalni and her adventures at world's end, but remarked easily enough. "I know Tirjella, I have already caught up with the events by dropping into Jerritol on my way through. Thinking she might need your protection, I have brought Jalni and her Uncle with me, but they can wait your pleasure. We have more immediate matters to deal with.".

The sound of desperate sobbing had come from the sickroom as Shiarjha opened the door, so Tirjella could go to her patient. The Sorceress confided in a low voice, as they passed within.

"Sarann is one of the drover's women. She took a knife to her wrists, not wanting to live, or bear the child he left her.".

"Show me.", Shiarjha commanded and at her steely tone, Tirjella led her into a discreetly screened area of a treatment room, where a girl (almost as bleached as the sheets) groaned, feebly clutching her belly with closely bandaged hands. Positioning herself to examine the girl, Tirjella nodded discreetly at the woman who wept over her, and Shiarjha led her away, as Healers silently stripped the bed. Sobbing, Sarann's mother clung to her daughter with terrified eyes, and it was some time before the Guardian could focus her attention on providing answers, but finally she blurted,

"Sarann's pains? They came before the drove, when it wanted three sectors to middle night. Her father thought it better that Joem (her little brother) and Markay (her husband) went with him as helpers, so we were alone when word came through.". The tight pinched voice was shamed as she agonised.

"Don't let Sundreth take my daughter into the dark Lady! He already stole our men.".

The weary hopeless voice faltered, as Shiarjha eased her feet on to a stool, and went back to watch Tirjella tenderly palpating Sarann's belly. Silently taking pulses at temple points, Shiarjha joined the brief consultation in the ante-room. Tirjella's voice was bitter.

"She carries twinlings, the labour is barely established, but she is too weak with blood loss to survive. So, do you have any ideas Shiarjha?".

The young Guardian spoke cautiously, "If I prepare, I might delay her labour long enough. First I need a wash, and time to gather my thoughts. Will you excuse me?". Thus instructed, Adeya took her two doors down the corridor to the facilities she'd requested. Shiarjha lost no time in instructing the novice further, as she sat at a long mirror, contemplating (with some trepidation) her next course of action. Finally she commanded.

"Adeya, summon my Ranger, telling him to bring the grey carrisack to this door. Fetch an enscrasure and message tablet at the same time please.".

As swiftly as the novice departed, Shiarjha stripped, washing in cleansing solution. Binding her hair back tightly, she focused her thoughts on the Opal she wore and found herself chanting an appeal.

"Serinahm Selunsanni, Ichspeller Selunsanni, Serinahm Selunsanni…". The Opal warmed and Daro was there in her mind, with no need for explanations.

"How do we heal Sarann?", she asked, intrigued as he replied cryptically, "Why not ask the Ranger at your door?", as Shiarjha drew on her workwear, then opened the door, commanding the Healer briskly.

"Adeya, my carrisack contains items for the birthing room. Please lay the contents on a steam-clean tray, cover it, then send word to Healer Jalni that she will be needed later. Tell her to wait for me in the study Hall.".

She took the Ranger to Sarann's sickroom saying abruptly, "Come, you are needed.".

Searching the man's calm brown eyes with no further hesitation she confided, "Daro told me to "ask the Ranger at my door" how to treat one who tried to end her life by slashing her wrist's.". She elaborated as she cleansed her hands once more, watching the sympathetic creases in his face deepen before demanding urgently:

"She is set apart from any treatment we can provide, for we no longer practice or teach the methods of surgery. However, to defeat the dark, Sanctuary must accept its revival. If we are willing to learn another Way, will the Rangers share that knowledge?".

He looked long into her eyes before he spoke.

"Write the words of Sanctuary Guardian, and Saharn will take them through the Sheer to the one who must decide if our links with the Sands can be forged again.".

This reply was non-committal but encouraging until he added, "I must see this woman if I am to convey the details accurately, but will she accept our help?".

She opened the door saying quietly, "You can ask her mother.", the Guardian instructed, turning away from the screened bed, closely followed by the Ranger. Tirjella (sill chanting quietly), blinked as the man in blue went to Sarann's mother and knelt, taking her hands in his. After a moment her dull eyes fastened on his face and she whispered his name.

"Ranger Skellin? Something dreadful happened …", and the dry horror that had held her frozen melted as she choked on her husband's name, repeating it like some mantra. "Ranir…", she sobbed, "O Ranir, Joem, Markay…all gone, all gone.".

The Ranger's thumbs smoothed the backs of her hands, deftly working tension points, soothing her sorrow with his calming voice.

"Hush. Hush, Meriend. We'll look after you. Its time to sleep, so you can help your daughter and her babes".

The low hypnotic timbre of his voice crooned suggestively, "Sleep safely Meriend, sleep…Sleep and forget your pain. Sleep my friend, you are in safe hands.".

Exhaustion took her, eyes rolling helplessly as he swung her up on to his shoulder. It took little more than a flickering glance at her Healers, then Draille Skellin was led from the room with his unconscious burden, to the sound of Tirjella's satisfied announcement.

"The shock has stopped the birth pangs. Sarann also sleeps.", but her eyes still lingered on the door that Draille had just passed through, thoughtfully.

She slid her stool back from the bed, dimming the night glows, whispering instructions to the Healers who came to sit by Sarann, then Tirjella led Shiarjha through a connecting door into her rest room, throwing herself down on a bench muttering under her breath.

"Poor child doesn't stand a chance!", then catching sight of Shiarjha's expression, she admitted gruffly.

"Go on Shiarjha. I know I often question the Way. I just wish that there was someone who knew more than I. Someone who could help, bring justice, or a cure for that poor child!".

Much relieved Shiarjha swiftly raised a hand towards a long robing mirror, in which a flickering stream of light formed, filling the centre with gleaming mist. Beyond this, the familiar image of the Council Chamber in Selesh appeared, behind the worried features of Beneva who frowned, saying crossly,

"Curse this fogginess, Shiarjha. I suppose you can hear and see me? The One only knows we have the devil of a sandstorm running down the rift at the moment.".

Shiarjha said patiently. "More pressing concerns take precedence Beneva. Recent events involving Jalni have been settled and I have brought her, with her uncle to report to Clan and Guild. I have requested the help of the Rangers to assist Tirjella in undoing the work that Jalni interrupted. It is time for everyone to turn unique knowledge to saving this world, rather than jealously guarding information to the detriment of others.".

Shiarjha continued solemnly.

"The Heart of Darkness would have swept all our beliefs away on a tide of terror. Even one life saved from such evil must be worth the attempt. In that light we ask Tirjella to search her heart and ask those who follow another Way to contrive what we cannot. Remember, we once held such knowledge and practised it ourselves, so we cannot condemn the use of practical magic if it undoes the aim of evil.".

Beneva said softly. "As we were taught by those who preceded us, the time would come when the knowledge of the ancients might be used to save us from annihilation. We, who have been trained to recognise the symptoms of decline must act in accordance with our beliefs, to preserve life, and honour the One. Proceed in faith my Sister Guardian and may the One watch over us in all we do!".

Just the wisdom of the words she spoke settled the matter. Tirjella nodded agreement as Beneva concluded this strange meeting, and as the image of Beneva faded and the mirror cleared, Shiarjha turned to Tirjella ruefully.

"Jalni waits for us in the Hall of the Weavers. Your healers will hold the threads of Sarann's life in their keeping until the Rangers arrive, with Beneva's help. She's been working on remote healing techniques quite successfully during Eshima's recent decline. Look!".

In the mist of the mirror, another image formed, Sarann's bed bathed in light, the girl sleeping naturally. Then the light in the room shrank to bathe her body, as a gentle thrumming beat began. The liquid melancholy of Beneva's voice drifted gentle as a tide of tears, wrapping the girl in a cocoon of sorrow.

As they left, the Sorceress said softly, "I forgot how amazing Beneva is. How wise not to turn Sarann from tears, but to support them, understand and work beyond them.".

They regarded each other sombrely, then Shiarjha spoke. "There will be time to explain everything later Tirjella. We have no time to cover the ground before Sarann wakes, and I must undergo a Teaching of Tapestries before tonight, for such was the advice that sent me here. So my Sister in Sorcery, lead me to your Hall of Weavers and let me learn what I can.!".

However, the lesson was not for her, but for Jalni who patiently waited in the depths of Darnesh.

Chapter 19- The Teaching of Tapestries

In the vaults where the Weaver Guild had placed their repository, Jalni felt a strange pulsing in her blood. Whiling away the time since Orto left her here, she had applied to read the dyers daybook, which was nearer to her own inclinations than the plying of thread. Soon absorbed in recipes that included ground minerals in combination with plant and animal extracts, she ruefully recalled her childish disgust at using human urine to make the fateful blue dye that had led her to seek safety in Selesh. Sat in one of the study booths, her own notation tablet in front of her and the fine parchment pages of the daybook open, she steadily refreshed her memory of dyer symbols, occasionally raising a hesitant hand to Master Dyer Grovan who presided here.

He, noting the symbols tattooed on her hands, had known instantly who she was and had greeted her with astonishing deference, begging her indulgence while he sketched them.

"For posterity my dear.", he had exclaimed in delight, and Jalni had found herself laughing up at him, submitting to having her hands impressed on a fine wax sheet and the precise position of every motif recorded.

Orto had gone to the Weaver Guild with a closely written parchment supplied by Shiarjha. Jalni smiled grimly, imagining the confusion once the Master's accepted that another del Orto (with a far stronger claim than hers) survived. Grateful that Shiarjha had persuaded the Steward that the less the Guild knew about sabotaged looms and unnatural death, the better for the Halt's continuance, she turned back to her studies, considering the Steward as a far from reluctant ally.

Madiv, accepting Shiarjha's advice that the distress of the previous night was better forgotten, had never noticed when the Guardian "smudged" the memories she had culled from his well ordered mind, leaving only the image of Renna vaulting the garden wall, and the Weaver's spiteful tongue as Orto's prior claim on the Halt emerged.

Shiarjha, ruthlessly eliminated every recollection of unexplained death. Removing (in the course of the morning rituals) all physical evidence whilst "exorcising" the Halt. As the void was replaced by delighted acceptance of Orto's return, Jalni waited, aware of a rising sense of anticipation but still relaxed until a small retinue entered the far end of the Hall.

She stood, wriggling stiff limbs as she watched a positive throng of Masters (Weavers in blue, and Dyers in bronze), fall in behind Tirjella. Body throbbing with anticipation, Jalni waited as Tirjella, then Shiarjha were ushered into view by the Master preceding them. He walked along the bank of desks, leading the party directly to Master Grovan, who solemnly produced a massive key and dropped into the procession behind the Weaver. Jalni snuffed the glow over her desk then, folded the stitched parchment of the day-book and left it on Grovan's desk, as she fell into step behind Shiarjha.

Leaving the dyer's study Hall, they turned into a long well-lit passageway, that culminated in the huge doors that Edrith and Madiv had describe so eloquently. Suppressing a gasp at the immensity of the outer framework, she almost danced with curiosity through the inset door, into the treasury of Darnesh.

In the shadows of the dimly perceived cavern, only the echoes of their feet gave credence to the reported enormity of this vault. However, when their guide paused, waiting for the visitors with barely concealed impatience, something about his inner excitement stirred Jalni's soul as though he was physically engaged in raising her expectations with his urgent strides. Then, they turned into a dimly lit recess, and found themselves mounting a series of shallow steps, as the Master turned and addressed them, the timbre of his voice lowered by emotion.

"Look up Gentles all. Look up at the skills of Weaver's and Dyers long past.". This whispered exhortation was followed by strict instructions.

"Let me advise you that the light we can provide is very restricted. We have no way (other than taking each tapestry to our examining rooms) to display these wonders in the light of day. In fact, this would be so destructive to their integrity that the Guild forbids any research other than those carried out by Master's trained in preservation of ancient fabric. However, at the request of the Guardians, we have permitted this examination. Deshun Tirjella, Seris Shiarjha, Healers, apprentices and all must submit to the instruction of Master Weaver Arrell, Master Weaver Madiv, Master Dyer Ollarun, and Master Dyer Shern. Only gloved hands may touch the fabrics, and then only when and where instructed.".

His voice, though formal and utterly inflexible still hid a hint of mischief and Jalni was keenly aware that he anticipated their reaction with almost the same wonder that he had undoubtedly experienced himself, at the first sight of the treasures in his care. Then Tirjella raised her Staff, and the cavern was flooded with light.

There was a faint stir above them, a sibilance whispered in a thousand voices, rippling down the Rotations as though every Weaver and Dyer involved was trying to tell her something. Jalni stared up at the first Tapestry, open mouthed. It hung suspended on a frame, which curiously hinged seemed to tilt the weaving so that the immensity of the project became obvious. Struggling to marshal her thoughts as they soared, touching here and there on individual motifs, she found they fluttered away before she could grasp their meaning. Shiarjha's pointing finger finally underlined the realisation that what she saw related to the Opal Sands, but this was not the place she knew so well.

She peered up in blank dismay. Mount Torrenesh seemed smaller, the Highlands had shrunk and whoever provided the design had filled the great southern desert with something that glittered suspiciously like water. The strange pulsing in her blood increased as she lifted her hands, palms upwards, sensing a radiance from the weaving. The faint tingle in her palm, flushed through the tattoos that had carried the secret of her mother's blue dye into Ikella's protection, then the next tapestry was swung into place, but not before Jalni's mind recognised what was wrong with the Opal image.

"No Divide!", she thought abruptly, then suddenly felt a blossoming along her spine, her entire body quivered and Daro whispered in the depths of her inner mind.

"Dear heart.", he chuckled indulgently, "You're looking at images composed long before that rift was visible. Now use your brains my girl and remember for me.".

The hot hungry hands of her intellect searched every inch of every Tapestry as they appeared in order. The riftless Opal with its glittering field, flecked with symbols she couldn't interpret. The astonishing Azure, riven with flames issuing from a mountain that could only be Scartel, suspended amidst a border of buzzy bugs, vetali plants inside another glittering band that seemed to flash and ripple. As that was superseded by a Tapestry so green it caught the breath in her throat, Jalni saw the very image that she had shown Tjerri as she died her lonely death in Selesh. Framed in towering trees flyby's danced, glittering mountain peaks shimmered a stream of sparkling threads down one border and in that torrent strange creatures played.

Jalni held up her hands to each Tapestry, drinking in the strange sensation of feeling wet, when she knew she was dry. Hearing again and again that rhythmic rushing sound, and as Tapestry after Tapestry passed in a glorious suffusion of colour and confusion, the one thing that linked all nine, was the powerful lure of the continuously present theme of water. She felt thralled by the teasing glimmer, thrust into some world she couldn't comprehend. There were many symbols to pursue, ideas competed for instant attention, and through it all came the pulse. It was so powerful, so demanding that she felt drowned by its surge in her blood. Instinctively, she "knew" that in the threads that glittered so alluringly there was a message for all the Sands. Drunk on a surfeit of impressions, she followed the slightly dazed contingent back to the Healer Hall, before retiring to sleep the short practiced "cat-nap" of trained healer before Shiarjha called her to duty once more.

The sand-glass turned four times after Sunfall, before Adora, the new Senior Healer of Darnesh woke her with a whisper.

"Healer Jalni, I have roused Seris Shiarjha already. Deshun Tirjella requires our assistance at a birthing this night, and it is at her behest I invite you to join her supper table before the event.".

She grinned as Jalni grimaced, adding sympathetically, "I know it is hard to force oneself to eat before duty, but you can't get faint during a twin labour. My lady asked if you would assist the children's team?", and as Jalni dressed to obey, Adora recounted Sarann's story.

"After supper, change into workwear with me and I'll show you the drill and where everything is to be found. We are on the other side of the birthing suite, where we have moved Sarann. Seris Shiarjha is consulting on this and begs your attendance also. A Ranger contingent is taking charge because of the circumstances. It will be very strange having men about a birthing suite, but Deshun Tirjella has agreed.".

They left Jalni's room, turning into a private refectory on the same floor. Tirjella was dipping bread into soup, and Shiarjha nibbled half-heartedly on a slice of greenfruit, but Jalni felt sick. Her head pounded as though still filled with rushing water.

Remembering the twists of citrine and ginger she had in her pouch, she obtained a pot of boiling water, and steeped the mixture, regretting her lack of porrisroot, as her hands paused in frustration. Shiarjha gazing wistfully at Jalni's preparations, produced a familiar shaped root and a grater with a grin, and Jalni immediately brewed two more cups and placed them in front of her seniors. All three sipped in companiable silence then Tirjella said abruptly.

"I always make a birth plan with my mothers. How strange it feels that Sarann's wishes are unknown to me. Will Meriend know what she wanted to call her babies? Did she know that she bears twinlings?", but neither of them could answer her and she subsided muttering.

"Seems to me that we'd be better healing those wrists, getting her more hydrated before we plan on live births. I only hope that the one they call Kilda is as skilled as Ranger Skellin professes, otherwise your Rangers have come a long way for nothing Shiarjha.".

Jalni didn't betray by so much as a blink that she knew nothing about the Ranger involvement, keeping her knowledge of their Kilda and customs to herself, under the unnerving scrutiny of a Guardian. She forced herself not to think of her intimate knowledge of Renna's fate, but grimaced as Tirjella admitted that they could easily lose three more lives to that evil before dawn.

All too soon Adora appeared, and the three Healers and the Guardian of Power went to prepare. Adora said apologetically, "Jalni, I am sorry but we have to share your room with robing Rangers. They have come fully prepared with their own Apothecary, the Kilda, her apprentice and someone called Terris…", but she was speaking to thin air for Jalni had run ahead, throwing open the door to her room and launching herself into the arms of her friend.

"Jalni!", exclaimed the surprised girl in delight. "I never thought to find you here. Are you well?".

Jalni hugged her briefly, then keeping her voice low so as not to disturb the conversation between Sushanna and Kilda, answered as she tied back her hair.

"We are all well, but I am alone here.".

Seeing the rush of sympathy in her friend's eyes, Jalni said swiftly, "His duties took him to Selesh, but I had ghost's to lay, so I went to Jerritol and found I still have family living. I came to report that and have stayed to support Shiarjha.".

"Oh, will you return to Selesh?", Terris asked innocently, and Jalni sighed as she felt Adora's eyes rest on her thoughtfully.

"Oh yes.", she made herself respond naturally. "I must see my Uncle settled and his claim on family property allowed before I return, but I must go back to finish my training.", then the most ridiculous thought crossed her mind.

"Terris.", she'd turned away to wash herself in antiseptic solution. "Do you remember Orto?".

The girl stared at her nonplussed, then said in startled tones.

"Of course I remember him. He was Solana's right hand and a more lovely man you couldn't hope to meet. He liked everyone and everyone liked him. He'd help harvest the strip fields, fetch and carry, dig ditches and help irrigate gardens. Why do you ask? I didn't think you'd ever met him, though Daro knew him. He went to get help at Darnesh, but we think he died of plague because he never came back again.".

"No Terris, he didn't die.", said Jalni happily. "He got very ill with dehydration and lost his memory for a while, but when he recovered, he discovered that there was no-one left in Scartel, and hearing of Solana's death, he assumed that you had all perished. The Guild of Weavers took him in, and he is to be apprenticed to them, but the funny thing is that he is my Uncle!".

Terris raised her hand to her mouth gasping at the scope of the coincidence, but Sushanna smiled and said gently, "Synchronicity Terris! This is beyond coincidence and should be recognised. Good evening Healer, are you and yours well?".

Wishing desperately that she could answer that question, Jalni followed the Ranger party in a strangely subdued mood, but in the birthing room, the sudden rush of homesickness for those she had left behind fled in the face of Sarann's need and the company of friends that rose to greet her.

Chapter 20 - The River Sings

The treatment room was large, with the central area well lit under free standing glow baskets. Under the light, The birthing bed was discreetly curtained by an arrangement of screens behind which, one end of the room remained in shadow. Here, sitting cross-legged on the floor with her medicines ranged in ceramic bowls sat Sushanna with Terris hovering nearby to do her bidding. On one side of the room two Healers consulted over wrapped baskets full of linen and a small group of attendants hovered at the bedside. Her interest quickened as she saw Kilda's assistant laying out the familiar racks with their equipment, but she could see little, and hear even less, until she moved forward. Like some unseen signal, activity around the bed unfolded as she glided silently down its length, and turned towards the bed end.

The Kilda was examining Sarann's sadly lacerated wrists, cleverly engineered rolling rests were being manoeuvred under her arms, one to each side of the bed, and in their wake came Sushanna to stand by Kilda, and Terris to the side where Iskilda burned crushed leaves in a pot, waving the sweet scented smoke over the bed. To Jalni's trained eyes it seemed that Sarann felt no great pain, though she panted and strained with the effort to give birth, so Jalni feeling her presence demanded, passed the last screen, and found herself gazing in bewildered silence at Garald.

He beckoned her towards the end of the bed, where Tirjella sat on a high stool, ideally positioned for the process of birth, which (judging by the increasing moans of Sarann) was imminent. Heart thudding, temples pounding combined with the rushing sensation that had accompanied her from the Weaver's vault), Jalni walked towards the Dream Walker on leaden legs, feeling as though she was caught in some strange dream. Tirjella's voice seemed to come from many Sands away as she approached them.

"She is sliding away Master Dream Walker.", her Sorceress was saying sadly. One highly trained hand tattoo's blazing Azure hovered above the discreetly covered mound of Sarann's belly as the Sorceress turned a bleak face to the Ranger. Garald sighed and said softly.

"We must turn her away from death before anything we do here can succeed. This is her only hope and it is not in my giving, but in that of this Healer.".

His eyes sought Jalni's as he explained.

"You know that imparting a truth is no guarantee of gaining acceptance. Showing anyone proof of facts beyond their current understanding cannot reverse values ingrained since birth.".

His wide grey eyes held Jalni's as he made an outrageous suggestion seriously.

"For example, I could say that there is a Sandsinger in this room, but if there was, would anyone admit that they believed it? No!.", he said abruptly, "No they would not because from birth we have believed such things to be lies, or

158

phantoms of the past. In such a way Sarann turns towards death, surrenders to the dark she believes she deserves, because one moment of maddened grief made her reach for the knife.".

Tirjella nodded emphatically.

"You believe her greatest danger comes not from her wounds but from her beliefs then?", and Jalni saw the bright intelligence leap in Tirjella's plain face, transforming it into that of an avid student sitting at a Master's feet. Garald spoke simply.

"Healer Jalni has already shown herself able to enter into a hypnotic state that can promote a mental change in a deeply unconscious patient. Seris Shiarjha confirmed this ability is all that saved Deshun Ikella's son after his recent serious illness. Having persuaded him from a deep coma, I hope she may turn Sarann from her path towards death. The Guardian herself has agreed to assist by supporting her dream walk, if you will give your permission?", he didn't wait for Tirjella's reply but glanced around the room listing preparations.

"The girl's mother is ready with the children's team in the other room, your Healers will convey the infants there once safely delivered. Our Kilda and Iskilda are prepared to seal her wounds, the birthing team are ready, all we need now is Sarann to want to live, to want her babes to live.".

His voice had dropped to a murmur and in that hypnotic space between waking and dreaming, Jalni was sat on a stool, back leant against his bracing chest, as she had seen Marran some ninenights past. Dimly, she heard Tirjella's question.

"Jalni? Tell me clearly that you consent to this?", and heard her own voice whisper through thickened lips.

"Yes, oh yes.", then Shiarjha's cool hands grasped hers and her crisp voice said sharply.

"Jalni, you will obey Dream Walker Garald implicitly. I will support you only if you agree to obey him. Think of Selesh if you need my help to escape.", and the pressure on her wrists told Jalni that the Guardian sat facing her, with hands firmly clasping hers. Someone passed burning herbs under her nose, warm fingers threaded through her hair seeking pressure points, then Garald's voice in her ear said calmly, "Ready?", as she felt the rushing waters of life close about her.

The cold black glimmer flowed sluggishly, caught in some dark eddy that whispered loneliness and despair. She was washed against sullen roots that sought to entangle her with a moan of "Markay, O Markay.", as she slid, languid as a veil of exhausted tears into a chill backwater that rolled indecisively at the junction of Sarann's choice. Too cold to initiate thought Jalni floated, her mind caught in the listless flow of Sarann's sorrow as she became aware of another voice, no, other voices.

Instinctively curious, she turned towards them, tugging Sarann's reluctant attention with her own. A flush of warmth seeped into chill bones as her mind quickened, seeking the whispering chant of life as she steered herself away from the black depths that drew her drowning, into the swirling shadows beyond. The pace of the river had changed subtly. She heard a background chant that seemed to lift her, sweeping her towards a mighty torrent that rocked her, rolled her, pounding her powerless and gasping into the rapids. Jalni's hands quivered and seized Shiarjha's wrists, closing about the circlets of guardianship as if they had ceased to exist. Shiarjha, stunned at the images she was sharing, winced but hung on, aware that Jalni had set herself to turn the labouring woman from the choice to doom her babies.

Jalni, oblivious of everything outside of the rushing of her mind noticed that the pace of the dream-walk had increased. Her attention, riveted on the lift and curl of the river, heard something beyond the blend of voices, and she frowned, struggling to identify every part of this plainsong. There were deep male undertones in counterpoint to the strong pulse of a heartbeat. She caught the driving compulsion of feminine urgency, the toll of Tekrun's bell, a rising pressure within the chorus as voice became othervoice but from no human throat. She was surrounded by light, as the river threw her ashore crying out in wonder.

"O Deo...! The River Sings!".

Then she broke from the grip of the current into the peace of Ranger chant. Their voices blended in close harmony, neither song nor speech, it seemed to speak of wide open plains with secret places teeming with life. The deep throbbing beat of male voice synchronised with Jalni's heartbeat. Kilda and Iskilda interweaving a rhythm with the chiming clarity of Tirjella's othervoice, as the first babe slid into her hands.

Garald continued to steady Jalni's shoulders as she became fully aware of her surroundings, hearing Tirjella urging Sarann.

"Come my dear, one more brave push for Markay!", as the second twin was born. Relaxing against the Dream Walker as the child cried out, Jalni heard a mumbled question from the new mother, then a little chuckle from Tirjella.

"Unusual but good names my dear. Amira for the eldest, after your father, and Markaya after your husband for the youngest, yes!", Tirjella's habitual twinkle was in her voice as she mused.

"Your daughters are fine strong babies, small but in no danger. They will feed and thrive while the Clan supports you. Your brother's name will be added to the family name as was his right. At Jentaroth we will honour them, so you need not fear for their souls, they are safe in the care of the One.".

A murmured conference took place around the bed as the Rangers withdrew. Jalni felt Garald releasing her and sat forward. He smiled down at her, then retreated to the shadowed end of the room, accepting a light caress from his Sushanna, and a drink from Terris, who to Jalni's critical eye seemed to be glowing with subdued excitement. She found herself wondering what was going on, jumping as Shiarjha pronounced severely.

"She's celebrating a waste of good Healer material I suspect! Your friend is pregnant Jalni. but although motherhood will suppress the development of a true othervoice, at least she has apprenticed herself to their Apothecary, so her talent won't be completely lost!".

Staring at Terris in awe, Jalni hardly noticed as Shiarjha disengaged her wrists from the Healer's grasp, rubbing them ruefully as she enquired.

"Are you recovered my dear? The verian used to prolong the hypnotic state is not harmful or habit forming, although the effects remain in the blood for a few hours. The Rangers stay until Sarann and her babes can travel, then they will live with them for the first Rotation. It is all settled apparently. The Clan will offer a good price for Amir's holding, ensuring it passes to family members when the time comes for a nephew to start out on his own, so this matter is closed.", she paused as Terris presented Jalni with a tall sand-paste glass containing a blued green liquid.

"Excuse me Seris Shiarjha, Sushanna begs you share this tonic. It will restore your strength before you leave for Selesh, and before the Kilda adds this dream walk to Jalni's skin record.".

Jalni blinked, but Shiarjha grinned, accepting the restorative. She sipped delicately from one side, proffering the other to Jalni speaking confidentially as Sarann's bed was adjusted, and the new mother washed.

"I must return to Selesh now my work here is done. You are on your own again seeking your destiny, but recent events mark a turning point that you cannot ignore. You have found family, friends, the respect of your Clan and recognition by your own Sorceress. The One only knows how many lives you have been instrumental in saving, but I am to tell you that it is not only the Rangers who wish to recognise your contribution to the continued safety of the Azure Sands.".

She broke off as Jalni (mutinous scowl in place) rose to join the Rangers.

"Don't fight it Jalni. You'll recognise the Source, long before you work out what its up to. This is the beginning of your journey of discovery, and one thing you have learned already.".

She held out her hand in the manner of Seleshanni farewells speaking sotto voce.

"When times are hard, or you are in great danger, never forget that the river Sings. For those of us who hear that song and are committed to our world's salvation, that song is our watchword and a beacon of hope.".

Jalni stared at Shiarjha, then said quietly. "That's the first time I ever heard you sound like a Guardian Shiarjha, I think I like it, but please don't turn into Ikella!".

She turned away, following Terris to find the Decrian waiting and missed the swift calculating look that crossed Shiarjha's face, nor did she hear the muttered plea.

"The One guide your feet my girl.", as the Guardian met the steady gaze of Draille Skellin who had entered the room to collect his charge. She smiled into his serious eyes and said lightly,

"Our Healer is talented (if not as obedient as we would like). Her inventiveness will take her a long way in her endeavours. However, her temper was forged with lightening rods, she has a rebellious streak wider than the Divide and an overly suspicious nature.".

He took Shiarjha's carrisack from Adeya, considering these comments, head on one side. After a moment he added.

"Qualities Guardian, that may already have saved her life.", then, as they nodded discreet farewells to the knot of Rangers, continued reeling off a list that surprised Shiarjha into temporary silence.

"She's impulsive but generous. Quick tempered but not ill natured, fierce to protect those she cares for and totally dedicated to Daro. She's remarkably intelligent, appears to learn quickly and is not afraid to admit her lack of knowledge when she encounters something new.", his lips quirked as he added, "She's not bad looking either and I suspect that she could end up with half the men she meets at her feet should she want them there!".

Shiarjha looked up in surprise, and caught a far away look in the Rangers eyes, but remained silent as the thought crossed her mind.

"Including one First Class Ranger if I am not mistaken.", but the moment for comment passed as they left the room with no more ceremony than that afforded them on arrival, slipping away to take the ride through the Sheer that would return Shiarjha to Selesh before Seleus lit the Sands.

The Healers clustered round Sarann's bed bustled away as Sushanna stood with several stoppered flasks and Tirjella joined her to confer over restoratives and the like. Jalni sat on the stool in front of Kilda holding out her hands for the Decrian to examine. The woman bent over the delicate symbols tattooed so long ago by her mother and said softly.

"Your skin record is very unusual Healer. Some of the symbols are not native to these Sands, do you know the Decrian who placed them here?", a question that left Jalni stammering apologetically.

"My mother was Nishanawa, from the Temple of the Winds Kilda. I only know that the secret of a blue dye was hidden in these tattoos. I ran with them to the Opal Sands and sought protection there, just as my mother told me to before she died. Deshun Ikella took me in, translated the symbols then admitted me to the Guild school.", she broke off in confusion, aware that she was babbling, then Garald's hands rested lightly on her shoulders. His amused voice hovered at the edge of her hearing as he suggested,

"Lean back Azureling, listen to the story of the River.", as he swept her away on a torrent of words.

In the recitation, Jalni was rocked and swayed as the verian took her deeper into trance. Under Kilda's practised hands, a delicate tracery in blue linked her mother's secret symbols together, flowing to the back of her hand like some magical cascade. At one point, she roused to find her forearms being wrapped in moist dressings and shifted position, complaining that her arms itched. Then she slipped into exhausted sleep, unaware that Garald lifted her, bearing her away in strong arms to share a room with Sushanna and Terris, until she woke in the blued shadows of the following afternoon.

"My mind feels as thick as a coatan's winter pelt.", she complained, rolling out of bed and seeking the necessary in sleep befuddled urgency. Terris giggled behind her, calling her attention to her arms.

"Take care Jalni, don't knock the back of your hands. I'll change the dressings if you like.", and Jalni smiled to herself, thinking how much happier she felt in the company of trusted friends as she returned to the room they shared.

She found out that Draille had indeed taken Shiarjha back to Selesh, returning discreetly after Height of Sun had cleared the Sands of observers.

When Jalni languidly enquired where his unusual mount was stabled, Terris promptly exclaimed, "Sheerwolves look after themselves silly!", but it was evening before the befuddled girl felt like moving out of their room or catching up on events. Taking the advice of Sushanna, the two girls dressed with elaborate care, Jalni braiding her hair, found herself wondering where the Azure ribbons that marked her as a fourth year Healer had materialised from. Terris was likewise agog at the elaborate patch dyed blues and wristband that marked her as the wife of a First Class Ranger. The Apothecary chuckled with real amusement as she explained.

"These came back with Draille. He hadn't planned on doing anything other than escorting Seris Shiarjha home. However, he insists that another Guardian pounced on him, dragging him off to a room full of books, asking him so many questions that his head still spins.".

Jalni grinned, exclaiming, "Beneva!", then, "Poor Draille. Did she suck him dry of all Ranger knowledge?", and giggled at Sushanna's eloquently rolling eyes.

"Oh my!", said the Healer, then she stroked the ribbons, luxuriating in the feel of the clean clothes that had arrived carefully folded and packed.

"Where did he get my clothes from then?", she demanded, subsiding into a fit of laughter as Sushanna elaborated.

"Apparently having survived one interrogation, Draille escaped, straight into the arms of a Healer, who failing to pin him to a wall physically, did so verbally!", Sushanna shook out her hair laughing. "I'd pay good exchange to have seen that.".

Jalni, stricken with guilt identified Mina easily. "Mina fostered me from the time I entered Selesh.", she said seriously. "I'm afraid I resented her attempts to help me, playing terrible tricks on her, and she still cares for me bless her.", and she dwelt sadly on her bad behaviour, only brightening as she recalled Terris's new clothes.

"Where did those come from Sushanna? Draille couldn't have gone back to Holmgarth as well surely?", and the Apothecary said wistfully,

"No, indeed not. The poor man was almost dropping when he got here. These my dear are Daro's bride gift to you. Somehow he already knows your good news for they are sized for your increase, and are of such quality that they will last for many Rotations, though how he knows the manner of our dying I can't imagine.".

Terris smoothed the long tunic over her belly laughing at Jalni's quizzical expression. "Still absolutely flat.", she said with great satisfaction. "I only knew this ninenight myself, so that's very kind of him.", and hummed as she robed. Jalni watching her pleasure felt her heart warm and reached for the link to her lord, but he didn't respond, so she allowed Terris to drag her out of the visitors quarters and go to mingle in Tirjella's Hall.

Other Rangers were present already, and on enquiry Jalni found that Tirjella had very kindly conducted her visitors on a tour of Darnesh, covering most of the communal areas, and all the facilities that the Sorceress was most proud of. She was, as the girls arrived, introducing a small gathering of Weavers to Draille and Garald, entirely aware of the envious eyes of Master Dyer Grovan, who was only prevented from demanding an explanation of the patch dyeing process by the imperious tilt of Tirjella's head and the normal constraints of hospitality. Jalni plucked at Terris's tunic, pulling her friend closer so that she could whisper in her ear, but almost as thought translated into words, Tirjella caught her eye and nodded a discreet summons.

"Healer del Orto.", she greeted Jalni formally. "I am glad to see you recovered after your exertions on behalf of Sarann and her family. Have you eaten yet?".

Strangely tongue-tied in these formal surroundings, Jalni said shyly that neither she nor Terris had eaten and that it had been their plan to share evening refectory together. Chuckling, Tirjella declared that if Jalni (used to the bell ordered life of an enclosed community) expected that here, she would be sadly disappointed. The youthful Sorceress linked her arm through Jalni's, treating her as a favoured student, and explained, taking her current retinue of Rangers with her as she introduced Guild Masters and Clan Elders.

"We are still excavating this ancient settlement and to be frank, facilities here are rather thin on the ground. Although new developments are springing from the bare rocks around us, every day an influx of new settlers need them, so we are a bit like a frontier town. I still have trouble controlling tribal warlords who would prefer to fight over, rather than farm their holdings. I am praying that your Rangers may assist me in that endeavour.", and so saying Tirjella swept aside a heavy curtain, inviting her entourage to take their seats and eat with her.

Terris gasped at the sumptuous display of food, Draille looked mildly disconcerted, but they took their seats alongside Master Weavers and Dyers, Healers and Elders amongst whom lively discussion was soon advanced. Jalni sat with the junior Healers, Terris beside her and tackled a meal of milta grains and mixed vegetables miserably aware that by Ranger standards Azurians ate to excess. However, the meal passed comparatively easily, although Jalni was more than aware that neither Garald nor Sushanna had appeared. The reason for that became obvious when after a whispered consultation with Adora, the Sorceress turned a smiling face to her guests.

"We are invited to the nursery to meet the youngest members of Clan Zurias my friends.", she said with open delight. "Will you attend me, one Guild representative for each calling, my faithful Recorder and the Rangers involved?", and standing she clapped her hands to signal her departure.

They followed Tirjella to a long corridor lit by brilliant glow baskets. Several people Jalni had never met before had joined them, and finding herself aware of intense scrutiny from a young Master Weaver, was about to draw her friend's attention to this, when the party ahead turned through a brightly painted set of doors. On the threshold of the nursery she met an imploring gaze and found that far from unnerved by his attention, she was intrigued. She held out a hand in greeting.

"Good Sunfall Master Weaver.", she gave him a brief smile. "I think you wanted to speak to me?", and the young man smiled openly, and gave her hand the type of warm, dry clasp that she liked. He had a sunny smile, good fresh features and honey coloured hair. A quick glance told her that he wore his own weaving and that it was good, hard-wearing cloth. Catching the direction of her gaze he coloured faintly, but returned her greeting with equanimity.

"Good Sunfall Holder. I am more than aware that this is not the time for full discussions, but I wanted to introduce myself. My name is Dinnot del Lyn and I am the younger son of Jando del Lyn, Master Weaver at Anempor. Today I was informed of an opening in Jerritol with Master Madiv, who has received my credentials from my former master. I would relish the opportunity of applying to your Halt and beg your pardon for interrupting your progress.".

Jalni smiled into warm hazel eyes, and found herself responding positively to this man. She said swiftly, "If you are here to visit with Sarann and her babies, it won't hurt to split the numbers in two. Sarann will be very overwhelmed by the many who will want to help her, and with two babies she will tire easily.".

She saw the joy flee from his face, but his eyes didn't flinch as he said softly, "I wish her joy in her sorrow. For me the sorrow was to lose my wife. She laboured too long when our daughter came. Trishanna is well now and the Guild let me visit her as often as I want, but I need a home where I can be on hand to raise her, for that was my oath to her mother. I swore solemnly that she would come before my ambition to weave at my own Halt, before I took service with another Master even. My Jerym did not demand it of me, but I promised, and that oath cannot be broken. Where go I, so goes my child and her needs come first.".

Jalni didn't have to listen for the river's Song was in her ears, in her blood and then the memory of a small room, vividly painted for a child ran through her mind, and the decision was made. She said sympathetically, "Go visit your babe, while I attend my duties here. Tomorrow Madiv and I will discuss the matter with my fellow Holder, who is also apprenticed to the Guild, and then we will talk to you. Meet me at the Guild before Height of Sun and we will consider the matter together.".

He took a deep breath of relief, touched his fingers to head, lips and heart in the manner of true believers and turned away, but not before Jalni had seen the glitter of tears in his eyes. Sobered, both girls tiptoed into Sarann's room, accepting their share of the thanks and accolades, before hanging awed over the twinling's crib. Jalni whispered to Terris.

"One is such a miracle, but two is almost too much to believe!", at which Terris gulped and whispered her reply.

"I know. I just realised that by next Rotation this could be me! Although I know Garald left Marran in good hands when he was recalled, I can't help worrying that I might have to face raising our child alone.".

Jalni felt a sudden throb in her blood and was not surprised by Daro's inner voice in her mind.

"Terris should not be fearful dearling. Tell her I promised to sponsor all the Children of Scartel. Whether they be Clansmen or Rangers I will be there for them, their children and quite possibly their children's children. I will always provide for them and that goes for Sarann's daughters as well.".

The voice of her inner mind tried to respond, but suddenly she began to yawn uncontrollably, and amidst much laughter was forced to retire to bed, where she slept till long after dawn, dreaming of an endless river that sang in her blood.

PART 3 - THE LIGHT DAWNS

Chapter 21 - The Sandsinger's Weave

Jalni woke and stretched deliciously, finally feeling fully refreshed. The backs of her wrists and arms felt tight, but when she examined the new tattoos they looked healthy enough beneath the scabbing. she rose quietly, aware that Terris was not in her bed, and went into the guest room's necessary. She made herself comfortable, before washing, careful to use only the minutest amount of the cool water some thoughtful drudge had left in a jug.

Assuming that the Rangers had gathered together for their breakday meal, she dressed, swiftly rolling her discarded clothes for packing, then sallied forth to find food, catching up with Sushanna and Terris on the outskirts of the lively market that fringed the Gathering Square. She admired their purchases, watched carefully as the man who served them marked a notation on a tablet slung from his belt, then asked him curiously," Forgive me Master, but I recall another who used the same kind of notation. Are you by any chance one of the Guild of Master Builders?".

Warm dark eyes smiled into hers, white teeth flashed in the morning sun, and a melodic voice said softly, "Yes indeed Mistress Holder.".

Jalni grinned to herself, "How odd it is to be addressed with such respect, just because I wear the Weaver blue surcoat that Madiv gave me.", but accepted the situation with as much equanimity as she could muster. She took a glance at the tools the man had on display, and added warily, "Are you not engaged in your trade then Master?, and saw his grin diminish with reluctance.

"Needs must when children cry of hunger!", he remarked cryptically, following his comment by serving another customer, while his hopeful gaze locked on Jalni.

"I come from a poor farming community up in the Drekkens lady. My brother and I inherited our fathers bakery, which my sister by marriage runs. My brother acts as intermediary for village affairs, and when there is building work or repairs to do, I attend to those, and when not, I use my secondary training as simple Smith to craft tools, which I sell for just enough to feed those who need help.".

As his words closed the circle of fate that Jalni felt building around her, she was compelled to enquire..

"Are you from Dovodan? Is Bernot your brother, Trellin your sister by marriage?".

He glanced at her, saw her braid and hissed, drawing in breath so sharply that she instinctively moved closer. He stilled, examining her face, then, seeming to come to a decision, he said urgently.

"Are you who I think you might be Mistress? You have the look of one who may have seen marvellous things. My brother talks all the time about a blind man and his beautiful young guide. Is he here with you? It is you isn't it?".

Jalni was aware that Sushanna was preparing to leave the area, staring at her curiously as she talked to the trader, and said swiftly. I am here on family business, but my lord is not with me, he is in Selesh, where they are in desperate need of a Master Builder. Your knowledge of smith-work would stand you in good stead, and my lord would see that your village was well rewarded for your work, should you chance to apply. I am returning to Jerritol with my Uncle and fellow Holder. I can only offer an introduction, because my business here is not yet complete, but I am sure that there will be a regular trek train to Caranchar should you wish to accept my hospitality for a night. There is a shipment of goods due out from my Halt directly to Selesh if you care to tag along with that, as well.".

He nodded thoughtfully, his eyes lighting on one of the men who was also serving at this stall.

"I am lucky that this time, I travel with Bledwin, Master Smith at Shoranal. I can ask him to take word to Bernot, retain my goods, and pay over my takings. I don't have my own pack animals anyway, so I don't have to consider their stabling. When do you leave? Where can I send word to you? My name is Brand by the way.".

he smiled engagingly, and Jalni chuckled as she turned to follow Sushanna and Terris. She called back over her shoulder.

"I am Jalni, Half-Holder del Orto for formality. I will be engaged on Weaver business, or Clan records until Sunfall. That gives you a full days trading before my travel plans are made. You may leave word for me at the Guild of Weavers, with my Steward Master Madiv.".

She turned towards Sushanna and a small gathering of Rangers and did not look back, but somehow she was also aware that Brand had raised a hand in farewell, and smiled to herself. Terris pounced on her critically, hissing out of the corner of her mouth as the three of them walked towards Draille Skellin and his entourage.

"O Jalni, what a flirt you are becoming. That poor man was dizzy with interest! How could you be so bad when I know you are bond to Daro?", but there was merriment in the demure face the young Apothecary turned to hers, so Jalni grinned back.

"I wasn't flirting Terris, just setting bait to draw a good applicant for the position of Master Builder to Selesh, where my lord can....".

Her voice tailed away, her attention diverted as one of the men dressed in Ranger blues turned towards her, hands held out in welcome.

"Roast your victim, and serve him up decorated with spiced milta grains?", the amused voice in her head enquired, as he stepped forward, and caught her hands to his mouth.

She was speechless, blood surging through her veins, pounding in her ears and threatening to suffocate her. She struggled not to cling to him, she was weak at the knees, hands trembling, as he hugged her briefly then set her on her feet again.

"How?", she queried, eyes huge in a face that glowed, and he said softly, "I called Draille. You should know that although apparently recovering, my mother is far from well. Beneva has asked to meet both Sushanna and the Kilda. They may know of some treatment that can help Ikella. Shiarjha temporarily carries the Staff, Carolus never leaves Mother's side, and the worst of it all is that dear old Eshima is fading fast. I promised that I would bring Tirjella into the circle of those that know my status immediately. She is second in Sorcery, an old and trusted friend, and Shiarjha will need her if Mother doesn't respond soon. Draille will look after me, get me safe back to Selesh. There is no need for you to break off your adventuring or worry about us.".

His voice was light, but she heard his shaken whisper in her mind as Draille led him towards what appeared to be a reception committee.

"Stay safe dearling, and come home soon!".

She was silent, dazed by the strength of her reaction to him, as she followed the others to their breakday meal, remaining thoughtful through a morning of documentation and records with the Clan archivist, only returning to her usual humour as she rejoined Orto and Madiv at the Weaver Guild Hall. Madiv greeted her deferentially.

"Half-Holder Jalni.", his low bow was perfectly respectful, but suddenly irritated, Jalni scowled ferociously. He grinned impishly, murmuring for her ears only.

"So nice to discover I can return you to your normal self without resorting to the help of our Sorceress!", and highly entertained, Jalni sent a greeting to her smiling Uncle.

"How did you get on with old Larold?", Jalni enquired as her Steward led them into the fastness of the Guild. "He seems mightily cautious to me. He was very suspicious of my ability to recall my father's features, and said he would need more than that before handing half a Weaver Halt to a mere apprentice.".

Madiv nodded agreement. "I know!", he said ruefully, "However, he is not insensitive to the need for settlement and closure. He has spent every waking hour pouring through Sowdin's records (such as they are), discovering the whereabouts of two of your Aunts. They have been asked to appear at a formal hearing during Zenitheon gather. The Clan all favour this arrangement, and so Lady Tirjella has ruled. In the meantime, your Uncle has agreed to suspend his entry to the Guild, and will come back to Jerritol with me, in order to track down old Weavers and Dyers who might uphold his claim.".

He smiled down at her.

"Don't worry. Neither of them wants for anything, other than to find their brother, and a niece. They are settled well to the South, have no interest in pursuing anything other than the occasional yardage, and news of their youngest brothers child.".

Jalni considered this, then asked quietly, "So where are you taking us now?", and Madiv opened a door to a small gathering area, saying confidently.

"The Masters wished to thank you for exposing the evil in our midst. For removing that threat from the Halt at Jerritol, and for representing us in a favourable light to Guardian Shiarjha. We entertain her representative at the moment, and he too wished to express their thanks.".

Caught completely by surprise, Jalni felt for the presence that she knew they sheltered, and found him, head tilted on one side, listening to a low voiced description of the great Opal Tapestry suspended on a rolling frame above him.

Immediately aware that Daro wore ordinary travelling garb, she tilted her head in recognition, merely murmuring a greeting as Madiv introduced her to the Senior Masters, she nevertheless stepped in close to him, accepting immediately the task of guide without question. The small group of Weavers and Dyers spoke with authority about the tapestry displayed. Its probable age made Jalni's head reel in disbelief, the terms the Weavers used were familiar, but the technical details were as foreign to her as the complex terminology used in medicine used to be. However, she had one question to ask, it tingled on her lips, but before she could speak, Daro asked it for her. Supremely indifferent to any speculation amongst the Masters of thread, he asked Madiv serenely.

"I can feel odd harmonics around the tapestry. Tell me is there something metallic, something glittering in the design?".

The silence that fell was profound, and Jalni bit her lip, praying that Daro had not in some way betrayed his sensitivity to all things magical, then one of the Elders of the Guild cleared his throat.

"That is a very significant question young Lord.", he said before lapsing into thought. Daro waited calmly, as the man searched his memory, and then pronounced in the rustling throaty wheeze of an ancient.

"When I entered the Guild, the practice of enhancing a weaving by wrapping a fine foil around a plying thread had largely been discontinued. It is very costly, renders the textile open to denigration by virtue of wear, contamination, or rust caused by damp. However, there was a school of thought that said the ancients used minerals to achieve certain effects, although we don't have the knowledge of which minerals or how to weave them any more. To my mind this sets the date of this Tapestry further into the past than our current records imply, back to a time when a long dead class of mage was rumoured to have had a hand in the creation of certain textiles, including weavings of this nature.".

Daro's voice in Jalni's ear was triumphant. He streamed a hysterical image of himself turning cartwheels round the Gathering Square, shouting.

"I knew it! This is a Sandsinger's Weave.", then, as Jalni thought bleakly, "Yes indeed my Lord Sandsinger, and I know precisely what it feels like to be caught in one of those!", he turned a polite smile to Master Toluran as he developed the theme.

"I have always felt that these glittering areas referred to water.", the old Master said, ignoring the frowns and gasps from his fellows. "I know it seems ridiculous now, but if I am right, vast areas of the Opal Sands were once under water. There is no hint of the Great Divide between our Sands, just a continuance of the sparkling metal or mineral. I can't think that this applies to anything other than water. Even if it were snow, or ice, the water would have been there to produce either of those substances, and in other tapestries, there are flows of the same substance which clearly relate to rivers.".

Daro's imagination was immediately fired.

"Just think how many could survive with so much water to spare.", he commented, sounding quite awed, but then he seemed to remember the reason for this gathering, turning to Jalni.

"Ah well, we must do as we can, with what resources the One grants us, and it is my fortune to convey the thanks of the Guardians, for your part in diverting the evil, so recently visited on these Sands.".

Unaccustomed to accepting thanks or compliments at all (let alone gracefully), Jalni bit her lip and blushed, hanging her head to hide the habitual birth of a scowl, but Daro continued blithely, apparently unaware of her confusion.

"It is the pleasure of the Guild of Weavers to present you with their thanks in the form of garments specially woven and dyed for you.".

As he spoke an elderly woman stepped forward, and Jalni gasped. A pile of clothing neatly folded lay across the woman's arms, but it was the fabric that caught Jalni's eyes, her breath faltered, and her throat clenched about a sob of joy.

"O, how wonderful.", she eventually managed to force her voice to say. "My mother's dyeing, ", as Madiv delivered the final surprise.

"Yes indeed.", he agreed gravely. "While you were waiting to see the Tapestries, don't you remember Master Dyer Grovan recording the ancient dye recipe?",

There was a mischievous twinkle in his eyes. "We have been working the dye that Seris Ikella sent to us, but her scribes Interpretation of the recipe didn't cover one element, which we also failed to note until Grovan compared your late mother's discovery with a historic reference in one of his scrolls.".

"Which was?", Jalni prompted, and Madiv chuckled in delight. "It seems that we can achieve the colour and fix it, using the prescribed mineral compounds all right, but we neglected to identify the filtration method. We discovered that a significant difference had crept into our understanding of the dye.".

Jalni stared at him, confused, and Master Grovan himself stepped forward, clearing his throat.

"Yes Mistress Jalni. That is what we missed. It is common to strain or refine compounds in the making, sometimes filtering them several times. Because in the Opal Sands there is ….", he hesitated observing the amused twitch of Daro's lips as that worthy suggested mildly,

"Only Opal Sand?", to the obvious relief of the Master Dyer, who plunged on regardless of the grins around him.

Harrumph, yes precisely Lord Daro. Only Opal Sand, (which we have been importing ever since the dye was revived) without considering that the original recipe just mentions "sand". This dye seems to be a secret bound up in rituals that we know nothing of, but the fact remains, that ever made in the Azure, in the far north-east on the border with the Ashgenar, only Azure Sand would have been used.!".

"Dear me yes.", into the silence born of consternation, the Master Dyer continued to expound the theory.

"In that region there are a number of significant mineral deposits, which we now realise must have an effect on any dye filtered through the sand. Your mother was Nishan, born and brought up in that region where she obviously learned how to create these jewel bright colours. These then Mistress Jalni truly are the Colours of the Zurias, lost at Cataclysm.".

His perceptive gaze was fixed on Jalni's face, but she was withdrawn, face immobile as she recalled her mother's absorbed look. She remembered now, a stack of trays, the top ones filled with clean washed pebbles each one suspended over a bucket, dye pouring through the pierced base on which they sat. She may have seen more than she remembered right now, but she did recall the brilliance of her mother's smile when the bubbles rose from the final steeping in which the original dye had been made, and a tear sprang to her eyes.

On cue Daro said smoothly. "I am sure that Jalni will have many reasons to thank you for this wonderful gift, but you must also be aware that her mother's gift to the Azure's repository of knowledge is also recognised.", and at this suggestion there was a positive buzz amongst the Dyers. Thus distracted from their guest they gathered to discuss a possible response, and Jalni was able to recover herself, while Madiv, Orto, and Daro protected her. She cradled the garments, stroking them gently, amazed at the gleam and ripple in the fabric. It shivered under her hand, livened to her touch, and suddenly she was "aware", in touch with her sand, and had she been looking, she would have seen her Lord smile in silent sympathy. He cleared his throat softly and as attention turned back to him, said mildly.

"I apologise Masters all, but I have a duty call to make on Lady Tirjella, and I have not yet presented the compliments of the Guardians to Mistress Jalni.".

Jalni, who had placed her robes on a nearby table straightened, moved away from the lure of her trophies and came to stand in front of Daro. She gently clicked her fingers as he reached forward, and he took her hands in his. There was no mistaking it, the Lord of the Opal was "in magic", and yet no-one around them seemed to notice. He spoke with grave deliberation.

"Jalni, adopted daughter of our clan, as first son of the Shalhanhi I confer upon you the freedom of our Sands. Such is the will of Ikella, Sharall deir Opal and Guardian of the Way. Your welcome and a permanent home in Selesh is guaranteed in thanks for those actions which first revealed the hold of the Gattarene on a member of this Guild, and secondly permitted the actions which removed such a threat from our borders..".

His inner voice, his *othervoice* whispered in her ear. "Walk always with me my Azure, know that you are not alone, that I am waiting for you to answer the call.", his hands moved upward, dropping something around her neck on a smithworked chain, and her hands flew to her bosom where he had settled something that glittered. It was brilliantly enamelled a wheel shape, silvery metal enclosing Azure and Opal shades bounded by more of the metal that formed the hub.

"Oh.", she gasped as it touched her skin and warmed. "Its beautiful, thank you Lord Daro.".

"It is one of Selesh's most treasured possessions.", he assured her gravely. "When I saw it, ,I knew it matched your eyes. Keep it safe, and bring it back to Selesh one day soon.", and then he was gone, surrounded by an entourage anxious to conduct him to Tirjella.

Jalni, stunned by all this finery however, went directly out of the Guild Hall, into the Gathering Square of Darnesh, where two men waited for her anxiously.

Madiv gestured to Dinnot del Lynne, and he came forward eagerly, waiting as Madiv said quietly, "This man is certainly the best applicant so far. However, he brings complications with him. He has a child who is motherless, she is a new-born and whereas here, there is a nursery, wet-nurses, and Healers if they want them, at Jerritol we can't provide for the baby. I would suggest that a short period of trial without moving the child might suffice for all parties. It would give Master del Lynne the chance to find out if Jerritol and its Halt is what he and his daughter need. It would give me the opportunity to test his skills for myself, and it would give Orana the chance to brighten up the nursery and advertise for a wet-nurse.". Jalni watched as her Steward conveyed the same statement in hand-code for her deaf Uncle's benefit, and watched Orto's fingers flicker approval. Her eyes were drawn to Dinnot's face and caught the widening of his eyes, and understood that he too knew the language of the profoundly deaf.

"Better and better still", !said the voice of her inner mind. "Orto will have someone who can understand him to train him when the time comes, and the baby will have the best of worlds. I wonder how Dinnot learned hand sign?".

As if she had spoken aloud, the young man turned to her. "My older sister was deafened by some illness in childhood. My father sent her to an old Healer who taught Dreean to sign. I married her best friend, and it never occurred to me that there was any difference between signing and speaking. I always knew what they were chattering about.".

Jalni made up her mind instantly. "That's fixed then.", she said briskly. "Won't you mind leaving your daughter so soon?", but he shook his head smiling. "To take up this opportunity while she is too young to remember is far better than leaving her later.", he assured her, as Madiv turned to Brand.

"Master Brand?", he enquired, and swiftly Jalni explained.

Her Steward said softly. "He and his brothers are known to me Holder. They helped rebuild at Jerritol, and I would embrace his advice on extending the Halt.".

So it was that with journey plans made, the group agreed to take supper together, and turned back to the Hall to pack, ready for the morning.

Chapter 22 - An Overture in Opal

Saturated in the history of textiles, dyes, (and the manner of their creation), Daro walked quietly with the Masters of those matters, led by Toluran. The old man said simply, "I have a long history in guiding. If you permit?", and Daro placed his hand into the crook of Toluran's arm, saying gratefully. "I appreciate that offer good Master. I find it difficult to adapt when I change guides, it will be a relief to use your experienced arm. I really miss Jalni sometimes!".

The old man chuckled. "Only sometimes?", he enquired lightly. "Now, I miss my wife every second of the day, may the One grant her peace. She was the one I learned to lead you know, and I miss her humour, her gift of understanding, her insightfulness.", he sighed dolefully, then brightened as he asked.

"I take it that Guardian Shiarjha told you about Renna?", and paused while doors ahead of them opened. Daro considered briefly. He must first break the news he bore to Tirjella. He had to restrain the impulse to tell Toluran more of this story than his Sorceress might want him to know, and suddenly realised that he was missing his Songfather badly. He had never felt that he had to shield Carolus from anything, and was still considering the matter when Toluran said comfortably, "Of course, you don't have to answer that question young Lord, but when you are ready to talk, don't forget that I can remember what most of these fools spend hours searching records for. I have achieved eighty Rotations in my craft, am both Weaver and Dyer, and was brought up believing in the Old Path.".

Daro hesitated, then saw his way forward clearly. "When I have made my bow to Lady Tirjella, may I visit you before I leave?".

He heard the smile in the old man's voice.

"That would be greatly appreciated young Lord, I would value your opinion on something I have guarded for a long time. It may be of interest to you.", then, the last set of doors were flung open, and Daro was taken into Tirjella's reception Hall.

If he expected the formality that he was used to in Selesh, he was to be sadly disappointed. The Sorceress simply bustled up to him saying briskly, "Good Sunfall Daro. Have you dined? I had in mind a quiet supper together, you can tell me your news and I can pass on some remedies my Healers have devised for your poor mother. I hope you will be my guest tonight ?".

Gravely taking his leave of the Guild Masters, Daro agreed to Tirjella's plan, whereupon he was shown to a guest -room off the Sorceress's own apartment, and was left alone to unpack his battered travel bag. A hesitant knock at the door made him wonder if Jalni had come to rescue him, but it was a young man. Nervously, his visitor explained that he had come to help Daro prepare, so, accepting Tobin's help gratefully, Daro set about "disguising" (with sleight of magic), the rather impressive ceremonials hiding in the bag.

176

His helper was reserved but supportive, laying out what appeared to be simple desert wear, telling Daro gruffly that he would take his other clothing to wash. Wondering what a laundress would make of clothes that cleaned themselves, Daro resisted the temptation to refuse this hospitality and concentrated as Tobin explained that unlike Selesh, Darnesh had very limited water with which to maintain cleanliness.

Making a mental promise to investigate, Daro allowed Tobin to lead him through an internal doorway, into a small washroom, where he listened to the familiar sounds of personal washing implements being laid out. He mused thoughtfully.

"If Darnesh and Selesh were built to the same plan, there must be underground springs. They must be there, or such a centre of population would never have been built.", and so his thoughts ran as Tobin showed him into a private necessary and waited for him discreetly.

Daro's thoughts seemed trapped in the maze of Darnesh itself. He mentally retraced every step of his journey from the Guild of Weavers, up and into the cavern complex proper, then to Tirjella's apartments. He stood patiently superimposing the plan of Selesh on the much larger complex at Selesh, convinced he had the pattern of it, as Tobin poured water into a shallow bowl. He was still deep in thought when Tobin tapped him unceremoniously on the shoulder and said cheerfully, "You can stand there all day friend and get not a jot cleaner. Here's a wash cloth, find the bowl (which I'll tap for you), then spruce yourself up. I don't mind checking you over, I'm quite used to that, but didn't they rehabilitate you back in the Opal?".

Daro was riveted. Here was someone who wasn't going to do things for him all the time. Here was someone who knew what independence meant, and he grinned.

"Sorry.", he apologised. "I have complex messages to deliver and my mind was elsewhere.".

"Right!", Tobin said, then continued briskly. "You can strip down where you are. Drop your clothes to the left of you. Directly in front of you there is a wash stand, with two shelves. The top one is just above navel -height. That has a bowl on it. I am holding a drying towel ready, two paces to your right. Your wash cloth is in the bowl. It needs wringing out well before you add soap to it. Run your hand down the stand to a short lower shelf. On that to the left is soft soap in a tub, to the right is stuff for washing your hair. I'll do that for you if you like, it'll be easier.".

Perhaps it was this calm practicality but Daro suddenly felt confident enough to tackle this task, and in no time at all, he was sat in a chair, freshly washed and carefully groomed, wearing clean clothes and a beatific smile. He felt good, and touched his Seguidor calming his rising excitement as the Summoning bell sounded the time for him to join Tirjella. Tobin came back into the room, and Daro thanked him as he gathered soiled linen and rella towels together.

He replied cheerfully enough, "It is no trouble Master, but I hope your mission to Lady Tirjella goes better than mine did.".

He continued carefully, "She has been kindness itself, but she could only give me part-time work here, and to be honest young Master, visitors of your rank are far and few between. I help out in the hospital two days a ninenight, but make myself scarce when the warlords come to court.".

Daro heard the tension in the light voice, then asked simply, "Are you free of bond or service to another Tobin? You're not a runaway are you?", and Tobin gave him his full attention.

"No Lord.", he answered, (as though he was holding his breath).

"Will you swear to that if I am given leave to approach you?", Daro asked curiously, and Tobin chuckled.

"Are you going to offer me work then Master?", he enquired, but before Daro could ascertain the reason for the sudden increase of tension in Tobin's voice, There was a clack of approaching sandals and Tobin moved hurriedly towards the door.

As he passed Daro however, he spoke swiftly, in a voice threaded with hope.

"I am not in service or by articles bound, but I have commitments. If you decide that you have work for me, that is if you want to talk to me, ask anyone to call me, I will come to you. I am a practised guide, have worked rehabilitating those with sight loss and am very discreet. I need very little for myself, just regular work with time to attend to my commitments.".

Daro heard the tap at the door, and was grateful that Tobin was in the room, for he was still disorientated. A voice he recognised said swiftly "I have come to fetch my guest myself.", and then Tirjella was there drawing him through the doorway into a corridor redolent of age and the secrets of the past.

They left Tobin discreetly tidying Daro's belongings away, and strangely Daro felt no alarm. As if she read his mind Tirjella said comfortably, "It is certain that his ways are strange to our men, but Tobin is the most honest man I know. He takes care of guests who come without an entourage sometimes, mainly those Greeeyn with interest in our rock formations, visiting Masters, but never my warlords. They do not like his type, and he fears them greatly.". Her words were light, but Daro was more than aware that she was advising him, and thought for a few moments before asking questions.

"He was gentle, confident enough to help a disabled man attend to personal matters. He's clean and well presented as far as I can tell. He seems polite, and behaved with propriety.".

Unaware of the sharp glance aimed at him, Daro tried to form a mental image, guessing height, but sure that Tobin was delicately built, with a light pleasant voice. He frowned, as they turned a corner and Tirjella spoke more openly.

"Daro, have you travelled for Rotations without meeting those who pair with their own gender?", and understanding dawned.

"Is that anyone's business other than his own?", he queried as they entered Tirjella's private dining room. He waited while the Sorceress led him to a chair and saw that he was seated, then she said softly, "Of course not, however, many (particularly young men uncertain of their own persuasion), take against such pairings. Others fond of brutality have used such couples very badly, and to my shame Tobin's partner was singled out for such treatment just before I moved my court here. The poor man was crippled as a result but Tobin supports him valiantly, despite my inability to give him more work. You see, he still loves Andrau. I pray for guidance but I am angered every time I see the result of such bigotry.".

Daro silently broke bread, dipping it into the delicious vegetable soup set in front of him, and thought carefully. His own Sands were very easy about such matters, but they had got that way over millennia. Since the coming of the Inesh, a small Clan held in slavery. Forbidden to breed, and with few men of their own, they had changed perceptions. Since Ikella had freed them, more women had borne children, but not all did, many choosing to remain in single sex partnerships. He ate and thought, then as a light cheese was placed on the table, and his plate replaced by a platter of the herb biscuits he loved, he came to a decision.

"Can Andrau be moved?", he asked casually. "How long ago was he hurt, and what are his injuries?".

Tirjella frowned. "His back was broken after someone towed him on a rope behind a galloping Zeglur.", she spoke harshly, her face severe. "We have stabilised him, but infection is a major problem, he has not recovered the use of his legs, and is doubly incontinent. I don't think Tobin has really understood that his lifespan will be severely limited, but he nurses him as tenderly as any mother, and seems to understand that he will never recover. Why do you ask?".

Daro said softly, "Because if I offer Tobin a place as my body servant, I will also have to provide for Andrau, however limited his lifespan may be.", and Tirjella stared at him astonished. He saved her the trouble of further comment by saying with a smile.

"Deshun Tirjella, I have been here half a day, and still have no chance of breaking the news my mother sent me here with. Don't you want to hear the news of Selesh, of Scartel and othersands as well?".

She sat forward, avid interest written in her face and said gently. "I can't wait young man. You came through here four Rotations ago, and I haven't heard the results of that escapade, let alone the latest news. Ikella has been ill I know, fluctuations and odd harmonics in the Source tell me that much is afoot magically, but I must wait the Guardians pleasure before I find out what!".

She uttered a small growl of frustration, and Daro grinned, seizing the opportunity. Sliding his chair back, he asked politely, "May I have permission to rise?", then as if by mutual consent, she too stood, stretched and suggested that they go to her dayroom where there was a fire, no attendants to disturb them, and they could talk as late as they liked.

It was perhaps the matter of a few minutes to walk the small distance to Tirjella's day-room, but as they traversed a corridor where ancient sconces lit as they approached, Daro felt as though he was walking back into the past of the Azure Sands. Tirjella paused at a lavishly banded door, saying thoughtfully, "I wonder if I showed you our Inner Sanctum? So much has been discovered since you were last here and if I remember it correctly, you and Ahnell spent most of your time arguing about where you intended to travel.".

She turned away from the doorway, without noticing the sudden stillness in her guest, then she was expertly guiding him into an extraordinary circular room at the end of the corridor. She held out a hand commanding, "A Lecthos!", and Daro felt the walls flush blue. His Seguidor, hanging around his neck on a chain trembled against his flesh, until he raised a hand and touched the Azure segment gently. A deep sonorous chime sounded, and Tirjella tilted her head listening, even as she guided Daro down a long slope which ended in a bare arena, surrounded by banked seats. He could hear odd harmonics, detect that whoever stood here would command the attention of any gathering, and couldn't resist commenting.

"How many seats are there? Do you use this room for Council meetings, Clan gathers or What?", briefly regretting his impulsive demands as Tirjella seemed to shrink into her robes, almost withdrawing from him as he spoke.

She turned towards her own chair, saying in a odd, choked voice.

"Sorry Daro. I just had the most ridiculous thought cross my mind. I thought I heard a bell, as we entered the room and the two things together have left me feeling quite shaky! I must be working too hard and I know that we can't afford to have both Ikella and myself ill at the same time. Let an old lady sit and catch her breath will you? You have a chair in front of you, about six paces away. Do you want to explore a little, or sit with me till I get my breath?".

Daro regarded the faltering Sorceress with an indulgent smile on his face. Tirjella was (as all the Sisters of Sorcery were), a great deal older than she looked. However, she had given him an opening that he had to seize with both hands, so he tracked her position following the sound of her voice, and suggested gently:

"I could tell you the news Aunt Tirjella, then we could move on, back to warm drinks and fireside chats, but this would be ideal to start off with.".

When Tirjella became aware of some subtle change in Daro's posture, she found the lethargy that had drained her of strength melting. When his clothes started to shimmer, changing fluidly from the travel garments she had initially seen to the flowing robes depicted in rare sketches of the ancients, she leant forward, a look of intense interest on her face. Glancing round, she saw that the light quality of the chamber had altered. The deep blue of the arena was flooded with Opal. Its brilliance embraced the one seat in which she sat, and the man who faced her, encircling them both in his aura. Her jaw dropped, her mouth opened to speak, but with a warm smile, he raised a silencing finger to his lips, and opened his eyes.

Caught by surprise, caught like a gully-hopper in the gaze of a sandrigal she clung to her seat as he lifted his head and sang. She saw it all. The story of his exile, the endless wanderings, treatments for obsession, and the weary closing of the circle as he returned empty-handed. She experienced his strange dream, the heartbreak of those final days and his terror driven run across the Opal Sands from Tirjhinar to Selesh. She felt his anger, his despair, heard the challenge leave Ikella's mouth, then in the flicker of a scowl, understood that he had decided to sacrifice himself in order to break Ikella's stony wall of indifference. She gasped as she realised that the only reason they were again bathed in the light of Seleus, was because thinking himself unloved, Daro had set out to impress his mother!

At the end of this "overture in Opal", she still sat, trying to grasp the enormity of his achievement, and in the dying cadences of his voice heard the regret, that without sight he might fail to reunite the Sands. He wanted nothing more than a world fit for those who lived in it. That he still didn't know what he could do to provide more food, more water, and heal their troubled world. She caught the plea of a novice, blended with the power of a mage as yet untested and felt her loyalty engage. The light dimmed, Daro was disengaging from magic, as she sat up, regaining authority in the flickering blue of her own aura, and said quietly:

"May the One always guide our Way Lord Daro, but be assured that the Clan Zurias, these Sands and all I have to offer are yours to command. You spoke of others rising to power also. Do I presume that there will be an Azure Sandsinger as well? Do you have any idea when that will happen?", but Daro was grinning and shaking his head.

"Not yet for a while I fear, but be sure that by that time I'll know more. There are quite a number of people who seem to have expected something of this sort, dear Solana was one of them. By the time it happens, you'll all be ready for it.", but his inner voice was warning him maliciously.

"You're mad! How in Hadda's Hall could anyone prepare for the erratic influence of Jalni?".

By an unspoken yet mutual agreement, the evening was drawn to a close. Tirjella was frankly overwhelmed, and quite ready to accede to Daro's demands, grateful that she wasn't expected to break the news to her Clan, or in fact confide her knowledge to anyone else. Concern over Ikella's sudden descent into frail old age had quite frankly distressed her enough, so it was not long before Adora, dancing attendance on her Deshun, found herself escorting Daro back to his guest room, and the welcome attentions of Tobin.

He was transferred from the hand of the Senior Healer with the cheerful acknowledgement.

"Ah. Well done Tobin. Our visitor and Deshun Tirjella have talked themselves to a standstill. I think a hot sweetdrink, cool sheets, and peace and quiet are prescribed. If you can take care of Lord Daro, I'll tackle our other problem!", and wishing Daro a peaceful night, she turned and was gone in a swish of robes and the clicking of sandals. Daro teetering on the brink of sleep himself, let Tobin guide him to a chair, and help him disrobe. When he was just clad in nether clothes, a sleeping robe of soft Azure wool was thrown around his shoulders, as Tobin suggested that he massage Daro's feet. Sandals removed, a light oil, redolent of the tall trees that still graced Mount Darnesh's peak, was applied. Strong fingers kneaded knotted tendons, flexed his ankles and calmed jangled nerves, and still Daro waited for Tobin to speak. Eventually the servant stood, tucked a cloth round Daro's legs, then turned away to tend the brazier where his sweetdrink bubbled. With his back turned to Daro, the man spoke gently.

"Thank you for considering my employment Master. No doubt our Deshun will have put you in the picture, and I am sure that you have re-considered your position. I should like to attend you while you remain however and wouldn't like you to feel under any obligation to continue our earlier conversation.".

Daro knew with certainty that this was not the first time that tight, painful little speech had been made and came to a decision.

"Hadda hang you high if you've been less than truthful over wanting a permanent position!", he exclaimed wrathfully. "I had to work on Tirjella to get her to consider transferring Andrau to Selesh.".

Tobin whirled to face him, eyes alight with joy. "You know and don't care?", he gasped, hands clenched about a tall drinking vessel. "Do you mean it Lord? Andrau needs a lot of care. After what happened to him, his back was broken, and he slept like one dead in Darnesh's deepest chamber. He says he dreamed wonderful dreams, and it is true to say that even a Master Weaver of Andrau's skill couldn't have imagined what he says he learned whilst asleep. He will never recover, but what he knows all the Master Weavers want to learn and I cannot write it fast enough, and work to feed us. However, I have a childhood friend who is a scribe at Selesh, Brannith would write the skills, while I work for you.".

He looked at Daro searchingly. "Are you well Lord?", he demanded, as Daro's skin prickled, his inner mind ringing under the assault of Tekrun's Bell, as yet another part of his magical jig-saw fell into place.

Chapter 23 - Loom of Legends

In the half-light of dawn the Rangers gathered silently. The road out of Darnesh was deserted, as sleeping babes were swaddled in furs, and tenderly disposed in riding slings. Drowsy passengers were lifted to the saddles of mounted men, and in the shifting shadows of a blue-grey desert the sands softened the shapes of the Sheer Wolves they rode. Patch dyed blues disguised the riders, a drift of rising mist enveloped the party turning northeast, then at the signal of a raised hand the massed riders moved forward... and were gone.

Jalni who had risen especially to take her leave of Terris and Sushanna, blinked. If she hadn't seen it she wouldn't have believed it. One moment there had been Rangers, wolves and passengers, the next, only the sand, and a cold wind rising. She shivered, pulled her Holders surcoat around her shoulders, and walked quietly back into the Healer Complex.

Few people were about yet. Some drudges swept floors, a Healer slipped into a sickroom, and Jalni used to earlier hours than most, quietly went to the room she had shared with the Ranger women, and closed the door behind her. She packed her travel bag swiftly, swept the last of her possessions into a carrisack and prepared to leave herself. She had made her formal representations to Tirjella the previous evening, so there was no need to remain, but although she was in no way bound to Darnesh, her mood was whimsical and she lingered. Wondering if she should seek out her Sandsinger and return to Selesh with him, she leant her head against the cool rock wall as the sun began to rise and with the chime of warming stone in her blood, was enveloped in a pure surge of energy.

Her breath caught in her throat, her body leapt in joyous response, but coming to herself long minutes later, she recoiled with a shudder of fear. This was the very sensation that had accompanied her childish tantrums. Flushed with such power, She had revelled as she suspended Tjerri over the waste pits at Selesh, glowed as she "silenced" Mina, and they had paid the price, not she. Tjerri long dead from plague, Mina nearly killed by her cruel attempt to silence her chattering!

"No! If these great underground places threatened her ability to control her erratic powers, she would journey back to Jerritol where she had lately felt safe, then, out across the Sands in search of her destiny. Mind made up, she stopped searching for Daro, glanced round the room once. before hoisting her carrisack over her shoulder,. Somehow, despite the lingering thrill making her legs tremble, she forced her self away from the place where the walls whispered honeyed temptation to explore and went in search of her party.

The gathering square was still quiet, though a light burned in the forge. There was a clatter from the kitchen as she crossed to the stable yard, just in time to see her Steward ordering a groom to bring out their Zeglurs. She was wondering how three riding animals could carry the new members of their party, when Orto crossed to join her leading two extraordinary beasts, already saddled and bridled, ready to ride. She stared at him blankly until Dinnot del Lynne appeared, taking the reins out of Orto's hand, and commenting.

"Do you like my Cherl's Half-Holder Jalni?", to which enquiry she simply had no answer.

"I never saw anything like those in my life.", she eventually said, taking note of the height of the beasts nervously. They swayed above her, jaundiced eyes regarding her down the length of the most supercilious of noses. Their golden woolly coats surmounted by tufty manes making them look and feel exotic and strange. Great long legs and powerful haunches spoke to her of speed, and Dinnot grinned as she peered up, trying to see the ornate high crested saddles above the elaborate woven blanket bedecking the strangely curved backs.

"They look fast.", she eventually remarked, "but where do they come from? Are they yours and if so where would we stable them? They are huge!".

Dinnot smiled, saying cheerfully. "Oh they are used to rough grazing. They never had anything else since I won them at dice in the Carnelian Sands rotations ago.", and he patted the arched neck nearest him. The Cherl groaned softly, turning its head towards Dinnot and he fussed the animal gently, murmuring to it tenderly. Jalni sighed, and signed to Orto.

"Can we put Cherls with Coatan?", she enquired, elegant fingers making the unmistakeable shape of the Coatan males heavy curled horns. He appeared to consider the matter, but eventually shook his head and shrugged. She sighed, as Dinnot said encouragingly.

"Your signing comes along swiftly Holders, the only problem is that you need a lot of patience to be sure that the person you sign to understood what you said. Yes, Mistress, your Uncle understood you perfectly, he just doesn't know the answer.", he finished with a grin so confident that Jalni had to resist the urge to put him down. Seeing her flush of irritation the young Weaver said soothingly. "Fortunately Cherls are quite docile, and get along with most domestic animals. The only exception being when they are breeding and have young to protect. These two are mother and daughter, from whom I plan to breed, but first I must find a place to settle.".

He said nothing more but cupping his hands assisted Madiv to scramble inelegantly into the saddle of the older Cherl, as Orto helped Jalni up onto the back of one of their Zeglurs. She was mildly disappointed that she wasn't riding the more elegant creatures, but changed her mind as soon as she saw their strange swaying gait. She whispered to Brand as he took the halter of the last Zeglure and mounted.

"I hope Madiv isn't needed in the weaving rooms immediately. the poor man looked quite nauseous as they passed.", and the builder grinned.

"He'll adapt soon enough I reckon Healer Jalni.", was the only comment, but there was a sly twinkle in his eye as Jalni, (reminded of her calling), touched her scrip and recalled what she carried for the treatment of saddle-sickness. Thus, in the cool of dawn they left Mount Darnesh and turned north to Jerritol and home.

Back in Darnesh, Daro had woken, aware that Jalni had gone. He lay still for a moment, then after refreshing his memory of the room's shape, he sat up, then swung long legs out of bed. The rock walls were "singing in the day, still vibrating with the soft surge of power he recognised as the signature of the Azure. Along the passage doors opened as the community went about their business, and hastily, Daro threw off his sleeping robe, and found his way to the necessary. He was trailing the wall, trying to locate his wash-stand when he realised that he was no longer alone. The whisper of bed linen, then the gentle tap at the door forewarned him of Tobin's arrival, and he turned with relief. His body servant seemed rather subdued, but Daro said warmly, "I'm glad you came before I broke something.", and Tobin swiftly sprang to his aid.

In no time he was sitting in the sleeping area, sipping a sweetdrink as Tobin said abruptly, "Forgive me Lord, but I find Andrau reluctant to come to Selesh, and where he stays, so stay I.".

Daro heard the misery in the servants voice, and raised an eyebrow, silently interrogating that statement, as Tobin hastily explained.

"Andrau is a Master Weaver. He is unable to contribute to his Guild in any other way than using his knowledge to complete their records. He has been working with one of the Guild Elders using ancient techniques in an attempt to recreate a missing Tapestry.".

The freshly washed hair on the nape of Daro's neck was by now, standing on end, as Tobin confided, "He thinks these Sands were once home to a special class of Weaver who was able to use Sorcery to create a magical Tapestry. Both that knowledge, and the Loom of Legends that created it were lost long ago, but there is a belief that if we only knew where to look, we might be able to recreate the conditions that would bring back a better world for all of us. He is so convinced, that even if he might not see it himself, he must stay with Master Toluran and test the weavings he dreamed.".

Daro's mind reeled. So many beliefs teetering on the edge of truth, every one of them a huge leap of faith, and yet so many nearly right. He was silent, absorbing what Tobin had said, understanding that he was going to have to stretch their credulity further, but relieved that in some strange parallel of his own search, good people everywhere were looking for salvation, not for themselves, but for their world. He asked gravely.

"Does Andrau have a large room to himself?", and Tobin replied nervously.

"Yes Master. Toluran persuaded the Guild that they should support him. His injuries need a lot of careful treatment, and he gets tired very quickly, but Toluran (who set up a small loom to occupy himself), often keeps him company while weaving samples from the records.".

Daro grinned. "So, we can talk to Toluran, Andrau and Tirjella in one place.", he observed thoughtfully, and arose, intent on gathering his thoughts in quiet meditation. Reluctantly Tobin guided him to Tirjella's dayroom. She was puzzled, but willing to let Daro use the chamber where he had revealed himself, for a period of quiet reflection. She agreed to meet him in Andrau's room, and to ensure that Toluran was present also, then guided him herself, letting Tobin go to warn his Andrau that she would visit in two turns of the sand-glass.

At the door of the Council room, Daro said briskly, " There are a number of things I need to do Tirjella. I must talk to Shiarjha and prepare them for Andrau's transition to Selesh. I will take you into my confidence later, but for now dear Aunt, I must be alone.". He half expected some resistance, but after initial hesitation Tirjella said calmly,

"If it so please you my lord, but can you manage without a guide?", and hearing only concern for his safety in her voice he allowed her to open the door and guide him through. With the door shut against other eyes, Daro flexed shapely hands into a complex gesture and in his grasp was his staff (powerstone alight). He smiled at the hiss of Tirjella's indrawn breath, then turning away from her, allowed the Staff to guide him to the centre of this small amphitheatre, and knelt. Tirjella's concerns answered, he felt relief flood him at the "snick" of the door, and sat back on his heels, lowering his Staff and freeing his Seguidor.

He held it between fingers and thumb, positioned carefully on the metallic hub. Feeling it starting to spin in his grasp he mentally "opened " himself to his environment, and knew that the Stillglass in the council Chamber would show all the shades of Azure. Shortly thereafter he heard Shiarjha's voice.

"I am here Ichspeller .", and in relief he began a short but comprehensive list of commands. She listened without comment, then said quietly. "All that can be done quite swiftly, but I fear to tell you that we have company here. It is not too surprising I suppose, but Suraya is home.".

Brow furrowed he absorbed this in detail, then asked mildly, "Has she been any trouble?", and pictured Shiarjha's face screwing up in concentration while he awaited her reply.

"In honesty Ichspeller ?", she deliberated over his title (subtly reminding him who held the balance of power at Selesh, but as he remained silent continued softly.

"She is the very model of rectitude. Calm, polite, and I feel, honestly distressed by Ikella's decline. She arrived without notice yesterday, spent two hours in retreat, then arrived at my door professing herself ready to do anything she could to help me. So it would appear that Kerisima has been a very strong influence, and Suraya is indeed ready to return to Beneva's tutelage.".

Daro sighed, but chose not to remark on this latest test of his restraint, merely checking that he had remembered everything he needed.

"I will have the rooms you describe cleared and prepared for your patient. I am certain I know which one you mean, it had looms in a workroom, storage for materials, both raw and finished, a large bedroom and a living area as well. I will ask the builders to check it over and fit a door. Mina will be warned and have Healers in place ready for your return, and I will definitely keep Suraya right out of all and any preparations!".

This last was definitely not one of his requests, but a brief smile lit up his face, as he imagined Shiarjha's indignant expression. His hands rotated his Seguidor once more, and this time his fingers touched the Azure filled section.

"Jalni my love.", he barely breathed sending his voice directly to her inner mind. "Stay safe in your travels, know I am returning to Selesh where you will always be welcome.", but before she could answer him, he withdrew, ruthlessly shutting down the link so that he might more clearly focus his energies on more pressing matters.

He changed position, sitting cross-legged, resting a hand on each knee, dropping easily into the meditation that would most refresh his powers, focussing his mind's eye on his powerstone, dreaming the Opal and slowing time. After a while the creases on his brow smoothed, and his eyes opened revealing their gleaming depths, as he explored a method by which he might safely conclude this day's work. Twice more he summoned Shiarjha through the Seguidor, then with calm deliberation he stood, holding his Staff aloft. He touched Seguidor, Anduigor and powerstone, then said calmly, "Virinesh.", and disappeared, leaving behind just a sparkle in the atmosphere.

Materialising seconds later in his own study at Selesh, he fingered his Seguidor once more, knowing that the glow of Opal filled the scrying table in the Council Chamber, and Shiarjha (who had been waiting for just such a signal), said briskly, "Where?".

"In my own study.", he answered her enquiry, then asked curiously, "Are you alone?". She chuckled gently, "Not exactly, she's in the Djellim with Beneva.", and into his mind floated a picture of a small demure looking girl with a mane of dark hair, piled up and pinned to add to her height. He considered for a moment, then said placidly.

"Fine. I'll be back some time after Height of Sun. There'll be fewer people about then, and we should be able to get my guest settled before I tackle Suraya. Is everything ready?".

She said briskly, "Yes, or it will be by then.", and broke their connection immediately. Daro tilted his head, checking his memory once more then, apparently satisfied, lifted his Staff and commanded, "Revistas!", materialising in the Council Room of Darnesh, just as Tirjella entered to take him to Andrau.

He walked steadily, his hand tucked into the crook of her arm, and wondered at the informality of these Sands. He knew (and admired) his brave Inesh warrior guards, but privately chafed at their constant presence. Ikella's position had always been a barrier to a normal life, but he recognised the place Selesh occupied in Pelshar's social structure, and if he looked at the freedoms of Darnesh enviously, it was only briefly. Tirjella talked about the constant search for any sign of water at Darnesh, saying grimly that the inhabitants spent more time in gathering moisture since the cloud cover had gone, than they had during the artificial Winter following his birth, and guiltily Daro touched his Seguidor's Azure segment, marshalling power to search Mount Darnesh for underground aquifers. They were descending now, the atmosphere cooling as they plunged down broad ramps, then Daro caught the sound of rushing water, as Tirjella said quickly. "How are you on stairs my boy?", turning right as she did so.

He came to a stop, holding up a hand for silence, and surprised Tirjella stood stock-still, as Daro turned left, called his Staff, and lit the powerstone with a simple gesture. Tirjella stirred restively, obviously longing to demand explanations, but stilled at the expression on his face. He concentrated for a moment longer, then placing a hand on the wall to the left of the corridor he sang a long low note, which culminated in the magnification of the sound he had heard. Tirjella immediately held out a hand cloaked in Azure, and following the line of the wall, harmonised her voice with his, sending out a harmonic which seemed to resonate with the wall until she stopped suddenly, as the note soured and dropped. Daro heard a deep thrum, then Tirjella had her own Staff in her hand, which she struck to the wall at the point where she had stopped.

There was a dull "thunk", then Tirjella shrieked with excitement.

"Water. I found water, Daro look, I mean feel!".

She guided Daro's hands (mysteriously free of magical Staffs), to where water was bubbling through a crack, then she stilled suddenly, concentrating on summoning help. It wasn't long before a small group formed to collect water, followed by the builders to investigate its source, and Daro and Tirjella were able to complete their journey, turning at last into a deep cavern room, where Andrau, Toluran and Tobin waited their pleasure.

It was a comfortable room. A shelf held books and scroll-bags, a bed central to the room was provided with a cunning table piled high with sand and wax tablets, but what held the eye was the man who lay back on banked up pillows.

"He must have been a commanding presence before he was robbed of his health.", was Daro's first thought, for the life force physically radiated from the man. He could feel it as Tirjella crossed the floor, leading the Sandsinger right up to the bed. He heard a rustle, then a shaky laugh as Andrau said softly.

"O my! I thought I had problems, but at least I have my sight! How In all Nine Sands can a blind man provide what I need Tobin, or are you too far gone in hero worship to notice that small blemish?", to which Daro heard shocked murmurs as Tobin tried to apologise for his partners rudeness. Daro grinned amiably and retorted (just as rudely).

"Yes, I can tell you're a difficult customer to please, but thank the One, I didn't lose my mind when I lost my sight. It must be doubly hard to manage with no legs and no brains either!", at which Tobin failed to stifle his giggles, while Andrau considered his next tactic. Daro Forestalled him.

"Good day to you too Master Andrau.", he said pleasantly. "Shall we put our tiles on the table? It will save everyone a great deal of time and trouble. I am quite sure that Tobin has told you that I am Seris Ikella's son, and that I offered him full employment at Selesh as my body-servant and rehabilitation advisor. Whatever your concerns about that are, that offer is still in place. However, I wanted to put your mind at rest. Your situation notwithstanding, I am prepared to extend that offer to you, and to Master Toluran as well.".

He heard the rustle of robes as bodies shifted, looking at each other, then Toluran said gently.

"Andrau, dear boy. I told you that Lord Daro has no designs on Tobin. That he would facilitate your move to a place which is the centre for all Healer training, and is not too far away for us to communicate.".

Tirjella agreed, adding briskly.

"Selesh is our new Sanctuary. You will be surrounded by ancient texts, all three Guardians, the greatest Healers in Pelshar, and have your friends with you as well. What more do you want?".

Daro said kindly, "Whatever happens Andrau, I promise to take care of Tobin and ensure his safety and comfort. I will take Master Toluran as my pensioner as well, he has the run of the Djellim of Sanctuary in order to pursue your research, and he may use the looms we found in the ancient part of the settlement as well. Furthermore, that can all happen fairly quickly, without pain or fatigue, if that is what you want.".

The sick man's voice quavered. "How can you promise such things young lord? You don't know the agony of movement, the pain of treatment day in day out I wouldn't even survive the journey, and I am too near death to want to make the effort. What about your warlords? How will you protect my love from the fate that befell me? Even the ancient Sandsingers couldn't be everywhere all of the time, and although I think you very beautiful, a Sorceress you'd never make!".

Despite Tirjella's "tut" of outrage, Daro couldn't help grinning. He liked Andrau hugely. He had a mind and spoke it clearly, what was more he had given Daro the opening he needed. He took a pace or two back from the bed, then said sweetly.

"No, you're right Andrau. A Sorceress I'll never be, though I thank you for the compliment, but what about a Sandsinger?", and cloaked himself in Opal.

Chapter 24 - Dreaming the Opal

Daro lifted his hand, as He heard fearful gasps from Tobin and Andrau. Tirjella spoke soothingly, using a local dialect to steady her patient, then she said simply, "Dear Toluran. Do get up, you're far too old to kneel for so long on this cold floor, my lord wouldn't expect it of you either.".

Daro, (feeling the particular severity of her gaze) banked down the fire of his power, ceased to glow, and came forward hands extended, saying with a smile.

"No indeed my friends. Gurayen alone knows how cold those floors get, and I don't need two nursing cases more at Selesh.".

In the brief time his powers had been fully engaged, he had used "true-sight", to test the integrity of those present, mightily relieved to find three true men beside Tirjella, outlined in the eerie flickering view that power afforded him. He realised that anxious eyes were turned on him, so to relieve the tension, he asked for chairs and a sweetdrink to be provided, and was amused when Tirjella invoked her powers quite casually to produce these items. Old Toluran tapped his hand on the back of a chair, and Daro moved towards the sound, and was enthroned by his companions, as Tobin took charge of the small table that had materialised filled with drinking bowls and stoppered jugs. In a short space of time, Daro heard drinks being poured, and then Toluran cleared his throat and addressed the company.

"Lord Daro, Deshun Tirjella, I have lived near Mount Darnesh for most of my many Rotations. I have seen many strange things, otherworldly things, and much magic in my life, but I never thought to see a living Sandsinger. I have for many Summers travelled back to Anempor, often using the cooler evenings there to search for more information to go with this.", and as the old man produced a tiny book from the pocket of his surcoat, Daro distinctly heard a tinkle of tiny bells, and caught the perfume of the great velvety flower that Jalni had identified as a "rajah", back in Scartel.

He sat forward demanding, "What have you got there Toluran?", and the old man said gravely, "Just a simple book my lord. It is very tiny, only a mans thumb in length, but very thick. It has many old dyers recipes in it, most of which are unusable because we can't identify the plants, or even some of the minerals recommended, which adds credence to my theory about its antiquity. However the part which I believed might interest you or the Guardian of Knowledge is written in some arcane script which jiggles about and can't be read. Even the most highly trained scribes say it is bewitched, being unable to focus on it for more than two characters, which means it is impossible to copy.".

Silently Daro held out his hand, feeling Toluran's old dry fingers tremble as the book was placed on his palm. Simultaneously, the cool breeze of awakening power fanned his neck, as his Seguidor quivered, his Anduigor pulsed, and the voice of Sentinel reminded him.

"Take care Selunsanni. Some things this world is not yet ready to know. You may learn at your own pace, but mortals often need to be protected from a knowledge they don't have the capacity to understand.".

He felt the Sorceress stir, and half wondered if she too had heard the warning, but she was interested only in his intentions for Andrau and Tobin. He reluctantly held the book out to Toluran.

"That will undoubtedly require a great deal of research, and although I'm very tempted to try looking into it here, we simply don't have the time or resources that we have in Selesh. Tirjella, you have my word that if the contents simply refer to the Azure, Beneva will return this after she has translated it.".

Duty done, he turned his attention on Andrau and Tobin, who had been engaged in a conversation of fierce whispers.

"Come now you two. I need to make clear the terms that I offer. You will be installed in rooms that were once used by another Weaver. There are looms (which have been successfully used in my lifetime), and you may order what threads and materials you need. There is more than one room in this apartment, judging by echoes the living area is bigger than here, which will make caring for Andrau easier. There are bathing facilities, store rooms and sleeping quarters. There will be Healers on call, a refectory where you may choose to eat, and as we have a lively group of permanently disabled inhabitants in the infirmary, Andrau will be less isolated. All your needs will be provided for, and you will be part of my household.".

Andrau spoke bitterly.

"Which is all very well my lord, but what about Tobin's safety? Every time there is a Clan Gathering he has to go into hiding. Your warlords and their underlings can very easily do to him what mine did to me, and I cannot bear that he lives in fear alone.".

Daro spoke gently.

"Some things even a Sandsinger cannot do Andrau. I am not a God and my powers are limited. I cannot heal your back, or prevent your death when your time has come, but this I can tell you. In the Opal Sands we have no warlords. We have our warriors of course, known as the Inesh, for they are members of our second Clan. However, they do not ride Zeglurs or any other animal. They are dedicated to the service of Selesh, which is the Mother house of Sorcery, and like their distant cousins the Nishanawa, they are all women, from whom I believe Tobin is totally safe. Your status as a couple won't affect anyone else, for the Shalhanhi have learned to respect each other's personal persuasions.".

"I tried to tell you Andrau!", Tobin was agitating, "I knew Lord Daro wouldn't let us walk into danger. We will be safe in his household, for I doubt that even Rodjeos or his enforcer would pursue us there.", and so it was that Tirjella, Sorceress of the Zurias watched in total amazement as the complicated boy she had known since birth, encircled Andrau's bed, the two men standing on either side, a heap of hastily gathered possessions and himself in a shimmering cloak of opalescence, and with a single word, vanished. However, long after Andrau had been settled into his new home and the rest of Selesh slept, Daro fretted over Tobin's words, eventually recognising their significance as he too drifted towards sleep.

"Rodjeos enforcer", was a term he had heard before, and it applied to one man who would have positively delighted in the performance of such a cruel act. Half asleep, as the words ran through his mind, he sat up, sweating in terror. Andrau's comments hadn't seemed to relate to the past, although he could be wrong. The Sandsinger threaded his fingers through his hair, wide awake and thoroughly unsettled by one thought.

"Rodjeos enforcer was Sowdin! Yet Tobin was still going into hiding every time the warlords came to Council. If the cold stone sensation in his chest was right, Tobin was in hiding from the same man, yet Sowdin had been reported dead Rotations ago.", he forced himself not to panic, not to summon his love in the middle of the night, for nothing would be achieved by that.

"However,", he promised himself grimly, "I must speak to her in the morning, for if I am right and Sowdin is alive, Jalni is in terrible danger.".

He rose when Seleus warmed Mount Torrenesh, and silently padded through his apartment, familiarising himself with rooms grown suddenly cold, vast and lonely. He missed Ahnell, he missed Jalni, and hard on that thought, he was reminded of the dreadful thought that had haunted his dreams. He bathed, sliding into the deep pool warmed by the hot springs below the complex, and wrapping himself in towels, ventured back to his bedroom, and stood irresolute wondering how he would choose appropriate clothing.

There was a soft tap at his door, then a firmer one, and he sighed, feeling that his brain needed peace and quiet rather than visitors, but he held out a hand calling "Come!", knowing that if he didn't, others would worry.

The door swung open, and Diras (remaining out in the anteroom said gruffly. "Your body-servant Lord. Shall I introduce him to the Watch so that he may pass where my lord permits?", and Daro was suddenly relieved of the problem with clothes.

He sensed Diras's disapproval as a bewildered Tobin was ushered through the door. Smiling Daro called Diras into the room in Tobin's wake.

"Don't go Diras, I have something to show you.", and swiftly seating himself on a low backless stool he said to the awed retainer, "Tobin, I have just washed my hair, while it is still wet will you show Diras that plaiting and beading technique the Zurian men wear for festival gathers?".

Swiftly Tobin obeyed, neatly dividing Daro's long hair into fine sections, his nimble fingers gathered and parted strands, weaving them together and embellishing every second strand with a bead, plucked from a long strand worn around his own neck. Under the unsmiling scrutiny of the tall Guard commander, Tobin had appeared frail and effeminate, but with his innate neatness and economy of movement, under his flying fingers Daro's hair became a work of art.

Diras was captivated. She held her breath as Tobin placed the last bead, then gathered and twisted the plaits into a neat club at the nape of Daro's neck. He came round to stand in front of Daro, and skilfully re-plaited Daro's Clan braid, and the tall imperturbable warrior whispered in admiration.

"For a high celebration the look is magnificent. For everyday however...?", and Daro chuckled.

"I wish I could see it!", he remarked, "but I don't want my mother to worry about me, nor would I tease Andrau unnecessarily either. Perhaps the style but not the beads?", then realising the work that had gone into the style, he said gently, "Here Tobin.", and held out a hand full of beads. Tobin captured them in a soft cloth bag, and escorted Diras to the door out into the ante-room, and Daro relaxed as he heard her chuckle.

"I can certainly get those rethreaded.", there are enough girls skipping in the Gathering Square to do that task quickly.", then the door closed and Daro turned to Tobin.

"I have urgent matters to deal with Tobin, so sadly I must dress and go about my work, but you are at liberty to explore, make lists of whatever you need, and Diras will tell you if we have it, or where and when you can get things ordered. Before you order vast amounts of toiletries for me, talk to my Songfathers. You will find them in our underground pastures. The elder is Carolus the Apothecary, and the younger is Master Trader Patris. When I have my duties organised for today then I will look in on Andrau and Toluran. Did you all sleep well?".

He was aware of drawers opening, the huge clothing press being investigated, then Tobin said with a gasp, "So many clothes, and all for one man. I have never seen anything like this. Are you sure that I'm not dreaming. Everything so elaborate, everything so beautiful, I won't know which garment to pick for you Lord.", and in his bewilderment Daro heard a great truth.

"There are robes of great antiquity in that press. They were certainly not designed just for me, but I have inherited them, and they possess magical qualities. However, I can only wear one set at a time, so pick one for today, and remember that I may have to travel so choose something easy to pack as well. I will wear pants, tunic and surcoat this morning, for I particularly want to impress a certain young lady!".

Wordlessly Tobin laid out shaving tackle on a dresser, and under Daro's direction fetched water from the bathing room. He was gone so long Daro nearly went to find him, but was reassured when Tobin returned full of astonishment at a deep bathing pool.

"I never saw anything like it Lord!", he babbled joyously, "I will enjoy cleaning and polishing in there!".

Daro was humbled. He (who had never had to clean or polish anything), could not imagine taking any pleasure from such an activity, and he said rather abruptly, "No you won't Tobin. That is what drudges do. Your job is to take me in hand. Make sure that I am clean, tidy and well turned out that I do not by my appearance let my mother or Selesh down. While my bondswoman is away, I may need a guide sometimes. I mean only in Selesh, which you will soon get used to, I have not thought of taking you out into the Sands, Andrau needs you too much for that.".

He shrugged himself into the clothes Tobin produced, suffered himself to be sprayed lightly with a musky perfume and have his Opal *redic* positioned on his brow, then said swiftly. "I must go Tobin. Lives here are governed by the Summoning Bell, and my people expect me in High Hall for the first service of the day. after I return, we will take break day with Andrau and Toluran, but I must go, I have a new Sorceress to impress.".

The people of Selesh crowded quietly into the Hall of the Healers. Members of the community, villagers from Selesh Minoria, student Healers filled the aisles. Standing in the Syndarial with Beneva, Shiarjha gently adjusted the belt on the girl who trembling, waited for her introduction to the community she would one day rule. She had been warned by Kerisima, Sorceress of the Tourmaline Sands, that she had made a very poor impression as a precocious child, deeply offending Ikella's adopted son, and her legs shook as she remembered the white shocked face of the boy on the day she left. He had given her his precious Dolcan, and now fourteen Rotations later, she could understand the nature of that gift, for Usticus had been her only companion and confidant in the lonely Rotations that followed. She had grown to love the little creature, carried him like a child (arms round her neck), and wept bitterly over his little corpse on the day he'd died from extreme old age, and now she was back, and would likely pay the price of childish taunts.

Earlier in the day she had stared incredulously, as a substantially unchanged Apothecary crossed her path. He had said nothing to her, but with the perception of power, she had been overwhelmingly convinced that he disapproved of her. She hoped that she could improve on her situation with hard work and loyalty, but trepidation was hard to keep at bay as she waited for the third Guardian to appear.

When eventually Ikella entered on the arm of Senior Healer Mina, Suraya was shocked into silence. The Sorceress of the Opal seemed like a shadow of her former self, and close inspection showed the Sorceress-Elect, that the fine lines of extreme old age had seamed her face. As Ikella stopped by her Sister Guardians, her gaze fell on Suraya and she smiled grimly.

"In the north Somishen Suraya, I heard that when Rangers are about to die, the ravens gather. In my case however, it seems that for ravens we can substitute magic-users.".

If she was aware of the discomfort these words caused, she didn't acknowledge that fact, but continued talking to Suraya.

"You have returned at a time of momentous change child. You are about to be initiated into the greatest mystery of our time. Kneel before me Suraya, voice, hand and power subject to my will. I bind your obedience, your silence, and your service in life and in death to the one who will command your allegiance this very day. Look up child, look into the Opal and dream.". Feeling the rush of a far superior power, Suraya mutely bent her head obediently and dreamed.

The man with the Opal eyes was holding out a hand, and smiling down at her, perfect teeth gleaming in his tanned face. Long hair caught back in elaborate braids gleamed like the bloom on the black jay's wings. He seemed vaguely familiar, but try as she might, the ensorcelled girl could not recall where she had seen him before and she was becoming very aware that she should not (in all modesty), remain staring up into his face like a moon maiden. She lowered her eyes modestly, or tried to, but her gaze was fixed on his, she could not look away, as his smile widened. Her head was swimming, his eyes were glowing like living Opals as he pinioned her by power. She felt her legs tremble, locking her knees had absolutely no effect and gracelessly she slid to her knees, still caught in his thrall.

At last he spoke, his voice running through her blood like fine old wine, but what he said made no sense at all, until she'd run it through her mind twice.

"Well little sister.", and his voice trembled on the edge of laughter, "Here we are again, and you have returned to show me your powers as you promised, but I hardly think I'm nothing now!".

Chapter 25- Azure Rising

In Jerritol, Madiv and Orto leant on the kitchen table, hands flashing in silent argument. Jalni had dropped out of it long ago, unable to keep up with the pace of accomplished signing. Attention wandering, she drifted out of the warm kitchen into the cool interior passage, making for the garden door. Letting herself out into the quiet evening, she crossed to the family funerary plot, and stood in the shadow of the citrine tree, in quiet contemplation. She touched the stone her mother had placed to mark the spot where her father lay, leant against the tree, and wondered where her mother was buried.

Her Grandfather had only said that Viness had been provided with a far better funeral than she deserved, so, skirting every other issue invoked by the memory of Sowdin, she turned her considerable concentration on that statement. Forcing herself to try and recall anything that might help her search, she became so absorbed in her thoughts that she nearly collapsed with fright when a voice came out of the dark.

"Puhrr aow?", it enquired delicately, as heart thudding with relief, she felt the pressure of a velvet head, and Echo was once more stretched out beside her, lying full length on the wall. Running skilled fingers through his coat, she soon encountered little nicks and scars he had inflicted on himself during her absence. Rubbing his ears, her hand had fondled the crest of his head, and passed to the arch of his neck before she paused, realising just how long she had left her faithful friend.

"Had he been hungry or cold in the chill of night?", she questioned herself guiltily, tugging her fingers in a combing action through the dense pelt. The mystcat casually draped a restraining paw over one hand, staring into her eyes as a strange hued miasma rose around her.

She leant half against the wall, half against the great cat, mesmerised by that brilliant gaze, finding herself caught in a stream of non-verbal communication. There had been a pile of old sacking in the store room, generous kitchen scraps, not to mention the large gully hoppers Echo himself had caught. Absently, she fondled his shoulders, captivated by this new turn of events, then became more alert as she tried to tell Echo that things round here would change soon. Beginning with the arrival of new Weavers, then passing to the possibility of a little child living here, she concentrated on making Echo understand that man and mystcat didn't belong together, to no avail.

He rolled over, displaying his throat and licking his paws reflectively until Jalni played her trump card.

"Of course.", she murmured conversationally, "It will be too late once I've gone.", at which Echo fell off the wall outside the garden and Jalni knew she had hit home with that remark.

"Uww raor?", the mystcat scrambled back onto the wall, daring her to impugn his dignity as he arranged his tail around his feet, but the spell was broken. Wishing Echo really understood human speech, she buried her face in his coat in frustration, as a peculiar sensation shivered along her neck. Her hair quivered like some living entity. Her skin prickled and she felt giddy. Breathlessly, she remembered experiencing something similar on the night she found the spell-charts back in Selesh. She was teetering once more on that same pinnacle of power, and yet this was different. Here in her family garden with those she trusted around her she felt safe enough to explore, so, in the deepening dusk of an Azure night, she turned blazing blue eyes on a creature from the wild and softly sang her dream.

Her world was filled with water. It spread across the broad horizon of her vision from Mount Darnesh north, to lap at the base of stark soaring cliffs below the Drekken Heights. There was an unusual rocking sensation, as though she *was* the water, washing up against shallow dunes to the East, turning at the barrier of strangely seamed sandstone cliffs below a shining palace, then sweeping northeast, as a dense mist descended.

Was she the wave that lifted and fell to speed the searchers on their way? Or was she the craft that running before the wind, sought shelter from some impending doom. Ahead, fog streamers billowed as she approached an enormous Temple complex set into a cliff. There were rocky promontories here, then the wind shifted and she was gliding westward, a drum driving the rhythm of her song, the rhythm of the paddles, and there was smoke in her eyes. Vision blurring, she leant forward, the boat swung around, and as the paddles dipped again, they swept away from her. In the distance she saw a great mountain, fire gushing crimson and gold from a crater half-way up its side. The mist of the vision rolled on, and Jalni's voice dropped as the last thing she saw was a group of paddle driven long boats disappearing into the rolling fog. She had been abandoned! Left behind on an unfamiliar shore disguised by an immense Azure sea.

With a cry of utter desolation she woke, pillowed against the mystcat, understanding at last that she was not the sea, nor the ship, she was the Searcher! In the long ago of her vision, she had seen another launched on such a search. Tomorrow, she would begin her own, starting with the retrieval of her mother's body. She turned to her father's grave and made a vow, one that she would see through, even if it resulted in all three of them sharing this family plot.

"I will find you Mother, and reunite you with Father, however long it takes and at whatever cost!".

She had not known that she spoke out loud, or that Madiv reluctant to disturb her had entered the garden on last rounds, but his voice said quietly out of the dark.

"Then you will have company, for this is precisely what Orto intends to do, may the One guide you both.".

Echo sealed the pact, rubbing his great head submissively against Jalni's hand, with a contented "Puhrr Aow.", before slipping into the night to hunt, as Jalni turned weary feet towards her bed.

The following morning, Orana had no qualms, greeting Jalni's decision with surprising equanimity.

"Of course you must make the effort my dear.", she said easily. "Will your friend Seris Shiarjha help you with your search. Perhaps Deshun Tirjella has some reports you could use?", but Jalni shook her head.

"Deshun Tirjella has enough problems of her own at the moment.", she mumbled through a mouthful of milta grains boiled in milk. "When I left, she had a loft full of Rangers, a high ranking Shalhanhi visitor and a newly traced spring to sort out. I dare not ask for help in that direction. Shiarjha had to go back to Selesh, but she gave me leave to stay and search. I have credits to exchange, Orto for company and I think the mystcat will follow us. We will try and get him back to the Ashgenar where he belongs, for if I am right, Sowdin took my mother back to her own people.".

She glanced round the table, seeing Madiv signing to Orto, and added. "He told me that my mother had a better funeral than she deserved, which means that someone must have provided that. He dared not take her to any Healer, because they would have seen the signs of malnutrition and abuse. The Nishanawa however, are a closed society. They do not intermingle with outsiders, and could not have known what brand of evil they were dealing with. Mother's whole life (before Father) was bound to the Temple of the Winds, then Sanctuary. One has fallen, but the other still stands! Who but her people would have provided her funeral?".

The entire company were looking at her with varying degrees of surprise on their faces. Orana said slowly, "Why didn't we think of that? He was far too much of a coward to bury her himself. When she died he was panicking, I heard him say that Healers could tell what killed a body now, so he wouldn't bury her here, in case someone pointed the finger at him, or that slavering bitch he took to wife. He could easily have taken her to the Temple, claim he'd found her body and recognised her as one of theirs, and be thanked for his wickedness!".

The bitterness of this speech was not lost on Jalni, who caught her Uncle's eye and said firmly.

"Then, if no-one has objections, tomorrow we leave for the Ashgenar, the Temple of the Winds, and whatever lies beyond.".

Later that day she consulted Edrith, who with the serenity of long practice had installed Dinnot Del Lynne with his own weft of Weavers. The young man's intent face told Jalni what she wanted to know, long before Edrith drew her to one side and pronounced himself well pleased with her "find".

"Oh yes Mistress, he is going to prove a valuable asset to this Halt, provided he wants to stay. His last Master thought very highly of him, and he is certainly a quick study. He had six samples from Madiv this morning and just working on a hand loom he has recreated three perfectly already, and even suggested time saving developments for the fourth. He's a full Master, but today he dressed plain, and made himself useful, helping the others dress a loom. He even showed young Shangle how to tie a weavers knot successfully, and I don't know how many times I've tried that trick.".

Jalni couldn't recall the last time she had seen Edrith so enthused, so relieved on that account at least she went into the hallway to see Madiv escorting Brand through the front door, into the street beyond. Hastening to say her farewells, and wish him success in his application, she was a little withdrawn and pensive as she returned to the Halt with her Steward. Following her invitation, Madiv joined her in the garden room where Orto was laying out travel packs for both of them. Shutting the door quietly behind him, he watched her squatting down to check her pack, and was entirely thrown off-guard when she asked abruptly, "Do you think my journey unwise Madiv? Edrith said nothing, but he pursed his lips and wriggled his face ,the way he does when he disapproves. When I told him what our plans were, even Dinnot looked worried, although we seem to have solved his problems with the Cherls. We will ride them back to his family in Anempor, and take Zeglurs from there on.".

She bent over her pack, turning her face away from Orto in case his skill in lip-reading made it impossible to confide in her Steward further. She continued talking about their potential new Weaver.

"Dinnot has already decided that he very much wants to stay here. He is of course, ready to fulfil your methods of selection, but Edrith will be devastated if you don't offer him at least a Rotation's tenure, and you know he's not easily impressed. However, both Dinnot and Edrith also brought up the subject of my slow signing. I am sufficiently aware that my Uncle takes a great risk in accompanying me, but he seems set on the idea, saying if he can't go with me, he'll go by himself. Can you talk to him for me? He seems to be hiding some sort of secret and I must know if he has discovered something that would substantially change the nature of the risk we take.".

She stood, tapped Orto on the back of his hand, and signed firmly. "I am going to find Echo. I want to tell him we leave at dawn.".

Without waiting for the deaf mute to reply, she slipped out of the garden door, and went purposefully to the store -room where the mystcat sprawled in a patch of sunlight, sleeping off a very large meal. Behind her in the garden room Madiv had placed a restraining hand on Orto's shoulder.

"She needs to think, and she wants to know what it is that you haven't told her.".

Jalni's Uncle grinned, and sat cross-legged on the floor beside his backpack, hands flickering at speed. "Don't know if it matters.", he signed, "Couldn't tell her anyway, she doesn't follow signing that well yet.", and Madiv's brow cleared.

"Tell me then.", his hands commanded, and Orto's eyes creased in concentration.

"We go to Darnesh, then to Oplaya and on to Tregeth.", at which point he smiled happily and with both hands to his ears, pantomimed a Zeglur braying.

Thankful that Orto couldn't mimic the awful sound, Madiv nodded tacit understanding. Orto laughing silently raised two fingers, tapping his scrip to indicate exchange of some kind, and then signed clearly.

"Take beasts to Anempor.", circling his head to indicate a Master's tokrun, then touching the Weaver blue of his surcoat. Madiv then saw uneasily that Orto was looking furtive. He placed a finger on his lips, then made the sign for "secret", as the Steward leant forward.

Orto frowned, creasing up his face as he laboriously explained, fingers slowing, repeating signs until Madiv at long last understood what he was being told. Then it was the Steward's turn to frown. He signed carefully.

"You are not going to the Temple Villeth? Why in Azure not?", and the Steward stared at the deaf man in consternation, for Jalni had been right. To divide a small search party was risky, but for a pair to part company in the Sands spelled disaster. However, Villeth del Orto had a determined streak, and although Madiv interrogated him sternly, all he got was an emphatic re-affirmation in sign language.

"Not my secret to tell. Someone else told me. Can't tell anyone. Secret.".

When they eventually went into the kitchen, the travellers ate in silence. Edrith and Dinnot chatted easily about weaving methods, and Madiv gave Orana instructions for rations to carry Jalni and Orto as far as Oplaya where they could buy more. Orto withdrew immediately after their meal, and Madiv said unhappily (in response to Jalni's look of enquiry).

"Couldn't get as much as a brinkle bean out of him. Says he's not going to the Temple, wouldn't tell me why, but says he knows a secret which isn't his to tell. Seemed quite animated about going to Tregeth though.", and Jalni's frown cleared like magic, though she groaned softly.

"Of course! I should have guessed. That snarrelled Apothecary gets everywhere!", she chuckled deep in her throat, and added, "Carolus is Ambassador for the High Council of Selesh. He also trades in Zeglurs, was Solana's great friend and knows Orto well. I have no doubt that we'll be picking up rather more than two hired Zeglurs at Tregeth when we get there, but it'll be good to have the old man come along too.".

At Orana's confused expression, Jalni "improvised" happily, "You wanted me to get the help of the Guardians Orana. Well, Carolus is the next best thing. He may even have messages from them for me.", and on that happy note, with last minute directions for his home from Dinnot del Lynne, Jalni retired, snuggling down in her old room. She was prepared for a wakeful night, but despite everything looming like unplanned disasters in the making, she slept long and restfully, waking at first light without any difficulty. She rose, slipping into travel wear silently in the shadowed room, only pausing briefly on the threshold to take stock of a place that she was convinced she'd never sleep in again, then left soft footed down the stairs to find Orto ahead of her. His weathered face lit up as she lifted her pack, and suddenly overcome with a huge rush of affection for this silent man who was all she would ever have of her father, Jalni's eyes glistened. They turned towards the garden door, (hinges well oiled precisely for this moment), and slid into the grey pre-dawn light.

From there it was but a simple step, up onto a rock casually positioned that evening by Orto, and onto the wall. In the shadows beyond there was a restive sound, then Dinnot del Lynne stepped forward, and it was an easy matter for both Holders to settle themselves in the saddles of the hump-backed Cherls he led. Jalni took Dinnot's message bag for his family. He said nothing much, but his eyes were haunted as he handed it up to her, and Jalni realising that it carried the sad news of his wife's death, pressed his hand in simple sympathy and slipped the package into a convenient bag strapped to her saddle.

It was time to go, the night was dissipating rapidly, and if they stayed the household would rouse and they'd be caught up in lengthy farewells (which Jalni hated)., She twitched the ear of the Cherl she rode, and felt it surge forward with pleasure. As they turned south east towards Mount Darnesh once more, Jalni wondered where Echo would pick up the trail, marginally concerned by the thought of the Cherl's reaction to being followed by a mystcat. She was looking forward, seeking out the lie of the land, or she might have seen Dinnot tap on the store room door, summoning those who had concealed themselves within to join him at the garden wall. Had she looked back, she might have seen a row of anxious faces and waving hands in the glow of early light, as her friends watched them out of sight of the Weaver's Halt. She might even have seen the strange phenomenon of hoof marks in the Sand, blazing blue where the Searcher passed. Azure rising, she rode on intent on not only seeking her destiny, but the salvation of her world.

Chapter 26 - Trial at Trididge

At the beginning of the journey Jalni had been excited, thoughts streaming onwards towards the goal she'd set herself. However, she soon discovered, Cherl riding took total concentration, besides requiring the adaptation of the few riding skills she possessed, starting with the odd position of the rider.

She'd crossed her legs (half sitting on one), as Dinnot instructed, but utterly unprepared for the peculiar rocking motion of his beast, she'd clung to the saddle in a vain attempt to counteract the nauseating sway. Realising with mounting concern that the lurch and swing was making tense sweat-soaked thighs chafe, within the first turn of the sand-glass, she raised her hand in the traditional signal, and brought her Cherl to a stop, with a muffled groan of defeat.

Sliding from the saddle, she'd tethered the beast, looping a leading rein around a large rock, before perching on its flat top to ruefully examine her inner thighs, rolling up soft leggings to do so. Dismounting, Orto watched the horizon, maintaining studious indifference to the length of pale golden skin exposed, as Jalni applied a soothing gel and wondered how to overcome this setback.

"This is horrible!", she managed to sign, creasing up her face to signify the depth of her distress, but Orto (dressed in soft leather leggings) seemed puzzled. Moving off her rock, Jalni adopted a comical stance. Bow-legged, hunch backed, she'd twisted her spine into the posture she'd noticed at fairs, which Orto found highly entertaining. However, as his hilarity died away, he hauled down his blanket roll producing another set of riding pants. These (made in fine kid) were obviously cut for a woman and threaded at waist and ankles with the dark blue braid of a Master Weaver. Staring in dismay at the new costume Dinnot had intended for his late wife, they'd been sobered by his selfless forethought. Wordlessly, Jalni measured them against herself, before exchanging them for her light weight trousering. Seleus was climbing, the light was intense and with a fair days travel ahead of them, they used the scatter of large rocks to remount and rode on.

By the time they turned east at the crossing below Mount Darnesh, she'd almost become accustomed to the movement, and when they climbed down at Drojan's Well, (a comparatively large oasis), Jalni was resigned to the ungainly beast she rode. Having unstrapped her bed-roll, saddlebags, and saddle, she handed the reins to a bright eyed boy, who waited for Orto's before hauling both Cherls towards a corral. Handing him one of Tirjella's markers, Jalni called after him.

"We'll stay tonight. Make sure they're fed, watered and rubbed down. We'll need them at first light.".

Slightly open-mouthed at her generosity, the lad pulled his jerkin down, acknowledging her instructions in a slightly adenoidal voice.

"Yarr Healer. That be done right away. I'll do it myself, and check their feet as well. They be clean and comfy afore sunfall. They're fine looking beasts, I like Cherls.", he moved off, talking to the Cherls happily, as Orto shouldered their saddles, and walked towards the stone built yard that nestled into the astonishing greenery that surrounded them. Jalni slung her bedroll round her neck and grabbed their bags, amazed at what she saw. Looking up into the canopy of foliage, she asked faintly, "Those can't be Driands surely?".

Hardly expecting an answer, but nevertheless, she got one. A passing grower replied proudly.

"Indeed Healer, they are Driands, just coming to the fullness we need if our Deshun is to enjoy them at Zenitheon. These plants are mature enough now for us to lay the first cluster on her table at the gathering festivities. I think they will be the first grown so close to Darnesh, and they are proof of our success. We have invested much in this crop and I can't wait to see her face!".

Thanking the man, Jalni was forced to run in order to keep up with her Uncle, but at last, she felt her adventure was beginning. Unusual experiences, rare plants, and stretched out ahead of her, days to be her own person, with no-one demanding she keep to their time-table, or fulfil their plans. Revelling in that feeling, she was utterly unaware that a greater plan than she could ever have imagined, lay in her path, ready for her to fall headlong into.

Neither Jalni nor Orto slept well, though they were both more than ready for their beds when night fell. Orto had fallen in with a group determined to play a game of dice. Jalni, concerned about her Uncle's ability to play a complex game involving six players, watched until her eyelids drooped, then took herself to the women's quarters across the courtyard and might have fallen asleep, but for the brush of cool air, that blew away her sleepiness. In the morning as they mounted well-rested and sprightly animals, Jalni signed to Orto.

"We camp alone tonight!", and received his nod of acceptance with relief. He grinned as his sitting beast rose to its feet, and Jalni was scandalised as he shrugged, and signed slowly.

"took these fools ten throws to realise I'd played dice before!", he gave her a savage grin, and patted his pockets so meaningfully that Jalni was glad she'd not looked into the stables to say goodbye. With a roll of her eyes, and a flick of her reins she stirred the younger Cherl into motion, and headed back into the Sands. This was to be the easiest part of their journey, though both of them had expected difficulties when they reached Sangan's Shelves, a series of extraordinary steps in the sands, where (had they been riding Zeglurs), they'd have lost days leading the beasts, who loved the tough grassy reeds that grew through the sands.

Along the edge of a landscape that rose in ever increasing terraces towards the sheer cliff face on the eastern flank of Mount Trididge, the Cherls maintained steady progress. Jalni glanced up at the third peak in the Darnesh range, trying to remember an old story her mother had told her, but she was too aware of the increasing heat, and the need to find shelter from the incandescence during noon, to give it any more thought. Then Orto was signalling, turning south-east, and as her own high stepping mount picked up the pace, heading directly for the highland itself, she shortened her reins and prepared to give chase.

Curious, the Healer stared ahead as her mount pricked up its ears, and began a soft ululation deep in its throat. They hung on grimly as both Cherls surged into a lumbering run, then Jalni smelt something on the air. Gathering up the reins she shouted joyously.

"Water!", as all else about her was forgotten or ignored in the dash to find the source of that scent.

They were not disappointed. A small group of droitch's clustered about the natural water-course, and as they approached at the run, several men stood, hefting large rocks in their hands, as if preparing to defend their rights. Orto wheeled his Cherl about abruptly, and Jalni's slithered to a stop in its mother's wake. The Healer leapt from her mount (and praying that her Uncle would follow her lead), slapped him on the back laughing.

Something tickled the back of her neck, and seizing the thread of power that had tormented her for the last half turn of the sand-glass, Jalni's hands flickered adroitly signing.

"Keep calm, ignore the threat.".

Showing no sign of alarm was the hardest part of this exercise, but she turned quite naturally and as if she had only just noticed the nomads and the small encampment, she freed her hair from the knot she'd tied it in, advancing, hands held out in greeting. Ignoring the menacing aspect, identifying the leader and pinioning him with her wide smile, she prayed that they would see her Healer braid, as they stood their ground.

Facing these fearful strangers She waited until they recognise that she posed no threat to them, and with relief watched taut mouths and unsmiling eyes relax. One of the men carefully placed the rock he clutched back on the ground, and cleared his voice self-consciously.

"Forgive us Healer, we have twice paid taxes, and twice been run off our camp, progressing only a short distance before being attacked again. Some warlord of these Sands says we must have permits to trade northern Sands before we venture there. One of my men is badly hurt, another is still recovering after they stole his woman, and her with a babe at the breast. When we heard the pace of yon beasts, we thought they'd come back for more.".

He choked on the last words, and Jalni accustomed to the way shock took some men, retreated to stand near Orto while the nomad collected himself, taking the time to sign the news in a briskly efficient manner that left her Uncle staring. Irritably she demanded with a complex gesture, "You could at least acknowledge that you understood me!", before stalking back to the nomads, hands already delving into her scrip for the medications she carried.

She had never entered a droitch, and frankly stared up at the large central aperture in the roof, noting how the smoke from the hearth escaped. The skins that covered the framework made the interior gloomy, but knowing that her eyes would soon adapt, she followed the silent men in. Familiar with other customs, she nevertheless watched and followed the example set by the man she now knew as Sherith. She took off her boots, handing them to Orto, and went swiftly to the side of the man who groaned painfully in a ring of anxious women. She noted his pallor, the way he clutched his gut, and felt the Sands whisper sounds of encouragement to her. Kneeling, she pulled her carrisack from her shoulders, once more laying out Syndalware bowls, and raising her shantana. She felt odd, somehow divorced from reality as she methodically prepared to harmonise her othervoice with the fluctuations of this man's life force. Completely oblivious of the smoky atmosphere, the unspoken terror of the girl who clutched her patient's hand, she prepared herself, withdrawing into that calm, quiet place from which she would follow the pain, seal the wounds, and drive the injuries away.

She was no longer Jalni. She could hear a great torrent of life thundering through her veins. She was rooted in the Sand, anchoring her patient, sliding effortlessly through the shallows of his breath, to listen to the tide flushing his life away, as she watched. Something in the way he lay jarred and she held her hand over his body, seeing with interest how her fingers glowed blue in the shadows of this unfamiliar structure.

She signalled to the two older women huddled beside her patient, that they should strip him, turning eyes that blazed compulsion on them, when they demurred. Time was so short and she could sense blood pulsing fainter and fainter as she struggled for the note she needed. Briefly she remembered Brus, how Daro had held the threads of that young life tethered by the sheer power of his voice, and then she heard Shiarjha say quietly, "There are those of us who hear the River sing, knowing that we hear the Source…", then once more she found herself borne on the torrent as she tuned her empowered voice to heal.

A long time later she roused, hands cramped and stomach surging. Someone she thought was Orto, swung her up, wrapped a warm blanket about her, and held her gently as she reeled from the droitch to their own modest tents. She remembered gulping cold spring water, refusing food, and collapsing inelegantly onto her sleeping mat. Then she knew nothing.

She didn't feel the touch of a familiar breeze, nor hear the voice that whispered for her ears only. "Jalni my love, where are you? I feel your presence in the Source, so I know you live. Touch the trinket I gave you dearling, find the Sand and I'll come to you.", but she was too far gone to respond, and the breeze died away to leave her sleeping.

When she woke in the early hours, her mouth was dry, she had a low sick headache, and her eyes felt gritty, but as she rolled over and sat, her Uncle was there. He had obviously lain just outside her tent in the open, and she smiled her gratitude as he handed her a damp cloth to wipe her face, and followed that with a steaming cup of citrine tea. He caught the enquiring lift of an eyebrow and hastily signed.

"Orana said, take care of you. Men are frightened, but stand guard. You better now?", and she wearily nodded, then stood to go to her patient. They left the tent together, Jalni carrying her treatment bag, Orto ready to protect her as they approached the dull gleam of an entrance. Sherith appeared silently, drawing aside a curtain to let them in. Two of the women were gently bathing the face of the man Jalni had worked over, but at her approach, they knelt, foreheads touching the Sand in her honour. Hugely embarrassed, Jalni ducked away, bending to examine her patient, and was astonished as she saw, where a knife blade had slashed his belly, only a pale pink line. Confused, she ran searching fingers along what looked to be a week-old scar, and wondered if the water she'd bathed the wound with had some unknown healing properties, but with no-one to answer that query, she turned her attention to packing her precious bowls.

She was replacing a stopper in a flask when the first sound came from outside. Just a "chink", as though someone had stepped on something metallic, but it was enough to cause the colour to fade in the faces surrounding her. Deliberately, she retuned her attention, switching from the thready beat of returning life on the pallet at her feet, to the stealthy approach of violent death, as it patrolled the parameters of the encampment. The hair on the back of her neck was rising, a frisson of fear ran up her spine, then she was angry.

Her inner voice chanted furiously, "By what right do you invade peaceful law-abiding camps? By what right do you demand payment to pass. By what right do you take young women from their babes, slaughter men who would protect their own, and by what right do you sully my Sands?", but what her mind thought and her mouth said was totally different.

She was on fire. Every nerve, every sinew blazed, and that strange miasma that had engulfed her in her vision had returned. She was the Searcher, the seeker after dreams, and no man born could stand against her or those she protected while her feet were planted bare in the sand of her birth. Her hair rose and flowed around her like a living cloud, her clothing shivered, flowing with the breeze that had sprung up, and her eyes blazed Azure. Her connection to the Source wide open, she turned towards the entrance of the droitch, lifted both hands and launched her othervoice.

"Ansarash mi, sherranath mi, Gurayen sek moi!", she commanded, and the wind of the Azure rose to her bidding.

If she was aware of the howling terror outside, she gave no sign of it, simply standing four-square to the entrance, eyes blazing, one hand clutched to her breast, the other pointing into the distant dark desert night. Long moments later, when the disconcerted shouts and screams had faded and the wind had died away, her attention returned to the man who lay at her feet. Gravely she bent over him once more, reading his body heat with the same hand that had snatched the lives of his attackers, as she smiled down at him.

"The One be praised.", said Jalni the Healer. "His fever is cooling, and he will survive.", at which there was a devout chorus from the nomads.

"The One be praised!", they agreed, but all eyes were fixed on the entrance of the droitch, and the empty Sands beyond.

Chapter 27 - Ranger Falls.

They remained in Sherith's droitch for the rest of the night, Jalni reluctant to leave the injured man while he was still so weak. However, once he slept normally, she posted the girl (who still held his hand) to watch him, while she turned her attention on the one man who sat apart, sunk in apathy. Refusing food, drink or encouragement, he turned his face to the hide wall, until she withdrew, wrapping herself in a blanket, and joining the women near the hearth. Despite their unusual dialect, Jalni soon discovered that Master Craftsman Jorn had lost his wife in an earlier raid.

Unwilling to interfere with natural grief, she leant back against the comforting bulk of a saddle watching Orto "talking" with the men, in a mixture of hand-codes. Gesturing emphatically, he was demanding they report the attacks, despite the obvious misgivings of their hosts, forcing Jalni to realise how little she knew of the territory or its customs.

The nearest settlement, Oplaya, lay half a day's ride to the east on the other side of a natural break in the highlands that dominated this region. Standing at the eastern gateway to the southern Sands, the rough collection of buildings huddled behind walls, half swallowed by the same Sands that had buried a fertile Fringe. This, lost in the great Storm before Partition, had left only a scatter of oases between here and Darnesh. At this thought, Jalni roused briefly.

"I must report to Tirjella, in case those reptiles escaped to make mischief elsewhere.", but too exhausted to think, her eyes closed, although the warming sand sang in her veins as Seleus rose.

Rousing (only three turns of the sand-glass later), she eased herself upright, bewildered by the feverish activity around her. Orto was stood by the entrance of the droitch, Sherith and the other men clutching a variety of implements backing him up. Even the women were plainly preparing to defend themselves, but "reading the Source", Jalni could detect no threat nearby. She turned her head, hearing the susurration of sand shifting on the ridge, then a whisper of soft footsteps before silence fell once more. Staring into the frightened faces opposite, she felt a flutter of apprehension, then she "reached", searching with the eye of her mind beyond the skin covered framework, out into her beloved Sands, finding the cause of those sounds almost immediately.

There were Rangers nearby and greatly relieved, Jalni told the others , before passing them in one fluid movement, leaving the shadowy interior of the droitch for the brilliant blues of morning. It was a bit of a shock, but she shaded her eyes as a familiar face came into view.

"Garald! I have never been so pleased to see a friend!", she exclaimed in delight, before turning astonished eyes on his companion, suddenly unsure if she was allowed to speak to the young man sitting at the Dream Walker's feet. Marran laughed up at her.

"Healer Jalni, how are you? How is Daro?", he asked, then his eyes narrowed as he gazed up at her, and for a moment she thought she saw something very disquieting in his expression. Garald smiled gently at her, saying quietly.

"We came as Soon as I felt your signature in the squall, but though I tried a reading dream, there was too much confusion along the Sands to be sure of anything other than Ranger's Fall. However, I fear we bring you trouble. We found bodies, men , women and their beasts, and we have need of your services for one survivor.".

Marran stood, a stranger in patch-dyed blues, already half a head taller than Jalni remembered him, and beckoned her urgently towards a heap of blankets that resolved itself into the shape of a woman. Speaking in a low voice Marran sounded concerned.

"That storm came out of nowhere, and the Dark Riders never stood a chance.".

Stealing a sidelong glance at her, he added.

"The raiders deserve no pity, although good beast's drowned in the sand. However, this girl is too young ,too respectably dressed to be the usual type they attract. I suspect she's an innocent victim, but whether her family will own her now, lies between them and the One.". His voice dropped to a whisper.

"The Kilda detected magic in the squall. May the One defend the Innocent if Daro looses the winds again!", and in his eyes Jalni read fear for the first time.

Blinking at this, she turned to the girl who lay moaning softly in the sand. Kneeling to look into a face that must have been pretty a night ago, she hissed at the sight of blackened eyes, split lips and bruised cheeks. Without lifting a hand the Healer "read" other injuries in the way the girl held herself, protecting breast's and stomach, hands curving about her body instinctively.

"Take her to the side tent Garald. ", Jalni instructed, "Marran, can you go to the droitch, and get Orto to make up this remedy. He must add the contents of this slip, to two cups of boiling water, then infuse. I'll be with the girl.".

She'd half turned away when she remembered that Marran knew Orto well, turning back to catch his look of surprise.

"Yes, I did mean your "Orto". It is all he remembered of his name when Solana took him in. He is Villeth del Orto, my father's older brother. Small sands we walk do we not?", but under her breath she remarked to his departing back, "and incidentally Ranger Dorenard....Daro had absolutely nothing to do with last night. Sometimes it takes a Healer to purge the Sands of filth!".

Ignoring all the sounds of delighted reunion and new introductions in Sherith's droitch, she followed Garald and the girl to her own tent, where she collapsed weeping in a huddle on Jalni's own sleeping mat. Gradually, through an incoherent muttering, Jalni heard (with chill recognition) the familiar story. The fear of capture, the isolation followed by threats, taunts and physical humiliation. Enduring these indignities without protest until the leader of the band had appeared, she'd made the mistake of appealing to Rodgeos better nature.

With a flash of spirit the girl confided, "He didn't have one!".

Jalni (engaged in anointing minor wounds with a salve) asked curiously, "What happened next?", but Junith flinched and |Jalni watched her pale. Deciding to divert the girl's attention, she asked softly, "Do you belong to this swage?", using the local term for a group of nomads.

"Yes.", she muttered in a hopeless voice, lowering her head, tears splashing onto Jalni's hands. "I an wife to Master Craftsman Jorn, we have a fine son, but he will set me aside now I'm shamed.".

Abruptly, Jalni was reminded of the man, rocking in the depths of intolerable grief, and took a risk.

"If he loves you, wants your child to follow loving parents, last night won't matter.", she argued, but Junith sighed saying simply.

"Healer. Surely you know the law. There is no way back for us, not after …". Dramatically she raised her head, flung the hair out of her eyes and slid out of the soiled robe she'd been clutching. Oblivious of Garald, she displayed the unmistakeable signs of rape, as Jalni hissed in pity. Bleeding bite marks adorned both breasts, blackening bruises revealed the savagery of violent abuse, along with scored thighs where welts rose dark on delicate skin. She saw the parody of love, huge red blossoms along the white throat, the injuries around her neck, the places where thongs had secured fragile wrists, then looking beyond to the deadly acceptance of a fate yet to be decided, she felt the "blue" upon her.

As rage surfaced cold and clear, Jalni (surrounded by a nimbus of Azure tinged light) took Junith's hands in hers. *Othervoice* engaged, flushing the stigma and all its footprints away, she crooned softly, threading a ripple of forgetfulness (culled from Shiarjha's repertoire) into the Weave. The Dream Walker watched in disbelief as the evidence vanished. Bite marks and bruises melting into unmarked skin, as last night's events were undone. Seeing the shadows lift from Junith's eyes, Garald (alerted by cries beyond this magical place) went out to greet her family.

Her husband was first, a wary eagerness in his eyes. He was followed by Sherith, who seemed rather remote, (as if the man was in shock.) Garald intercepted them, as Sherith declared heavily,

"I love her too. She's my daughter , but I'm Reader and the law is specific. Any woman defiled is a shame upon her swage, and though she lives, she cannot bear children who may carry the taint into the bloodline. You must put her from you, unless she can prove she's untouched.".

The craftsman responded in a hard tight voice.

"I won't even consider that possibility until I've seen and spoken to her myself.".

Garald, still with his mind full of the magic he had seen in the small side tent , threw caution to the winds. He seized Jorn by the hand, declaring inventively (in a voice that he did not recognize as his own).

"Good fortune greet you Master. We happened across a dead fellrunner, beneath which a woman hid. She says she was abducted from here but before her captors got to their camp, the storm overtook them. When the animal she was thrown over perished, it sheltered her and thanks to the One she survives.".

Assuming the wide eyed look of a prophet, Garald completed Junith's rehabilitation by adding ingenuously, "She is convinced that her determination to return to her baby son saved her. I just handed her to a Healer, who's mending a bruise.".

Jorn smiled tentatively, but Sherith greeted the comment with disbelief.

"A bruise? Is that all the injury she's taken?", Garald almost chuckled as he countered innocently.

"Well yes. It seems her captors believed she'd brought the Storm down on them, by praying that they would be healed of all wicked intentions. They left her to the mercy of the Sands, but they received no mercy themselves. Whatever wickedness ailed Rodgeos crew, they have been healed, of the ability to rob, terrorise or even breathe! The Azure has taken her vengeance, freeing the daughter of this swage without injury or stain on her reputation.".

Instinct took hands to head, heart and lips as they quietly entered Jalni's tent, to find the Healer gently smoothing porrisroot oil onto Junith's chafed wrists. Mind and body purified, the girl flew joyously into her husband's arms as he said her name. In that moment, every inflection of life, laughter and love was in his voice, so Jalni rose, and left the little tent discreetly. Whatever fluke of power had enabled her to undo Junith's experiences and rewrite her memories might have to be paid for, but happy to foot that bill at the appropriate time, she could leave love to strengthen the repairs she had made. Tilting a serene face in Garald's direction, she saw from his abstracted air that he was composing another of his hypnotic dream-walks, little realising that the account of the last days were to become a legen for posterity.

That night they gathered in Sherith's droitch again, settling themselves into groups as formal introductions were made. They learned that this swage were harness and saddle makers. Trading primarily at Gathers, or with other craftsmen practising skills in sympathy at events throughout the Sands. The visitors listened aghast, as Jorn explained that most of his newly tanned hides had been stolen, along with precious smithworked mounts for creating bridles, belts, or harnesses. Every credit they owned had been stolen, and even the great Biron that hauled the collapsed droitch coverings or carried the bundled frames had been slain. Hueth the tanner's pack Zeglurs had been scattered and the only good thing was that they were safe, with water that they could catch from the rivulets that brought high condensation from the peak of Mount Trididge.

Caught between yawning and a sneeze, Jalni asked innocently, "Garald I meant to ask you why this place is called Ranger Falls?", but was sufficiently distracted not to notice the stillness that came over the Dream Walker and his pupil.

"That's a long story Healer.", the Ranger replied evasively. "Something to be told on Winter nights, and I don't have the number of Rangers present to do it justice. Suffice it to say that once a Ranger gave his life to save another's young, and from that day to this, there has always been water here. The amounts vary, but we see that as the favour returned.".

With that enigmatic comment, it was time to leave the droitch and seek their beds. Garald and Marran taking their leave, intended to continue their interrupted journey long before the others rose. The night was still and safe again as Jalni slept, dreaming about heading towards the east and Tregeth where the best Zeglurs on Pelshar were bred.

Chapter 28- The Advent of Bleckons

In another Sand far to the south west of Jalni, Drex, (Official Recorder to the Temple of Skyrrh) bent over an ancient parchment. Running inquisitive fingers down the worn roll, he carefully revisited what appeared to be nothing more than a collection of vague ramblings. At last, he tapped a finger on a single sentence, covered the parchment with cold cloths to relax its curl, then faced the inevitable with resignation. Considering previous attempts to turn an ancient mistake to his own advantage, he realised that he was forced to share his jealously guarded knowledge (in order to succeed). Pacing restlessly, spinning an arcane web around his prey like some malevolent spider, he made his decision, then went to the Temple below.

The evening rituals were beginning as he scurried into place, processing into the Truth Hall behind Koth (its sinister High Priest). Wondering who (if anyone) he should entrust with plans (laid long before Adruna abandoned the Way), he nearly jumped out of his skin as Koth's spokesman invited sibilantly, "Stay after sacrifice Drex. we'd value your confidences.".

In trembling delight, Drex ducked his head in acquiescence, standing aside as a dark eyed girl (no more than a Rotation old), was lifted onto the High Altar. her Head turned towards her fainting mother, as she passed into the care of the heretic Sorceress. Gurgling as Adruna tickled her nose, the child arched her neck, innocently presenting her throat to the sacrificial knife, as Adruna lifted it high. To the accompaniment of a faint wail of protest, drowned by an anticipatory groan from the crowd, Adruna's hand flashed down, and rose again red with blood.

Unmoved, the wizened Recorder watched the ecstatic throes of the priestly caste, hugging his intoxicating fragment of knowledge to himself. That habit underpinned the subtle menace on which his very survival hung, and tonight he was about to show his hand. His twisted psyche thrilled at the thought of so much risk, but nevertheless, he crossed stares with the smooth cheeked priest who served the tongueless Koth, unable to resist wondering what secrets Krej held.

The dark oily light at the altar flickered, the ritual drum beat slowly, as with his life's mantra running through his mind, Drex prepared to leave the Temple, possibly for the last time. Adruna, Koth and the priests kissed the dripping blade, then left the unholy altar as Drex slipped inconspicuously to the rear, mentally chanting.

"Knowledge is power, read and retain.", as he prepared to share that knowledge with Adruna, Sorceress of the dark path to enlightenment.

Entering the innermost recesses of the Temple, Drex (true to the God of knowledge) opened his mind, using his rather remarkable faculties to file mental images of everything visible. Doors stood open as he followed the retinue along a well lit passage, so (using peripheral vision), he began filing images of wall hangings, costly robes and thick furs for future reference. In comparison to the simple austerity practised by most priests, these apartments spoke of decadence unknown, but then (albeit temporary), this was the court of Adruna, where nothing should surprise him.

Entering the large room ahead, he found himself facing the girl Sorceress who had defied Ikella at Partition. She sat on a divan, feet curled under her, indulging her pet sandrigals with tasty morsels from the nights sacrifice, as Koth leant over her. Drex quailed under her darkly brooding gaze, then, without a flicker of expression, she said in a bored voice.

"Well Drex. What is it that fills those eyes of yours with dark sparks? Out with it, before my pets tear out your tongue!".

Keeping his voice steady (by will-power alone), he spoke quietly.

"Your Magnificence, long ago I found a way of destroying at least one of your enemies, although I didn't see it in Gatta's holy light at the time. This information lay buried in an ancient text, which I rediscovered a while ago, seeing then the potential use.".

A glimmer of interest coalesced in her eyes, as Drex added conspiratorially, "The scroll refers to a plant, grown in these Sands, which provided a tall canopy for the speedy protection of small isolated water sources. However, the first time these plants went off sands, something strange happened and the plants mutated. The experiment was abandoned and all memory, or written records have passed into obscurity.".

Adruna sat up, letting go of the High Priest's hand, suggesting harshly, "Of course you'd be the only one who knows how to repeat the experiment through that thrice cursed barrier!", and throwing back her head she loosed a peal of hysterical laughter, provoking a growl of rage from Koth.

Drex schooled his face to impassivity.

"This is the most dangerous part of the process!", his mind warned him. "Its crucial to make them understand that we can beat the barrier, by staying inside. They'd never connect the sudden unexplained deaths with us!", and was relieved when Adruna calmed.

"Most Excellent.", he whined apologetically. "Our vengeance is already planted deep within the Azure. All we need is a confident man to substitute one item for its deadlier twin, ensuring it is conveyed to whoever you choose to destroy.".

He felt the paralysing gaze of the High priest lingering on him, then Adruna said brusquely, "Explain!", and Drex hastened to obey.

"At the base of Mount Darnesh the Fringe began to fail long before the Opal rose to dominate the Sands. Gradually the water courses along the central region dried up, Darnesh itself was abandoned, and the northern Sands became virtually uninhabitable. Only the occasional oasis survived, and the growers moved to other sands. One of them came here, to tend the gardens of Skyrrh, it is from his writings that I report to you my Sorceress.".

Darting crafty glances under lowering brows, Drex saw he had her undivided attention, and continued his scholarly lecture smoothly.

"Fra Keord succeeded in seeding the warm caverns here with fungi and shade loving edibles, which (in our current situation) is what stands between us and starvation, so his work has merit. If half of what I have translated is true, he has also provided the perfect means to force the Guardians into submission!".

That statement brought a calculating look into Adruna's eyes, even Koth sighed wistfully, but Krej reacted exactly as Drex had predicted. Jeering, he mimicked Drex, embellishing the words with his trademark lisp.

"If *we* can believe *your* translation! *If* what you read is true? What is this wonderful solution? How can we use a history lesson about the Azure to bring the Guardians to heel? Have you lost your mind dear fool? I take it that you've consulted someone about your suicidal tendencies?".

Palely bulging eyes fixed on Drex, the priest declared bitterly, "You should value your knowledge only by the pain you'll suffer for this empty rant!", then the priest gasped, as Koth casually knocked him aside, to let Adruna speak.

"Very interesting Drex.", she purred, "What is this solution? More importantly, where can it be found?", and her eyes flashed ominous warnings.

The Recorder bowed his head, and elaborated so that only Adruna and Koth could hear, aware that over his shoulder, Krej already plotted his downfall. Forcing himself to remain submissive, he asked humbly, "May I explain everything your Glory? This is a matter so serious that you must understand the concept, so that you can decide the likelihood of success.", at which she nodded permission, and Drex began to speak.

"When growers had access to all Sands, they discovered that over time, oases develop around pools, or where underground water surfaces. However, this takes many Rotations, and depends on visiting animals and birds to drop seeds and fertilise them. In natural oases, the tallest plants form a canopy under which shorter ones develop. They are never large enough to support more than a family, and a few passing visitors, but they can and do produce some of our luxuries, like fruit. At a time when food became scarce, and water even scarcer, the ancients devised the principle of "seeding oases", making tall, straight, fronded plants especially welcome to growers. The man who came here seeded Bleckons, with all the properties I have already mentioned. Moreover they are incredibly fast growing.".

Aware that his dry delivery was beginning to bore his audience, he continued hastily.

"Fra Keord planted Bleckon seeds keeping strict records on successive generations, which I've been reading. At first he thought that these Bleckons were related to Driands. However, it soon became clear, that he had something new, something dangerous. Left unchecked, his Bleckons started to mutate, demonstrating a rare potential. It would seem that without being poisonous themselves, they can poison nearby fruiting plants, along with those who eat them. I thought you'd be interested.".

Adruna threw off Koth's hand, insinuated with insulting familiarity under a fold of her robe. Drex, (unable to resist noting this occurrence), forced himself back to the subject in hand.

"Most Exalted One, !", he spluttered, choosing his next words cautiously. "When I was young and impetuous, I journeyed in search of ancient things, even then unwilling to believe in the Way. I am the second son of a grower and had long held a wish to discover an ancient plant that could feed us, or cause other foodstuffs to flourish.", he lowered his eyes as though admitting his guilt with appropriate shame.

"I spent half a Rotation finding a suitable oasis, planting a few Bleckon seeds to see what happened, but had to return before I could test the theory. However, a disaffected Weaver offered to help me, taking my seeds and an artefact (said to encourage their growth), repeating my experiment every Rotation. Just after First Rites of Spring this Rotation, one of our Seers told me that my agent was no more, but the experiment had succeeded. At an unfrequented oasis near Jerritol, Bleckons grow once more".

He felt the air quiver with the sigh of delight as he continued slowly. "I rather think that Bleckons have been forgotten. Fra Keord has slipped into obscurity here, and as the Way forbids examination of the past, no-one is likely to remember. If I am right, anything grown under Bleckons will be poisonous. Fra Keord observed that just before Zenitheon and Jentaroth, the Bleckon plant sends out a fine tendril like root. Through this, they implant their seeds deep in the root-stock of surrounding plants. He seemed to think that under Gatta's influence, a substance was pumped into the host plant, which can be any one of a thousand edible varieties.".

Adruna squealed in delight. "Will you tell me what you plan, and where?", she demanded, and Drex outlined the plot, fully aware that his very existence hung on every word.

"For our purposes, the most interesting feature of Bleckons is that they only survive a Rotation, maturing in ninenights. They survive pollution, dry seasons and damage, then disappear into the Sands after they seed for the second time. If we only use the poisoned edibles from a second seeding, there would be no evidence to show what caused the poisoning. It took Rotations of study to realise that they were dangerous, mainly because until they seed themselves, they behave exactly as expected. Only under Gatta's influence does seeding take place, and only plants within a short distance are affected. I only need access to one of your most confident agents, then I can begin.".

Curiously reptilian eyes flickered over him, sending icy thrills down his body, then Koth's head turned and Krej said huskily.

"I will locate the one man who can be guaranteed to take pride in this work. He will succeed or die with his knowledge, who have you set your sights on Drex, and when?".

The Recorder battled to appear nonchalant, but there was a squeak of excitement in his voice as he declared, "Tirjella. She is the mainstay of the Opal once "she who shall remain nameless" dies. In fact, the opportunity arises at Zenitheon as Gatta rises .", and Krej (speaking as the voice of Koth) hissed.

"Then I have just the one for the job. He is in place already, and can easily get to Darnesh. I can arrange for him to deliver poisoned fruit. What sort grows under your Bleckons Drex?".

His voice told Drex to proceed very carefully indeed. His eyes both cold and cunning told Drex that Koth was not deceived for one minute. That he knew plans this elaborate had been laid with escape clauses built in. Drex steeled himself to meet Koth's considering gaze with equanimity, thinking that with his co-operation, Adruna could pull down those who had condemned the Amethyst and all who dwelt there with her, even as he replied casually.

"Driands Exalted One. They'll fruit by Zenitheon, then die, along with Tirjella who simply can't resist them.".

Chapter 29 - Rendezvous at Tregeth

If Jalni hadn't heard the mournful call of a distressed Zeglur, they might never have entered Oplaya. However, rising wind blowing sand directly into their faces, forced them to dismount to put on riding capes. With no hope of reaching Tregeth in this weather, Jalni paused in the act of remounting her Cherl and listened intently, before lowering herself to the sands.

"A-haw, A-haw.". The baby staggered into view through the skin-rasping bluster. Orto frowned as it stumbled, a lurching woe-begotten youngster, barely two days old, nodding head over wobbly legs. Trembling, it wearily turned away, braying piteously as a faint response came from somewhere close by., Orto needed no further encouragement to follow the foal as it staggered through driving sand, collapsing two steps from its dying mother. He turned a stricken face as Jalni hobbled their Cherls, signing, "Stop. No choice. I have to kill them!".

As their Cherls sank down, (legs tucked under them), she ran to the baby, feeling its life-signs fluttering ominously. Incandescent rage shook her. She was angry with the wind, angry with the Sands, even angrier that she could do nothing. Scarcely able to reason, her hands flew to Daro's trinket, as rage became power, once more the River singing in her blood.

One hand on each of the crumpled forms, she struggled to make her othervoice resonate with the barely detectable thrum of life beneath her fingers. At her snarl of enraged frustration, hurtling sand stopped in mid-air, cascading down impotently as the wind ceased squalling and fled. Amid this sudden cessation of hostilities, she found the power -note, and a gaping wound in the dam's belly closed. Staring into Orto's worried face as he steadied the floundering foal, she impulsively cupped his right cheek in affectionate reassurance, returning those blazing eyes to the dam's injuries as she chanted. Even by her critical standards, her empowered othervoice sounded exactly as she'd always imagined it might, and watching entranced she saw open wounds glow, then vanish, never realising that a "blue space" had formed around her patients.

Healing and calming, Jalni sang until the mare staggered upright to nuzzle her foal. Filling their feed bucket from an apparently bottomless flask, she crooned to the baby, as Orto encouraged its mother to drink. Gradually, With only exhaustion and hunger left to mend, normality returned and the Zeglur stood feeding her foal, leaving Jalni to work out what had happened.

She stared into space, unable or unwilling to discuss it. However, Orto unabashed signed in grandiloquent gestures. Indicating the animals, he strutted (nose in air), beating his chest, finally patting the Sands, before placing a silencing finger to his lips. It was so swift that Jalni had to get him to repeat it three times before she understood.

He was saying "Only the animals know you're a Sandsinger! I'm so proud, but if they don't tell anyone, neither will I!".

"Ridiculous man!", she laughed out loud, vision blurring as exhaustion swept her from conscious thought to dreamless sleep.

She woke to the dark velvet night, golden highlights flickering in the lee of a semi-circular group of rocks, and stirred reluctantly. Immediately, a shadow rose from the small fire it tended, as Orto brought an unusual savoury drink to her. She sat, back against the comforting bulk of a basalt outcropping, hands clasped round her travel mug, and thought quietly about the strange occurrence. She remembered the sandstorm beginning, the shock of the Zeglur cry, and finding the foal's mother. After that, nothing made sense, except a recollection of anger. Ruefully, she sipped the drink, until Orto spoke.

He rarely tried using his voice, deeply frustrated by his inability to communicate verbally, however, this time (to Jalni's amazement) she understood him perfectly. Vocabulary limited, delivery awkward, but, she heard it from his own lips.

With much clearing of unpractised throat, Orto said self-consciously, "Jalni? I can hear you.".

His hands (either from uncertainty or habit) signed as he spoke, then his face creased as the tears came. She sat, gently patting his shoulders, until he stuttered, "Sssorry. Sssilly really.", then the Healer in her took over.

"Not silly at all dear.", she said firmly, "You're entitled to cry. Happy tears I hope?", and found that she too, was caught on the cusp of weeping. Grinning ruefully, he repeated the words.

"Jalni, I can hear you!", adding the information, "With my right ear.".

This time he didn't sign, but patted his ear, just to make sure she followed his slightly flattened intonation. He seemed subdued, perhaps more tired than he wanted to admit, but brightened when she asked anxiously, "Zeglurs?".

"Good.", he responded, pointing to a cluster of rocks that formed a natural shelter, where mother and foal rested. The foal's eyes no longer had the sunken, inward look of death, his mother showed little sign of her ordeal but they would need more nourishment (and rest) soon. Reassured for now, Jalni began processing each stage of the event. Remembering her hands holding Daro's trinket, she instinctively clasped it again.

Energy rushed through her, then she heard Daro's othervoice, shaking with strain.

"Dearling, the Source is very disturbed, pulsing from Azure to Amethyst then back to Opal. Beneva has scryed for the cause, but the disturbance is too great to penetrate. If you hear me, be very careful of strangers.", his voice faded to nothing, then she heard him say (wrathfully):

"Damn this howling! How can I tell her Sowdin lives and she's in terrible danger?".

Her mind reeled.

"Sowdin lives?", she was struggling to control the terror in her voice as she stared hopelessly into the fire. She'd forgotten Orto, forgotten he could hear, but she saw his head lift, nostrils flaring as his lips thinned with fury.

Unable to express his feelings in sign or speech, such a howl of rage was wrenched from him that Jalni's hair lifted. Then words came in a chilling vow.

"If my father's path crosses mine again, I'll kill him, or die trying.". This time, he didn't need to sign and Jalni believed him.

When her Uncle discreetly withdrew (to take care of personal needs), then patrol protectively, she trembled, steeling herself to continue purely domestic tasks. Berating herself for such timidity, she watched for his return, anxiously aware of restless animals, twitching nostrils and flattening ears. She stood uncertainly waiting for whatever prowled to show itself, relieved when Orto returned to sign swiftly.

"Guard on patrol!".

She stared at him blankly, (seeing how incredibly like her father he was), totally unable to make sense of what he'd said. Clenching her fists in the sign for "warrior?", she rudely tapped her head, questioning Orto's sanity, but he just grinned, then squatted to bank up the fire for the night. Quite deliberately he raised a hand, curled it into a paw and mimed licking it to wash invisible ears. Jalni, who was kneeling on the opposite side of the fire-pit said joyfully, "Echo!", and half rose to her feet, until Orto placed a restraining hand on her shoulder. He signed and whispered confidentially.

"Sssh! Don't scare the Zeglurs. He always guards us. He'll be pleased you didn't know!", then he gave a childlike chuckle and purred loudly until Jalni collapsed in helpless giggles. Gradually, the light of the fire died, only a wisp of smoke betraying its presence as they rolled into hollowed sleeping pits and slept, secure in the knowledge that no-one could harm them.

The following dawn, they reluctantly turned towards Oplaya, with its narrow streets and broken ramparts. Having by passed it earlier, after the nomad's described a dying settlement, this was a step in the wrong direction. However, after due consideration, they'd decided the Zeglurs couldn't make Tregeth without rest and refreshment. Persuading her Cherl to a slow walk, she encouraged the Zeglurs to follow, but as the sun crept higher, flushing the sky turquoise, the baby was soon crying weakly. At last, Orto leapt from his mount, and gathered it up in his arms. Muttering curses, he remounted his docile beast, laying the exhausted foal on his lap as the Cherls rocked and swayed their way into a deserted market-place.

Grumbling softly, (mainly to hear his own voice), Orto knotted a rope around the foal's neck, turning the animals into a loose box next to the inn. Jalni stood in the courtyard, slowly rotating on one leg as she swept her eyes over the buildings, seeing no smoke, and little evidence of occupation. Somewhere a dog howled, a fell -runner whickered from a small corral then only the comforting sound as Orto bustled about broke the unnatural silence.

She concentrated, listening intently but there was no hum of conversation, no shouting cooks, and finding herself reluctant to look over the half-door into the inn, she turned to her Uncle, signing and speaking simultaneously.

"Something odd is going on here, or the natives keep late hours.".

Looking confused, Orto tipped his head, and banged his good ear, then Jalni realised that he'd thought his hearing had gone again, and said sharply.

"You could need a knife! Its too quiet here!". He moistened his lips asking gruffly.

"Trouble? Bad trouble?". He ducked into a fighter's crouch, the knife she'd never seen flashing in his hand. He pursed his lips, emitting a shrill whistle, that caused the sand to shiver where it lay along windowsills, until Echo shimmered into view above them.

"Ouh raow?", said the mystcat conversationally, but Jalni heard a voice in her mind. "Only dead people here"!, it announced.

She thought back to the caverns of Scartel and how she and Daro had used "speech without speech", wondering if she could hear Echo through their mutual bond to the Opal Sandsinger. However, Echo (lying atop a wall which over hung both herself and Orto by three handspans), simply blinked lazily and licked a paw in reply.

That day was to linger in Jalni's memory for a long time. She took her shantana from a pocket on her tunic, and donned it, shaking back her heavy fall of hair in order to position the half-veil correctly. She spoke before she lowered it, pleased to see that Orto was regarding her steadily, without undue alarm.

"The cat smell's death.", she reported without signing, and her Uncle nodded soberly.

"I smell it now.", and that was all she remembered for a long time afterward. House by house they searched for a living person, meeting only savagery in the butchered bodies of men, women and livestock. The cat preceded them into every room, checking with a greatly augmented sense of smell, and reporting back with lowered head and rasping growl. By Height of Sun they knew the worst of it. Empty shelves and scattered belongings spoke volumes about Rodgeo's final frenzy. There was no end to the horror, slashed, skewered and violated the dead filled every home, bed and byre. Silent accusing hands pointed to their suffering and prolonged starvation and for once Jalni was glad that Daro was not present. She could not envisage his reaction to such brutality, but she knew his vengeance would be monumental and at that moment, she could do with less death around her.

Sighing heavily as they headed back to the inn, they made a check of that last premises, then drawing an overlooked wine-skin from its hiding place at the back of the blood-soaked bar, Jalni said abruptly, "Let's get out side, where the air is clean!", and turned to see a small boy standing uncertainly in the doorway. He seemed to be oblivious of the bodies at his feet, but Jalni saw the shadows of shock and said coaxingly. "My name is Healer Jalni. Would you like to see my baby Zeglur?", as Orto lifted him up, and they went to join the animals.

They spent the rest of the day laying lines of wax soaked cord between the streets of death. Their animals rested and drank, slept and ate the enriched fodder they found in one lavish warehouse. Here there were riches, hand spun wool, barrels of wine, casks of oil, and many things that neither could identify. The building was stone, including the flat roof, and soon Orto (and Echo) scrambled up on to it, and made a camp for the night. They managed to erect a kind of tent by dint of hanging rugs over a set of ropes, and by Sunfall, Orto had made a ladder by which Jalni and Drue (their small charge) could ascend.

Every luxury was present in that strange camp. Thick pelts to keep out the nightly chill, warm beds and pillows abounded, and so did food.

Recalling the horror of the homes around them, Jalni began to realise that the renegade pack had starved and stolen for months to amass so much. she also saw that the nomad swage would have been perfect cover for the gang. Amongst the animals and droitch's their booty could have been concealed as goods and taken south to Rodgeo's lands, just another caravan going South to sell.

Drue was a different problem. He, (it seemed) was nothing to do with Oplaya. Just a lowly coatan herd from Tregeth, he had driven his father's herd onto the pastures above Oplaya, and leaving them there, had brought a message from his mother to the inn. He was shocked and shivery, wary of the mystcat, but only seven Rotations old, was too naïve to question Jalni and Orto about their part in this horrible story. He slept innocently as Echo patrolled, waking unconcerned to the new dawn when Orto touched him.

Barely able to make out their path, the adventurers helped him collect a sizeable heard of the goat-like coatans, and turn back for Tregeth. Orto loaded their increasing herd of animals, (fell-runners and Biron) along with their own Cherls, with items from the warehouse. They collapsed their impromptu camp, packing and folding covers, slinging them onto the massive travois they'd discovered, then with Jalni paying out cord from a huge reel, they withdrew to a safe distance. This time she sang hand-fire, sending it along the Wax impregnated cord she'd laid, watching it take hold of the first street, cleansing Oplaya from the taint of death, before setting out for Tregeth.

The morning flew by, as following in the wake of Drue and his coatans they made good time down the widest part of the canyon, and then just as it started to narrow, Jalni caught sight of grazing to their left. Drue was racing on ahead now, sturdy legs sending up little puffs of blue sand as he raced into a sizeable courtyard created from beaten earth, and it was only then that Jalni saw the group waiting to greet them.

On a covered dais sat the old man of Tregeth, resplendent in the hairy costume of a beast handler. by his side were four men, all wore the hukvah of Mastery, and with the noon sun blinding her, Jalni was forced to lower her rehenas to see anything other than vague outlines. Trudging wearily she walked slowly forward, certain that she knew those shapes, jumping back as she was swamped in a bear-hug.

"The One bless the child !", said a familiar voice, "She's dead on her feet.", and the Master of Tregeth stared down at her laughing.

"Carolus!", she exclaimed furiously, then gaped as Patris Rowbet and Somner gathered round her laughing.

Finally she got her breath back, saying with a muffled squeak.

"All I need now is Olneth and a parcel of Rangers, and my future is secured. "At that, the fourth figure stirred and said solemnly.

"Olneth is in the Carnelian, with Daro and Ikella as Eshima takes her Long Walk home. There are Rangers a-plenty on the station, but won't I do instead?", and Jalni stared numbly into the eyes of Jashell.

Chapter 30- Gurayen's Gully

From the time they arrived in Tregeth, Orto, their Cherls and Zeglurs moved into a roomy pasture of their own. There was a large herders hut where, (Carolus assured Jalni), Echo would be welcome provided he didn't frighten the stock. There were Rangers about, but she saw none that she knew, and it seemed that the main business of Tregeth continued on a series of shallow plateaux, each climbing in a gracious sweep much like the reed entangled "steps" they had already negotiated north west of Tregeth, along the edge of the central highlands.

Carolus cheerfully allocated a wing of the stone Master's house to the women, suggesting that they would probably feel more comfortable without the company of men for a few hours. To be true, although Jalni giggled at Jashell's elevated eyebrows, and agreed with the warriors amused comments, all she wanted was a wash, and to sleep. However, Jashell had a surprise waiting as she took Jalni into what Rowbet had described as "modest bathing facilities".

Still dragging her carrisack wearily, Jalni followed the commander of Ikella's household guard into a room lined with clothing hooks. The stone walls felt hot to the touch, and Jashell grinned as Jalni hissed in surprise.

"This is an idea that Master Carolus "borrowed ", from an ancient text. There is underground water here, but not enough to indulge in bathing like we did in Selesh, so he has provided a steam-room.".

Jalni goggled as Jashell stripped to a thong, hanging her masculine attire on a peg, and taking down a large towel from a shelf. She struggled to copy her, feeling about as elegant as a coatan herd, until Jashell said sympathetically, "Come, let me help you sister.", and became tongue -tied with embarrassment as Jashell gently stripped her to the buff, eyeing her critically.

"You need to strengthen your upper arms if you intend to lift and turn patients without harming your back.", was the comment as Jalni wrapped herself in the thick towel, then the tall Inesh woman led her into the next room where hot rocks lay on a kind of altar.

Jalni gazed in amazement as Jashell dipped a long handled ladle into a small tub of water, pouring it over the stones. Steam billowed around them, and Jalni felt the first prickling of sweat form, cutting a runnel between her breasts. Casually Jashell laid her towel on a bench, and laid on it, superb muscles rippling along her back as she waved Jalni to the next bench.

"Lie here Sister,", she invited easily, and too tired to argue, Jalni gave in and enjoyed the experience. At first they simply lay and sweated, allowing the dirt to lift from their pores easily. Jashell showed Jalni how much water to use, and they took it in turn to replenish the steam. They must have been there a full turn of the sand-glass, when the warrior suggested that they oil each others backs, and then if Jalni wanted, she could massage her legs. They chose aromatic oils from a selection on a shelf, and set about clearing the detritus of the sweat bath, (literally scraping themselves clean with horn scrapers) before anointing themselves with oil. Somehow, it was easy to accept Jashell's strong hands, unknotting tired calf muscles, and easier to reciprocate, Jalni applying gentle pressure to Jashell's energy points, as she worked.

When Jalni rose however, she found herself staring at a new tattoo on the nape of Jashell's neck. Positioned at the top of her spine, strongly inked in red (for mourning) she saw Indeera's sigil. Shock stopped her hands flexing and kneading for a moment, then, (before she lost the courage) she asked "When?", regretting the intrusion as soon as she saw Jashell's body quiver in distress. However, the guard Commander's voice was very calm and level when she spoke, but Jalni saw the minute tremble in her hands, as she turned her face towards the towel draped bench.

"Indeera was very tired, a little perturbed by some odd rumours she'd picked up. Three nineninghts ago, she consulted with Beneva, then went to the cavern Temple she served, intending to fetch the scroll containing all we know of our ancestors, but she never returned to us. Driss and Sorrill found her, sitting at the entrance which looks out over the Great Divide, where she often went at Sunfall. She had her finger on a line which refers to a great River and she was smiling. Quite dead, and smiling as if she had finally understood a great truth.".

The rich voice, so used to bellowing orders across a huge Gathering Square, shook as Jashell added. "We were together from first training. She was, is, and always will be the only love I ever had. It was she who helped show me the way to gain our freedom, it was she who told me the legends, and she who recognised Ichta Selunsanni. Now I am Commander no longer and I bear her ashes home to Gurayen's Gully.".

Shocked, Jalni pressed Jashell's shoulder sympathetically, silently returning to her own bench and wrapping herself in her towel. Jashell rolled over one arm across brimming eyes and said formally, "My apologies Healer, you must forgive me. I am too long used to sharing my sorrows with my sister's freely. I forget that you are so young, that you choose to remain solitary.".

Fascinated, Jalni moved toward Jashell. She had no idea that the Inesh were so perceptive, it gave her a strange feeling of kinship, made all the stronger when she remembered how they had handled her during her all too recent disgrace. They had controlled her physically, without undue force or humiliation, choosing instead to bolster her confidence, giving her courage to endure what she must. Then she recalled Jashell calling her "sister", during that ordeal and blushed for shame, kneeling to press Jashell's free hand compassionately.

They stayed locked in the silence of sorrow, until she started to shiver, and instantly Jashell roused from her lethargy, sat up, and pulled a comb through her hair with rough familiarity. Finishing their toilette both women were glad to withdraw into separate bedrooms and sleep. Jalni too full of the days horrors to deal with another death easily, Jashell, too uncertain of the path she had chosen to take another step today. Perhaps, somewhere in their dreams they could find the courage to face a rapidly changing world, but for tonight they both needed rest.

When the first light of dawn strayed into Jalni's room, she sat up, crossed her legs and tried to meditate. She cleared her mind of all extraneous thought, sitting erect, a hand on each knee, and controlled her breathing, willing her heart to slow, her mind to disengage from the world, and follow her thoughts, on and outward, listening for the Sand to warm her mind and blood. The gentle chime of crystals filled the air, tingled along her veins, as Seleus rose, but she was filled with foreboding, aware of a dark shadow cast across her path, and true meditation eluded her. Somewhere nearby, she could feel an angry aching cold. Not that far from here, something malicious awaited her, and unwillingly her mind went back to Oplaya, but that abomination didn't seem to have the right "echo", when she examined her memory. So, she tidied herself, dressed and went down the stone steps, to the kitchen at the back of the house, and found Carolus, happily dipping a spoon into a thick porridge redolent of spices and honey. Saying nothing, he pushed a ladle, bowl and spoon into Jalni's hands, and nodded at the large stone range where a pan bubbled. She caught on easily, serving herself and ate silently, until he rose replacing used dishes with brimming mugs. She picked up her drink, then paused, eyebrows raised in enquiry.

"This is different.", she said evenly, "Usually I am the one dishing out tonics and restoratives. Doesn't this contain vetali? I remember the taste.". She cast the Apothecary a suspicious glance, refusing to be mollified by his twinkling eyes.

"Vetali is a wonderful pick-me-up for all forms of debilitation Healer.", he responded easily, but Jalni called his bluff.

"You also left a load of slips back in Scartel containing something Solana called "Sandsingers Friend!", she retorted, and the old man grinned.

"Well my dear.", he said challenging her directly. "As you seem to have shared your Sandsinger's Remedy with said Sandsinger, why deny yourself the benefit of a different version? He may be the only Sandsinger around right now, but shouldn't the remedy benefit his friends as well, or did I misunderstand the warmth of feeling between you two?".

Totally mortified, Jalni retreated behind the contents of her mug, and drank, feeling a subtle warmth stealing through her body, in preparation for a very strange day.

She was somewhat nonplussed to discover that in fact she had been the last to rise. Carolus grinned saying dismissively, "Oh, birthing Zeglurs have absolutely no regard for time. that's why Patris and all the crew he can spare have come to help me out.", he spread expressive hands in a gesture that embraced the large kitchen, and (for all Jalni knew of it), half this odd little kingdom as well. Tregeth enjoyed a somewhat unusual position in as much as it was not strictly in the Azure Sands, but marooned on the edge of what was known as the unexplored territories. These badlands, composed of soaring pillars of rock, stretching from the north eastern border down the perimeter of the highlands on the eastern edge of the Azure formed a wilderness of such depth and complexity that from Cataclysm it had remained empty. With no water for more than a day's walk to the east, no areas of cultivatable land, and no apparent access to the range of mountains beyond, the Clans had abandoned any attempts to annex a territory so unusable.

Jalni accepted a mortar and pestle containing dried porrisroot to grind, as Carolus busied about, setting a pan of water to boil. While he chopped unfamiliar roots and pungent smelling leaves, she heard how he had come here as an outcast boy.

The old man's voice wove a spell that seemed to take Jalni back to a time where things were simple and easily explained. She saw an awkward lad, one who questioned everything he heard, collecting nuggets of information from his travels with the step-father who had never cared for him. She felt the warmth from the ancient range enfold her in much the same way as Carolus described his welcome here, long ago, when as a lonely frightened boy, he had dragged himself to the door of the Master's house with his step-father dying in his arms, and had been taken into safety. She handed over one ground ingredient and accepted another as she followed that long ago boy, from the summer he had spent recovering from that ill-fated expedition, through his triumphant return to the Selesh of his youth, to discover his mother ill.

He had apprenticed himself willingly to the resident apothecary, only to discover that the man had no intention of teaching him anything useful, being only interested in gaining a bed-mate in his mother and a slave in Carolus. He had bitterly resented the travels that his Master put him through, because he saw so little of his mother from then on, but eager to learn anything he could, he used his eyes and ears to his own benefit, making friends with many who were to directly influence the rest of his life in his travels.

Jalni stirred the simmering contents of the pot, while Carolus found dispensing jars to hold its contents, then set the pan to cool as he sat comfortably at the table with her. They sipped fennis tea, nibbling oatcakes as he told her of the theories he'd been unwise enough to expound in Selesh, but she saw the sorrow as he told of his eventual exile, and heard sympathetically how he had returned to Tregeth, and taken up the offer of trading in Zeglurs, along with his expanded medical studies, clapping in delight as he finally explained.

"I travelled far and wide, through the Sands and into the Eternal Snow for Tibrettta and Briona. When Terolld inherited I travelled for him. Here vetali grows in special beds, highly fertile soil allows the growth of allowort, saltwood, sterrish and many other rare herbs. The herd is healthy and increasing, so now I inherit the Mastery of Tregeth, and a headache in management.".

He took away all the dispensing paraphernalia, carrying pots, pans, pouring funnels, moulds and more around a corner, into an old sluice, which he had altered to suit his own needs. While Jalni watched, leaning against an ancient settle, he skilfully skimmed the top off his brew, tossing the contents of his ladle into a press, and squeezing the last ounce of goodness out of the thickened mess. Discarding the solids, he strained the rest of the concoction through a fine gauze, until the sediment was dry. His hands busy, his tongue enchanting, as he told Jalni of the journey north, to the Ashgenar and beyond. Eventually his liniment decanted into storage jars, he turned, held out his hand and said, "Come child, let's go find your Uncle and that damned mystcat. I might find a use for all of you yet.".

They set out on Zeglur back, trotting towards a slope that took them onto the next level. Jalni (to please Carolus) had agreed to wear the rough jacket and trousers of a herder, topped with a brimmed leather hat. They were comfortable (if loose), but she felt odd, and wondered why she had to wear men's clothing before the Apothecary settled happily.

"Bless the One.", he'd exclaimed in surprise. "A Healer, a woman past eighteen Rotations, and still an innocent!".

Jalni blushed, remembering with sudden intoxicating effect the memory of passionate kisses and an aroused male body in her arms, and knowing eyes lingered on her averted face for a second, then turned away as they arrived in front of a large hut. They were just looping reins onto a rail, when the door opened, and Jashell strode out laughing. Echo loped at her heels, and for a moment Carolus gazed at her speculatively, then she said cheerfully.

"I grow old and stiff Master Apothecary. I have undertaken to exercise Ichspeller Selunsanni's friend. He is going to chase me to the top of the valley and back for his supper.".

Before either Carolus or Jalni could respond, she lifted an ornate lead that was clipped to the obesh collar that Echo now sported, unclipped it, saying sternly.

"After Amethyst! Right?", then she eased into the smooth action that Jalni remembered watching enviously round Selesh. From the half open door behind them chanted Orto's slightly flattened tones.

Opal, Azure, Malachite, Cynabarr, Onyx, Amber, Carnelian, Tourmaline, Amethyst!".

The cat sprang away up the slope behind the loose limbed runner, and Jalni heard the challenge from the ridge, as Ikella's Guard Commander called.

"Last one back's a worm ridden gully hopper!", followed by a querulous "uhr raow".

Grinning she turned to find Carolus unusually silent, but at her querying look, he turned abruptly, making for the door even as he said gruffly, "Come my dear, let's go explain your journey to Gurayen's Gully, and why only you can seek what is to be found there. Then I'll walk to the top of the valley with you, and show you the unexplored territories.".

Chapter 31 - The Temple of the Winds

Long after that evening, long after the strenuous ride north, Jalni was to remember how she first heard the legend of the Tapestry of Tten and the Searchers who had sought it in vain, over the past thousand Rotations.

They had sat together in the herders hut, Orto (immensely proud of his new found hearing), Jalni and the ancient Apothecary, sharing a strangely intimate Sunfall supper, after which Carolus drew a long breath and suggested slyly.

"Perhaps I should tell a bedtime story?", and for a moment Jalni was overcome with the feeling that "someone other" occupied the old man's place. He twinkled at her gravely however, so she dipped her head and blood tingling with expectation, leant back to listen, as the Apothecary's tale began.

"Long before Cataclysm, when Pelshar was a different world, scholars studied the stars at night.", he stated in his soft, velvety voice. "In those times, all men wrote or drew, needing no help to record their impressions of the world they lived in, and during my many Rotations of travel, I have seen the proof of their writings inscribed on the walls of broken cities, or written in the Sands themselves.".

He glanced at his rapt audience briefly then continued, "voice weaving", a picture of the long dead past with absolute authority.

"In the days leading up to Cataclysm, although they could do nothing to save themselves, our illustrious ancestors in magic set about weaving a great spell-plan. One that would protect Pelshar and its surviving people until a time when we would understand their culture, and embrace their beliefs once more.".

Jalni sighed, she could sense truth when she heard it, and right now, she could feel the frisson of old magic stirring. Even Orto seemed aware of something outside the norm, leaning forward, eyes intent as Carolus spoke gently.

"Since the time of Adaria, magic has been building, repairing itself, preparing for something to happen. As the ancient's spell unfolded, we have made many discoveries and Guardian after Guardian collected these in the repository of knowledge. Strengthening the ancient spell where they could, until the protective weave placed around Pelshar was ripped away, during the re-emergence of the next race of Sandsingers.".

The old man's voice died away as he reviewed the events of that Rotation, reliving the moment that he had lifted that new-born and heard the winds paying homage to the child, starting visibly when Orto questioned in a wistful voice, "Daro?", smiling as Carolus nodded.

"Daro.", he confirmed, as Orto said regretfully, "I wish Mother Solana could have known that. She must have died still waiting for him to arrive.".

Jalni reached out to take her Uncle's hand lightly.

"She knew dear. She knew before she died. I was there when he told her, didn't I tell you that she died in his arms, all her work done, her children safe and her Sandsinger ready to take her spells?".

For a moment she saw Daro "in magic", felt the power brush her, heard the song-spells pass from the aged Healer, into the protection of the mage. then a tear dropped on to her hand, as Orto shook his head mutely.

Carolus returned to his story, abruptly steering them away from emotive to practical issues.

"Well my dear young friends, now the search begins in earnest, but the Tapestry of Tten has eluded all who sought it previously. Beneva fears that it won't be found in time to avert a second Cataclysm. Since Ikella's recent illness, we understand that the time is short, and growing shorter, but we lack the means either to understand their warnings, or unearth all the clues we need. Daro must do what he shies away from and declare his status openly, so that all current knowledge can be brought to bear on this subject, but with Eshima's impending death hanging over the Carnelian like a shroud, the time is not right. Until that day, we must continue to search covertly.".

Jalni chose to remain silent, huge lilac blue eyes fixed on his, as he continued unperturbed.

"Daro came to Darnesh to seek advice from the Guild of Weavers recently. During that time he found an interesting connection in Master Toluran and one of his students (now sadly crippled). Toluran held a relic which Beneva recognised, so Daro brought Toluran, Andrau (and his life partner Tobin, to Selesh, where they are searching the old Weavers rooms, looking for what they call the Loom of Legends.".

Jalni barely glanced at him, but said vaguely, as though correcting a mistake.

"Both Andrau and Tobin are male names Carolus. The loom was in Sanctuary's repository when it fell.", and stopped abruptly, one hand clapped to her mouth, and whispered forlornly. "How did I know that? What in the Nine Sands is happening to me?".

She had spoken almost to herself, but Carolus shaking his head and staring fiercely at Orto, said comfortably, "Nothing to worry about my dear girl, merely the maturing of body and mind under the influence of your own Sands. Time was when youngsters like you stayed home until all three could take place under a mother's guidance, but things change and....", he never got the chance to finish the sentence as Jalni added harshly, "... and mother's die!.

The Apothecary frowned, but said nothing, remaining calm while Jalni fought temper and tears under control, nodding acceptance as she finally sniffed, dragged a sleeve across her eyes and muttered "Sorry.", as the old man cleared his throat.

"Well, I don't often ask favours from untrained spies, but I understand that you two are going north to Gurayen's Gully with Jashell tomorrow. I know the Maidens of the Temple only welcome female visitors at this time of the year, however, I have a question to put to the Oracle, and I would count it a favour if you would convey it for me?".

He slid a ring from his finger as he spoke, and Jalni accepted it, tucking it into her scrip asking hurriedly, "What is your question then?", as a soft footfall sounded outside.

"The question is in the ring.", the old man answered smoothly, as a soft knock sounded on the door, and Orto stood, throwing it open to reveal a gaggle of grinning Rangers. Leaping up impulsively, Jalni exclaimed in delight.

"Marran, Garald, Sushanna, oh my! Here's Lladro, Torvin and Calar! Whatever are you all doing here?", and was instantly silenced as a familiar babble rang out around her.

"Sand walking Jalni.", or "Buying Zeglur shenns Jalni.", then a quiet voice said gently.

"Guiding you Lady.", and in the shadows beyond her friends stood Draille Skellin.

They went out into the dusk, Jalni touching hands with adults, hugging Solana's "children", marvelling at the change since she last saw them, less Than half a Rotation ago. She turned as Carolus stepped out toward the rising terraces, and followed listening in awe to the happy chattering throng, and caught Draille's eye.

He smiled saying softly.

"Your lord is well I trust?", to which she said candidly.

"I have no idea Draille. I have been detached to deal with family matters in the Azure as you know. I now find myself at a crossroads, but I am journeying to find my mother's grave, then ask the Oracle a question for the Guardians before I return to my training. My lord is about his mother's business in othersands right now, and I truly hope he's well. However, do me a favour Draille, for the sake of the One, tell me quietly what Zeglure shenns are? I don't want to advertise my ignorance!".

He grinned, and asked quietly. "Have you never wondered what material the windows here were covered in?", and at her blank look, he prompted her, waving towards Orto's hut below, where an aperture glowed brightly illuminated from the lamp within.

She stared at it thoughtfully, then said slowly. "Skin I suppose, but its so supple, far finer than a vellum, yet strong enough to stop the wind. Whatever is it?", and was totally unprepared for the answer. "It is…", said the Ranger seriously, "The dried casing of a Zeglur's afterbirth!".

She peered at him through the gathering twilight, then chuckled and said cheerfully, "I wonder who thought that one up? It's a brilliant use of waste material, although I wouldn't like to process it!", and was rewarded with his shy smile. They were climbing towards the setting sun, and as they mounted the ridge, gazing east over the badlands of the Unexplored Territories, Jalni's breath was snatched away in a gasp of wonder.

In every direction immense monoliths jostled for space. Great fissures slicing mauve shadows into odd shades of pink, overlaid with streaks of copper green. No growing plants or hint of life was visible and above this desolation, the sky seemed to churn, as if liquid lightening flowed along the horizon, leaking magenta shadows into that ravaged lunar landscape. When Seleus spread his Sunfall mantle over the distant land beyond, fiery shades of gold and red glimmered a tracery along soaring peaks, jutting outcrops, vanishing into the blued depths of night as the first stars gleamed.

They were not alone however, nearby Jashell leant on a spear that Jalni didn't remember seeing when they parted, at her feet, perfectly poised the mystcat lay, eyes gleaming inscrutably. It was a long time before Jashell's voice rang out in the evening call to prayer.

"Eh yeh. Morou soutann. Eh yeh. Domune soutann.", she called as the sun dipped below the horizon, and suddenly Jalni was convinced that the call had not been heard here since Cataclysm. The echoes rebounded, a multiplicity of voices, Jashell and every shade of Jashell calling the faithful to prayer.

"Eh yeh Morou soutann. Eh yeh Domune soutann.", and they all knelt on the heights of Tregeth, and prayed for their world and its safety.

When they finally stood, only the odd gleam of pale rock reached tantalising fingers to the sky. Solemnly, the Rangers gathered around Carolus, as Jashell led the way down the deepening gloom of the valley toward the herdsman's hut that Orto occupied. Echo prowled sedately at Jashell's heels, and suddenly Jalni realised that what she was looking at, was the gathering of spies.

"Of course!", her inner voice chided relentlessly. "The Rangers pass in every Sand without fear or challenge. The Mystcat can disappear at will, and who would notice an Inesh warrior travelling anywhere in the Opal, but where do I fit in?".

She was still pondering over this as they approached the hut, and saw the outside fire-pit alight, dark clad figures moving round the cooking hearth, and delicious aromas rising. Jalni held her breath.

"Surely that can't be Terris?", she exclaimed, as she ran forward to investigate. Terris it was however, her pregnancy just beginning to show, as she officiated at the cooking stand. She grinned as Jalni hugged her lightly, then turned a serious face to Marran.

"I hope you've bought your appetite with you Ranger.", she exclaimed, telling Jalni (sotto voce), that he had lost his appetite after a difficult foaling, patting her own belly meaningfully.

"He is unlikely to let me travel again before our Rangerling arrives, but I have enjoyed seeing the baby Zeglurs born. I am not afraid for myself, I just hope he can stand the strain!", and chuckled as she placed a baked gourd of some kind, stuffed with leaves, nuts and grains on Jalni's platter.

They ate and talked, until the youngsters withdrew, heading in a chattering gaggle to the next hut down the valley to sleep, Echo prowling in their wake. When drinks were poured, and the cat returned, Carolus spoke earnestly to the group, who gathered close to the fire-pit, blankets draped round shoulders to listen.

"The Guardians summon thee Searchers after truth.", he stated clearly. "Those of you who know the legend, listen one more time, for those of you who know nothing, listen and learn.".

Jalni caught Orto's eye, then saw he had positioned himself by Draille who was illuminated by the firelight, and signing for him. Carolus sighed and spoke.

"We don't know what the last days before cataclysm were like, but writings both scroll and book have begun to emerge as if some architect planned us to find them at certain times. We have been warned that the end of Sorcery is upon us, but that is not inevitable, although the warning can be read several ways according to the Guardians. Recently it came apparent that several artefacts (which still have to be found), may hold the clues we need, one of which is this Tapestry. We are reminded that it holds a message for every Sand of our world, the symbol of each Sand is indelibly woven into the work. It promises us the hope of reunification for every Sand must work together to combat some evil fortune that faces us, and from which there is no escape without the Tapestry's powers unleashed. We know that every Sorceress holds a clue, without knowing to what it refers, and that the return of the Sandsingers, heralds the time in which the Tapestry must be found.".

There was a concerted sigh as the old man's voice died away and Jalni closed her eyes sending her memory soaring into the high vaulted ceiling of the Guild of Weavers. Again she saw the Opal Tapestry, noting the strange shimmer that old Toluran had diagnosed as water. She felt a light frisson of apprehension as she forced her mind to reveal what she remembered of the Azure weaving, and was immediately aware of the intoxicating aroma of the wild raja flowering not two spans from her. As a nearby fell-runner jingled its harness, a clear voice reached her.

"Go sister.", it said in the depths of her mind, "Go north, to the Temple of the Winds, and ask what they did with my Tapestry.".

She met Draille Skellins bland gaze across the fire-pit, and while her mind exclaimed, "Feydora!", her lips said, "I have reason to believe that the next step in this plan takes me, and Jashell to the Ashgenar. There is trouble coming, I can feel it, so the sooner we start the better. If Carolus can help Orto discharge our business in Anempor, Jashell and I can travel faster. Something huge looms over us, something bad, I must go north or Sorcery may even die.".

Chapter 32 - The Nishan Trail

Before first light touched the Sands Jalni and Jashell took their leave of Orto and Carolus. They ate sparingly, drank their breakday stemmis, hoisted carrisacks over their shoulders and stepped out onto the beaten earth of Tregeth's marshalling yard. They had spoken very little as they rolled bedding, folded clothes, and swept personal possessions into drawstring bags together, until Jashell touched Jalni's hand as she picked up an elaborately carved container, and the Healer stilled as understanding dawned.

"Indeera?", she questioned, as the taller woman fingered the sealed lid tenderly, and Jashell nodded, eyes brimming, then, overcome with a sudden conviction that this time, she was the one in command, Jalni slid an arm round the warriors heaving shoulders and rocked her while she wept. Wordlessly she helped to slip the funerary urn into a soft woven bag, drawing the string tight, then took Jashell's hand whispering softly.

"Thank you dear sister for letting me share your grief. I am honoured to serve Indeera in death as she helped me accept the Rule of life.".

Jalni stepped back, hoping she'd comforted Jashell, unprepared for the warrior's reaction, as she slid to her knees saying blankly... "but Jalni, we failed you. Indeera sent me after you, to beg forgiveness, then travel to the Temple of the Winds where they may tell us more.".

Impulsively Jalni reached out, pulling Jashell upright saying urgently:

"How can I forgive what I do not understand Jashell? As far as I am aware I have not been wronged by you, by Indeera or your Clan. Would it not be better to journey then seek enlightenment if that is what Indeera wanted? Draille will be waiting outside.", and so, cutting short their leavetaking, they stepped into the courtyard and gasped in astonishment.

All the Rangers were gathered, squatting comfortably with packs and bedrolls, ready to mount when the travellers arrived. Near them, large forms fretted in the shadows, and Jalni marvelled at the sibilant shifting, the low rumbles of enquiry and endearment as the Rangers fondled their Sheer Wolves. Not a muscle on Draille Skellins face flickered, but the humour in his eyes betrayed his pleasure at their reaction. He gravely bowed to Jalni, then turned and with a single movement of his hand his company rose and lined up, as Jalni recognised the full Tawn. Marran stepped forward, saluting Jashell gravely, then conducted her (with her precious burden), along the ranked Rangers. Ever the Commander, Jashell graced the formality, touching the hands of all present in sombre greeting, until she drew level with Draille who had mounted his wolf. He leant down extending an arm, and as if she had been doing it all her life, the warrior grasped his forearm, put her foot on his, and swung up into the saddle behind him. Jalni was nonplussed as Marran led forward a young wolf, staring at its silver pelt in wonderment, as the boy grinned.

"Grey?", she hazarded, to Marran's delight.

"Yes, how great you remembered her. She's old enough to carry one rider on a leading rein and short training rides are so necessary for youngsters.".

He swung the stirrup forward, assisted Jalni up into the saddle, and as Garald appeared on his mighty black Dorval, the wolves surged forward and they were off.

Misty outlines flowed past her, interspersed by flickering shadows and shimmering lights. Nothing seemed solid, not even the sand, and she was aware in some vague way of immense speed, even though the Sheer wolf's pace was smooth. That rippling thrust of power bore her effortlessly within the heart of the pack, strangely isolated from her companions, feeling only her face, chill in the frozen air of the Sheer. She dared not move, holding her hands low to the saddle to balance herself, mindful of the ranger's reminder.

"Just don't fall off. We've never recovered anyone who did yet!", but she could sense that leading rein, connecting her mount to Marran's "Blue", and relaxed.

Time stretched before her like a tunnel, yet she felt she was flying, and was immediately reminded of her dream vision. She was skimming above an Azure sea, the rhythm of the wolf became the sway of the boat, there was a pulsing in her blood like the beat of a drum, and she could smell the fiery gases from the heart of Scartel once more. Her grip on her saddle tightened as she sensed a change in direction, a slowing, the gentle break in rhythm as the wolf's pace shortened, then in a jumble of impressions, Grey came to a standstill, and they were there.,

Friendly hands lifted her down, someone said quietly.

"Leave her be for a moment, she was wolf-dreaming!", then Draille was there, checking her over impersonally, gentle hands rubbing her upper arms and easing the chill out of her bones. He held a flask to her lips, urging her to drink something he called Rinnish.

She gulped, spluttered, then laughed through tears starting from her eyes.

"Rinnish? Bottled wild-fire more like!", she complained, but fell silent as Jashell dismounted.

Garald raised a hand and the Tawn lined her route. Tall and silent, a guard of honour in patch dyed blues, watching solemnly as Jashell bore Indeera's ashes to their rest. She walked (alone and unchallenged), up a great scar in the cliff-face, until the path enfolded her as it turned. Ascending in great diagonal swoops up the sheer face, it levelled out on the rocky plateau where the Temple of the Winds kept guard over Gurayen's Gully, a natural ravine that led to the Ashgenar and the wilderness beyond.

Until Jashell reappeared on the ramparts above they stood at the ready, then as a breeze lifted the hair on Jalni's neck, there was the distant sound of a voice raised in command, followed by the slow thud of drums. The Healer glanced around nervously, but the Tawn had relaxed, Draille was smiling, and Garald ,was instructing young Rangers to examine wolf pads and paws. Jalni unslung

Jashell's carrisack, adding it to her own as Marran checked Grey. Then she too turned towards the Temple until Garald stopped her with a gesture.

"We return to Anempor and wait for the rest of the party. the Tawn takes a detachment back to Darnesh with messages for Lady Tirjella. Have you any thing to relay with them?", and Jalni was suddenly aware that Marran was looking rather pleased with himself.

"He must be leading that complement.", she deduced, suddenly feeling very isolated. Her young friends were growing up, sure of their place in life while she still foundered on the sea of uncertainty. However, there was one service she could perform for her own folk.

"When you meet up with Master Madiv, please ensure Master del Lyn has been reunited with his daughter.", adding softly, "I won't return to live in Jerritol.".

Garald's eyes were on her face as she said to herself.

"No. Holding isn't for me, although I love the Halt, it is Orto's birthright not mine!", then with a wave of her hand, she stepped out, up the cliff path towards the Temple from which her mother had taken the Nishan trail.

Garald watched her go as Draille joined him, (the Tawn gathering around Marran), he said prophetically.

"If the Halt is Orto's birthright, these Sands are yours Lady. Take your time, you have a particular duty to fulfil first.".

Saying nothing more, Garald the Dream Walker rose, and mounting Dorval, sent out an eerie cry across the Sands. It echoed up the steep incline behind Jalni, sounding both greeting and farewell as the wolves collected themselves and leapt into the Sheer.

Jalni paused as the Ranger's winked out of existence below. Adjusting both her own and Jashell's carrisacks, she felt the weight of some unknown decision descend upon her, marooning her half way up a cliff, from which she might never return. Almost as though she walked the strange twilight dimension they called the Sheer by herself she trudged onward and upward, Unsure of what lay ahead, fearful of what lay behind, but there was a shadow looming over her path, which thought made her shiver. The sudden clatter of a pebble falling roused her heartbeat to a near throttling pace. Somewhere ahead of her, a fluting call told her she had been observed. She adjusted her pace, slowing her heartbeat by force of will, as she rounded the last corner and found an enormous Gathering Square laid out before her.

It was filled with ranked women. Spears flashed in the rising sunlight, medallion bearing oath cloths twinkled as heads snapped in her direction, then in a familiar tongue a command rang out.

"First Watch ready! First Watch salute", then the presence at Jalni's heels made itself known, shifting shades to prowl around to her left hand, announcing its presence softly.

"Puhrr raow!", said the mystcat, and in her mind Jalni heard the muttered comment.

"They could do with practise!", as Echo sauntered past her, then sank down beside Jashell.

She was magnificent. Standing erect, spear held slanting from grounded haft to glittering blade. It was only then that Jalni saw that the spear was Indeera's ceremonial weapon. Once more she felt the thin, icy trail it had traced on her skin, once more she tingled with the expectancy of pain as twin lines flared from the nape of her neck and passed behind her ears in an elaborate trail. She felt the ground vibrate as these others, the Nishanawa surged around her, then she heard the whispers.

"She bears the insignia.", then, "Look at her wrists.", followed by a soft chanting.

"Sheyah Nishanawa. Sheyah Nishan. Sheyah Nishanawa, Sheyah Ineshanawa inexis Tawn.".!

She faced her friend, seeing the pride, the relief and the poignant smile on Jashell's face, and found herself asking doubtfully, "Do I understand any of that correctly? Were they saying that you brought the proof that the Nishanawa and Inesh are but two parts of one Clan? .

Jashell almost too full of emotion to speak, knelt on one knee, Indeera's urn beside her, close to the haft of her ceremonial spear. Bewildered Jalni asked quietly.

"I understand that you have proved a prophecy by returning Indeera's spear, but if I remember the words correctly, they spoke of a coming together, on the point of the Nishanawa and Inesh spears. They say that on the point of those spears the fruit of a Nishan is bound? That is the literal translation of Tawn isn't it? A fusion, a weld, or kindred bond, but I only see one spear!".

The flat puzzlement in her voice made Jashell's explanation all the more exquisite, a s smile transformed that stern face, illuminating it with sheer joy as Jalni said gently.

"O little sister, you remember an ancient dialect, but have never known what my name means? I am Jashell, Spear of the Inesh.".

Later, in the room they shared, she confided.

"Indeera was strictly "old school. She believed that somehow the Temple of the Waters at Selesh, and the Temple of the Winds here, had some ancient connection. It was Adaria who noticed the similarities first, when she discovered Sanctuary. You will know some of the stories of how Sorcery was first discovered, but Adaria always said, that the words should have been "re-discovered". Indeera always believed that one day there would be proof, and spent long nights reading after Ichspeller Selunsanni came to his power. She had found a writing of Adaria's which said, "When the Son of the Light returned, we would be reunited with our sisters.".

Jalni looked at her askance, then said slowly and deliberately, "Why did she think that somehow I was to be involved Jashell? I am not Nishanawa, though my mother was. I am not Inesh for I am born Zurias.", but Jashell was shaking her head.

"That isn't as I understand it my dear.", she smiled, clearly delighted to be teaching Jalni something of value.

"The Nishanawa are but one part of a Clan structure unique amongst other Clans. Lacking the number of males necessary to maintain a healthy breeding stock, they decided to split themselves up. The true tribal name is Ineshanawa, who were somehow displaced from their Sands, but who found a purpose in serving Sanctuary. The Nishan who actually guarded those who lived there were our finest warriors. trained from childhood, they were dedicated at ten Rotations old, and sent to Sanctuary as virgins when their training was complete. They were never expected to return alive.".

For a moment, Jalni's mind touched the gentle mother she'd adored, wondering how it was that she'd come to marry Sowdin's son, then Jashell's gentle voice turned her back to those who had followed the Nishan trail north to the Eternal Snows and the magic it guarded.

"When the Guardians foresaw the fall, they sent word back to the Temple of the Winds with Viness (your mother), who also carried a dispensation. Because of her youth, because she could be retrained, she was to remain here and serve the Oracle. However, long ago, another Oracle predicted that a Clan that had been rent in two, would be reunited by the child of the last Nishan warrior. At the time, no-one gave that prediction credence because the Nishan were virginal, and never likely to return, let alone bear children. They were unaware of your existence, and would have remained so, but after celebrating Izaneth (a festival between first Rites and Zenitheon), Indeera and Shiarjha started researching a book of predictions that a Weaver under Lord Daro's protection found long ago, in the Tapestry store in Darnesh.".

Jalni's skin prickled, she couldn't help her natural curiosity getting her into scrapes, but there was a pattern building, linkages that even a minor magic-user could feel entwining her in its machinations.

"What did it say?", she demanded, shifting position to lean back on Echo's flank.

Jashell lowered her voice conspiratorially, "It says that a daughter of the Clan will return the Spear of the Nishanawa, lost since Cataclysm, together with the Spear of the Inesh, that the Tawn of the Rangers will once again unite what has been divided by disaster.".

Jalni was frowning. "I'm not Nishanawa ", she protested, "My mother was however, does that count?", and Jashell grinned.

"Nishanawa.", she intoned as though reading a definition. " Girl child. Born of a Nishanawa woman and brought up within the Clan boundaries at the Temple of the Winds. Inesh. Male or female children of a Nishanawa woman (not brought up within the Clan or under its auspices). You however are unique. You were born to a Nishan warrior, who should never have been able to conceive. You are entitled to claim your mother's birthright as Nishanawa, while retaining your status as Inesh. Brought up outside Temple constraints. You bear unique markings, which Indeera discovered identified you, which led her to mark you with the spear. On the night she died, her finger lay on this statement. "She bears n her hands the marks of natures work, on her throat the trail of a sister's spear".

The lines on Jalni's neck flushed as she recalled her terror at that touch, then Jashell said seriously, "Whatever you achieve in your life Healer, you have healed a rift set in antiquity. Time and time alone will reveal the rest of the story but from today forward, you will be my sister through affection, through respect and through blood. Welcome home little Sister, welcome home.".

Chapter 33 - Eve of Disaster

The long days that followed her arrival at the Temple filled Jalni's soul with the kind of spiritual peace she had always been denied. She seemed to be hanging on the cliff of forever, no-one cajoling her to join in their activities, nobody preventing her from wandering as she willed. At dawn each day she rose and meditated on the tiny ledge outside the window of the room she shared with Jashell. It looked north, over the dramatic wilderness of the Ashgenar, for which she was grateful for it stirred no memories, aroused no desires. Hidden beneath the tangle of vegetation, precipitous paths ran down the ravine into a vast scrubby wasteland. Shrouded in mist, colours and shapes blurred into an indistinct mass, too ephemeral to provoke Jalni's natural instinct to explore. Here, in this unique place she rested, poised between one life and another, the first dictated by the whims and fancies of others and the next, which she must choose for herself.

Around the Temple various bells tinkled from time to time, gongs would sound imperious summons across the gardens where women tended carefully irrigated growing beds, but nothing and no-one troubled Jalni, who content to simply exist, drifted around the ancient buildings, mind in limbo.

However, around midnight on the last day of her second ninenight, she was roused from restful sleep by a violent surge in the Source. She sat up, feeling as though she was choking, so hot, so tight in the chest she could hardly breathe. Despite her best efforts to stumble out of bed without waking Jashell, she failed dismally and the warrior found her on all fours, panting for breath and struggling not to vomit.

Jashell, calm and controlled, only demanded, "Are you sick?", then raised the alarm. Lifting Jalni (who couldn't speak), she draped her across the window-sill, rubbing her back with brisk compassion, urging her room-mate anxiously.

"Relax Jalni. Just rest and breathe slowly, don't panic. Help's coming.".

Feet were running along the passageway, a door was opening, then as Jalni's senses swam a calm voice said swiftly. "Stand aside Commander, you've done all you can for the moment.", and then a hand waved something so acrid under Jalni's nose that the tears started from her eyes involuntarily. Roused from the dangerous lethargy that had seized her limbs, she swam back to full consciousness, and heaved a huge sighing breath, as she heard a slow solemn chime that shivered in her blood. A friendly arm slipped around her shoulders supporting her as a clamour started ringing around the walls, then the unknown woman said sharply.

"She is in psychic shock. No-one told me she was this sensitive!".

Jalni stiffened her backbone, dragging air into her lungs with painful care. She bent her head, pinching the bridge of her nose to quell the dizziness, then struggled upright to find herself confronting a slender woman with bird bright eyes.

"I'm sorry.", she gasped, not entirely detached from the reverberation in her blood, "The Source is very disturbed.".

Dark eyes surveyed her coolly from under arched eyebrows, then the clear voice observed.

"Daughter, if you feel the disturbance that strongly then the Guardians should test your powers again. In the meantime, we will go to the Inner Temple, where you can rest with the other sensitives amongst us. Come, Jashell can accompany you, and so can that dratted mystcat that you've been trying to conceal.".

Jalni struggled to her feet feeling foolish, but the other woman had already reached the doorway. "Bring your bedding by all means, wrap yourselves against the chill of night and follow me!".

Teeth chattering Jalni obeyed, wondering whose commands she was following as Jashell steadied her against another sickening bout of dizziness. They were half-way across a guarded cloister when Jalni heard Daro's voice in her ear. He was singing, empowered voice drifting poignantly into a gentle lullaby and then she knew what was happening. She paused, holding Jashell's arm, restraining the Inesh warriors progress with contemptible ease.

"Deshun Eshima is dying Jashell.", she muttered, "Since we spent so long together, sometimes I feel what Ichspeller Selunsanni broadcasts, particularly if he is in pain or very distressed. I only wish I could be with them, to comfort them or support them. Here I'm on my own, and a damnable nuisance I'm being. Too much magic is bad for me!", then she strode after her benefactor, ignoring the peculiar glance her friend gave her.

Far to the south, beyond the southernmost reaches of the Azure, beyond the complex highlands of the Amber Desert lay the sullen plains of the Carnelian Sands. Streaked with patches of mineral deposits and brilliant skythe, they presented a lavish palette of colour for visitors to wonder at. However, even the exotic perfumed air, and the sound of busybugs harvesting pollen could do little to relieve those who clustered round Eshima's deathbed. She had chosen to die (as she had lived), in her favourite hold at Ignef, which had lately ceased to be just her summer residence, but had assumed the air of a temporary capital. It was (after all said and done), by far more accessible lying at the crossroads used by most of the skythe traders. Here, the aged Sorceress had founded her Audience Hall, a wonderful tented pavilion which was cool on the hottest of days. Now she lay on the dais from which she had interviewed and argued with most of her subjects, her devoted servant Yani crouched at her left hand, the Guardian of the Way at her right. Her court had gathered as night began to fall, now the room was tense with expectation as the velvet night enfolded her pavilion, while her subjects wept softly.

Daro stood behind his mother, hands lightly resting on her shoulders for comfort as they waited for the inevitable. There was no sign of magic, but the air around the bed trembled and somewhere a mere whisper of energy caused a glimmer of light to touch his sombre features, as though a candle flickered somewhere nearby. Time slowed to the failing beat of the heart within that bed, a wind sighed, stirring the Sands with the measure of that infinitesimal breathing, songbeads slithered through praying hands, then, to the accompaniment of stifled sobs, a small procession passed through the throng and ascended the stairs to the bedside.

Serafina, Sorceress Elect, was calm but pale as she knelt. Beside her, Yani shuffled her ancient knees and tried to withdraw, but Serafina reached out a gentle hand and steadied the old servant, whispering kindly. The Senior Healer bent over the Sorceress, taking her pulses before retiring to the end of the bed, with the priestess who held the Carnelian Staff, angling its subdued glow to light Eshima's well beloved features.

A collective sigh went up as the wind began to strengthen. A bell chimed softly, then the powerstone of the Staff flickered and faded, before recovering once again. Slowly Ikella rose from her chair, to gently kiss her old friends withered cheek. Serafina touched Yani's hand, delicately extending permission for the aged servant to kiss her mistress goodbye, then the powerstone flickered, glowed brilliantly one more time and faded, down to the last beat of Eshima's failing heart.

As the aged Sorceress drew her last breath, a soft groan ran through her court, and the Carnelian Staff flew to Serafina's hand. Ikella raised her head as the air above the bed transformed into a cascade of Carnelian red petals, and Eshima's body glowed, dissipating into a stream of power returning to the Source from whence it came. The Guardian of the Way drew the new Sorceress forward, accepting a trembling obeisance, kissing Serafina's forehead in recognition of her accession, then as Tekrun's bell tolled Eshima's passing she turned away and left, discreetly guiding her son, leaving the Jedrun to mourn their own.

In every Sand the blow was felt. Bells tinkled the passing rotations of Eshima's long life, her Sister's in Sorcery knelt in prayer, each of them sorrowing for the days when the autocratic old Sorceress had overruled hosts to stay up all night telling outrageous stories of her youth. Gradually as the dark gave way to dawn, across the Union of Sands minds turned to the future, to welcoming a new young Sorceress, but not all those minds in harmony could have predicted what new terrors nipped at their heels, what new sorrows awaited them.

In the deepening shadows of the Azure, a man was crouching close to the bitter waters of a ruined oasis. He had been staring into the murky depths for many turns of the sand-glass when he became aware of the livid reflection as Gatta swam overhead. In that moment he heard the voice. It came to him more regularly now, taunting him, tormenting him in his sleep with memories he'd prefer to forget. Somehow provoking almost incontrollable rage, sometimes plunging him into furious activity, sometimes whispering thoughts of revenge on all those who would like to see his downfall. He hugged his hatred closer, praying for vengeance, particularly if it involved that girl with the vivid eyes, the one whose very presence had brought back Rotations of impotent rage. Jalani they'd called her, "little Weaver."

"Well, she'll weave no more at my Halt!", he thought bitterly, face twisting into a mask of malevolence, as the silken whisper tormented his ears.

"Sowdin del Orto, are you man or are you minkrat? Are you going to allow either one of those boys Serba insisted on adopting, or the misbegotten get of a Nishanawa to take your birthright?".

He wanted to scream, to rip that voice out of his head, and clutched it in despair. His own father had wandered in his wits before dying, his mother had a sister who was insane, surely that couldn't be happening to him. He gritted his teeth, snarling softly, and that damned voice chuckled.

"I can see that you hear me Sowdin, now, stop building an apoplexy and listen. I can help you get your revenge. On Serba and her plans, on Jalani who humiliated you, and on all the Sisters of Sorcery, but you must do it in the order I tell you, using only the weapon of my choice! Do you hear me del Orto, or are you determined only to destroy yourself by torturing weaklings and cripples? Can't you imagine being able to take down those who really deserve to pay the price of your pain?".

Sowdin glared into the reflection of the dark moon, but this time he grunted assent, and the slick voice dripping with venom advised.

"You have work to do then. In that grove yonder there are tall trees. You may recognise the Driands that cluster amongst them. These are the weapon of my choice. Now don't argue, they have been properly treated, but will not be ready until the EVE OF Zenitheon. They must not be harvested before midnight, but must be cut and prepared before dawn. You have two ninenights to wait, and during that time you must take yourself (discreetly) to the first oasis beyond Darnesh in the old Fringe. There a grower is desperate to train a fruit gatherer, having lost one through accident. You are sensible, strong, and the grower will teach anyone willing, to harvest and prepare his Driands, ready for Tirjella's table at Zenitheon. Once you have done his bidding, he will likely send you with this offering to Darnesh, but you will be diverting to Simlan's Spring en route. Here by the light of Gatta, you will harvest a few of your own, and mix them with those that you are sent with. Simply deliver them to the kitchens at Darnesh and leave. Your revenge on the Sisters of Sorcery will echo around the Sands. Do nothing to draw attention to yourself, and you may assist us again. Now, so that I can find you when I need you, or protect you if necessary, dip your fingers in the pool and make obeisance to the dark moon. Touch your fingers to your heart and lips, savour the bitterness on your fingers, then go about your business.".

Too awed and terrified to ask questions Sowdin did as he was bidden, withdrawing into his camp and waiting for the dawn to allow him to identify the Burgeoning Driand clusters in the sickened grove. Satisfied, he turned north east and set out to find the oasis, and the training he would need, passing Darnesh in the billowing bluster of a convenient sand-storm, as he set out to destroy its ruler.

Chapter 34 - The Oracle Speaks.

As dawn lit the Azure Sands below the Temple of the Winds, Jalni joined the Nishanawa who waited patiently in the courtyard below the Inner Temple. Dark circles under her eyes betrayed a sleepless night, but she stood erect, thoughts directed to the Jedrun, who would wake this dawn without their adored Sorceress.

The expectant hush was broken as a hawk screamed overhead, swooping along the terraces as it descended to the gloved hand of a Temple attendant. Momentarily distracted, Jalni almost missed seeing a door open on the interior wall ,as a covered carrying chair was borne in on the shoulders of eight statuesque women, a small procession following. Around them a host of girls fluttered, gold draped limbs shining, tiny bells tinkling as they passed, but Jalni (never having suspected the presence of young children here), gaped. They whirled and pirouetted seriously, eyes lowered demurely, followed by three shrouded figures, so heavily veiled that they seemed sexless. Belatedly, Jalni grasped the significance, and glanced at Jashell, who was standing rigid with concentration as the palanquin drew level with their position.

The curtains parted fractionally, a regal hand beckoned, then Jalni and Jashell were hustled forward to be enveloped in celestial blue robes, their boots exchanged for slippers of fine blue kid. Thus prepared, they were thrust into the retinue as it passed into a passage, through another courtyard, then into the Hall of the Oracle.

Neither of them had been aware of petitioners arriving, but the Hall was filled to overflowing. Its great height alleviated the sensation of claustrophobia, but Jalni dreading some return to religious ritual sighed despondently. She had come to consult the Oracle however, she sternly reminded herself, she just hadn't planned on doing it in front of all these others. However, she was to be pleasantly surprised, for of this entire assembly, there were only nine petitioners, all dressed in blue robes similar to theirs. Other pilgrims passed simply to make offerings, presumably for past favours and it soon became apparent that the Hall was emptying fast. She watched intently as the carrying chair disappeared behind a screened wall. Incense burners filled the air with a musky perfume, then a door slid aside, and behind an ornate grill, one of the veiled attendants approached those who waited silently.

A few words were exchanged, a servant brought forward an offering and Jalni hissed impotently. She had forgotten the offering, but with that thought came the memory of Daro's trinket .As a lowly Healer, all she could ask (in return for her skills) was a bed and some food. Her hands fretted through the pockets of her under-vest reluctantly, and froze in relief as she encountered the Apothecary's ring. She paused considering, then decided that as Carolus had told her to give this to the Oracle, he must have understood the Temple's rites and practices. She slid the ring from her pocket onto her thumb, bending that digit to secure it in place and felt her heartbeat return to normal as she settled Daro's trinket near her heart where it warmed briefly.

Someone touched her hand, and dragging her attention back from the memory of a soft amused voice, and the seductive curve of Daro's mouth, she looked up, into the face of the woman who had conducted her into the shielded rooms of the Temple dormitory, and smiled in relief.

As Jashell and Jalni slipped along the row of petitioners, a curtain was swept aside by unseen hands. Led into a comfortable room, where their friend of the night indicated two seats, sliding on to a bench, as they settled. She addressed Jashell gravely,

"I am Orchis. For many Rotations, I have studied the predictions of those who went before. Have you a request for the Oracle O Spear of the Inesh?".

Jashell bowed her head, whispering her request in a tear choked voice.

"I was the life-partner of Indeera, priestess of the Temple of the Waters at Selesh. It was she who finally understood the writings we had treasured from Cataclysm. She who consulted the Guardians, and she who guided me, trusted me to do what she could not. I ask only to return the Spear of the Ineshanawa, then to lay the ashes of Indeera to rest amongst her ancestors here in Gurayen's Gully.".

Orchis closed her eyes, then after a few moments she said quietly, "Your request is very moderate and will receive due consideration. Have you brought Indeera's ashes with you?".

Jalni blinked as Jashell lifted Indeera's urn across the table to Orchis, one hand lingering on the urn in farewell. She had been so self-absorbed that she hadn't noticed Jashell's sorrow, and castigated herself as she struggled to phrase her own questions. However, Orchis had risen silently, was already beckoning her through another door, and bemused, Jalni followed. Soft footed, they filed into a tiny room where narrow piercings allowed light to penetrate in thin golden streams. The whole atmosphere was hushed, as they approached a draped altar. Bewildered, Jalni watched their host light a taper, touching it to glows set in the walls, then Orchis passed behind the altar, sweeping aside the golden covering to reveal a crystal casket, containing (in unaltered grace and beauty) the body of a warrior.

"Was this whom you seek child?".

Their guides voice seemed to change, but Jalni's whole being was riveted to her mother's beloved features. Viness, (once again clad in silvery blue Nishan armour) seemed merely to have fallen asleep. Her face was young, unlined, all her pain fled away as she slept within her crystal casket, and tears held back too long streamed as Jalni crouched, hands outstretched, whispering brokenly,

"Mother, oh there you are.", as relief, sudden and strange shook her to the core of her being.

She was barely aware of Jashell's indrawn breath, or the ceremonial salute, one warrior to another at rest. She was only aware of a hand clasping hers, then

Orchis saying gently, "Come now child. Now you know she is safe with her sisters, in the heart of her family, you can rest.".

Numbly, she allowed them to lead her away. It seemed like a lifetime before she managed to state her other request, stumbling over the words, still lost in her own emotional turmoil.

"I also search for an artefact of High Magic.", she had eventually muttered.

"It has been sought from time to time before, but the Guardians now believe that our world is doomed unless we find the Tapestry of Tten.".

She glanced up at Orchis who sat framed in the brilliant light of day, gleaming highlights sparkling on her silver hair. She seemed to be consulting some inner memorandum as Jalni redoubled her efforts, pleading.

"Would it be possible to Search your repository? I haven't come empty handed.".

She slipped the Apothecary's ring from her thumb, and held it out to Orchis who touched it with a trembling hand. Jalni intent on her own search hardly noticed, as she added quietly, "My friend Carolus said that the Oracle would recognise that ring, and I should make sure that it reached her hand myself.".

Orchis smiled at her, taking the ring, and placing it on a surprisingly masculine finger.

"It will not leave my person until it is on her hand.", she stated firmly, and Jalni relaxed, but not for long, as Orchis raised her head and spoke again.

She had become remote, eyes glazed silver, voice transformed into something other-worldly. It echoed round that anteroom a threnody of voices in chorus, thrilling and disturbing in both tone and content.

"Welcome Searcher.", she sighed. "Welcome daughter of the doubled Clan. The Tapestry you seek was never here, though we long for its discovery and pray for its safekeeping. The ripples of time are closing in, once more the Lords of Sand walk amongst us, once more the Searchers appear, but your path Child is written in two Sands. In one you will love, in the other you will lose, but your future is sealed into the House of High Magic, where you will become the mother of the Tenth Wind.".

Jalni stared at the woman who had helped her through the night and suddenly understood.

"May the One protect me.", she turned a stricken face towards Jashell. "Last night she called me "daughter", I should have realised. Orchis is the Oracle!".

She had risen to her feet glaring mutinously, with no apparent recognition of either of her companions as she wrenched open a door and stalked forth, fury etched on every line of her face.

"I won't!", she hissed into the dampening atmosphere of the Oracle's Hall. "I won't be constrained by tradition, religion, prediction or the hounds of Hadda's own Hall! I can't be a mother, I only just stopped being a child myself.".

She strode through deserted passageways, muttering dire imprecations, steered only by a vague idea of where she was going until she found herself in the small dim room that she was to remember as the Crystal Chamber.

She faced her mother's casket defiantly.

"You shouldn't be here.", she stated flatly. "You belong to Father and me, not to this crazed Oracle! What am I to do with you?".

There was a whisper of sound, the tinkling of a long forgotten wind chime, the powerful scent of citrines, and a memory stirred. The anger faded as a breeze tickled Jalni's face, and she murmured confidingly.

"Tirjella said that if ever I needed refuge, I was welcome at Darnesh. Well if I leave tomorrow, I can easily get there before Zenitheon, perhaps there I'll be able to think, for I am never going to accept that my life is pre-ordained. I would sooner be walled up alive in the Amethyst Sands than follow some ancient prediction.".

She didn't wait for a moment longer, rising swiftly from where she'd knelt, going to her room where she packed, while she considered how to free a hawk. She would send it to Anempor, where she devoutly hoped her Ranger friends would have met up with Carolus. She scowled, contemplating the questions she would ask him, and sat on her bed, turning her problems over helplessly.

The room was full of light as Jashell returned. Jalni sat up yawning, aware that she must have fallen asleep, and mentally groaned as she realised how late it was. Dawn had barely broken when they had been conducted to the Oracle, she hadn't stayed for long in her mother's resting place, but here it was, wanting only three turns of the sand-glass to Height of Sun, and she hadn't sent for the Rangers. Jashell chuckled, as Jalni struggled up scowling furiously.

"Come on sleepyhead!", she challenged provocatively, "Half the days gone and you're still in your supplicants robes. Take them off this minute, go get a sand bath and eat before you travel.".

She casually threw a pair of boots onto the floor, and pulled off Jalni's slippers as the healer turned a shocked face to her room-mate.

"How did you know what I planned?", she whispered, glancing at Jashell's throat to see if she still wore the Opal insignia that marked her as a priestess, but Jashell's neck was bare of all jewellery. The warrior looked at her seriously, then squatted on the rush matting, eyes level with Jalni and spoke softly.

"I travel no further little sister.", she announced gravely. "I have said my farewells in the Opal Sands and have relinquished, my authority there to my natural successor. I have followed the path of the Opaz as our writings decreed, bringing with me Indeera's ashes which will now rest here with our sisters. It was Indeera's last wish that she make the journey home with her spear, and my joy to bear her home in triumph, having reunited our Clan. Today, if you would but stay your journey till Sunfall, the spear of the Ineshanawa will be rededicated and will stand in the crypt of the warrior where your mother rests. I am, and will always be the living Spear of the Inesh, and for that reason I shall not leave here, so that my sisters and brothers can return home.".

Jalni was stunned into silence. The immensity of Jashell's faith brought a lump to her throat and for a moment tears glistened as she thought of Selesh bereft of that stentorian bellow, those bright intelligent eyes and the statuesque figure of command, but then Jashell grinned.

"Don't worry little sister. ", she chuckled. " I have left plenty of trouble behind me to occupy both my Clan and the Shalhanhi for Rotations. The new Master Builder is exercising his prerogatives' in examining the farthest reaches of Old Selesh. The Guardians are busy with accessions, and appointing Searchers. The Weavers add their own kind of confusion. Everywhere they go we get a history lesson in weaving techniques and…", she broke off, obviously considering something that led to much merriment, for she chuckled before continuing.

"Then there's the matter of Ichspeller Selunsanni's new body servant, who has (singlehanded), turned our Sandsinger into a bit of a peacock.", she announced straight-faced, going on to muse provocatively. "Unusual perfumes, distinctive clothes, elaborate hairstyles!", she rolled her eyes expressively, adding with a smile.

"Deshun Ikella hovers between approval and wondering if her son has developed an unnatural tenderness for this man!", she whooped with mirth as she described Ikella's confused expression when Daro had paraded Tobin's latest extravaganza. She glanced sharply at Jalni, but got more of a rise when she commented dryly, "Then of course there's Shey Somishen Suraya.".

Jalni's eyes flashed Azure fire as she leapt up.

"Hadda's balls! I'd forgotten her. I suppose they had to send for her with Ikella so ill?".

For a moment jealousy seethed in her eyes, then she suddenly whooped with laughter, astonishing Jashell by sniggering. "Whoo hoo! She's in for a shock if she looses that spiteful tongue on him now! Does she know?".

She hauled Jashell to her feet, patting her bed in open invitation, and they sat side by side as Jashell admitted,

"To be quite honest I didn't stick around to find out. I had my feet on the path when Diras ran after me to say she'd arrived. By that time I wanted only to leave, and finding Master Carolus below Emblem Rock was more in my mind than returning to a life I no longer wanted.".

Jalni hugged her impulsively then said carefully, "Do I understand that after the ceremonies of the day, I can leave for Darnesh without hindrance?".

Jashell replied soothingly.

"Of course. Draille and his Rangers are bringing a few Inesh foundlings back to us for Zenitheon, and the hawk this morning was to tell us that they will be here before Height of Sun. Hadn't you better get changed and washed dear sister. I can't possibly have you late on parade. My reputation would be utterly destroyed!".

Joyously, Jalni bounded to her feet, and hastened from the room, failing to see the shadow of regret on the brooding face of her friend, as the warrior contemplated the rest of the Oracles's prediction, the part that Jalni hadn't waited to hear.

Chapter 35 - Flight to Darnesh

Jalni, intrigued with all the preparations going on in the Great Courtyard, found a comfortable alcove from which she could watch swathes of blue cloth being spread around the base of its ancient walls. A gaggle of children supported the edge of the longest piece, manoeuvring it experimentally, causing it to "ripple". She closed her eyes, inwardly focussing as the events depicted in the Azure Tapestry, were staged for all to see.

"A river.", she murmured, as a thudding rhythm encouraged young voices to chant, unaware that she too, was under observation., She sat forward musing, as a second chorus echoed the first. Voices twining, advancing, retreating, skipping in eddies that flowed like water, until she breathed the words again.

"The River sings!".

A quiet voice agreed, "Yes, the river of life sings to all in its own way Lady.", and she turned to see Draille Skellin leaning against the ancient wall, watching her with those warn brown eyes. He smiled, creases crinkling his sun bronzed face with ready humour as she slipped down from her perch, and took his outstretched arm in greeting. Gazing back at the preparations, she said outrageously, "All this drives me crazy! Why don't we run away together and breed skythe-hounds for Deshun Serafina?".

It was meant as a joke, but suddenly a pit yawned under her feet. Wondering how she had misread Draille's calm self-assurance for disinterest she tried to withdraw from this dangerous conversation, lowering her eyes, trying to hide those inviting azure glints she'd turned on him. He tilted his head, regarding her placidly as she stubbornly rejected the unfolding disaster. A tiny flame warmed that grave countenance, as he guided them back to a safe place reluctantly.

"Aah yes, and I would go with you anywhere in a heartbeat Lady, but your lord might have other ideas. Remember, I have no magic to offer you.".
".

Steady eyes held hers, gauging her reaction as an unaccustomed flush stained her cheeks, then he relented with a sigh. Now it had been said, Jalni stared at Draille dumbfounded, until he held up a hand in submission.

"No matter Lady. I will always be here for you, for you both if necessary. Without question, without claim, just to be your Ranger. Do you understand what I am saying?", and Jalni nodded, heart too full to speak. She had known that Draille admired her in that strangely potent way that all women understand, but she was totally unprepared to discover a devotion. Suddenly shy, she glanced down the path and saw others in the Ranger party approaching.

"Garald!", she exclaimed then, "Carolus, Sushanna, Orto, oh everybody! How lovely.", and the unexpected intimacy with Draille was broken (but not forgotten).

Then there was a horn blowing, a summoning that rang out from the higher terraces, and the ceremony began. Jalni watched it all as the second Tapestry came to life in front of her. A carrying chair made up to look like some predatory creature hovered just above the rippling swathes of material. Children wearing oval frames around their middles, surged out from a hidden door, and slid amongst billowing folds, plunging wooden paddles each side of them energetically. They gathered Jashell in their midst, watching closely as Indeera's theory came to life in dance and mime, in front of them.

There was a roll of drums like thunder, as children surged out across the courtyard like a miniature armada, paddles dipping an accompaniment to the thudding rhythm that echoed around the Temple from hundreds of stamping feet. To the left, a cone shaped peak emerged from the fabric "waves", and as Jalni watched, golden material (clearly weighted), spurted forth, followed by red streamers and showers of glittering dust.

It seemed to issue like fire, spreading around the conical rim, then spilling forth as triumphant children rolled it towards the crowded walls. Heads turned as a carrying chair made up like some watercraft emerged, its stately bearers solemnly dipping imaginary paddles into a fabric sea as it retreated.

Suddenly silence fell, followed by an unearthly keening as the billowing fabric stilled and stretched taut and lowered to the ground. The watercraft had turned, was approaching the steps where astonished eyes perceived that it did not carry the Oracle as suspected, but six Inesh warriors wearing the familiar uniform of Ikella's guard were emerging. The chant was changing, deepening as Jashell leapt to her feet, challenging them joyfully.

"Ho Seleshani.", that stentorian bellow rang out, then Jalni saw Ikella's First Watch surround Jashell proudly. She blinked, counting the seniors, naming them silently to herself and wondering who protected Selesh while they were here.

"Driss, Sorrill, Nyman, Diras, Farill, Madrian.", every one of them commanded a Chapter, but still they lined up, smiling at their old Commanders bewilderment, then Sorrill said softly,

"We are all here Commander, we are all here!", and Jalni saw that Sorrill carried Indeera's urn. Somehow it looked different, it gleamed flickering all the shades of Opal. Then the one whom they had protected for Rotations, materialised in their midst, greeted with a huge roar of approval.

Ikella's voice rang out, embracing Inesh and Nishanawa alike.

"Greetings O Ineshanawa. Now are your sister's and brothers returning to seek the affirmation that you are sprung from one root. After so many Rotations of exile, may their journeys bring them safely to settle in retirement with their kin,

The entire Temple seemed to come to its feet, as Sorrill nodding to Jashell to take Indeera's urn, called. "Ayah so speaks the Guardian of the Way, Ikella Sorceress of the Shalhanhi has spoken.".

Still pale with astonishment Jashell bent her head as her Deshun held out a hand, then understanding she held out Indeera's urn.

"Gurayen sek moyen, Gurayen noi shominen.", (Gurayen shelter us, Gurayen defend us).

The invocation to the Wind of the Azure brought Jalni's attention sharply into focus, as she saw the magic enfold the Sorceress, her Honour Guard, and half the courtyard. There was a fluttering of flags, a steady billowing of blue fabric, and then Ikella lifted her hands and Gurayen received Indeera's ashes in a glittering stream.

For a moment the light eddied around Jashell, drying her tears, and then the flare streaked across the Temple, flickered along the rift they called Gurayen's Gully, and vanished. For a long moment the wonder held them all motionless, then wordlessly, Sorrill, Diras and Ikella faded from view. Those left behind closed ranks, and slowly marched towards the Temple, intent only on attending the re-dedication of Indeera's Spear.

It had been an extraordinary event, and Jalni was feeling quite exhausted by it all as Carolus approached her alcove where she sat in company with the Rangers. He listened quietly to her complaint, then said cheerfully,

"Well, I'm sorry that you can't take your mother back to join your father, but had you considered doing it the other way round? Your uncle has some news for you, that I think he celebrates, so while I ask Orchis if Rowin can be re-interred here, perhaps you'll speak to him. He can rid you of at least one ghost I suspect.".

He shuffled off, leaving Jalni staring after him suspiciously, as Orto arrived and put an arm around her.

"Hello.", he said simply, "I can still hear you love, but you're as cross as a sticklebear without berries!".

She turned laughing, and said seriously. "Would you mind if Carolus gets permission to bring Father here? I don't, so long as they are together, but he was your brother and I wondered if you wanted to keep things as they are when you return to hold Jerritol.".

He looked at her oddly, then said shortly. "I may not be able to hold Jerritol unless the Guild of Weavers is content to prove the old Weaver's will.".

He spoke so oddly that Jalni faltered. He had come a long way in his speech in under two journeys of the moon, but she was bewildered and said so as she walked towards the Temple to say goodbye to Jashell and her mother. Orto's voice was very gentle as he said, "What would you say if I told you that Sowdin del Orto was not my father, Rowin's father or your Grandfather. We dear niece, are all Ineshanawa!".

Jalni froze in mid stride, and Orto grinned as he hopped around her.

"Yes.", he agreed, "Took me that way too, but yon Apothecary seems to have a lot of contacts in Anempor, and it didn't take him long to find a Healer able to swear that Serba was barren. The Healer was very old, but clearly remembered Rodgeo's enforcer, and recalled sending them to a young man who was dying. He had settled with a Nishanawa woman until his condition was known. Having discovered his own family had disowned both him and his sons, he needed to settle them before he died. At that time Sowdin and Serba had been in the South for Rotations, so returning to Jerritol with a toddler and a baby complete with wet-nurse wasn't remarkable. However, it all backfired on Sowdin, when his father left the Halt to us. No wonder he turned bad!".

Jalni shivered, her face pinched as Orto exclaimed.

"No dear, its alright. I'm still your Uncle, just not a del Orto, except by name. If the Guild uphold the original will, we're still half-holders. I shan't lose you whatever happens, we've still got a Tapestry to find. Carolus swears he will help us if Tirjella can't. We're only Zurian through an unregistered adoption you see, so she may not be able to do much.".

Later that night when she once more travelled the Sheer a-wolfback, she wondered what she would do if Tirjella turned her away. She had taken Orto to the Crystal Chamber, and had stared in disbelief at Indeera's spear clasped in her mother's hand. They had lingered talking until it was time for her to leave, Orto remaining with their Inesh kin for this Zenitheon.

As those returning to Holmgarth, whooped farewells before vanishing into the Sheer, she leant back against the extraordinary man who had appointed himself her Ranger, as his wolf sprang into that odd dimension, carrying her into impending danger, where the celebration of midsummer solstice would change her life forever.

Chapter 36 - The Bleckoning

So utterly weary that she hardly noticed the peculiar sweetness of her welcome, Jalni sank like a pebble in a sand-trap, straight to the bottom of a lowly bed in the Healer Hall. Allowing the citadel to enfold her in its mysterious embrace, she gratefully followed Adeya to a dormitory, as Draille slipped back into the dawn. Night turned to day, and back to night before she woke, rousing with a vague sense of apprehension, as she realised that Eve of Zenitheon had already arrived.

Finding her way to the dining hall, she slipped along the edge of the noisy, exuberant crowd who gathered in earnest conversation, determined to find Adora and beg admittance to the training Hall. She had no illusions; Ikella would certainly tell Tirjella of her erratic protégé's fall from grace, but she had little to lose, and a Selesh trained Healer was bound to attract Tirjella's interest.

A bubbly woman in Healer blue was holding court in the second dining alcove as she approached. Jalni tried to slip past unobtrusively, but a cheerful voice (with a distinctive Southern accent) called out.

"Jalni? It is Jalni isn't it? Welcome back my dear. I'm Ellandra, Novice Mistress (for my sins). We would have met before you left, but for fever in the hall. Won't you join our table and tell us about your travels?".

Quite disconcerted by this friendly overture, Jalni forgot to scowl, and soon found herself surrounded by girls not much younger than her, all proudly wearing Fourth Rotation ribbons. She dined, chatting to qualified Healers and novices alike, and all her nervousness departed as she described her journey to Scartel. It never occurred to her that such an undertaking was highly unusual. She didn't notice trained Healers nodding in approval, but as she described how she had befriended Solana's orphans, and her presence at the old Healer's death, Ellandra spoke wistfully:

"If only you'd been full Healer, Solana's spells would have survived!", and Jalni (for the first time), considered what an invidious position she was in.

Solana's spells were perfectly safe, but how could she tell them that a living Sandsinger had retrieved them to pass on to Adora later? She glanced up, looking for Tirjella, wondering if Daro had revealed his status to her, retreating into anonymity when she saw where the Sorceress sat.

The high table groaned under the weight of food and the attentions of Clansmen. Tirjella seemed a flower amongst Biron as Jalni stared fearfully at the warlords. Hair and beards long, they had apparently sat to table straight from the saddle. Nearby, riding coats and helms piled high. Gauntlets thrust into belts, alongside knives that glittered wickedly, naked blades honed razor sharp, ready to draw in an instant. The loud rumble of male humour drowned all but the closest voice, beakers jumped and rattled as they rapped the table insistently, and

Jalni sighed glumly, knowing she could never get a private audience during Zenitheon.

Perhaps the loss of her earlier gaiety attracted Ellandra, who moved round to sit with her, encouraging her to talk. Jalni, glanced at her fellow students busily engaged in merry argument, and decided to confide her plans. When she asked if Ellandra could transfer her last Rotation's training to Darnesh, Ellandra propped her chin on her hand demanding curiously, "Are you serious? Most of our girls would tear your throat out for a chance to train in Selesh, and you want to give up elegant living, a purpose made Hall, and Deshun Ikella's handsome son for life on the frontier?".

She studied Jalni's betraying blush, then said shortly, "Aah. The old problem!", and fell into an enigmatic reverie, while Jalni struggled to keep indignation at bay. Her reasons had nothing to do with the strange feelings Daro provoked. That was just sex, and she was not bound to lead a celibate life as a Healer, but as yet she hadn't even contemplated Daro in that light. He was so far beyond her reach. He the son of a Guardian, she without a familiar name, the daughter of a simple weaver and a Nishan warrior, besides, he was her patient and she was sworn to duty, but Ellandra had noticed small white teeth worrying her lower lip.

"Never mind me dear.", the comfortable voice said. "You'll get over it, we all do one way or another. For the time being, you need to recuperate, attach yourself to Adora for assessment, then, when all the Clan business is conducted, we can ask Tirjella's permission. Do you think that would suit? Of course you could also give me a hand tomorrow. We have more guests to entertain than a hotchpig has fiddle-fleas, Some of them learned, some of them arrogant, most of them men! Tomorrow I need an entertaining Festival hostess.".

Jalni shuddered at the thought of the warlords, and Ellandra laughed.

"Silly girl.", she chuckled. "I meant only as table companion. It is quite usual for whole families to attend, but Tirjella's guests are far from home, or single.".

Jalni only hesitated fractionally, but Ellandra noticed and said reassuringly, "I can offer you a place down the table, sitting you with visiting craftsman?". Not liking to refuse, Jalni nodded, returning to her dormitory and sliding into bed.

She woke, the call of the desert stirring her blood as she rose and crept from the room. Hands trailing the walls, she drank in the spirit of Darnesh as she passed out into the "dark before dawn". Nowhere was she challenged, Darnesh slept without warriors prowling, but her senses were tingling, attuned to some hint of danger. Ignoring the sensations teasing the nape of her neck, she paused at the foot of the steps above the Gathering Square, certain that she had been summoned in some way.

"Lady?", the soft voice made her jump, as Draille Skellin rose from a stone seat and stretched. She stared at him, half annoyed, half anxious as she demanded quietly.

"Have you been sleeping there all night, waiting for me?", as he held up a package grinning.

"Not guilty Lady. I had messages to deliver to Master del Lyn at Jerritol. Mistress Orana specially asked me to bring back your Colours for tomorrow's Gather. She forgives you for not calling on her before hiding yourself back amongst the Healers, but begs you to wear your surcoat tomorrow. She felt it would give you more consequence amongst the Clansmen.".

He handed over the package and Jalni fell on it with a cry of delight. She had forgotten the wonderful gift of the Weaver Guild, and was more than thankful to have something of such startling elegance to wear. Impulsively she hugged the Ranger, and said (before she thought about it).

"What would give me consequence dear Draille, would be to have you attend me tomorrow! Please stay near me, I have a terrible sense of apprehension, but of what I cannot tell. I am to sit at Tirjella's table and entertain, which is bad enough, but I cannot do it alone!".

If she saw the flash of pain in his eyes, she didn't react, and after a moment's reflection Draille nodded saying cheerfully, "Its just as well that I ordered new blues then, we will really set tongues wagging with our turnout!", but she was yawning, sleepily withdrawing from him, and he let her go with a heartfelt sigh.

"See you at sunrise Lady.", his hand raised, he watched her drift back to bed, back to her sisterly comforts, as evil stalked her relentlessly in the shadows of Simlan's Spring.

Sowdin scowled as he compared the second set of Driands with those he had harvested legally. They were not noticeably different, but felt much lighter, and he surveyed them critically. His back and sides hurt from the harness he had used to climb the awkward swaying trunk, but that was a small price to pay for striking back at the Sisters of Sorcery. He glowered down at the means of exacting his revenge on those who had foiled his attempt to seize his inheritance. They could not have known that they had, (by so doing), nearly put a period to the intricate supply network he had established across the Sands, trading in pepparezad. A hallucinogenic substance extracted from fungi he'd discovered in Rodgeo's territory. He'd used it to influence his master for Rotations, amused himself by feeding it to the warlord's followers, and now he intended to destroy those who stood against him. One by one they would die, the only pity was, no-one would know who had done this. He grinned malevolently.

Now Rodgeo had been swallowed up in the sand-storm, he had only to return to Salatin, continue working his lord's saltings, then he could move in on that tasty little widow who would inherit Rodgeo's leavings. His eyes glittered dangerously as he contemplated success, but the irritant voice in his ear reminded him to finish his task.

He carefully cut the sticky fruit, leaving them clinging to the tendrils from which they grew, and spread them apart. String after string he sorted and discarded, keeping only the best ones to lie on the huge platter he had prepared over the last four days. Carefully draping the last one in place, he took a quick look into the faintly gleaming pool where Renna had died, then having adjusted his clothes to suit the part he was playing, he set out on foot for Darnesh.

The call to ascend Mount Darnesh echoed its weird brassy tones wildly, setting everyone's teeth on edge. From the Gathering Square, the young Clansmen raced each other, fierce determination on their faces, as they pounded up the steps and onto the steeply terraced growing grounds. Draille surveyed their progress with an expression that left no man in any doubt of his feelings. Jalni fought not to giggle as she saw indulgent fathers strutting proudly as they waited for the race to end.

"Hopeless!", Draille said softly. "For one they run on their heels, slamming feet down so hard they threaten to bruise the soles. They also fill themselves up with liquid before they run. It must slosh around their bellies until they're sick. Give me a Clansman a ninenight, and I'll break them so far down, sand grains will stand higher. Can you imagine what any one of those would make of Holonogarth?", at which Jalni had to turn away, eyes streaming with mirth when she remembered Marran's final test. She spluttered to a stop, hand obscuring her mouth as she gurgled.

"They grasp the vine, they'll ask not why. It hangs so close at hand.", and Draille chimed in.

"They'll swing aloft, then fall and die, Drowned amid the Sand.", mournfully repeating the refrain (in chorus with Jalni), "Drowned dead amid dry Sand!".

They roared with laughter at the age old stanza from an epic Ranger poem, then hastily altered their expressions when a tall Clansman beckoned. He was smiling faintly as he extended his forearm, clasping Draille's firmly, as he questioned the Ranger.

"I'm Andreth of the Far Reaches South. You two seemed to find our young men's race hilarious, but let me in on the joke? I suspect that not all of us would find it that amusing.".

Jalni glanced at him sharply. He was (for a Clansman) almost clean-shaven, hair and beard neat, clothes immaculate and he was twinkling at her in a very disconcerting manner.

Draille spoke cautiously, introducing Jalni, then himself, adding quietly:

"If we offended you Lord Andreth please forgive me. It was their sheer enthusiasm that reminded me of the Biron run at Perilherm.".

The Clansman surveyed him coolly, then chuckled.

"A good analogy friend Ranger.", he said, apparently satisfied, "but how else would you train them?".

Relieved, Jalni turned to see large tables being set up in the Gathering Square. Something like Eshima's pavilion had appeared overnight, and now, sides rolled up, cooks and skivvies were preparing for the feast. She was just about to turn away, when she saw a grower, approach the head cook with a platter held high. Too far away to make out his features, or what he offered, she was nevertheless convinced she knew him. Idly wondering whether it was the enthusiastic grower she had encountered on her trip to Tregeth, she went back to Draille, who was taking his leave of Lord Andreth, smiling.

The horn sounded again, and they moved out of the way as a stream of Clansmen clattered down the steps and poured into the gap beyond the Festival tents, cheering and waving pennants above their heads. she watched them assemble in groups, then Draille muttered thoughtfully. "Next Zenitheon, Andreth's son enters the contest and he'll run them all ragged, or I'll serve his father for the following Rotation!".

Jalni had no doubt that Draille would succeed, and hoping he would instil some Ranger philosophy into the southern territories, She accepted his arm, walking down to join the Gather, happily unaware of the eyes that watched their progress.

Immediately pressed into service, Jalni followed Ellandra, settling on the seating for the feast, until it was time to change into Festival finery. Draille made for his camp, leaving Jalni to slip into the deserted dormitory to unpack her Colours. She washed swiftly, and slipped into them smiling as they shivered against her skin like a lover's caress. Her hands found and adjusted Daro's token, sliding it out to hang between her breasts, caught up in thoughts too intimate to share as she turned to the polished bronze mirror. She was still gaping at the supremely elegant creature who flickered like a living tongue of Azure fire in amazed delight, as the horn sounded and there was no more time to spare.

Draille was simply stunning in an understated way. He stood at the edge of the crowd, totally ignoring the "come hither" signals of the women who had lined up to gaze at him. Jalni blinked; where was the highly trained backhillsman in this graceful courtier? He wore patch-dyed blues cut to reveal his strong, sturdy body to its best potential. His hair (cut short as always) gleamed dark bronze, only the narrow plait at the nape of his neck was swung forward over his shoulder, its length and feathered embellishment declaring his seniority. Leggings over tied with elaborate leather braiding encased his legs, finished off with soft Irix hide boots (patch stained blue to complete his camouflaged look).

She gaped at this display, until his amused voice said enquiringly, "Do I wash up well enough to accompany my Lady to the Feast?".

She flushed, and the gentle tint in her cheeks set off the natural peach of her complexion as he confidently steered her through the crowds, to stand by the chairs he had marked as theirs. Men were hurrying to their places now, guiding wives or lovers, dictating the behaviour of teens, all busily making sure that they had engaged a servitor's attention. Jalni glanced nervously up the length of the table, looking for this Weaver that she must entertain, then relaxed as Dinnot del Lyn was led forward to grin into her astonished face.

"Well met Mistress Holder.", he sighed with pleasure. "I have been scarcely able to rest since Madiv told me I was to represent my father's interests in Anempor, rather than have the poor man dragged away just as business there is needing his attention. He sent me loving greetings from my parents by marriage as well, so it seems he has reconciled himself to my travels. He bade me give you his thanks and wishes for a good Zenitheon also.".

During the meal they caught up with all the news, but Jalni's attention was diverted by little pricklings along her skin. Draille plainly felt it too, for after he had eaten sparingly, he silently rose to his feet, and asked permission to withdraw. For a moment she questioned his steady brown gaze, her own blue blaze radiating from an anxious face, then Dinnot said gently;

"Better tell me the worst then. Have you done away with your Uncle? Did you find what you sought, or are you merely resting from the search?".

Before she could answer, a stray breeze stroked her cheek compelling her to turn her head as her hair whipped across her brow. It was then that she saw Tirjella reach out a hand and lift a Driand fruit to her lips. Time slowed to the thudding of her own heart. People laughed, plunged knives into tasty morsels, drank their fill of Southern wine, or joked while a junior Healer watched her Sorceress bite into the fruit in mute despair. Unaware that she had risen to her feet, Jalni brushed aside Dinnot's well-meaning enquiries, and put her fingers to her lips, shrilling out the two toned Ranger signal for immediate danger. Half a heart-beat later, she whistled again the long tremulous call, the signal that would gather any Ranger in earshot to his immediate superior. Hardly had she done that when Tirjella choked, flushed an ugly purple, and fell, hands clawing at her throat. Adora was closest, and sprang to her Deshun's aid before a single Clansman had reacted. Loosening clothes, peering into eyes and taking desperately racing pulses, the Senior Healer worked rapidly, as Jalni's fingers flew to Daro's trinket. She pressed it firmly, calling in the depths of her inner mind, "Daro, Ichspeller Selunsanni.", but answer came there none and she reluctantly accepted that he couldn't hear her cry for help.

The Clansmen were rising, pushing back chairs under Andreth's command, dishes and food discarded as they lifted Tirjella up and laid her near the fruit that had killed her.

"Not yet!", Jalni's fierce determination galvanised that command. It surged from her central being, flared along her mind, lighting her incandescent like a living torch.

"Not yet!", she ground out as she strode towards the table, hair crackling around her shoulders as she silently demanded.

"Tirjella te Syrene, your Sands are in grievous danger. You cannot go, you must remain. Anchor yourself to your sand my Deshun. We cannot spare another so soon.".

she towered over the little Sorceress, silently willing her to live, silently daring her to die, and found herself winding limp fingers round the trinket she had discarded. The sorceress groaned suddenly, head turning as a fragment of sparkling Driand escaped her lips, then the Clansmen were raising the table like a litter, and rushing the Sorceress into the Healer Hall, leaving her guests reeling in shock.

Jalni slipped through the crowds, feeling as though some magnetic force drew her to Adora's side and there was nothing to prevent her, no guards, no interference, even the outer door to Tirjella's apartments stood open as she entered.

Ellandra was handing Adora a mixture made up in a jug as Jalni swept in and her own eyes narrowed before the blue blaze approaching. However, she made no move to stop her, simply moving back to let Jalni stand next to Adora, who red-eyed was wringing her hands in desperation.

"Purging is the only treatment I know.", she remarked as Jalni stood beside her, " but Solana knew so much more, were she alive, or had her spells been saved I could have saved her.!".

She was still trying though, and Jalni saw the pain and confusion as Adora "searched beyond", using her empowered *othervoice*, trying to infiltrate the terrifying tendrils that engulfed Tirjella's body. Jalni was close enough to touch Adora, close enough to touch the medallion now clamped in Tirjella's dying grasp when she felt the air brush her forehead in a tender kiss, and knew what she must do. She raised a hand, murmuring "Let me give you strength sister.", and placed her palm on the middle of Adora's back, and opened herself to the Source.

She felt the room fade away, heard the ancient chant in her mind, and silently invoking the One, she recalled the serenity of Solana's face as she passed her spells to Daro.

There was a roaring in her ears, a pulsing under her hand, then she was holding the hub of her medallion, as her *othervoice* came to the rescue.

"Secralla moi, theraacsa moi.", the liquid beauty of that impassioned plea rose from the ancient settlement as something in Jalni's mind unlocked, and the magic flowed. How long she sang for, what she sang, or who received the wisdom she had accidentally gleaned on the evening of Solana's death, she would never know. The only witnesses were so engaged in supporting the dying Sorceress, that it was done, and they didn't question how a mere fourth Rotation student had not only acquired Solana's spells, but had effortlessly transferred them in time to save Tirjella from the ancient fate of "bleckoning".

Chapter 37 - Retribution and Return

Jalni came back to herself as Adora's enhanced *othervoice* took over the chant she had started. The woman's rich contralto throbbed in the high roofed room as the Healer kneaded Tirjella's chest, then flexed her throat by lifting her head. Tirjella gave a faint cough and with that, a blackened ball of writhing tendrils was expelled from her airways. Still the Sorceress lay limply as Adora changed the tempo of her empowered chant, tracing energy paths that had retreated under the vicious assault of the Bleckon seeds.

Content to leave Adora wielding Solana's heritage, Jalni took a step back and would have fallen headlong, but for the intervention of Ellandra. She was sick, giddy and the walls were shifting in a very disconcerting manner, but with Ellandra's help, Jalni made it to the washroom before she started vomiting. She was totally unconscious of begging the Novice Mistress to let her die, completely at the mercy of nausea and thankfully unaware of the worried glances between the two experienced Healers. Eventually, huddled miserably on a low cot, she prayed none of the Clansmen would notice her as they moved the Sorceress to her bed chamber. She only roused fractionally when Andreth's voice said slowly, "Poor little thing looks absolutely done in. I'll call her Ranger.".

The sweet cool air of evening woke her sometime later and she stirred, dismayed to find herself nestled into a pile of sweetgrass, feeling tired and rather sore. She sat as a shadow slipped out of the dark, and came to her side, touching her forehead with casual familiarity.

"Lady, lift your head so I can return your talisman, then I can get you a drink, and tell you what I know.", Draille's voice was calm, and Jalni, relieved to find him present, obeyed instantly. She clasped the talisman in both hands, drinking in the sights and sounds around her, deducing that they were above Darnesh, camped in the open pastureland where the Clansmen had turned out their riding beasts. She could make out the soft glow of other encampments, the occasional flutter as a roosting bird settled down for the night, and the chink and scrape of tethered beasts grazing. A nightlingby hooted, and wrapped in that drowsy reverie that follows recovery from sickness, Jalni's mind jumped back half a Rotation to Scartel, and a darkly handsome face. She sat bolt upright, eyes frantically searching for Draille as she gasped out a question.

"Draille! Is Tirjella…", and her voice died away, unable to frame the word "dead?". She relaxed as soon as he turned back from the fire, for he was grinning as he returned with a drink for her. He squatted quite comfortably, saying simply:

"Your Deshun is sleeping. She is well and has spoken with her Clansmen, who have put themselves at my disposal, so that we might continue the hunt for this would-be murderer. She is convinced that the blame for Deshun Ikella's illness may lie at the same door. She said there had been strange incidents around Jerritol recently, which is why I brought you here. You are safer with Ranger eyes on you, than down there.".

Jalni questioned her memory, silently digesting what Draille had said, then she drew a sharp breath, the connection closed, and she knew who her enemy was. Some intuition must have conveyed her comprehension to Draille, who spoke apologetically promoting a grin when he observed:

"You were so limp, so unresponsive that I thought you drifting to Sand. I had a few moments trying to compose what I might tell your lord and live!".,

"Only a few moments?", she queried making light of his concerns and he responded, laughing.

"Yes, a mere few. About the time its taken me to get to first class Ranger, plus the length of time I have to live!"., then he cocked an ear, and stilled so that the silencing finger he raised to his lips was unnecessary. There was a low warble as if a sleeping bird had roused, then a shadow slipped into the firelight as Roath, (one of the Tawn) sidled in and crouched by Draille. She caught the man's wondering glance though, then Draille said roughly. "Yes, you summoned all of them. The One only knows how, but they all came, and Darnesh hasn't a chink big enough for a sandrigal to escape Ranger eyes!".

Jalni shook off the sleep inducing sweetgrass and stood preparing herself, for she knew she was always part of this plan. Speaking in a whisper she explained (as she pre-empted Draille's request):

"Yes, I recognised him. Yes, I can identify him and yes I'll come with you and put an end to this.".

She moved gracefully in the Ranger's wake, slipping through the ring of sentries posted around the pasturage, feeling their eyes cling to her as they passed, encouraging her with a benevolent support. She knew them for Tirjella's Clansmen, and almost giggled as she remembered how afraid she had been of them. They were off the pastures quickly. Creeping silently around the Gathering Square, heading for the railed enclosure behind Tirjella's stable yard, when she paused, feeling the sand beneath her slippers. In sudden irritation she bent and slipped them off. She needed that contact, for as she straightened, tucking her talisman into her tunic, it warmed to her hand, as she thrilled to a surge of power.

As a large black shadow shifted ahead, deep harmonies awoke around her, quivering along her skin as her hair crackled with lightening. Then Andreth's voice said softly in the dark.

"Ranger, would you bring a mere child to this confrontation? As Tirjella's champion, I stand against this man.", but Draille protested, equally quiet, but infinitely more deadly in intent.

"If you insist on challenging one who has already nearly killed a Guardian friend, you and your children will lie in the Sands long before Jentaroth.", then he reached out and touched Andreth's shoulder.

Jalni's eyes had been straining in the gloom, but her feet had just slid into a clear patch of Sand, and like a switch being thrown, all her senses came to life at once. She saw Draille's hand grip andreth's forearm as the Clansmen tried to brush by, then the Ranger was whispering apologetically as he lowered the warlord gently to the ground.

"Sorry Andreth, I can't let you kill yourself or your family.", then he turned and beckoned her forward.

There was no denying the hasty preparations being made on the far side of this scrubby enclosure. A Cherl chuckled, shifting from foot to foot as unfamiliar hands attempted to saddle it. Jalni could smell fear overlaid with evil, underscored by insanity and shivered. It was cold, uncaring, and determined to kill, but she had her anger, her retribution to deliver, so she thought of her father, his brother, her mother, including all those who had stood in Sowdin's way and spoke that dread name just once.

"Sowdin?", she called into the night, hearing him gasp, feeling his terror before of its own volition, her hand rose, pointing at him as she hissed.

"Die!".

He stood fully revealed as a nimbus of blue flame surrounded him. He was older, balding and paunchy, pale with sweat and alone, but he was indeed Sowdin del orto, her nemesis. Draille saw those astonishing eyes darken, then fill with a glittering fire. Her shoulders braced as she lifted that accusing finger, then Sowdin cried out despairingly .

"No Jalani. No little Weaver! I am your Grandfather, you can't do this!", then he shrieked, hands clasping his throat, clawing at his chest as a glow burst from him. He writhed as he fell, flames leaping from his prone body. then they died too fast to be natural, and a great calm descended over the empty pasture. Of Sowdin there was no sign, not even a scorch mark mourned his passing, but Jalni knew that there were observers, for she had heard the distinct sound of a door closing softly. Too tired to consider what this meant, she numbly allowed Draille to lead her away, to sleep in the sweetgrass of the Ranger encampment.

The days that followed were a blur as she drifted aimlessly round Darnesh. She had withdrawn, sitting empty-eyed as the Faculty of Healers discussed her future. Tirjella, now completely recovered, took counsel of her Senior Healer and the Novice Mistress, then retired to the tranquillity of the small hall where she had heard a Sandsinger in power. She curled up in her favourite seat, desperately trying to rationalise what her Healers had told her, eventually giving way to the urge to contact the Guardians. She carefully took down the sand-paste bottle, gently easing the ancient stopper from the neck to pour a little Stillglass into a shallow dish. She focussed her thoughts, but the image that swam into view as her aura engaged, was nothing like a Guardian. She studied the young anxious face for a brief moment then acknowledged with equanimity, "Shey Somishen Suraya?", and the girl dipped her head respectfully.

"Deshun Tirjella.", the voice was one of peculiar sweetness, as she asked hastily, "Does the One protect your sands this Zenitheon?", to which Tirjella found it surprisingly easy to respond.

"We are so blessed my dear.", but the crease between her eyes betrayed Tirjella's agitation as Suraya murmured, "Beneva comes.", as her image wavered and was replaced by the Guardian of Knowledge.

"Well Tirjella, have you found the source of those disturbances yet?", she asked easily, but by the time the tale was told, Beneva was joined by both Ikella and Shiarjha. As she described Jalni's current mood, her aimless wandering coupled to morbid introspection, Ikella glanced at Beneva and said quietly, "We have seen her like that before, twice.", and went on to explain.

"After the fever took her fellow students she withdrew. It took Rotations to get her back, and then she nursed Daro.", she said no more until Tirjella whispered his name.

"Ichspeller Selunsanni?", and with relief all three Guardians smiled.

"At least he had the sense to tell you the truth.", his mother spoke with some asperity. "I don't know what this secrecy is about.", she grumbled, "I would have thought he'd be more effective if he announced himself to the sands, but he'll have none of it.", then Shiarjha interrupted.

"He can work better if they don't know what he is Sister. He is vulnerable in a way we cannot imagine, so powerful yet so dependent. He's very like Jalni really. He has no equal, no mentor, no rules to follow, no limits to obey. She too has been cast upon the Sands, and because of the way she arrived amongst us and the peculiar exigencies of those times we never tested her powers beyond those necessary to enter the Guild. We may have severely underestimated her potential, but she fears her *othervoice* and simply won't use it.".

Tirjella immediately rebuffed that suggestion, saying shortly, "I owe my life to that *othervoice*. There's nothing wrong with it, rather the opposite. Ikella, Telaya is a fine Elect, but Jalni may be like your Suraya. Had you not considered that she may have come to power unnoticed and untrained? That might answer some of the questions surrounding her. She needs a Guardian for guidance and Daro has to know that she usurped Sandsinger prerogatives in transferring spells entrusted to him, even in my hour of need. Adora and Ellandra are the only ones who know what she did, but I would feel happier if she returned to Selesh, where greater powers than mine can advise.".

Eventually it was settled, Jalni would return to Selesh, for her future to be decided. However, Daro had yet to be told. He had taken an unusual interest in altering the Eyrie, positively alienating his mother, by harnessing Brand (her new Master Builder) to the task. Only admitted when the work was nearing completion, Ikella stared as she entered a radically altered suite. The space revealed took her by surprise, the panelling was still there, but the small rooms, the confined areas seemed to have been swept away. To one side of what had been a corridor, she could see doors, and supposed what she was looking at had been Ahnell's rooms. Diras opened a door for her, and she found herself gazing at Daro's new body servant, who was happily engaged in loading hanging bars with Daro's clothes. He jumped up and bowed until Daro called out.

"Tobin, show my mother your sewing room!".

She stared at bolts of fabric, racks of trimmings, seeing all the accoutrements of a first class tailor, and chuckled.

"You have turned my ruffian into a fashion statement Tobin.", and was pleased to see the little man flush with pride. She regarded him coolly, then asked quickly. "Do you design for women as well?", in a diffident voice that betrayed her interest all the more clearly.

Tobin smiled and said cautiously, "If my Deshun pleases.", and in the main room behind her Daro groaned. She turned, closing Tobin's door, advancing on her son as a horn announced visitors at the Gate in the Rock.

"That will be a Healer returning Daro.", she announced firmly, "I will have to go in a minute, but I wanted you to know that this particular Healer has returned to face your wrath. In the last few days she has insinuated herself into Zurian society in a way totally unbecoming to her calling. She has kept company with a Ranger, abandoned family affairs to seek entrance to another Hall of Healing, and has usurped your own rights in the matter of Solana's spell heritage.".

She stared at her son speculatively, for he had straightened from his bored slump, and had turned his face to hers beaming.

"Jalni?", he begged eagerly, and Ikella sank into a chair, agreeing. "Jalni".

They talked long into the night, and more the following day. Arguments raged back and forth between the Hall of Sanctuary and the potential of her power, and stilling her, or retraining her more carefully. Meanwhile Mina swooped on the exhausted girl and took her back to the narrow bed in the room she had occupied before her downfall, made her a strong sedative, and left her to sleep. It was therefore four days later that she came shyly into Ikella's study to face the Sorceress, and found herself facing Daro.

she hesitated on the threshold, eyes turning to Diras in mute appeal, but the new commander of Ikella's Guard simply said, "Courage Sister!", and having reprised her predecessor, gently but firmly pushed her into the room and shut the door. She stood, clad in the simple tunic of a novice, hands twisting nervously behind her back, staring at Daro mutely. Then as a rustle betrayed another presence, she turned towards the fireplace and saw Ikella curled into her favourite chair. She hastily bobbed a curtsey, noticing that tonight the Sorceress wore the silver robe of a Guardian, and bit her underlip in quivering anticipation.

"Yes.", Ikella observed sternly, "You have the right to remain uncertain young lady. Conduct most unbecoming of this household of which you are a daughter.".

If there was a trace of amusement in those fierce green eyes Jalni couldn't detect it as Ikella enumerated her sins one by one. "Racketing around the Sands like some lordling on a Cherl, forgetting to ask permission not only of your House and Guild before leaving Jerritol, but neglecting to notify your host Clan of what you intended to do. Whether in the company of an unproven family member or not, travelling with a single male companion to whom you are not handfast is definitely detrimental to your reputation, and by association, detrimental to House, Guild and calling.".

Before Jalni could protest that Shiarjha had given her permission to attend to family matters, the Guardian changed her tactics.

"What about this Ranger?", she demanded. "He seems thoroughly besotted. Calling everyday at the Guardroom for news of "his lady". Do I presume that he is your lover?".

Jalni's temper began to rise at that. Her eyes became stormy, her teeth gripped her lip tighter, then Daro intervened gently.

"Draille is an honourable man Mother. If his intentions were otherwise, he would not have brought Jalni home. He had no need to, they both belong in othersands and Tirjella told us that she would not compel Jalni's return. She is here to settle her future once and for all I suspect.", and Jalni turned to face him, white with tension.

"Ichspeller, I can no longer remain a Healer.", she blurted suddenly, "I have offended every law of healing for I have killed, and must bear my shame.".

His head lifted, and for a strange moment Jalni felt as if he was watching her, but the moment passed as Ikella snorted derisively.

"Oh, Sowdin!", she commented dismissively. "Well, all things being equal I imagine that he would have killed you if he had the chance. No my child, that won't wash if you're looking for an excuse. He had already tried to kill me and we know about this bleckoning now Tirjella has supplied the details. If you acted in defence of your House my girl, not only are you forgiven, you have been rewarded. Tirjella has authorised the transfer of the Weaver's Halt at Jerritol in perpetuity to your Uncle. Sowdin's name has been expunged from Clan records, but the familiar name remains. Villeth (your Uncle) insisted on that, so the bequest of Sowdin's father would remain as the old Weaver wanted it. So then Jalni bin Selesh, what shall we do with you if you have finally discounted Healing as your future. Shall you prove yourself once and for all?", but Jalni was gazing at Daro, feeling a tingling awareness of him spreading through her blood, her skin and the tips of her breasts.

As if in a dream, Jalni listened to Ikella's pronouncement. The Guardians voice blurred as she listed her proposals, for Daro's beautiful blind eyes had opened and he was smiling faintly as he listened. With no magic employed, Jalni was mesmerised as her options were laid out before her.

"You have a peculiar command of power, too great to ignore.", said Ikella and Daro nodded, lips pursing slightly and into Jalni's mind came the memory of a torrid kiss. Oblivious of Jalni's distraction, or of her son's part in it, Ikella droned on.

"Too potentially dangerous to ignore, too potentially dangerous to Still.", she pronounced as the disconcerting sensation of a passionate mouth tenderly nuzzled the back of Jalni's neck. She flinched visibly, and as Ikella saw her flush, she dryly remarked.

"I promise you that I can still take that course however repugnant!".

Jalni felt his hands gentling the tempestuous rise of her breasts. She almost squeaked when he breathed (in her inner mind),

"Over my dead body or hers".

Then Ikella was listing again, to a shaking girl who could only hear the heavy mantra of love in her heart, and a man who wasn't listening.

"You must control your *othervoice*. It must never control you!".

"Wrong.", murmured the Sandsinger, eyes now glowing restlessly. "You may feed the power and direct it, but it is not ours to control". Jalni struggled not to react as the hands of his mind stroked her back.

"You must remain celibate in order to control power. Outside distractions or sensations severely impair your focus.".

"Like this? or this?", and the hands of Daro's mind sent sparks racing down Jalni's body, until she remembered that she too could engage her bondmate in battle, and mentally pushed him away. Ikella said softly,

"Do you think you could remain dedicated to the service of the Azure. Put all thought of marriage and children from you and Sing the Song of Sorcery?", and Jalni jumped as Daro stood Abruptly, and held out a hand to his love.

"You have a token of mine dearling. can I have it back? Beneva wanted to see it, and its hardly appropriate here while you are under my protection.".

He held out a hand, and numbly Jalni passed him her precious talisman, which he slipped into a pocket casually. Jalni felt his hand on hers, heard the ghost of a chuckle, then impossibly Daro was negotiating the desk, sliding his arm around her and saying lightly.

"Jalni has considered her position many times while we were in Scartel. This is why I detached my Ranger and appointed him to care for her while she made up her mind. We always knew of one decision that you have no power to influence Mother. Jalni may return to healing, but she will never make a sorceress, for she is bond to me, and tonight she will sleep in my arms.".

There was such tenderness in his supporting body that Jalni leant against him boldly, as he lowered his head to hers and asked gently.

"Will you come with me and be my love?"

"Yes, my lord.", the would be Healer said instantly. "I will.", and arm in arm, dazzling Opal against Azure fire, they left Ikella musing over the dying embers of her own.

"No good will come of that match!", the Sandsinger's mother predicted grumpily, but even had she known the truth of those words, she still might not have been able to intervene .

Chapter 38- A Summoning of Sorts.

They nestled together cocooned in comfort, content for the while to lie there holding hands. Such was their emotional response to the decision taken, that neither of them felt capable of doing anything about it. She had exclaimed in delight over the love nest he had prepared, reacting shyly as he led her into his private bathing room, then giggled helplessly as he reminded her of the "old Azurian custom", of bathing together. Wordlessly he lifted her into his arms, negotiating his way confidently back to the immense bed, and they had lain together, drinking in the wonderment of the moment.

They had slept a little, hands clasped, but she had roused instantly aware as he tentatively stroked the back of her hand. Somehow clothes removed themselves, hands gently guided to drawstrings and buttons. His eyes were alight with a gleam of mischief as he whispered in her ear.

"What about my rival? We didn't ask Draille's permission.", and was instantly appalled and apologetic at her reaction. She turned her head, face into his naked chest and wept, for the sake of the man who loved her, and knew he'd already lost, for the sake of the life she might have had if only she had met him earlier, and for herself, tormented by guilt for her part in Sowdin's death and the diminution of her own innocence in Draille's eyes. Uncertainly she tried to explain, until Daro took her chin, tipped up her head and stopped her mouth with his own.

"I adore Draille too!", he'd groaned, !but must we take your Ranger to bed with us?".

She hung over him with a wry chuckle, then lay back admitting entirely seriously, "Dearling, I never have you know?", as Daro shaken to the core, lifted her hand and kissed its sensitive palm.

"Me neither.", he breathed huskily, "but not for want of trying!".

He ran tender fingers down her body, pulling her against his, letting her sense his arousal, as she quivered beneath his exploring hands. She never knew how much of this was him, how much of this was her as his mouth captured hers again. They simply flowed together like the merging of two Sands, bodies slick with sweat gleaming, senses drowning as the Source rose and swept them away.

She clung to his strength, melting under his delicate ministration, thrilling to the ancient roar of desire as he took her. Her eyes sought his rapt features as they rocked and plunged in a surge of passion, his eyes were closed but his secret self was hers, laid bare to his naked soul as they clung. She was trembling, caught up in the moment, ascending that dizzying peak once more, as her lord lifted, implored, cajoled her upward, then locked in exquisite completion, she felt the lightening flare in her soul.

Still gasping with primal reaction, Jalni opened her eyes, as her world turned blue.

The End?

Now read on from

"Sword of Sanctuary" © Julia Cæsar 2011

Drex drew a shaky breath and tried to ignore his manacled hands as he faced Adruna warily. So extreme had been her reaction to Sowdin's failure, that even Koth removed himself from Skyrrh while she raged. Turning on courtiers, priests, and drudges alike she'd erupted in a frenzy of blood letting, until the halls were silenced, and only funeral pyres branded her fury across the Amethyst Sands.

"Tell me what you recall of your final incompetence.", she demanded again, as Drex drew breath, painfully aware of the dangers facing him. A soft footfall interrupted his train of thought, then as the entrance to his cell darkened and Adruna whirled round eyes sparkling, he caught a sense of something dry and deadly rustling past. The tip of his tongue wetted his lips as Koth was escorted through the door, then Adruna turned back, pinioning the unfortunate Recorder with a stare devoid of all humanity.

"Speak!", she commanded and as Drex fought the compulsion to tell the dark Sorceress his innermost secrets, Adruna reached out, tracing the elaborate tattoos that branded her tongueless inspiration of evil. He giggled, as Drex mentally recoiled in horrified understanding, forced himself to describe what he'd seen through Anieman's mirror. Choosing not to embellish the explanation with his usual flowery compliments, Drex spoke humbly.

"Lady, the subject was worthy of our trust. He learned much in the short time available and prepared well. The bleckoned Driands were delivered to Tirjella's table at precisely the right time. By all the indications Sowdin was accepted, as were the tools we employed, but one thing he couldn't have prepared for, someone recognised him. I heard him call that Healer by name, saying he was her Grandfather, but what manner of Healer could tell a man to die, causing him to burst into flames, clear across a gathering yard?".

"The Tapestry of Tten", a gripping series of Fantasy Fiction novels by Julia Caesar is published by Arima Publishing. To order, please visit our website, http://www.arimapublishing.co.uk , or write to us at,

Arima publishing
ASK House
Northgate Avenue
Bury St Edmunds
Suffolk
IP32 6BB

Why not follow the series progress on
www.sandsingers.co.uk

or find
The Tapestry of Tten
On Facebook?
Already available in Kindle Format
From amazon.co.uk, .com, & .de
&
In Braille
From RNIB's Talking Book Library.

"The Tapestry of Tten", what is it? Where is it? and why must they find it? The story begins at the

"Dawn of Darkness"

They were all doomed until the Sorceress remembered an ancient incantation, but as she chanted the forbidden words, what has Ikella unleashed on her unsuspecting world?

Hidden in the brilliantly hued deserts of Pelshar are the clues to its secret past. Strict obedience to the "Way", has prevented their discovery until, engulfed in an apocalyptic storm, a party of Healers accidently fulfils ancient prophecy. Now launched on a perilous journey of self-discovery and emotional awakening, Ikella reaches far beyond her previously circumscribed existence, as she adopts a foundling of the Storm. Facing a choice between the child she loves, and the security of a world teetering on the brink of ecological disaster, she must discover why the word "Sandsinger" haunts her dreams, and how their very existence depends on finding a mysterious " Tapestry of Tten".

The reader will agonize with her over baby Daro's future, relax in the reassuring company of an aged Apothecary, and be on the edge of their seats, waiting for the sequel, "Curse of Night."

■■

If you enjoyed this book, follow the unfolding mystery in

"Curse of Night"

After the Storm, Jentaroth (the annual Rite of Passage), takes on new significance. Amidst mourning rituals, Ikella must protect the Union of the Sands from treachery within, whilst resisting her growing emotional attachment to the frail orphan she longs to adopt. Beset by premonitions as she gathers her Sisters in Sorcery at Selesh, Ikella is forced to defend the Gathering as one of three new Candidates reveals herself as a practising heretic, with command of Dark Magic. As she confines Adruna and her followers to her own Sands, Ikella cannot prevent her cursing baby Daro, but did her curse have any effect?

As Daro grows up, how many Rotations must Ikella endure his relentless obsession with the ancient mages of the past? Is this something to do with "The Curse of Night? As his obsession leads him into perilous places, can he survive to find "Another Shade of Mystery?"

The Tapestry of Tten - Book 3 by Julia Cæsar

"Another Shade of Mystery."

Having exiled Daro for his obsession with the ancient mages of their secret past, life is still far from peaceful in Selesh. The aging Sorceress has found no relief from troublesome children, for she has given refuge to Jalni. The girl, hotly pursued into the heart of the community, has an intriguing (though erratic) command of power. Admitted as a novice, Jalni commits a catalogue of crimes, and is on probation when Daro returns empowered, to challenge his foster-mother's long held beliefs.

Determined to ignore the personal price he has paid for his power, the Opal Sandsinger takes Jalni as his guide, and sets out to save the children of Scartel. Encountering Myst-cats, Wanderers, Storm horses and a mysterious mentor, Daro must also find his feet in a strange new world, looking for "Another Shade of Mystery", to help him understand, "The Song of Sorcery".

■■

When you have read this book, you can continue with

"Sword of Sanctuary"

Marran Dorenard never thought he would find it difficult to follow the Ranger Code. Honouring the memory of the Grandfather who gave his life to save him, he must deal with a web of divided loyalties,. Can he support the Lord of the Opal in his desire to break free from the constraints of Selesh and his obligations, or should he protect the vulnerable girl who has been the mainstay and support for his Tawn of Rangers? As for Jalni….

Deeply distressed by constant bickering, worried about Ikella's increasing frailty, and concerned about her own erratic powers, she discovers she's pregnant. The Oracle's prediction was true! Frightened into running back to Scartel, she decides not to tell Daro, who seems intent on rejecting her. With the firm intention of surrendering the Sandsingers child to the Temple of the Winds, she returns to the Ashgenar with only Marran's sword for protection as she comes to terms with her destiny. Can she take the child where his father can't find it? Or has the Shadow of the Singer cast itself ahead of her?

Where can you find out more about the Tapestry of Tten and get regular updates about forthcoming books?

Why not visit

www.sandsingers.co.uk

The official home of The Tapestry of Tten, and find out more about the fascinating world of Pelshar. Get a feel for this troubled planet, find out about the Clans, the culture, and the ideas that drove Julia to write the series. Find out about the parallels between our world and theirs, follow the characters, study the maps and see where they lead.

Website designed and maintained by our friends at
Red Dragon I.T. Ltd

+44 1303 723456   www.rdit.co.uk

RNIB Talking Books - A message from the Author.

A proportion of the purchase price of this book, is being donated by the author to RNIB, The Royal National Institute for Blind and Partially Sighted People, and will be directed to their National Library Service which runs the Talking Book Service and the Learning and Skills Library. These provide visually Impaired people with an accessible source of entertainment and education, through the conversion of books into an audio format, known as DAISY (Digitally Accessible Information System). This is a unique system that allows navigation of audio books.

The resulting CD's dropping through the letterbox are a powerful tool in the battle for equality, giving blind and partially sighted people access to thousands of books which were previously not available. This lifeline service is invaluable to some tens of thousands of people across the UK.

"You have already supported this significant service simply by buying my book, but if you want to help further the aim of making it possible for all books to become accessible to Visually Impaired Readers, or need information about the RNIB Please call their helpline on
0303 123 9999 or visit www.rnib.org.uk

Thank you for your support,

Julia Cæsar

www.ingramcontent.com/pod-product-compliance
Lightning Source LLC
Chambersburg PA
CBHW071130260626
47162CB00003B/725